Praise for *Hex in High Heels*

"Wisdom does a truly wonderful job mixing passion, danger, and outrageous antics into a tasty blend that's sure to satisfy."

—*RT Book Reviews*, 4.5/5 Stars

"They just keep getting better and better... a very entertaining and sexy story."

—*Night Owl Romance*, Reviewer Top Pick, 5/5 Stars

"Hold on to your broomsticks! Sassy, smart, and so much fun!"

—Terri Garey, bestselling author of *You're The One I Haunt*

"Delightfully fun... the story is every bit as delicious as the title... Anyone looking for a fun, paranormal romantic romp will quickly find themselves under Ms. Wisdom's spell."

—*Blogcritics*

"Fun, flirty, with a dash of sex appeal, danger, and a double dose of witchy magic... a delicious must-read for the lighthearted paranormal fan."

—*PopSyndicate*

"A treat... Ms. Wisdom creates fun, magical worlds peopled with unique characters... Better still, she creates love stories that warm the heart."

—*Star-Crossed Romance*

Praise for *Wicked By Any Other Name*

"Fan-fave Wisdom… continues to delight with clearly defined—if somewhat offbeat—characters who face danger with pizzazz."

—*RT Book Reviews*

"I was absolutely entertained with this fun and magical romp! Linda Wisdom is quickly making herself a household name in the paranormal genre."

—*Armchair Interviews*

"Linda Wisdom weaves a laugh-out-loud spontaneity of hilarious moments between two unforgettable characters… an extraordinary read not to be missed."

—*Coffee Time Romance*

"It's sexy, silly, and in the end love conquers all… can it get much better than that?"

—*Marta's Meanderings*

Praise for *Hex Appeal*

"Jazz is as irascible, high-maintenance, and quick-tempered as ever, and Nick is the kind of vampire who loves her just the way she is… An intriguing look beneath the bravado of Wisdom's characters to their inner fears and vulnerabilities."

—*Booklist*

"Sure to charm and entertain readers from the start."

—*Darque Reviews*

"A spectacular supernatural story full of love, laughter, and plenty of magic in and out of the bedroom!"

—*Night Owl Romance*

"Simply one great read, filled with sensuous characters, laughs, and a bit of wild adventure."

—*Star-Crossed Romance*

Also By Linda Wisdom

50 Ways to Hex Your Lover

Hex Appeal

Wicked By Any Other Name

Hex in High Heels

DEMONS
ARE A
GIRL'S BEST
FRIEND

LINDA WISDOM

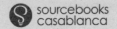
sourcebooks
casablanca

Published by Sourcebooks Casablanca, an imprint of Sourcebooks, Inc.
P.O. Box 4410, Naperville, Illinois 60567-4410
(630) 961-3900
FAX: (630) 961-2168
www.sourcebooks.com

Printed and bound in the United States of America
QW 10 9 8 7 6 5 4 3 2 1

For my fans who have embraced the witches
with such love and support.
Thank you!

Chapter 1

"OH YEAH, JUST ANOTHER SATURDAY NIGHT HITTING the clubs, watching the dancers, feeling blood stream out of my ears." Maggie O'Malley winced as Static-X's "Destroyer" screamed from the state-of-the-art speakers embedded in the club's walls. Still, she couldn't stop her hips from moving to the throbbing music. If she wasn't there on business, she would have been out there dancing. "Why don't you just shoot me now?"

"Any females get naked yet?" the voice of Frebus, one of her team members, rumbled from the mic in her ear. "It's only a matter of time 'til somebody gets caught up in the moment and starts tearing off their clothes. You gotta love shape-shifters cuz they're always the first to get down and dirty."

Maggie played idly with the crystal earring that dangled almost to her bare shoulders. She considered her jewelry a much better look for a mic and earpiece than the usual spy gear. If only she could mute the music for an hour. Or ten.

"Sorry, sweetie, I'm only seeing half naked, but think positive. The evening's still young." She grinned as she heard the low groan in her ear. Frebus and her other backups, Meech and Tita, were strategically placed around the interior, on the lookout for one particular degenerate in the sea of questionable characters.

She made her way through the hordes of glassy-eyed,

gyrating dancers, skillfully avoiding the groping hands on her ass and breasts. She muttered a spell against any who returned for another feel. Nothing like a magickal zap to the genitals to spoil the mood. Judging from the yelps that followed her, at least five tried.

Maggie didn't believe in giving anyone a second chance.

She viewed the large, creature-populated underground club with an expression of distaste and the desire for her olfactory senses to be on the fritz.

"Haven't some of these guys ever heard of deodorant?" she muttered, passing one scaly creature that fell in the "totally gross" category. It peered at her through red-slitted eyes and hissed, its forked tongue flicking toward her. Maggie hissed back and moved on.

The club's name, Damnation Alley, fit the interior with its glossy black walls, black glass bars with the interiors pulsing with ice-blue and black lights casting an unearthly glow on the preternaturals thronging the interior. Any unlucky human who managed to get past the door ran the risk of exiting in a body bag—or someone's stomach.

She'd planned to spend tonight with a bowl of popcorn and DVDs at home, but one of her team members got word that a fugitive they'd been after for the past month would be at the club tonight. Maggie and her team were sent here to bring it in.

She locked gazes with a vampire she remembered going up against a year earlier. He flashed fang. She responded with a smile that promised a repeat of what had happened before. The vamp wisely turned away.

At first glance, Maggie looked like a typical party gal

in her barely there black skirt and bandeau top. Shiny silver glitter accents covered the fabric that bared her shoulders and taut midriff, and only she knew of the protective spells woven into the fabric.

A dazzling, diamond-encrusted black widow spider with ruby eyes was tattooed on one bicep. Dangerous bling. Don't leave home without it. She'd slicked back her chin-length pale blonde hair with glittery gel, knowing that it made her features seem sharper than usual tonight. She smiled at one man who focused his attention on her legs and her black stilettos.

Maggie believed in themes, and tonight's was dangerous sexy female on the prowl. *The better to destroy you with, my dear.*

She cast her senses wide, searching for her prey. Her gaze skittered to a halt when it reached a man standing in the doorway leading to the private rooms.

A few inches taller than her almost six feet, he was also dressed in black, but he didn't look like the typical clubgoer. The silk shirt and slacks looked well tailored and suited his tanned skin, dark eyes, and spiked hair. He oozed danger. Judging by the hungry looks women were directing his way, they didn't mind the danger part at all.

Maggie didn't miss that most of the females were much more generously endowed than she was. She normally didn't mind her slender athletic figure, but sometimes she'd like to have enough to fill more than a middling B cup.

No time to play, pretty boy. Maggie's got other creatures to fry. But stick around, and maybe we can fit in a dance later on.

What a concept. Your everyday witch having an evening out where she could flirt with a gorgeous guy, get in some dancing, and just talk. When was the last time she'd had a date? Did she have enough fingers and toes to count back that far?

She purposely looked away until her gaze slammed into an odd-looking creature standing at the rear bar.

"Okay, that thing is butt ugly." Maggie noted the bloated body dressed in rags. She was positive he wouldn't smell all that good, either. Not that the smell seemed to bother those around him.

"Beauty's in the eye of the beholder, blondie," Meech's disembodied voice reminded her. She caught a glimpse of the big, blue-skinned monster on the other side of the room, guarding a side door. He was grinning as his voice continued through the mic. "While some think you're smokin', all I see is that you're damn scrawny, your nose is out of place, and those pearly whites aren't jagged enough. Plus, they're not healthy unless they're gray or yellow."

"Aw, baby, you know just what to say to make a girl feel good about herself." She took a quick glance down to make sure the girls were at their best advantage. Nothing like giving a perp something to look at while she took him down.

Not that anyone around here would notice. They'd just think it was another S and M show. Another thing Damnation Alley was known for. Although at present she wasn't seeing the kind of sex shows that had gone on here when Ratchet owned the club.

"Oh, Frebus, you bring me to the classiest of places," she purred.

"Better than that tavern two months ago. Plus, this one needs to be put down quick before he causes any more trouble. Him being here tonight is pure luck for us."

"Just stay on alert in case I need backup. Bloaters aren't the type to go quietly." Maggie put her hips to work as she glided over to the bar. She could feel the dark-haired man's eyes on her with a searing intensity, but she kept him on the back burner.

"Hi." She flashed her sultriest smile at her quarry.

The creature looked up, revealing a puce-colored fleshy face, round chartreuse eyes, and a dark slit for a mouth.

"You are witch." He looked at her from the top of her head to the tips of her shoes.

"No one's perfect." She rested an arm on the bar top, acting as if the putrid stench emanating from his skin didn't assault her nose. "Buy me a drink?"

"Witches do not drink maiden grog." His gray claws wrapped around a clay goblet.

"The main element in the grog is a virgin's urine," Tita whispered in her earpiece.

Maggie's smile didn't slip even as her brain screamed *euuwwww*!

"You'd be surprised what I drink." She cocked a delicate brow. "They have private rooms here." She ran a scarlet polished nail over his claws while moving forward enough to brush her breasts against his arm.

At the same time that the creature's gaze fastened on her bare skin, she whipped iron-laced restraints out and slapped them on his wrists.

"You bitch!"

"Aw, now you're just sweet talking me."

The Bloater roared, rearing back and striking her with his chained claws, sending her sailing onto the top of the bar.

Maggie didn't have time to react, finding herself thrown down the slippery slab. Drinks scattered everywhere, and earsplitting shrieks rose above the din. As she slid to a stop, she saw her quarry trying to escape, scrambled to her feet, and ran after him while others tried to stop her.

"Hellion Guard!" she shouted, even as she knew there would be those who didn't appreciate the authorities being there.

Before her prey reached an exit door, Maggie launched herself with a leap worthy of a football player and tackled him to the floor.

"You are under arrest," she began even as she realized he was inflating like a Macy's Thanksgiving Day balloon, and it didn't look like he intended stopping any time soon.

"We're on our way!" she heard Frebus shout from her earring.

The second her three team members shouldered their way through the watching crowd, Maggie's prisoner reached the breaking point.

And that's when he blew up, splattering pea-green goo everywhere.

———

"'Easy peasy,' he says." Maggie's fulminating glare sliced through Frebus as she and the hulking creature crossed the parking lot to the waiting SUV. Everyone else stayed out of range as the thick liquid dripped off her body. No wonder. She'd be a mile away if someone was walking around with Bloater goop on them.

"'It's just a Bloater. We'll be in and out in seconds. No one will even notice what's going on. No mess,' he assures me." Her fingers flicked angry magick in Frebus's direction.

Frebus hunched his shoulders up around his large head. "Intel told me—"

"Your intel sucks rocks." A shower of stones rained on the furry beast. She wiped the pea-green liquid cement from her chest. A few muttered words turned it to puke-green ash. She wasn't happy she couldn't do the same to the glop that coated her skirt and top. No way she'd go naked in front of her crew.

"Frebus, I am not happy about this. Plus, he managed to explode, so I don't have anything to take back but *this*!" She flicked the glop at him.

He hung his head in shame, his shaggy blond fur draped around his wide face.

"Where do I send the bill?" A new voice reached her from behind.

Maggie's temper was already at the boiling point. Turning around to face the sexy man she'd locked eyes with in the club was all she needed, considering her look was now somewhat less than "dangerous sexy female." She only wished they could have danced before she got slimed.

"I am impressed, Hellion Guard," he commented silkily. "You were in my club barely ten minutes, and you managed to destroy one of my bars and the surrounding walls."

"Two words. Soap and water."

His dark eyes glinted with laughter under the orange phosphorous lights that dotted the parking lot.

"Is this something you do on a regular basis? If so, I will have to look into sturdier furniture. I'm also curious. Where exactly did you hide those restraints?" His gaze swept over her with alarming thoroughness. "Tell me something. Do people tell you that you look cute when you're carrying a weapon?"

"Not if they don't want to end up seriously hurt."

Maggie walked toward the man. Her nostrils flared as she caught the faintest hint of sulfur before it drifted away to be replaced by a whiff of sandalwood and male.

Demon blood.

"And you are?" She already knew he wouldn't reveal his true name, since demons refused to divulge them. A body held too much power if a demon's real name was revealed.

"Declan."

His voice washed over her head like a warm shower. Not good at all.

Says you. The words raced across her skin, meaning Elegance, her spider tattoo, was making her feelings known.

Maggie lifted her chin.

"Declan what?"

"Just Declan." He tucked his hands into his pockets and rocked back on his heels. Just another guy looking to make time with a pretty girl who just happened to splatter Bloater goop all over the main floor of his club. Oh well, no one's perfect.

"And demon."

His eyes flashed red for a moment. "No one's perfect... witch."

"Aw, and here we were just getting to know each other."

"Are you this brave when your muscle isn't close by?" Declan asked, his gaze briefly resting on the creatures lounging against the SUV.

A smattering of laughter and guffaws sounded.

Maggie waved a hand. Bubbles of protective power enclosed each team member, but Declan had no doubt that they didn't hide behind the protection if their leader was in trouble.

"I'm the muscle, sweetheart. But I wouldn't discount my backup, because they don't like it if anyone makes me cranky." She cocked a shapely hip. "I suggest you vet your clientele more thoroughly if you don't want further visits from the Guard."

"We don't exactly run background checks." His dark gaze wandered over her body, sending prickly heat along her nerve endings. "Perhaps you'd care to come back in for a drink, and we could discuss how to better safeguard my club?"

She glanced toward the door where an oversize guard stood glaring at her. "It's not your club that needs protecting, Declan. The Hellion Guard is always ready to help those who need our skills, but we defend the innocent from... well, from the kind of riffraff that frequents your club. And once we've finished our job..."

Maggie's smile brightened as she lifted her hand and snapped her fingers. The parking lot lights winked out, leaving the area in total darkness, as though a heavy blanket had dropped over him.

"Fuck me!" Declan widened his eyes, and even then he couldn't see a thing.

Before he could draw a second breath, the lights came back on.

Maggie and her team were gone.

His shoulders shook with his laughter. "I must say the witch knows how to make an exit."

"I loved this outfit!" Maggie wailed, tossing the goop-covered skirt and bandeau top into the pink wicker waste-basket. "This is why I can't have nice clothes. Every time I have an outfit that rocks, some creature destroys it."

She pulled yoga pants, a T-shirt, and clean under-wear out of a dresser drawer. She glanced ruefully at the Barbie doll leaning against the lamp on her dresser. Her witch friend Blair had done a great job of making the doll look like Maggie, with a blonde bob, black tank top, and khaki cargo pants, complete with a variety of tiny blades and a wicked-looking rifle slung over her shoulder. The doll even had a tiny ankle bracelet with a broom charm around her booted ankle. Yeah, that was her, all right.

Maggie paused for a moment, looking down at a small painted portrait set in the place of honor on her dresser. Her fingertips trailed gently over the surface, and she whispered a few words before she moved away. She momentarily dropped her clothing on the rose-patterned bedspread so she could dig her fingers through the goo-covered helmet once known as her hair.

"And you looked very sexy in it, too." Sybil, a delicate-looking elf, was perched on a corner of Maggie's bed. Sybil's lavender wings wafted back and forth, emitting the faintest hint of French vanilla with lilac undertones. "You had protection spells woven into the fabric, didn't you?"

Maggie considered her friend better than any air freshener.

"The spells made the fabric stronger than Kevlar, but for some reason, they didn't do anything to deflect this gunk."

"You're not the only one who's a mess." Elegance, Elle for short, detached herself gracefully from Maggie's skin, scuttled down her arm, and landed on the dresser. She stopped at a delicate china bowl to gather up a scrap of blood-red silk before she moved up the wall to a corner in the ceiling where a web sparkled like diamonds.

A small square in the center glowed blue as Elle activated a teeny computer screen while she pushed the silk scrap together into a comfy cushion. In no time, she was surfing the World Wide Web. "Some of that disgusting goo ended up on me, too."

"Yeah, well, you didn't ruin clothing, Elle," Maggie muttered. "I'd like to know how it slid so easily off you."

"I am special." The black widow preened. "Ah! This could be it!" The tiny screen glowed, projecting an eerie blue against her face.

"Elle, you've been searching for the right hex to keep your lovers alive for centuries," the witch told her. "And so far, every hex has been either a total bust or a hoax."

"The perfect hex is there. I know it. And now the web can be cast worldwide. If you can't come up with one, *I* will." She clicked her tiny mouse and read away.

"There's nothing like a lovesick black widow spider," Sybil said.

Maggie half closed the bathroom door and stepped into the shower. The witch had no trouble washing off the protection sigils written on her bare midriff, but she found the thick mucus harder to deal with.

"I'll need a blasting spell to get this crap off! For Fates' sake, it's even in my hair!" She dumped half a bottle of shampoo on her head and dug her fingers into the mess, yelping when the bubbles dribbled down her face and into her eyes.

"Zap it out."

"This muck is so bad that if I did that, I could end up bald." Maggie's words were garbled under the strong shower spray.

Sybil examined her nails, painted a shimmery lilac to match her wings. "It's times like this I'm glad I don't work in the field." Her iridescent lavender hair hung in thick waves down her back. "Although there are moments when I think you have more fun than I do working here in the compound."

While she looked as fragile as a paper-thin china teacup, Sybil's sweet smile and calm nature made her an effective interrogator. If the smile didn't work, she always managed somehow to make their prisoners cry a lake of tears while making them give up whatever she wanted to know. In her own way, the elf was as strong as Maggie—and just as formidable.

The Hellion Guard was known as protectors for all creatures in this world and others. A form of supernatural military that was under the Ruling Council's mantle, the members were based throughout the world, set up to be ready for any alert that could harm any preternatural being or human.

They may have flown under the human radar, but they were there to keep everyone safe.

This branch of the Hellion Guard lived on a compound outside Houston, Texas, near a typical American suburb. The Guard was as close to a home and family as Maggie had known since being kicked out of the Witches' Academy with her classmates some seven hundred years ago. She'd come a long way from the frightened little girl that Eurydice, the Head Witch, had rescued from the disaster of a plague-stricken town.

"Now I'll have to clean out the shower, because there's no way I'm leaving that for the brownies to scrub when they come in to clean," Maggie grumbled, walking out of the bathroom with a towel wrapped snugly around her clean body and her hair wrapped in a second towel.

Thanks to the brownies that performed all the domestic tasks for the Guards, she never had to worry about dusting, vacuuming, and doing laundry. But brownies were touchy and secretive—they didn't like you to acknowledge their work, and there was a limit as to how big a mess they'd allow.

"I heard that the club has a hot-looking owner."

Maggie ignored Sybil's gentle probing, even though she knew she would eventually have to comment. The delicate elf had a stubborn streak that made a mule look downright malleable.

Wouldn't you know it? I meet a cute guy, and he turns out to be demon and owner of a club that's always been on the Guard's watch list of shady locales.

Not exactly boyfriend material. Like she'd know what a boyfriend was.

Dating didn't seem to be in Maggie's cards.

If she was smart, she'd get a new deck.

"Demon." She pulled the towel off and rubbed her hair partially dry before she ran a comb through it, leaving it hanging loose around her face. "I'd guess no more than half demon," she corrected herself. "But even a half-demon is too much trouble."

"All males are trouble. That's why we females were made." Sybil peered closely at her BWFF (best witch friend forever), who was standing there pensively. "I can't believe it. You're blushing! He's that cute?"

"Am not. It's from my hot shower. I practically had to put the water on boiling to get that cement off me." As if she wanted a male to mess up her life. Even a hot-looking one with a face made for sin and a body obviously created for...

Don't go there, Mags.

"The witch doth protest too much." Sybil's lyrical laughter rang in the room like silvery wind chimes. She stood up and raised her arms over her head in a lithe stretch. "Come on. We'll do some yoga before you go to bed, and you'll feel loads better."

"I just want a night out with dancing and maybe even dinner," Maggie muttered, following her friend out of her quarters into the hall. "I want to dress up and come home with my clothing intact."

"I want Orlando Bloom, but that won't be happening anytime soon," Sybil said serenely.

"O'Malley, why are you maiming my recruits again?" The roar echoed down the hallway and seemed to bounce off the walls.

Maggie winced.

"I believe you're being paged." Sybil's wings fluttered faster. "I'll be in the fitness center waiting… with bandages."

Maggie cursed under her breath. "Jeez, one tiny cut. Okay, more than a tiny cut, but the idiot needs to learn to move faster if he doesn't want to get killed. I was actually very easy on him."

She waved her hand over her head as she about-faced and headed outside the living quarters and across the compound's central courtyard to the administration building. She jogged down the stairs to what the team less than affectionately called the Dungeon.

Except this dungeon looked more like a Grecian temple complete with white marble columns and the soft sounds of lyres in the background. In the middle of the ancient elegance was a desk piled high with papers that every once in a while fluttered on to the gold marble floor and then floated back up to reside once more on the desk's surface.

Maggie wrinkled her nose at the harsh scent of cigar smoke permeating the air. While she didn't mind the aroma of a good cigar or pipe smoke, she did object to something that smelled like old, wet rope. Add in the haze of magick filtering through the air in purple coils, and the boss's office needed a good aromatherapy session.

"You shouted, old esteemed one."

A round face edged with a mangy white beard peered over the stacks of paperwork. "Bite me, O'Malley."

Maggie waved her hand in front of her face. "For Fates' sake, Mal, can't you buy a cigar that costs more than a penny? That smells worse than goat poo."

"Whaddya talkin' about? This sucker cost me a whole buck. They don't come cheap anymore." He held up the offensive item. "And don't think you can get me off the subject, either. What the fuck did you do to Arius last week? It was his first training session with you!"

"So the wuss did come whining to you?" She pushed papers off a chair and parked her butt. "You only needed a baby-size Band-Aid for the cut. Trust me, it was way less than he'd get in battle." If there was one thing Maggie would not allow, it was that anyone she was responsible for should go into a fight unprepared.

"He's threatening to file a grievance." Mal hopped out of his chair, revealing his three-foot height, and waddled around the desk. Faint wisps of white hair floated along the tips of his ears like antennae as he looked up at the witch who kicked ass and didn't bother taking names on a regular basis. A purple cloud of magick followed him. He made a face. "And you know how I hate paperwork."

Maggie's gaze drifted over the papers that covered the desk, floated in the air, and eventually escaped out the door. "Yes, I can see that. Tell Arius if he files a grievance against me, I will mop up the floor with him the next time he's in my class."

Mal's face, the color of aged oak, reddened to the point of explosion. "You do that, and he'll only file another grievance."

"No, he won't, because he wants to be on one of the major teams. So anything else, oh great lord and master?"

Mal snorted. "Cut the shit, O'Malley. Just tell me what happened at Damnation Alley." Dark-brown eyes peered at her with a sharpness that could cut titanium.

"I entered the club, encountered my prey, arrested said prey... and he exploded all over me. You do know this will all be in my report, don't you?" She kept her gaze centered on him. No way did your eyes stray from Mal if you didn't want him digging into your brain, which he had a habit of doing if he thought you weren't telling the truth.

Mal waved his hand in a dismissive gesture. "And Declan? What can you tell me about him?"

Maggie felt that warmth deep down again. *So gorgeous he's got to be illegal. Talk about eyes that make you wet. A smile that makes you flat-out melt. He could even be better than chocolate.* "I haven't had a chance to do any research on him. Since he's new to the area, I don't know if he owns the club or just manages it."

"Then what are you doing loafing around here when you should be looking into him?" Mal didn't blink when a towering stack of papers suddenly appeared on his already cluttered desktop. "We need to know why this Declan took the club over after Ratchet disappeared and just what Declan is, other than a run-of-the-mill demon. And we need to know it all yesterday."

Maggie already had the answer to one of those questions. She knew just where Ratchet had disappeared to. Actually, into. There was nothing like a psychotic losing the battle to a cursed chipper to make a witch's evening.

Blue Plate Special: Demon Burger on a toasted sesame bun with seasoned fries on the side.

"I think he's half demon, but that's nothing new, since whoever runs Damnation Alley has always been demon. I'll need Kittan if you want more intel on him." She named one of the compound's most thorough researchers. "I'm sure he'll come up with everything we need to know in no time."

Mal shook his head. "No can do. Kittan is busy with another project, plus we need the personal touch here." He grinned, displaying tobacco-stained teeth.

Maggie sat up straighter. "*We*? Whenever you say *we*, Mal, you really mean *me*. I have enough work of my own. You wanted me to go to Mexico and check on that new nest of chupacabras." *Please let me go somewhere and blow something up. Or even cut off a few heads. Go where I can grab one of those spiny bloodsuckers and pull off their spines one at a time.*

Mal smiled. Maggie knew that smile meant she wasn't going to like what he was about to say.

"I'm sending Calaban and his team to Mexico. Arius can go with them. He needs to get out into the field."

"Oh, no!" She shot out of her seat so fast she almost flew. "Exterminating chupacabras is one of *my* specialties, not Calaban's. He excels in Europe, and I do better south of the border. He loves going after trolls in the Black Forest."

"Then the next time I need to send a team to Europe, I'll send you, and you'll be even."

"Yo, boss." A two-foot streak of black fur burst into the room. "Maja wants sigs on these papers like three seconds ago." The ferret hopped onto the desk and leaned against a stack of papers, which threatened to fall over on him.

He pulled a tiny ferret-size travel coffee mug out of a hidden pocket and swigged down some caffeine. A small, purple baseball cap with the word "Cubs" embroidered on the front in bright green adorned his head.

"And Sand asked me to drop this off." Out of yet another invisible pocket the critter pulled a small, red silk pouch and handed it to Mal. Colors depicting a protective spell covered the pouch, indicating no one could open it except the recipient. Anyone else who tried would end up losing a few fingers at best, the whole arm at worst.

Ferret messengers populated the compound. Their energetic, sleek bodies could slide through the tightest spaces, making them excellent gofers, and the invisible pouch in their bodies was perfect for tucking away messages. All the high-octane caffeine they drank made them sound like demented chipmunks.

Mal sighed and waved his fingers over the papers. Each page fluttered as his signature scrolled across the bottom and then disappeared as swiftly as it had appeared.

"The damn paperwork alone will kill me. You'd think after all this time we could go digital, wouldn't you?" he muttered. He glared at Maggie. "Why are you still here?"

"To explain to you why I should be the one to take out that chupacabra nest." Maybe she could use witchflame this time. Once the chupacabras were destroyed, her team could finish up with an old-fashioned wienie roast and marshmallow toasting for s'mores. Maybe even a sing-along around the bonfire. She could really get into that. "I should be the one to go, and you know it."

"You need to remain here to keep an eye on Declan." Mal spoke around his cigar.

"My team can have the job done in one night. I'll be back before you know it." She feared she was starting to whine. She really hated whining, too.

"Fire demon Declan?" the ferret asked. "Catrina was

talking about him. She couldn't stop drooling. Said she saw him at Damnation Alley a few nights ago, and he could light her fire anytime."

"Fire demon? No wonder I smelled sulfur." Maggie turned to the ferret. "What else do you know about Declan, Trickie?"

"The obvious. That he's one hot guy," he chortled.

"Go." Mal waved his hand in his usual *Get the Hades out of my office* gesture.

"I need to be the one who goes to Mexico," she muttered, leaving the room with Trickie trotting at her heels.

"Don't think that's happenin' no matter what you say."

"Why is your Cubs cap purple, Trickie? Their colors are red and blue." Maggie eyed the garish cap.

"Forget Chicago. We're talking the New Orleans Cubs, babe. Those shifters know how to play serious ball." The ferret whistled a high-pitched tune as he raced off on his next task.

Maggie left the building and walked outside. She paused and looked up to admire the night sky dotted with stars and breathed in the crisp scent of sage. She'd lived in the five-hundred-acre Texas-based compound for the last hundred years and loved it. As the years passed, it continued to grow with additional teams and many Guard members starting families.

Protection wards meant their human neighbors couldn't detect the large area and kept it safe from supernatural predators. Not that any would dare to sneak onto the grounds, unless they wanted to be turned into a pile of ash.

The main buildings housing administration, the dining hall, the fitness center, and the armory were set in a semicircle at the heart of the compound, with living quarters for single members of the Guard and bungalows for families set off to the side. She headed to the fitness center, where she found Sybil seated on a workout mat with a pile of bandages arrayed around her. She looked up and grinned.

"Mal must have been barking rather than biting, since you're still in one piece."

Maggie reached down and pulled her friend to her feet. "Yeah, well, that doesn't mean I don't need some serious therapy."

Sybil's gossamer wings fluttered a calming scent. "Therapy as in...?" She raised a delicate eyebrow as they left the building and crossed the large compound that even past 2 a.m. was bustling with messenger ferrets busy with their tasks, as well as Guard teams coming back from assignments and others preparing to head out. The Hellion Guard worked 24-7 and was sent not only worldwide but also to other realms. Their work would put the Navy SEALs, Marine Recon, and Army Green Berets combined to shame.

Maggie nodded at some and spoke to others as she and Sybil made their way to a sprawling one-story building near the far end. She breathed in deeply, enjoying the scent of burning mesquite and smoked meat that permeated the air. She thought of the mega barbecue pit set up behind the dining hall. *Yum! Gonna be a barbecue later on.*

Sybil smiled at an Orlando-Bloom-as-Legolas look-alike, even spinning around and walking backward to watch him stroll away. The wild scent of the forest followed him.

"Focus, Syb," Maggie muttered with a grin.

"I am. But Elweard is seriously hot." Sybil returned her grin. "And his name means elf guard. How perfect is that?"

"Yeah, gorgeous, eyes that make you melt, a smile that's downright sinful." Maggie grabbed her friend's arm and pulled her along. "Forget the testosterone, woman. We have better things to do, as in girl bonding over an ice cream sundae."

"Shopping would be even better. We could take one of the jets and fly to New York City for a lovely breakfast, then hit the stores."

"Why do all my friends have this need to shop?" Maggie wondered if she'd missed out on that girl gene when she was born. She'd rather spend time training than at the mall. For now, she wasted no time heading to the building that housed a series of eateries covering every Guard species. A well-fed team was a happy team, and all the teams in the compound were extremely happy.

"It's more fun to go out and enjoy the great outdoors. And you don't need a snappy wardrobe and lip gloss to do it in, either."

"You wouldn't be so well dressed if we didn't brave the boutiques on your behalf. All you'd buy are more jeans, T-shirts, and yoga pants." Sybil followed Maggie through the heavy glass doors. "So what are we indulging in before you'll feel more like yourself?"

Maggie immediately headed for the dessert corner, which emitted mouth-watering, fresh-baked smells. "The hard stuff. I'm talking about a Snow Queen sundae that's over six feet tall."

The image of sexy Declan covered in yummy marshmallow crème popped into her mind.

Ha! I wonder what a fire demon would make of that?

Chapter 2

"ARE YOU READY TO READ THE DAMAGE REPORT ON THE club, Master?"

Declan looked up from the iced glass of vodka he had contemplated downing in the next few seconds. His half-demon self would metabolize the strong alcohol almost the same as spring water, but he could still savor the initial bite from the drink.

"How bad is it?" Not that he needed to hear the report. He'd already seen the disaster that had been his club. Months of work destroyed in seconds. But his second-in-command wasn't happy unless he could put it into a report for Declan to survey.

The imp that stood in front of him was about as ugly as you could get and scary enough to cause a lifetime worth of nightmares. Luckily Snips was as organized as a brownie, didn't tolerate bullshit, and was as loyal as you could get, considering imps were better known for pulling pranks than holding actual jobs.

But Snips had good reason to remain solidly by Declan's side. The demon was known for protecting those who were devoted to him. Declan was aware that Snips hadn't had a very happy existence before he took over the club. Now the imp didn't have to worry about being beaten, or worse, if he said one wrong word.

"That whole room will need fire blasting to get the Bloater shit off the walls, floor, bar, and the furniture. And that's not to mention the smell it left behind. That witch did a number on the place, Declan, and we're left to clean it up. We should send the Guard the bill." Snips frowned as he gazed with mismatched eyes at the ever-present PDA he was holding in his eggplant-colored claws.

"We can't totally blame her, Snips. To be technical, the mess came from the Bloater when he was destroyed." Declan recalled the ease with which Maggie O'Malley had caught the creature. A smooth efficient job—even if the oily mixture had ended up everywhere and he had been forced to close the club hours too early. Declan had heard stories of what happened when a Bloater was executed. Too bad those stories didn't tell all, or he would have barred it from the club.

"She just did her job, even though I wish she'd lured him outside to the parking lot before executing him." He leaned back in the buttery-soft, black leather chair, one hand still cupped around the glass. Steam curled upward in tiny coils as the once icy vodka now bubbled.

"The Hellion Guard prides itself on not going into a situation unless necessary. The questions I have are, what did the Bloater do to cause their attention to be directed on him, and why were they here to confront him? Is there a reason why we didn't receive any courtesy foreknowledge that this incident was going down?" He speared his assistant with a cold gaze. "Our intelligence claims to be as good as the Guard's. What happened?"

The imp didn't back down. "We have never bothered with the Bloaters. They are the lowest of the low and not worthy of our attention. While we are not happy when they come here, they do spend a great deal of coin."

"For something not worthy of our attention, it was still

spending that coin in *my* club and in some way should have been protected from the Guard interference—or at least escorted outside where the damage could have been better contained."

The scent of sulfur intensified in the room, and Snips instinctively stepped back as his boss's eyes glowed dark orange. Declan picked up a cigar and snipped the end. Not bothering with a lighter, he put it between his lips and puffed once. The end glowed cherry red, and rich aromatic smoke coiled upward.

The imp kept his slit-shaped eyes on his boss even as he struggled not to retreat any further. "No one sensed any reason to bar it from the club. Bloaters are known to battle more among themselves than with others. They have been in the club before and never caused a problem. Ratchet said anyone with coin that didn't make trouble could enter." Unspoken was what happened to anyone who did cause trouble in the club. They were never heard of again.

A dark-red candle that sat on the corner of Declan's polished ebony desk suddenly shot up in a white-hot flame that upped the temperature in the room a good fifty degrees. The flame soon settled into a gentle illumination, but the powerful heat remained.

"Then I am certain you will find out why the Bloater had the Hellion Guard on its ass. And you will tell me before nightfall." Declan stared at Snips as he set the cigar in an onyx ashtray. "I'm sure the club will be put back to rights as soon as possible, under your direction."

"I will need to bring through more workers to have the work done quickly," Snips warned.

"Do it, but make sure they are trustworthy and that they

understand it's only a temporary visit to this plane and that they will be returned as soon as the work is finished. No boons will be granted. This is purely a work-for-hire position, and they aren't allowed to leave the club under any circumstances. They are to be watched at all times."

The imp nodded and rapidly punched a few keys on his PDA. "The report is on your computer." He bobbed his head again and left the office.

Left alone, Declan stared at the candle, willing the flame to extinguish. As a barometer of his temper, the candle was infallible and an excellent way for him to work on not burning anything down.

He may have been only half a fire demon, but there was enough heat in him to level a large city in seconds. It only took a good sneeze at the age of four for him to burn down two houses. After that, his nannies were required to learn powerful fire-extinguishing spells and ordered to keep tight control over him.

He'd wanted a purpose to his existence. The chance six months ago to own this club was the beginning, even if it came with stipulations such as overseeing the portal. He was responsible for seeing that traffic was logged in and out and that certain demons didn't stay long in this realm. Some were to be barred altogether, but Declan knew better. If you had the right bribe, you could easily come through the magickal doorway. For demons, it was about what you had and were willing to trade.

But the excitement had started to wane right after he renovated the club to look as dark and dangerous as he felt and had named it as befitted his nature. He'd worked hard to erase all signs of Ratchet's influence in the building, so that it would feel all his. The underground club had been here for years, each new owner changing it to his personal specifications.

But there was always a price for that windfall, and if owners didn't follow the rules, they would find themselves dead. Declan's predecessors were well and truly gone. He didn't intend to follow their paths. He would do whatever it took to remain here, run his club, and create a new existence for himself. By agreeing to the terms of his new life, he could do that and more.

But lately, Declan felt the need to have something in his life other than the club. His existence had been lonely for so long, and now he felt the need for a mate. What caught his eye was a sassy witch who made him smile.

The question was if the interest was returned.

—∿∿—

"How you can eat all that in the middle of the night and not get sick is just… wrong." Sybil eyed what looked like a mile-high sundae that Maggie was consuming.

Scoops of peppermint ice cream were covered with marshmallow cream and dusted with tinted coconut, providing a colorful display. To make it last as long as possible, Maggie used a long-handled iced tea spoon.

Sybil returned to her one scoop of butter pecan ice cream topped with a spoonful of warm caramel sauce.

"Don't forget to clean up the mess before you leave," Tantris, the gnome that ran the kitchens, warned them. "And no taking it into the games room, either. When any of you do that, you forget to return the dishes."

"Spoilsport," Maggie muttered, spooning up her frozen treat.

"I have more to do than clean up after you. Do you

think a 1,000-pound boar can roast itself? Who's going to make sure the marinade is properly applied if I'm not out there to oversee the work?" He walked away with the rolling gait of a longtime sailor.

"Tyrant." The word held affection and not insult. After all, the teams wouldn't survive without Tantris ruling the kitchens that fed so many people and creatures at all hours of the day or night.

"One day you'll push him too far, and he'll cut you off," Sybil warned. "He comes up with more ice cream flavors than Baskin-Robbins could ever think of."

Maggie sighed. "True, although there have been a few that I'd never want to try. Remember when he had all those leftover oysters?" She shuddered. "That was totally disgusting."

The elf waited until Maggie had another spoonful of ice cream and coconut before speaking again.

"Tell me about this Declan, Maggie."

The ice cream immediately slid down the wrong way, and Maggie began choking. Sybil didn't have a chance to hop out of her seat to save her before a passing giant thumped Maggie on the back so hard she shot out of her chair.

"Thanks Otos... I think," Maggie choked, accepting his hand as he pulled her to her feet.

"Take smaller bites," he advised in a deep, reverberating voice before he walked away, each footstep sounding like the beginning rumbles of an earthquake.

"So he's that hot." Sybil's lips parted in a wide smile. "I'm beginning to think I shouldn't spend so much time in the compound. How I wish I were on your team. I'd love to see him in person." She spooned up more ice cream.

"No biggie. He's a fire demon. Not someone I'd care to hang out with. He hosts Bloaters at his club, for Fates' sake. I'm positive 'sarcasm' is his middle name."

"And here I thought that was *your* middle name," the comely elf murmured. Her wings wafted more lavender and vanilla.

"Mal wants me to find out what Declan's doing here," Maggie said.

Sybil raised an elegant eyebrow at Maggie's disgruntled tone. "But he said that Kittan can't do research for you, so that means you have to do all the grunt work."

"Mal's punishing me." Maggie waved her spoon in the air and then quickly lapped the coconut off the bottom of the utensil.

"Again?" Sybil giggled and then quickly backed off. "Sorry, I couldn't resist. Besides, why such a long face? If Mal told me I had to investigate a sexy male, I would be all over him."

"Okay, Syb, that word choice doesn't work. The image of you all over Mal is pretty gross."

Sybil ignored that remark. "We all know that demons are very private. They may mingle with others, but that's very limited. They are usually vigilant about who they hang with. I can imagine the only reason Declan is around so many of our kind is because of the club."

Maggie's mind clicked away like a computer. "I can't see Mal having any interest in Declan. It's got to be about the club."

"The club, as in the portal, since we know all their clubs have portals." Since Sybil had already finished her ice cream, she now dared to steal some of Maggie's. The witch was so occupied with her thoughts that she didn't think to object. "Demons coming in and out. Creating mischief."

"Creating turmoil and bloodshed is more like it. Hey!" She playfully swatted Sybil's spoon away from her dish. "Go get your own."

"I've already had mine, and now I'm saving you from a million calories. So when are we visiting Damnation Alley so I can see this demonic hottie for myself?"

Maggie stared at her friend, whose usual attire was lilac or soft cream in spider web silk. The short, angled hemline showed off slender legs and feet encased in ballet-style slippers. "Uh, Syb, even if you do a great job being truly scary when you're in interrogator mode, you still look more Tinker Bell than Xena."

"We're talking going clubbing and dancing, Maggie, not taking down any big bads," Sybil argued, then pleaded, "I wanna go dancing. I wanna meet some sexy males."

"Mal would draw and quarter me if I took you to Damnation Alley and something happened to you."

Sybil's ethereal features shifted to a rarely seen stubborn expression. One that Maggie knew meant the elf wouldn't back down. "I'll be perfectly safe if I'm with you."

Maggie swallowed her sigh. "The dress code at Damnation Alley tends to be black with a lot of chains, fangs, and claws."

"I have a gorgeous dark-purple dress, and I can appear as forbidding as you when you're doing the one-hot-mama look." Sybil sat back in her chair and stared at her friend. "What else is bothering you? There's something else on your mind, isn't there?"

Maggie made a face. "Arius filed a grievance against me. It seems he didn't like his last training session in the gym. One tiny cut the healer took care of in seconds. You'd think I'd cut off a limb."

"I think he has a crush on you."

"Sure. You always file a grievance when you have a crush on someone. He just wants to make my life miserable, and he's doing a good job of it."

"I'd call it a good way for Arius to get your attention, even if he went about it the wrong way. Come on, Maggie. You have to admit he's cute. He makes me think of a cuddly, awkward puppy you want to pick up and hug."

"The last thing I need in my life is a puppy. Still, as long as he doesn't hump my leg or pee on my shoes, I won't have to kill him. You'd think he'd know better than to file a grievance against me. It's just going to make it harder for him when he takes my classes. For Fates' sake, if Arius had done that to Zouk, he'd have been turned into something you could scrape off the highway."

As Maggie stared at the slowly melting remains of her mega-sundae, she realized that her eyes had very much outweighed her stomach. A buzz was rolling around in her head, and she was positive one more bite would send her reeling into a sugar coma.

"The club probably won't be open for a few weeks," she mused. "That Bloater made a pretty huge mess when it exploded. I wouldn't want to be on that cleanup crew." She took one look at Sybil's face and sighed. "Fine. You and I will check out Damnation Alley when the place is open for business again."

Sybil's squeal bounced around the room. "This will be so much fun. We haven't gone out together in ages."

"Oh, yeah, it's going to be a blast," Maggie muttered, picking up her dishes. "Want to play *Grim Reaper*

Blaster?" She grinned in anticipation of one of her favorite video games.

"I want to choose the game," Sybil groused. "You always win at that one."

"Who's in angst here?" She batted her eyes.

"Fine, but after one game, we play one of my choices." Sybil stood up.

Maggie thought about it. "Deal."

An hour later she entered her quarters, first noticing that her wastebasket was empty, the bed covers were pulled back, and fresh towels were set out in the bathroom. Even the mess in the shower had been cleaned up, and the tile sparkled.

But her biggest surprise was seeing her once Bloater-spattered top and skirt now immaculate and neatly draped over a chair. A small note covered with neat calligraphy topped the clothing.

Do not ever leave a horrific mess like this again.

There was no doubt the note was more than a warning. It was a promise that if she did, she'd end up without domestic service for centuries.

Maggie stopped at her dresser and gazed at the tiny painted portrait of a small girl's smiling face. *I love you, Margit.*

"I love you, too, Aleta," she whispered, thinking of the sister she couldn't save so many years ago and her vow that no one else would lose a loved one if she could help it.

She didn't bother undressing but merely fell on the bed, and, thanks to the beginnings of a sugar coma, she had no trouble falling asleep immediately.

Something was very wrong here.

"*My dreams usually involve old boyfriends who sud-denly sprout fangs and fur,*" *Maggie said from her seated position on a brick-colored couch that was as comfy as it looked. Scented candles were scattered around the room, the soft fragrance of spice permeating the air. She looked over the back of the furniture when she heard a door open and close and a familiar male figure walked in.*

"*What are* you *doing here?*" *they asked at the same time.*

"*You're in my dream,*" *Maggie told him, still not sure if this was a good thing or a bad thing. She cast a quick glance downward. Oh good. No sexy lingerie, leather bras, or corsets along with thigh-high boots. She was dressed simply in her favorite gray jeans and sage cot-ton T-shirt. Her feet were bare, and she caught a glimpse of her ankle bracelet.*

"*No, you're in* my *dream, Margit,*" *Declan stated, deliberately using her birth name. She wondered where he gained her real name, when there was no way of learning his. He walked around the couch and dropped into a navy easy chair. Like Maggie, he wore jeans and T-shirt, but in unrelieved black, while his dark hair stuck up in unruly disarray, as if he'd just climbed out of bed.*

"*I don't like surprises.*" *Feeling the need for protec-tion, she cupped her hand, waiting for the reassuring warmth of witchflame in her palm. Except nothing hap-pened. She scowled at her empty fingers.*

Declan smiled. "*Funny thing about that. You seem to forget I own fire. If I don't wish it in my presence, it won't make itself known.*"

Maggie looked around. "So what all do you do in here?" *She leaned forward and picked up the television remote.* "So what does a half-demon watch in the dream realm?"

"You can have flatter abs in just two minutes a day!" *A perky brunette with a bleached, toothy smile announced.*

Maggie clicked the channel button.

"This floor cleaner is a miracle worker!"

"This cookware set will be the last one you'll ever use!"

"How many foreign languages do you want to learn in a matter of days?"

"*Oookay*." *Maggie switched off the TV.* "You've got Hi-Def infomercials. That is so sad."

"*Tell me about it. No sports channels, no movie channels, just nonstop raves for diet aids, kitchen tools, cleaning products, and exercise equipment. Maybe this is a nightmare.*" *He stood up and held out his hand.* "What do you say we blow this joint?"

Maggie felt the heat of his fingers as she allowed him to pull her to her feet. "We can do that?"

"*Sure we can. It's our dream.*" *He laced his fingers through hers and snapped his fingers.*

If he hadn't been holding her hand, she knew she would have fallen. There was a dizzying sensation as the world spun around like a tornado.

Well, Dorothy, I don't think you're heading for the Emerald City.

Once Maggie felt as if she was on solid ground again, the first thing she noticed was the hint of sulfur, and it wasn't coming from Declan. She tightened her grip on his hand as she stumbled on loose rock. At least she now

*wore shoes. A rumbling sound rippling through the air
had her looking up and up and up.*

*"Are you kidding me? We're at the base of a volcano!
Don't you get enough eau de sulfur at the old homestead
so you feel you have to travel for more?"*

*"No, that's just a bonus," he told her. "I thought you
might like to stretch your legs."*

*"Stretch my legs as in hiking up a volcano?" By then
she realized the shoes on her feet were hiking boots.
"While I like long walks, I'm not all that keen on trek-
king up a cliff that looks like it's ready to blow."*

*"No, it's just having a minor tantrum." He wid-
ened his stance when the ground rolled under their
feet. "Besides, this is the best time to climb it. Makes
it more challenging."*

*Maggie burst out laughing. "Lead on, Sir Edmund."
She gestured upward.*

*Declan took hold of her hand and started up a rocky
path. "You're a Hellion Guard. That means you're in
top physical shape. This should be a walk in the park
for you."*

*"Yes, we all endure rigorous physical training," she
replied. "But I'm not a glutton for punishment." She
rubbed her nose against the acrid smell. "I've done my
share of hiking, but there are times when it's nice to curl
up with a good book."*

*He shook his head. "I can't see you as a witch of
leisure."*

*"When you've been on a mission that's lasted for
days and sleep was nonexistent, you think seriously
about a week-long nap." She paused to pick up an odd-
shaped piece of shiny lava rock and tucked it into her*

pocket. She was curious to see if it would show up once she was out of the dream realm. "So this is your idea of exercise?"

"I also like running. I'm not into joining a fitness club, so I use the track at the high school." He climbed easily over a tall boulder and helped her to do the same.

"I hope you have a dozen water bottles on you, because while you might not mind the smell, I do. And why doesn't it smell like rotten eggs?" She wrinkled her nose.

Declan laughed. "Sulfur only smells musty and acrid. The rotten egg smell comes from hydrogen sulfide."

"Great, a science lesson, too," she muttered, wishing for her perfume, although she wasn't sure the black-orchid scent would blend well with the pungent smell around her. "You must have been teacher's pet."

"You either received high marks in your studies, or you received a whipping," he said matter-of-factly. "A wonderful incentive to study hard."

Maggie stopped abruptly, pulling on his hand. "You were beaten?" She huffed a laugh and shook her head. "Of course you were. No wonder most of you turn out psychotic." She winced as her palm lost skin on a rough boulder. A whispered spell instantly healed the flesh. "At least some magick works here." She gripped his hand tighter when she started to slide on the loose rocks.

Declan pulled her upright, for just a moment holding her so close she could feel the hardness of his muscular body, waiting as she nodded she was okay.

"So tell me about yourself, Declan. What do you do when you're not in the club? Follow the volunteer *fire department? Go out to the elder home and perform tricks? You must save a fortune in heating bills."*

Declan chuckled. "You enjoy being a smart-ass, don't you?"

"It's a gift," she said with appropriate humility. "If I can't take my enemies down with my Guard skills, I talk them to death."

He smiled and shook his head as he followed the upward path. "Or blow them up."

"Now that was an accident," she defended herself. "I didn't realize the Bloater would burst into gooey bits so fast. I almost clogged the shower trying to get that nasty stuff off. So come on, dish, big boy. What do you do during your off hours when you're not climbing Mount Everest?"

"I'm actually a quiet guy. Like you, there are times when I'm happy to settle down with a good book and a glass of wine. What about you? What else do you do besides going into clubs and destroying them?"

"Not my fault, remember? Last week I played dog-catcher." She began to regret talking, since now the taste was in her mouth. She wondered if a marathon toothbrushing and using several cases of mouthwash would erase the nasty flavor.

"As in—?"

"Caught a hellhound that got off his leash and returned him to his owner. That critter decided I was his mommy, and yuck! Have you ever had one lick your face?" She mimed gagging. "A hellhound's breath is about as rancid as you can get."

"What about when you're not on duty? What do you do for fun?"

"*End up in someone's dream. So how do you think this happened? I'll be honest. I've never shared a dream with someone before.*"

"*I couldn't say.*" He stopped and produced a water bottle, handing it to her first. "*But I'm not sorry to see you here, Margit.*"

"*At least you haven't asked what my sign is.*" She was grateful to find the water tasted cold and refreshing without any tang from the sulfur around them.

"*I gave up pick-up lines years ago.*"

She handed the bottle back to him, experiencing an odd flutter in the pit of her stomach as she watched him drink. "*You're not what I expected of a fire demon.*"

"*Half,*" he corrected her. "*My mother was human.*"

"*It looks like you take after your dad.*"

Declan's expression darkened. "*Not exactly a compliment.*"

"*Fine, no more said.*" Maggie looked up, relieved to see they were almost at the top. She fanned herself with her free hand. "*And I thought Texas during the summer was hot. You really need to consider cooler destinations for your hikes, and I don't mean the Andes, either.*" She allowed him to pull her up the last few steps until they stood on the edge.

"*What do you think?*" Declan looked down.

Maggie followed his gaze, staring at the rich red, orange, and black colors that the molten lava comprised as it bubbled up amidst the dark smoke. "*I've never seen anything like this,*" she said softly, feeling in awe of the force of nature that was so close to them.

"*It's a humbling experience,*" he replied quietly. "*All it takes is one good rumble, and the lava bubbles up*" *and out." His gaze moved to the ground a few feet to their right. "What do you know." He placed his hands at her waist as he pointed in the direction he was looking. "Look there. Can you see it?"*

She looked down at the spot he gestured toward.

Among the gray and black earth was a tiny spot of color. Two green leaves framed a delicate white flower that looked too fragile for such harsh surroundings.

Maggie's face fairly glowed as she looked up at Declan's. "New life," she whispered. "Lava kills, and yet that small plant managed not only to grow but bloom amid the desolation." Tears sparkled in her eyes as she smiled at Declan, who smiled back. She tipped her face upward as he leaned down. She then straightened up when the air around them turned to a gray mist. "Uh, is this supposed to happen?"

Declan sighed and said with regret, "Sweet dreams, Margit."

"Dreams? That's what we're—"

"—having now," Maggie was still saying as she shot up in bed. "Lights." She looked around the bedroom, finding herself alone in bed.

"Do you mind?" Elle mumbled sleepily from her spot. "Some of us need our beauty sleep."

Maggie climbed out of bed. As she did, she realized she felt a pull in her leg muscles as if she'd been... been hiking up a mountain. She shook her head, trying to convince herself it was nothing more than a very realistic dream as she changed into pajama pants and a tank top. She crawled back under the covers and pulled them over her head. She whispered the lights off.

She lay awake in the dark, aware of a hint of sulfur on her skin. When she shifted in bed, she realized there was something hard under her. She reached under her body and picked up an odd-shaped piece of lava rock.

—⁓—

Declan paced the length of his bedroom. His skin felt tight and ready to combust, while his erection only added to the pain straining his body.

His dreams were infrequent and usually included blood and suffering. A few times, a portent of things to come would visit him during his sleep, but never had he had a dream like this.

He had brought females into his dreams before. They were always beautiful, knowledgeable in the sensual arts, and eager for the prestige of mating with a fire demon—even a half-breed. Some were rejected; others he accepted because they happened to show up when he felt lonely and wanted the surcease only a woman's body could offer, even if only in a dream.

The only problem was that his loneliness returned the moment he banished them from his dreams, and the sex was nothing more than an unsettling memory.

This time, there was no seduction. Just a normal conversation! Something he wasn't used to in the dream realm *or* real life.

"Too bad we couldn't have had that kiss before we woke up, Maggie O'Malley," he whispered. "I think you owe me one."

Chapter 3

"WHOA, WHAT'D YOU DO LAST NIGHT?" MEECH ASKED as he used the tip of his knife to pick his jagged teeth. Something that resembled a wiggling Cheeto was stabbed on the tip. "You look like shit. I hope the guy was worth it."

"Gee, Meech, tactful much?" Maggie practically chugged her espresso, waiting for the high-test caffeine to hit her system with all the subtlety of a Louisville Slugger. A past-dawn bedtime meant she hadn't woken up until midafternoon, and she knew her usual peppermint tea wasn't going to do the trick.

Her body clock was seriously out of whack. She could feel the weight of the small rock she'd tucked inside her pocket. "I'm going to tell your mate you said that, and she's going to cut your heart out with a spoon."

"That's nothing new." His usually sunny-natured blue face looked forlorn. "Reesa told me if I even looked at her funny, she would put a knife through my dick. Pregnancy hormones are a bitch."

Sybil's wings fluttered as she glided over to the table with a large cup of warm honey and nectar held firmly in one hand and a muffin in the other. "He told Reesa that perhaps her age might be the reason she's so on edge lately and that he was positive she'd feel more like her old self once the babe was born."

Espresso almost spewed out of Maggie's nose. "And

you're still in one piece? Meech, Reesa's in a delicate condition. The last thing you do is say something stupid like that."

"You couldn't have told me that before? I thought she would cut my balls off. And I'm very fond of my balls." He returned to cleaning his teeth.

"Reesa is older than most females when they bear their first young. We didn't think she could conceive. We had a lot of sex every time she was in heat, and this time it happened." His homely face suddenly shone with delight at the thought of a child in his household.

Maggie thought of her own childhood, short as it had been—she'd been only six when her parents died of plague. But she never forgot her baby sister, Aleta, who'd followed Maggie everywhere on unsteady feet. And the memory of how the little girl died was seared forever in her mind. The village bully had stampeded a herd of sheep that ran the little girl down, leaving her with what Maggie now knew were fatal internal injuries.

All Maggie knew then was that her baby sister cried constantly in pain and no one could help her. The young Maggie had held the little girl as she exhaled her last breath. Maggie vowed that she would grow up and do whatever it took to learn how to protect those who couldn't protect themselves. Three months later, the rest of her family died during a plague epidemic and Eurydice appeared to take her away to the Witches' Academy.

Meech turned to Maggie. "You will be there for the birth, true? After all, you are the vow mother. The one who will be there to help guide our child into a fulfilling life."

Maggie gulped. "I thought all I had to do was buy a nice gift."

"No, the vow mother is there to witness the birth of her charge. And to give her blessing when the child finds his or her mate." He pushed himself away from the table and lumbered off, still engrossed in picking his teeth.

"Nobody said anything about my having to be there for the birth," Maggie told her friend.

"It's a natural function of life. Their kind isn't so different from humans."

"If I'm lucky, I'll be sent out on an assignment when Reesa goes into labor."

"You know very well that the Fates won't allow it." Sybil glanced around and then leaned closer to Maggie, keeping her voice low. "There was some excitement last night. I got a message after I reached my quarters to go to the holding cells. Deets's team brought in a prisoner who was in a bad way. The jailer wanted me to talk to her since she was saying some alarming things."

"You mean they wanted you to calm her down and not bother waking up a healer." Maggie shook her head in disgust. "That had to mean that Xera was on call. She won't leave her bed unless a gorgeous man has something to do with it. You should have gotten tough and told them to drag her skanky ass out of bed and let you have your sleep."

"It was better that I went and not Xera, who may be an excellent healer but doesn't interact well with anyone with severe mental distress. The female is demon and was hysterical. I would have said that demons are never hysterical."

"Why do I feel you're going to tell me something

bad?" Maggie forked up her scrambled eggs spiced with green peppers and onions. Yay for breakfast served 24-7. "Oh, wait a minute… all we know is bad."

The elf nodded. "I'd say this could be as bad as we've had in some time. The female has dark knowledge of something about to happen. They did finally bring in Xera to use a sleeping spell because the demon wouldn't stop screaming. She probably won't awaken until late tonight, but I'd like you to listen in when I talk to her again. All I heard last night was a lot of odd rambling, but I sensed a strong core of truth in there—and not in a good way."

Maggie nodded as she worked on spreading black-raspberry jam on her toast. "What did Mal say when you told him?"

Sybil shook her head. "I wanted more details before I made my report. Once you hear what she has to say, you'll understand why I'm waiting."

"No hints before tonight?"

"Better if I don't." She sipped her drink and continued snacking on her muffin. "I want a fresh perspective."

"I thought that's what Boris was for."

Sybil made a face at the mention of her superior. "He can read about it in my report."

Maggie mulled over what Sybil *wasn't* telling her. "Now you're scaring me."

"Nothing scares you. Well… except for childbirth." Sybil flashed an evil smile as she finished her nectar. "I have to get to my office. Don't forget you promised to take me to Damnation Alley once it's running again. I want an up close and personal look at that demon."

"I don't recall promising a thing." Maggie flashed

Sybil a bright smile. "And if you've seen one demon, you've seen them all." *Unless they're so gorgeous, your teeth ache when you look at them and they take you on a hike up a volcano.*

Sybil leaned over the table to whisper in her ear, "And if I recall correctly, Mal doesn't know who left that bunch of henbane in his desk drawer. The same henbane that caused him to break out in an oozy case of boils that didn't go away for a week."

"That's blackmail."

"I learned from the master." Sybil sketched a snarky curtsey and left the dining room.

Maggie flicked a bunch of half-hearted magick sprinkles the elf's way. All they did was buzz around her head for a moment and then flitter off. "I swear, you can't trust anyone these days," she muttered, now concentrating on her syrup-soaked pancakes.

———

Maggie finished her breakfast, wondering why she hadn't mentioned her dream to Sybil.

She decided it was a good thing. Her elf buddy probably would have suggested Maggie talk to one of the people in the Psych department who dealt with dreams. That was one place she preferred to stay out of.

But what kind of dream found you seated in a living room watching TV with a half-demon?

She fixed herself another extra-strength espresso and snagged a cheese Danish on her way back to her chair. She figured some part of it was moderately healthy.

"Thank you." Her cup was taken out of her hand before she could sit down.

Her eyes almost crossed as she stared at the new blight of her existence. "You—"

Declan waved a hand as he sipped the super-caffeine. "Excellent. Perhaps you should get some for yourself."

Maggie's first thought was that he was very lucky she wasn't in the mood to pull out the silver stiletto strapped to her thigh. Or snag the short sword resting against her back... and there was also the PK Walther 380 snuggled in a shoulder harness. Not to mention a venomous black widow spider tattooed to her bicep. Elegance rustled in response to Maggie's sudden state of alertness.

Just because she was in her own territory didn't mean she went around unarmed. And if there was one thing she hated, it was somebody sneaking up on her when her guard was down.

But damn, the man was downright mouthwatering, and she had to admit he was a great conversationalist in the dream realm.

"How did you get in here, and who authorized *that*?" Her eyes fairly turned him to grave dust as she stared at the medallion around his neck that indicated he was a visitor to the compound and would be treated accordingly.

He continued drinking his—*her*—espresso. "If you have the right papers, you are allowed to enter the compound and they give you pretty jewelry." His eyes danced with laughter over the small cup. "It just so happens that I have the right papers."

"Forged, I'm sure." Maggie had to wiggle her fingers because of the magick that threatened to erupt from the tips.

"I don't need forged papers, Margit."

Maggie prided herself on not giving away her emotions

even when she was blindsided by a sexy half-demon. This was one of those times when she had to dig down deep to keep her expression serene.

Declan's black eyes smoldered with an eerie silver sheen. "You're more than an everyday witch, Maggie O'Malley." He paused. "Tell me something. How did a witch with Nordic looks like yours come up with a name straight from the Emerald Isle?"

"My father." She gave him her usual explanation.

He raised an eyebrow at that. "What was his name?"

Maggie flashed him a blinding smile. "Sven O'Malley." She stood up. "Now if you'll excuse me, I have work to do."

Declan also stood. "As do I. I was notified that you're holding one of my people."

I should have known the female demon belonged to him. Jealousy, party of one.

"That's not my department." She looked around until she spied one of the messenger ferrets. "Bickie, would you take Declan over to the holding cells?"

"I'd prefer you to be my guide." Declan continued, watching her with a heated intensity that flowed over her skin's surface.

"And I'd prefer a long weekend camping in the Outback. I have a meeting to attend. I should warn you now that the female had to be sedated because she was very agitated."

She ignored the look of anger on Declan's face as she looked down at the black ferret whose head whipped back and forth as if he were viewing a tennis match at warp speed. He continued slurping coffee from his tiny to-go mug.

"Have a good day." Maggie smiled as she sauntered off.

"Dude, you were so lucky," Bickie told Declan as he led him out of the dining room.

"Why is that?" Declan watched the sun bounce off Maggie's gilded hair as she crossed the compound.

"Maggie tends to break things or shoot someone when she gets that look on her face. I could tell you stories," he trilled in his overly caffeinated voice.

The half-demon looked down at what he considered his new best friend. "Really? Such as?" It wasn't easy to throw a subtle suggestion into a brain moving along at that high a speed, but he soon accomplished it.

And Bickie didn't stop talking about the comely witch as he led Declan to the holding cells.

"The next time we go after a Bloater, someone else will go in... *Frebus*." Maggie shot a grim eye toward the blond-furred creature.

"Bloaters don't like our kind," he defended himself. "They'd smell me a mile off."

"So do we," Meech muttered from the other side of the conference table. "Ever hear of taking a shower or even using cologne other than something that smells like a century-dead skunk?"

"As if you smell any better," Frebus snarled.

"Boys, boys," the witch soothed. "If you keep this up, I'll have to put you both in time-outs. We'll have playtime later. It's just that our last three missions have ended up as disasters."

"Not really. When you consider the end result, they were all successful." Tita, a tall sultry vampire and the other female on the team, chimed in. Her pale slender fingers were cupped around a mug of blood.

"No loss within our team and no damage. Unless you consider your outfit last night." Her nose wrinkled with distaste. "Too bad. Now, can we get on with this? Some of us prefer sleeping during daylight hours."

Since she was several centuries old, Tita could move about indoors from dawn to dusk, but she chose to keep the schedule she'd been forced into when she was first Turned. She specialized in night jobs and hypnosis, and could see perfectly in the dark, which made her a very useful Guard. Not to mention she had her own lethal methods. She leaned back in the dark-red leather chair and crossed her legs, with an evil grin at her colleagues that revealed wickedly sharp fangs.

"I heard that the owner of Damnation Alley is here on the grounds," Meech brought up. "Do you think he's going to file a complaint against us for destroying his club?"

Maggie opened her mouth to say something, then closed it. An odd prickling sensation skated along the tops of her arms, leaving her feeling unsettled. She already knew Declan was in the compound, so it wasn't some witchy warning system.

But she'd bet her favorite Hisshou fixed-blade military knife that her unease had to do with the sexy half-demon. Reposing in tattoo form on her shoulder, Elle offered spidery whisperings that echoed Maggie's thoughts—trust an arachnid with mating on her mind to be alert to those particular sensations.

"Maggie?"

She straightened up at the sound of Tita's voice.

"Sometime today? Tick tock." Tita tapped her watch. "Fine, last night was a cluster fuck. No one's fault." She glanced sideways at Frebus, who slid further down in his chair, trying unsuccessfully to minimize his seven-foot furry self.

"Perhaps a little. We all know that outside intel can be sketchy or not entirely accurate. We need to have one of the researchers look into the Bloater communities. There are clearly things we don't understand about them. That way, if we come up against another, we'll know better how to handle it."

Damn, I should have been the one to say that!

"I don't understand why this particular Bloater suddenly popped up on our radar," Meech said. "They always stay pretty much to themselves."

"Easy. The so-called 'blob from the swamp' had been seen cruising the human communities for the previous couple of weeks," Maggie said. "Dogs and cats were missing, and fear escalated when a four-year-old boy disappeared. Luckily, he was found a couple of hours later. The Bloater had nothing to do with that, but we needed to neutralize this one before something worse really did happen. Anyone know how we got the tip it would be at Damnation Alley?"

Frebus studied the contents of the file folder in front of him. "The call was anonymous and couldn't be traced."

"Then we need to find out if that was the only Bloater causing trouble," Maggie announced, getting up from the table. "Frebus, you put in the request for a researcher. Meech, it's your turn to write up the report for Mal." The creature groaned. "Consider it safer than pissing off Reesa any more."

"I'm willing to offer a personal apology to Declan," Tita volunteered with one of her patented smiles that were guaranteed to make a male offer up a vein.

"That's been done," Maggie said crisply.

"O'Malley, to the holding cells." Mal's voice boomed from the speakers implanted in the walls. "*Now*."

"Everything is now up to him." And she knew just why her boss was demanding her presence there.

It all had to do with a demon named Declan.

―᳁―

Declan paced the room with the impatience of his kind. The last place he wanted to be was in the Hellion Guard compound. But Snips's news that Anna had been brought here was enough to have him out of bed and in his car in seconds.

Not that the idea of seeing Maggie again didn't have its charm. The witch intrigued him, and he intended to find out just why she had invaded his dreams and his very being.

"As I told you, she won't awaken until late tonight," an elf with large lavender eyes informed him.

He sensed that the elf's delicate exterior housed a steel-like core. Tough as titanium, just like all Hellion Guards. Just like Maggie.

Except when she smiled up at him after he pointed out the flower—and what was it she had said? Something about new life amid the desolation.

"And she will awaken when I demand she do so. *All I have to do is see her*," he said between clenched teeth. He took one step forward into the elf's personal space. To her credit, she didn't back down.

He froze when a razor-sharp blade rested against his neck and one arm was smoothly pulled behind his back.

"I suggest that the big, bad demon back the Hades up *now*," Maggie purred in his ear. "Otherwise, I would be forced to grovel to the brownies so they'd scrub demon blood out of my favorite jeans. And they really hate demon blood."

Declan knew better than to go up against a Guard, especially when he had other activities in mind for the sexy witch.

"The elf..."

"The elf's name is Sybil," Maggie said tautly.

He tightened his jaw. "Sybil explained that Anna had to be sedated. I can awaken her." He deliberately relaxed his muscles to show he was as nonthreatening as a kitten.

He breathed easier when the knife was removed.

"The sedation used had to be very strong," Sybil explained.

"And she is mine," he reminded her. "I want to see Anna now."

Sybil looked as stubborn as the other two but finally nodded and gestured him out of the room.

Declan felt his temper begin to simmer as Sybil led the way and Maggie walked behind him down a dismal gray hall toward a guarded room at the far end.

"Why is she considered a prisoner?"

"She was a danger to herself. We had no choice but to restrain her," Sybil told him.

"Anna doesn't have one violent bone in her body." The half-demon looked ready to create some violence of his own as his eyes shimmered silver. The temperature rose a good twenty degrees.

Sybil pulled a PDA out of her pocket, tapped the screen a few times, and handed it to Declan.

"Blood! So much blood! Brutality. She must be found for the sacred sacrifice so the evil one may return!" The female demon's screams seemed to bounce off the walls even as she paced back and forth. Sybil could be seen in a corner in observation mode.

"Who is he, Anna?" The elf's voice was calm with none of the bite she was known to exhibit when interrogating vicious prisoners.

"The revered one. One who ruled the world to the south." Anna's dark eyes glowed with a fervent light. *"The Destroyer. The god of destruction."*

"What in Hades is she talking about?" Declan whispered.

"Sounds like she's talking about someone from your part of the world rather than mine," Maggie commented.

He pushed the PDA back at Sybil.

"Is Anna under arrest for something?"

She shook her head. "As I told you, she was brought here for her own protection. I know this looks upsetting, but she was better off being taken here than to our hospital, where she would have had to be restrained to a bed."

"If that was the case, I should have been called. She should have been brought to me, not locked in a cell." His jaw twitched with the emotions flooding his system. He despised being in a situation that was beyond his control.

"All we knew was that she was a demon. We certainly didn't know anyone was looking after her," Sybil said. "We only wanted her kept safe."

Declan looked through the small window into a room where a slight female body lay unmoving on a narrow iron bed. He pressed his hand against the shatterproof glass. It wouldn't have taken much power to melt it, and with the way he felt at that moment, he was very tempted to do just that.

He replayed Anna's cries in his head. She was too delicate to be here. But the alternative was unthinkable. Here, he could protect her.

"I want in there now. I will awaken her."

"It's dangerous to interfere with a healer's work when the patient has been sedated that deeply," Sybil argued. "Anna's mind could be damaged if she isn't handled carefully."

"Unlock the door, or I will destroy it." Declan felt the heat and fury flow through his body like molten lava.

Sybil opened her mouth to further protest, but Maggie placed a hand on her arm.

"It's all right, Syb. Perhaps Anna will be calmer with Declan here."

Sybil pressed her hand against a metal plate by the door and whispered a few words in her language. A soft click followed her words, and the door silently swung open.

Declan pushed past the women and entered the room. He knelt on one knee by the bed and rested his hand on the sleeping female's forehead before bending his head and lightly pressing his lips in the same spot. He felt the heat of her skin as bad dreams and fear infected her body.

Anna's eyes slowly opened. The dark orbs brightened as she recognized him, and she tried to sit up while talking rapidly in their language.

"*He wishes to destroy us all. We must stop him!*" She clutched at his arms.

"*You are safe, little one. I will never let anyone hurt you,*" he soothed, wishing he had the knack for providing comfort, but consoling someone wasn't something he was familiar with.

"Last night she talked about blood and danger," Sybil said, while she stood nearby.

Anna gasped and gripped Declan tighter.

He stood up and gathered Anna into his arms. "This is over. I'm taking her home."

"That isn't possible." Maggie stood in the doorway.

Declan knew she wouldn't harm him as long as he had Anna in his arms. No matter what, he considered his charge an innocent.

"We are leaving. There will be no interrogations." He glared at Sybil, who continued to look serene. "There will be no cells."

Anna whimpered as the tiny room's temperature increased. He took a deep breath, and the heat dissipated.

Maggie stepped back and to one side.

Declan left the room with Anna still cradled in his arms.

"We need to talk about this," Maggie told his departing back and then yelped as flames flared up from her toes. "Hey! These are my favorite boots!"

Declan fervently wished someone would try to stop them as he left the compound with Anna holding on to him. He knew it wouldn't happen when he heard the elf tell someone they were cleared to leave.

As if that would make a difference. He was getting them out of there no matter what.

"I am sorry," Anna whispered to him.

"You did nothing wrong." In a short amount of time, he was outside the compound and tucking Anna into the passenger seat of his BMW. "I'm just glad you're safe."

"But I'm not." She curled up into a tiny ball, her bronze-colored hair falling over her face. "You're not, and I'm so afraid."

He slipped into the driver's seat and reached over to cover her hand with his. "Believe me, Anna, you are safe. You are under my care. No one will ever hurt you." He started up the car, soothed by the sound of the powerful engine.

Anna pulled in a deep breath and exhaled. "She likes you." Her words were hesitant and shy.

"Who?" He knew even before she replied.

"Maggie, the Guard. She's very pretty."

Surprised laughter escaped his lips.

"I think she'd also like to fry me."

"But you forget that with our kind, that's an act of love." Anna arranged herself in the seat to look out the window.

"Perhaps we'd be better off just sending candy and flowers like humans do."

Chapter 4

"I AM SO STOKED." SYBIL FAIRLY BOUNCED OUT OF Maggie's venom-red Viper and walked around the hood.

"Sybil, hon. Please don't say 'stoked,'" Maggie begged. "It doesn't suit you."

She fixed the back strap on one of her plum leather sky-high heels and then shimmied to smooth down her going-out uniform of a black leather skirt barely long enough to cover the essentials and a plum-silk tank top. She was sporting her club look with sparkly gel in her hair to slick it back.

Sybil had chosen a hot-pink strapless dress and had pulled her lavender hair up into an artful twist secured with black lacquered chopsticks that Maggie knew would turn into weapons, if need be. Sybil slung the chain to her tiny black bag over her shoulder.

"I'm not allowing you to spoil my mood. I never get to go to the edgy clubs," she complained.

"You might not even like Damnation Alley. Edgy clubs are usually dangerous, and most only like Dark ones coming in." Maggie passed her hand over the Viper's hood. "Protect yourself. Allow no one to cross your boundaries, and if so, sic 'em," she ended with her usual relish for danger.

The car's response was a throaty growl and a shudder as a dark shimmer overlay the convertible. "Besides, I thought elves and Fae had their share of sinister and edgy clubs."

Sybil looked away for a moment. "We do, but as a member of the Hellion Guard, I am never welcome. They always think I'm spying on them. If it wasn't for you, my social life would be woefully pathetic."

"Pathetic? You date more than I do!" Maggie thought about it. "You're right. It is pathetic. Most of our social lives revolve around activities at the compound. Sweetheart, you're a total downer."

She walked swiftly past the long line waiting to get into the club until she reached the black leather rope and the giant guarding the entrance. Black flames covered the rope, ensuring no one would try to get through without permission. If they tried, they would end up as ash on the cement.

"What makes you think you're welcome here, Guard witch?" the giant bouncer growled even as he gave Sybil the typical male once-over. She smiled at him, but her eyes glowed with a green fire that sent the ugly giant a step back.

"Wow, where did Declan find *you*? Talk about someone who's not a people person," Maggie remarked. "Not a good way to bring in the business, big boy. You need to work on your conversational skills, because, guess what? I can go wherever I want." She wiggled her fingers before zapping the rope. The power died in the leather.

"You *will not* enter." The giant held up his hand, palm out.

"Shrink him, darling," Elle advised from her spot on Maggie's collarbone. The diamond-studded spider glared at him. "I would love to have him in my web. He might last longer than my last male."

"Patience, pet," the witch advised. "I'll find you something inside." She took a step forward.

"No." The giant presented himself as a wall with his hand still up.

"Hmm, guess what? I don't do 'no.' And I don't talk to the hand." She stared at his palm. "So I suggest you step aside, little man."

The giant growled again and took another step toward her, deliberately crowding her personal space.

"It's all right, Anton." Declan stood in a doorway that pulsed with tiny red-and-yellow neon lights lining the doorjamb.

"I haven't searched her for weapons yet." Anton looked way too happy at the prospect. "It's obvious she's carrying many of them."

"He's really looking for a whomp upside the head, isn't he?" Sybil whispered.

"I can search him." Elle skittered to Maggie's other shoulder for a better look at Declan. "He does look tasty."

"Hellion Guards are required to be armed at all times." Maggie stood her ground as she looked the giant square in the eye and ignored the demon standing behind him. "And even if we weren't, I wouldn't give up my weapons to anyone."

"Anton." Declan's quiet voice sliced through the stare down.

The massive creature slowly backed away but didn't take his eyes off Maggie, who displayed a toothy grin as she and her friend sauntered past the rope.

"I've got to give you credit, Declan. You have an excellent security force," she told him as she and Sybil followed him further into the club.

She was relieved that she had used a noise-dampening spell for her tender eardrums because the hard-core music battered them with the vengeance of an angry boar. She'd advised Sybil to do the same, but the elf insisted she wanted the entire experience. Judging from the pained expression on her face, she wished she'd listened to Maggie.

"You also seem to have a great cleaning service. I'm impressed you got the place up and running so fast." Maggie looked into the club's main room, which was packed with dancers and drinkers. She grimaced at the sight of a gremlin dancing on a table.

"The only difference I can see is your bartenders' uniforms." She gestured toward the demons manning the bar in blue polo shirts that mirrored the neon-blue lights buried in the black glass counter. She noticed the lights pulsed in time with Disturbed's "Into The Fire," which blasted from speakers embedded in the walls.

"Do you think that's some sort of code?" Sybil stared at the bar with the fascination of one who could be easily hypnotized.

"Could be, so I wouldn't look at the lights for too long." Maggie pulled her along and then stopped short when Declan turned around with two champagne flutes in his hands. He smiled and held them out.

"A product of France," he assured them.

Sybil disregarded Maggie's look of warning and accepted the flute held in front of her. "As if he'd try something here." She took a tiny sip and giggled. "The bubbles," she explained.

Maggie wanted to refuse the champagne, but she knew she couldn't with her friend sipping away. "I'm usually more a Stoli gal, but you did say the champagne is French." She took an experimental sip and then another. For a moment, she was transported back to a France of beauty and old-world elegance, where carriages were everyday transport and a lady never revealed a bare limb.

And Madame Guillotine would have had another victim if a rogue of a French pirate hadn't spirited her away from the dungeons holding the nobles awaiting their death. During that dark time, Maggie had learned that some of the cells below the earth held a magick-dampening effect. The experience had taught her that she liked her head where it was—and that a pirate ship smelled worse than the cell where she'd been incarcerated. Even after all these years, the memory of the stench remained in her olfactory memory.

"What stories do you have to tell?" Declan murmured in a voice that was meant for her ears only. "What adventures have you had over the centuries you've wandered this earth?"

"Very boring. I'm sure you have much more interesting stories of your time in the demon realm." She observed no reaction from him and decided to press further. "Or is that why you chose to come here? For a change of pace? Did you receive the club for good behavior or for your birthday?"

"I earned this club," he told her. "And I intend to keep it."

"Dancing, I'm going dancing." Sybil moved toward an elf that'd given her the eye. She set her champagne flute down on a nearby table as she swiveled her hips his way.

Declan stopped Maggie's instinctive motion to check

out the male her friend was pursuing. "Nothing will happen to her," he assured her. "By now, everyone in here knows the two of you are under my protection. Although I'm certain you don't appreciate the gentlemanly gesture," he teased.

She was chagrined to discover that he had managed to maneuver her away from the dance floor and toward the entrance of a long hallway. Every step of the way, she'd felt the heat of his hand resting lightly against her spine. The moment they passed through the archway, the music became so muted that she had to deactivate the sound-dampening spell.

Declan stopped at some double doors and threw them open.

"Come into my parlor," Maggie murmured as she brushed past him.

"You surprise me, Maggie." He opened a cabinet and pulled out a bottle of champagne, opened it with a thought, and lifted it in a silent question. He topped off her flute and then filled another.

"I've been known to throw people off-kilter." She walked around the office, noting the spare decor and a large desk of highly polished dark wood that boasted only a laptop, a telephone, and a six-inch statue carved from black psilomelane drusy. She wondered how he had obtained such a large chunk of the rich, natural-black metallic mineral. The quartz crystals covering it glimmered in the dim light.

She ran her fingertips across the top of the figurine and then lifted it, rubbing the tip as she gauged the magick that coated the stone. "I will admit curiosity. Why do I surprise you?"

"You were worried for your friend until I guaranteed you she was safe. You trusted me enough that you left Sybil out there. And you didn't hesitate to come back here with me, where you had to know we'd be alone."

He perched himself on the arm of a nearby chair, watching her movements with the intensity of a cat stalking its prey. He lifted the glass to his lips and sipped the sparkling liquid.

Except it had been a long time since Maggie had allowed herself to be intimidated.

"So, why are you here? You didn't come here to dance, and for obvious reasons, Bloaters are no longer allowed in here," he said.

She nodded. "Good idea, since I'm sure the speed-of-light cleaning service was pretty pricey. Although, with what I saw bellying up to the bar, I'd say you can afford it. Especially since you're wearing the monochrome wardrobe. What do you do when you get up and get dressed? Just open the closet and say, 'Oh, I guess I'll wear… black,' right?"

His lips curved in a smile. "Would you like to see my closet, Maggie? You might be amazed by what you find."

She shrugged. "You've seen one… you've seen them all." She savored the champagne as she studied the man across the room.

Declan didn't need to be a half-demon to be sexy. She knew he had what it took no matter what, and it wasn't just that spicy scent from his skin that she detected.

While his silk button-down shirt was the usual black, she saw a hint of silver gray in the shadow stripes, and the black slacks fit his lower half to the extreme. The two open shirt buttons allowed a hint of golden tanned chest, and she noticed a black fire-opal set in gold on his ring finger.

Hmm, left hand. Does that mean he's taken? And if he is, why did he march me up that volcano? Plus, is he the type to show he's committed to one woman?

"Are we through with the small talk?" Declan asked, getting up to refill his glass and then hers. Maggie tried hard to keep her eyes away from his seriously nice ass and the fluid way he moved around the room.

"I guess so. I never was good with small talk. I just like getting down and dirty." To her horror, she felt a blush creeping up her bare neck as she felt Elle's tiny chuckle skittering over her skin. *Terrific, Maggie, just shove your stiletto right smack into your mouth!*

Only the tiniest hint of a smile indicated he was tempted to follow up on her faux pas.

"We need to speak to Anna," she said in her most businesslike manner, deciding it was time to get to matters at hand.

"Not possible."

Maggie nodded, expecting Declan's refusal. Not that she'd accept it. Just that she knew he wouldn't give in too easily.

"It's obvious she knows about something that could threaten us all."

"What makes you think that?" This time he moved over to the black leather couch and sat down, leaning back.

Maggie likewise moved to sit in the nearby chair. "This is really comfy." She shifted her ass into the glove-soft leather. "Although, would it really have hurt you to buy this in, say, white? Or even navy, if you want to stay with the neutrals."

"Don't you ever say what's expected? What kind of witch are you, Maggie O'Malley?"

"I haven't carried a wand in centuries and never wore a pointy hat. Although my cauldron still gets used on occasion. There are some traditions you can't give up."

"But you work as a Hellion Guard, and as you say, you're never unarmed. I'm sure that puts many males off." He seemed to keep a wary eye on the glittering spider that now perched on her shoulder and watched him intently.

"They're not worth my time if they can't handle it." She set her glass on the nearby table. "I'm serious about Anna, Declan. The things she said to Sybil when she was first brought in mean something's going down."

"Who's to say it's not demon-related?" he asked her. "What is that phrase again? Oh yes, 'Everything isn't all about you.'" He leaned over and pulled a cigar out of a hand-carved box. He nipped the tip and then puffed on it once before the tip glowed red.

"I gather you also don't adhere to the no-smoking bans in public places."

One eyebrow lifted in amusement. "That's a human law, not mine. As you know, humans aren't allowed in here."

Interesting, he says mine *and not* ours. *And they say the Guard is a law unto itself.*

"Your predecessor Ratchet allowed them in. He thought they made excellent playthings, even if he knew his activities with them were illegal." Her eyes flared with anger.

Declan's features turned to golden stone. "He had his

rules. I have mine." He kept his gaze on Maggie. "Is that why he disappeared? Because he brought humans into the club even though he knew the Guard didn't allow it? Why didn't you just shut him down?"

Maggie thought of the horrifying mess she'd found in the middle of the desert with a bloodthirsty Ratchet in the midst of it. That was the night she'd experienced the pure pleasure of dispatching him to the deepest bowels of Hades. She hadn't regretted her actions since.

To date, no one but her knew exactly what had happened to Ratchet. She preferred to keep it that way.

"We didn't have to. He did it to himself. Ratchet was the lowest of the low." She settled back in her chair and crossed her legs, seemingly oblivious to how far her skirt inched up her thighs. Her shoe dangled from her foot. The brilliant emerald set in the broom charm on her gold ankle bracelet winked flashes of color.

"He watered down the drinks, drugged females so they could be used in private sex shows, treated the help more as slaves than employees, and I'm sure he skimmed from the top. Plus the rumors that he murdered many creatures weren't just idle chitchat."

Declan sat up, leaning forward to rest his arms on his knees, his fingers linked together. "Did you kill him?"

Her eyes didn't waver from him. "Why would I kill him?"

"Because he did as you said—and much more. Because the demon world won't argue against a lawful execution done by a member of the Hellion Guard. Because he would have deserved it." His eyes bore into hers, seemingly in search for answers.

"Was he a friend of yours?" Maggie asked.

Declan's laughter was harsh to the ear. "Ratchet had no friends, only those who despised him."

"Yet you inherited his club."

"I *earned* this club, and that is all you need to know." He jumped to his feet. "And as for Anna, no, she will not return to the Guard compound. No, she will not be interrogated by your elf, and no, I will not allow even you to speak to her."

"What if she gives us a written statement?" she suggested. "Something, or someone, greatly upset her. I need to know what sent her into such terror. Don't you see, Declan, it could be something that will affect all of us, not just your kind. I am bound to protect everyone, even the demons."

His lips twitched. "The only ones to protect demons are demons." His eyes turned even darker with lambent hints of flames in the depths. "But what of you, Margit? Who protects you? Who keeps the night terrors away?"

"I don't have them." She stood up, the soft leather of her skirt sliding down her thighs. "I can go over your head and formally request that I have a chance to speak to Anna."

"No." For the first time, his ironclad confidence seemed to slip. "Anna has done nothing to deserve your attention."

"She was picked up because she was distraught and acted as if she were about to do harm."

"Yet you didn't bring her to me."

"Sybil told you we didn't know she belonged to you." She still wondered just how much the lovely demon belonged to him. He'd acted like the adoring male with Anna when he left the compound with her in his arms.

"She doesn't belong to anyone but herself," he bit out the words. "But Anna is under my protection."

Maggie admitted she wasn't surprised often, but she was now, as the realization hit her with the force of a Mack truck.

"She's in hiding," she said. "How much danger is she in?"

Declan sliced his hand through the air. "Do *not* speak that aloud."

Without looking down, Maggie reached inside her small clutch bag. When she found what she wanted, she brought it to her lips and whispered a few words.

"Sometimes secrets are necessary. I will keep yours."

"If I give her over to you," he said bitterly.

She pressed what she took from her bag into his hand. "Have her keep this on her at all times. It won't make her invisible, but it will keep her under the radar you're obviously using."

Declan stared at the small, brown chiastolite sphere that held a black cross in the center. "Protection."

"I always carry extras, and I added some extra oomph to this one," she explained. "I'll make a deal with you. I'll talk to our Seers. If they don't think I need to speak to her, I won't push the issue."

"And if they do?"

"Then I'll be back, and I won't be as nice next time."

"Yes, I can see that." He continued to stare at the sphere as if he'd find all the answers there. "Why?"

"Over the years, I've had to fly under the radar a few, or a thousand, times. Now I'm going to snag my dancing friend and get out of here before something happens that would require my intervention. I really don't want to have another good outfit ruined." She walked toward the door.

"Maggie." He reached the door before she did, turning and leaning against the door frame so she couldn't leave. "You're doing this for me, aren't you?"

"What is it about the male ego that thinks it's all about them?" She laughed and shook her head in amusement. "As long as you want to protect her, I will help. The minute you try something else, I'll tear your balls off. It's been a long day, so I'll say good night." With a nudge of her hip, he was gently pushed aside. She pulled open the door, leaving behind the scent of black orchid.

"But I haven't had a snack yet," Elle could be heard complaining. "Could we at least stop by the bar? I'm sure I could find some nice insects there."

By the time Declan reached the main room, Maggie and her friend had reached the exit. He noticed that the pretty elf was smiling and wiggling her fingers in farewell to an elf he knew to be a club regular.

He also knew things about the male elf he didn't think the elf was aware he knew. He had no doubt that if Maggie learned about his proclivities, she would cheerfully disembowel the male without a second thought.

"What did the witch want this time?" Snips appeared at his side.

Declan kept an eye on Maggie's slim hips and long legs. "She only wanted to help."

"The Guard doesn't help. They only destroy," the imp sneered.

Declan felt the sphere in his pocket, where his hand

now warmed the stone. He felt the heat of her magick in the depths and the sense of safety it offered the owner. It was obvious it would shield Anna better than anything he could have devised.

"I want to know everything you can tell me about the witch. Go back to the day she was birthed."

"Why?" Snips's suspicion was at a high level.

Declan kept his expression noncommittal. Snips may have been an excellent personal assistant, and Declan wholly relied on him for the workings of the club, but that didn't mean that he trusted Snips with anything personal. Snips knew Anna by another name, and Declan made sure her true identity was hidden from the imp. He figured as long as he didn't slip up where Anna was concerned, Snips wouldn't discover the truth.

"It's always best to know all you can about your enemies."

"You don't look at her as if she's an enemy." Snips's ugly face showed disdain.

"It's better to allow her to feel as if she has me under her control." Declan surveyed the dance floor and bar across the room. Both were filled, as usual. "Use your sources, and if you run into trouble, give them my name. I can't imagine anyone would let her know I'm looking into her history."

Snips pulled his PDA out and began tapping the keys. "It will be done." He started to move away, then paused. "But you be careful of her. Many think she was the one who killed Ratchet," he spat out the name as if it left a bad taste.

"You didn't like your former master very much, did you?"

"No one did, and he didn't care as long as we did what he wished. But that doesn't mean *she* should have been the one to destroy him. And it means she's dangerous." Snips sniffed and then left Declan alone.

And that was exactly how the half-fire demon felt, even in a room crowded with creatures from every realm. He rolled the sphere in his palm.

For a moment, he imagined he could feel the light coolness of Maggie's touch against his skin.

He hungered for it again.

———

"He asked for my number," Sybil chattered away in the car.

"And you were a good little elf and didn't give it to him." Maggie downshifted as she turned a corner. Her silence was telling. "Please tell me you at least checked him out!"

"Definitely."

"Not his ass… him overall. You did some interrogation mojo on him, right?"

"He knows I'm with the Guard. Do you really think he'd try something?"

"Hmm, let's see. There was that gremlin we brought in two months ago. He knew you were with the Guard, and he also thought you were a total pushover. Which you almost were, because he trotted out a sob story worthy of a midnight soap opera on the Supe Love Channel."

"I went through my usual list of questions as we drank and danced, and his answers were all I hoped for," she assured her friend.

Her cell phone chirping "All Star" interrupted Maggie's

comment about sanity having more than one meaning. Without looking down, she tapped the Bluetooth button on her steering wheel to answer.

"O'Malley."

"Tell your friend that Algar has to cancel their dinner date this weekend. He's been called back to the Dark Country." Declan's voice flowed through the microphone like smooth jazz.

Maggie shifted uncomfortably in her seat. "How did you get this number?"

"What did you do to him?" Sybil demanded, practically leaning across Maggie.

"Trying to drive here, babe," Maggie told her.

"I want to know what you did to him, Declan!" Sybil's voice grew shrill even as she still partially obstructed Maggie's vision.

"Syb!" Maggie pushed at her friend's shoulder. "I can't see the road!"

"Algar's a great person, and there was no reason for you to mess with my social life," Sybil growled.

"Trust me, there was an excellent reason."

"I want to know how you got this number!" Maggie chimed in.

"Sweet dreams, Maggie." He clicked off.

Maggie muttered a variety of curses in multiple languages while Sybil added a few of her own.

"That's it. I'm dragging that Anna in tomorrow." Sybil fell back against her seat. "My eight brothers weren't allowed to mess with my social life, so there's no reason for him to think he can." A soft chirp sounded from her bag. She pulled out her cell phone and began reading. "Oh, boy."

"'Oh, boy' what?"

"Yours isn't the only cell number Declan dug up. He texted me a report on Algar. It seems that son of a whore has a few side businesses we need to check into." Sybil's delicate features turned hard.

Maggie grimaced. "So Declan did a good thing."

"Yes."

"Oh."

Sybil looked at the witch. "Did you do something?"

Maggie took a deep breath. "Remember Jim Morrison singing about lighting his fire? Well, I guess you'd say I doused Declan's."

Her friend gaped and then burst out laughing. "Let's hope he's wash and wear."

———

When Anna walked into Declan's office, she found him standing in the midst of a downpour that didn't touch one piece of furniture.

She pressed her hands over her mouth and just stared with saucer-size, midnight-black eyes as her shoulders began shaking with suppressed laughter. "Declan?" she choked out the name.

The long-suffering demon wiped his face as steam rose up from his clothing.

"Anna, would you get me a towel, please?"

Chapter 5

MAGGIE SAT CROSS-LEGGED ON HER BED WITH HER laptop whirring away. A bored Elle was navigating across the rose-patterned bedcovers with delicate steps. Morning sunshine streaming through the bedroom window reflected off her diamond-encrusted body and cast rainbows of light that danced around the room.

Maggie sang along with Beau Jocque and the Zydeco High Rollers as they played from her computer's iTunes library.

"Please, do not sing," Elle begged, making her way up to the shadowy refuge of her web and her miniscule computer. "A foghorn would sound more palatable to the ear."

"You should talk. Your singing is worse than mine." She clicked several more keys as she set the machine to search out every piece of information on fire demon Declan. "And FYI, you don't have real ears."

"Have you ever heard of a wizard named Akashik?" Elle asked from her ceiling perch.

"No, but that doesn't mean anything." Maggie's eyes were glued to the laptop's screen. "Why?"

"He wrote an article for the *Journal of Wizardry* saying that some magickal venoms can be reversed." Excitement lightened her voice. "If I can't find an immortality spell for my lovers, perhaps he could help me that way."

"Check him out first. There are a lot of fakes in the wizard world." Maggie put the laptop on a table and got up to dress. "Are you coming out with me?" she asked after pulling on a soft, blue cotton tank top and jean shorts.

"No, I will remain behind and supervise the brownies in their cleaning." Elle's gaze didn't shift from her computer.

Maggie winced at the piles of laundry, clean and dirty, along with shoes stacked in a corner. "This is why I prefer living in the compound to having my own place." She placed her sunglasses on top of her head.

"*Data scan finished.*"

Maggie returned to her laptop and checked the screen. "This is all there is? Declan really *does* have a boring life."

A few minutes later, she left her quarters and crossed the grounds to another sprawling building. Halfway across, she stopped and lifted her face to the morning sun, feeling the warmth seep into her skin.

She wondered how Declan felt about getting a surprise shower. It was small revenge for having to change her cell phone number, change all her passwords, and check her credit cards. Security was everything in her line of work. She still wanted to know who gave out her cell number, so she could come up with more creative vengeance.

If she'd been the one on the receiving end of a monsoon, she would have plotted the ultimate retribution by calling her witch friend, Blair, the revenge-witch queen. Maggie wondered if Declan was the vindictive type.

"Who doesn't want to get even?" she muttered as she closed her eyes against the bright light. "I would."

"Get even for what?" Frebus asked.

Maggie's nose wiggled against the reek of sweat and wet dog. Frebus might not be of the canine variety, but he did have enough heavy fur to rival a Saint Bernard.

His dark-pink eyes peered at her from under his shaggy blond bangs.

"Those new recruits are pussies," he told her. "They were crying for their mamas and pissing in their pants before we were ten minutes into class."

She grinned. "You roared at them, didn't you? And I bet you showed them your second set of teeth."

He displayed choppers resembling steel knives. They only came out when he was in the midst of a fight. "I'm nothing like what they'd face in battle. They need to learn early."

"Mal wants us to go easy on them in the beginning."

He snorted. "If we did that, they'd be gutted first time out." He looked around. "What are you up to?"

"My computer ran a search on Declan, which didn't turn up all that much. He's either been in the demon realm all this time, or he's managed to stay out of trouble. And now I'm going to see Ravenna." She thought of the Seer as she walked toward a tall archway sizzling with brightly colored magick. "If there's something in the wind, I'm hoping she can find out what it is."

"What about the female demon that was here a couple nights ago?" Frebus ambled along with her. "Word's out she talked gloom and doom. You know… the usual 'end of the world the way we know it' shit. Anything to it?"

"We weren't able to find out specifics, and Declan's not letting us near her again."

"Like that's ever stopped you before." He snuffled

loudly and then ran a hairy paw across his nose. "Drag the bitch's ass into Interrogation, and let Sybs do her work."

Maggie smacked his shoulder hard enough that the seven-foot creature stumbled. "What did we agree on about the B word?"

He hung his head. "That it's not a good idea to use it."

"And why is it an excellent idea to strike it from your vocabulary?" She used her schoolteacher voice.

"Because if any of us forget and use the B word, you'll boil us in oil—after you skin us."

"Good boy!" She reached up and patted him on the head. "Go take a shower, because you really stink. Euuwww!" she squealed when he laughed and hugged her tightly, transferring some of the smell to her.

Maggie reached the archway and stopped in front of the runes etched in the sandstone. "I, Margit, humbly beg for entrance." She pressed her palm against the runes, waiting until they blinked gold. Once they sparkled, the crackle of the magick died down and she was able to pass through safely.

Maggie felt a hint of disorientation every time she entered the Seers' Pavilion. The building's ceiling was a rainbow of colors that shifted in patterns like a kaleidoscope. The soothing music from chimes hanging everywhere blended with sounds of lyres and flutes. She wrinkled her nose against the strong scent of patchouli in the air and then sneezed.

"Who do you wish to see?" A young female dressed in the dark-orange cowled robe designated for apprentices suddenly appeared before her. The apprentice's hair, the color of a ripe peach, flowed down past her hips.

Maggie didn't blink at the sudden visitation, nor was she surprised she now wore a soft cotton robe of electric blue. Maggie knew that when she left the Seers' quarters, she'd find herself back in her tank top and jeans. Until then, she felt as if she had been catapulted back to the 1960s. Her bare toes curled into the floor, which felt like a cloud and was warm from magickal sunlight.

"I would like to speak with Ravenna to see if she might enlighten me about a dangerous situation that is in the air," she said.

"You really need to relax," the apprentice advised. "Let me see if she's free."

Maggie waited, listening to the music and voices singing. One archway led to what looked like a spring meadow where a group of Seers gathered in a circle. She was so engrossed in watching them that she didn't notice the apprentice returning until the young woman touched her arm.

"You should join us. We're having a skyclad brunch later," she told Maggie as she directed her down a hallway that hadn't been there a moment before to a simple door at the end.

"I really prefer reserving my nudity for more private parties," Maggie replied.

Her guide disappeared the moment Maggie placed her hand on the doorknob and gently twisted it to one side.

The interior was as dark as the reception area was light. The ceiling looked like a night sky dotted with silvery stars and a shining crescent moon. Maggie was relieved that the scent of patchouli was absent from the room, but she wished she could mute the sitar music.

"Good morning, Ravenna." She stepped inside, carefully feeling her way across the room.

"Margit, it is wonderful to see you!" The woman facing her was petite and garbed in a silver-hooded robe that matched the curly ringlets drifting down her back. She stood in the center of the room with a warm smile on her face. "I haven't seen you since the Winter Solstice. Wasn't that a wonderful time?"

"From what little I remember." Maggie hadn't forgotten the hangover that plagued her for a week afterward. The Seers worked hard and partied even harder.

"What can I do for you?" Ravenna waved her hand in the air, instantly bringing the light level up to full moonlight.

"A female demon is saying darkness and death are coming."

"And that's a new thing?" Ravenna laughed softly. "Margit, you live for danger."

"This seems to be more than the usual. I wondered if you could See what she might have tapped into and if it's something we can control." Maggie waited.

The small figure walked around the room, her robe glinting in the magickal starlight. She hummed an odd tune under her breath.

"Her real name isn't Anna. She's hiding from her sire and master, who wants to enslave her in a way that not even many demons can comprehend." She spoke in a soft monotone that flowed over Maggie's brain like silk.

"He cares not for her body, but for the gift of what she can See. He wishes to use her like currency to further his own causes, even seeks to auction her off to the highest bidder if it furthers his own purposes. He is looking for the right way to punish not only her but also her brother."

Maggie bit her lip to contain all the questions hovering on her tongue. She knew better than to interrupt the Seer when she was on a roll.

"She can only See what is dark in the world. Not just danger, but blood and death. What she has Seen is more than you can imagine, but her mind refuses to believe it. You will have to urge her to release the images so they will not haunt her. She is an innocent in this, as is her brother." A sly smile curved her lips.

"Are you sure there's any such thing as an innocent demon?" Maggie argued.

Ravenna's laughter rippled through the air. "As always, Margit, you are impatient. You need this female. She's the key to finding another innocent, one who requires protection, since she is the center of what will happen when the darkness descends."

"Another demon?" She instantly knocked Declan out of the running. If he was an innocent, she was Mariah Carey.

"No, this innocent has blood that has blended over the years. She has no idea who or what she is, but she is a crucial player in the coming time of blood and darkness." She tipped her head to one side. "I hear ancient chants in the ether and See blood sacrifices meant to begin the process."

Oookay, that doesn't sound good.

"How crucial?"

"She is the one who could open the door to the one that wishes to destroy the world as we know it and rule the new land through violence and death. She must be found and protected so that this being of darkness doesn't use her for his own purposes.

Maggie shifted from one foot to the other. "So there are specific targets?"

Ravenna looked upward as if the ceiling of stars and the crescent moon would offer an answer.

"No one specific. Just everyone who doesn't worship him."

Yep, so not a good thing to hear.

"This Anna is an innocent, and she's the only one who can find some person who's the key to something that wants to rule the world?" Mal chewed on his cigar. "Except Declan doesn't want us talking to her. Anything else?" He glared at Maggie.

She scowled back. "Isn't that enough?"

"What have you dug up on Declan? He's a demon, so what kind of havoc has he been wreaking?"

Maggie shrugged. "He doesn't seem to have done much, actually. At least, not in this realm. All that shows up is that he took over Damnation Alley not long after Ratchet disappeared."

She ignored Mal's questioning look. Even her superior didn't know exactly what had happened to the psychotic demon, and she preferred to keep it that way. There were some things this grumpy gnome didn't need to know.

"Give me the CliffsNotes version."

"I just did."

Mal sighed. "Are you telling me that with all the databases we own, you could only find out one tidbit?"

"Hey, you said you couldn't spare the researchers who might have been able to uncover more, but I don't think even they could find anything else. It's as if he popped into this world fully evolved. Maybe he did. It's happened before with demons."

Mal stared at the marble columns of his serene surroundings that warred with his intense personality. Curls of smoke wafted in the air.

"My therapist said this would relax me. All it does is make me want to take a weapon out and shoot all those fucking cherubs," he growled. "All they do is flitter about like demented butterflies. Do you know how annoying that is?"

Maggie looked upward at said cherubs. She had to agree their tiny wings did remind her of butterflies.

"Maybe you need a new therapist."

"Last time I hire one because she's got great legs. Okay, back to Declan," he said finally. "It seems as though he's become a major player pretty quickly. Who's his sire?"

"Victorio. His mother was human. Apparently she died not long after the child was born. I'm sure Victorio wasted no time taking the baby off the human grandparents' hands and taking him back to his realm. Wouldn't be surprised if money weren't involved. A son would be a great boon for him, even if the child was half human. For Declan to rise as far as he has shows he's more his father's son than his mother's. At least in personality."

"Odd for a fire demon to choose a human to mate with. The human usually doesn't survive the fucking," Mal mused. "She had to have something more in her bloodline not only to live through the sex but also to get pregnant."

"Unless Victorio did something to ensure he would have a child." Maggie thought of the charcoal depiction of Declan's father she'd found online. It was like looking at an alternate version of Declan. The same gorgeous sculpted features, but dear old Dad was clearly the usual psychopath demon with thoughts of evil and violence etched into his features, while Declan's mother's blood had been strong enough to allow a lot of humanity in her son's face.

"Forbidden magick," the gnome grumbled. "He probably bespelled her into thinking he was human to trick her into accepting him so he could get her with child. I bet she didn't have a clue what was going on until she gave birth, since the baby wouldn't look the way Declan does now." He used his cigar to sketch in the air.

She made a face at the smoky drawing of a baby that looked more like something that had gone through a meat grinder than flesh and blood. She settled back in her chair, waiting for the other shoe to fall. Mal was great at dropping a bomb on her when she least expected it. This time, she hoped she was prepared.

He leaned back in his chair, his stubby legs propped up on the desktop. He continued puffing on his cigar, sending the acrid smoke drifting among the pillars. "We need to talk to this Anna. You got the goods, babe. Use them." He raised his heavy eyebrows.

She shot up in her chair. "Oh, no, been there, done that. Wore the ton of makeup, skimpy clothes, and learned to pole dance. Never again."

"You do that every time you go clubbing."

"But I wear quality skimpy clothes and high-end makeup," she corrected him. "And I didn't need a pole to dance."

"The way I hear it, Declan's hot for your bod, so it shouldn't take much effort on your part."

"Stop pimping me out, Mal, or I swear I'll have a chat with Brigid," she threatened, mentioning the saucy gnome he'd been dating for the past five hundred years. The pool predicting their marriage had changed dates so often that everyone involved had given up. They'd finally used the money for a big party.

Even that didn't deter him. "Just do your thing, O'Malley." He waved his cigar at her. "Get outta here and do your job instead of sitting around looking decorative."

"My pleasure to leave your presence," she muttered.

"And hook up with the demon so you can talk to the female," he shouted after her.

While the thought of seeing Declan again was oh so tempting, she didn't think he'd be that happy to see her after the impromptu shower she'd sent his way.

"He deserved it," she told herself. She moved down the hallway, sidestepping speed-of-light ferrets racing from one office to the next as they made their deliveries.

"You're talking to yourself again." Zickie, a white ferret with a saucy red beret perched on his head, paused long enough to grin at her. The rich aroma of high-octane cinnamon mocha teased Maggie's nostrils. She vowed to pick up a mug of peppermint tea. "Oh, this is for you." He reached inside his hidden pouch and pulled out a small scroll that felt heavier than it looked. "From Ravenna. She said you'd need this."

"Thanks." She tucked it in her jeans pocket to peruse in private. She knew if the Seer insisted she'd need the contents, she'd *need* them.

"Later, gator." Zickie took off in a white streak of fur.

Maggie headed outside, only stopping long enough to get a tall to-go cup of her tea.

She reveled in the warm sunshine as she walked to the edge of the compound. The air glistened with the protective spells that kept the complex invisible to the human eye. It wouldn't bode well if the locals knew that all sorts of supes lived within fifteen miles of the small rural suburb of Houston.

Not when so many humans had shotguns mounted in the back of their pickup trucks. As if Maggie was one to talk, since she had a nice Remington racked in the pickup truck she sometimes used.

Along the way, she snagged a folding chaise lounge from the pool and dragged it with her until she reached a deserted area of grass some yards away.

Once the chaise was set up, she settled down and pulled the scroll from her pocket. A small heart-shaped stone fell into her lap. She picked it up, studying the colorful striations in the opalescent gem. It warmed in her palm and glowed with an eerie light the longer she held it. She finished unrolling the scroll, studying the elaborate calligraphy.

Carry this with you at all times. You will know when it is needed.

"Thanks, Ravenna. I just love it when you spell things out for me." She conjured up a pair of sunglasses and stretched out on the chaise.

There was nothing like some Maggie time.

～

The rich aroma of spices, tomatoes, and garlic tickled her nose along with her taste buds.

"Uh, I don't dream in the middle of the day." Maggie stood in the tiny foyer of a small restaurant that was below street level. Red-and-white-checked tablecloths dotted the small square tables and booths along the walls, and multicolored drip candles sent waxy colors down the sides of the Chianti bottles while music played in the background. Almost every table was filled with diners dressed in clothing more suited to another era. She noticed they ignored her as if she wasn't there. But then, maybe she wasn't.

She looked down to find herself wearing a drop-dead perfect little black dress along with black kitten heels. Wow, the girls have never looked better. *"Dean Martin and Frank Sinatra? How cliché."*

"Even though the restaurant was popular in the 1920s, I thought Frank and Dean were better musical choices." Declan walked out of a nearby hallway.

"What will I find out back? A cocker spaniel and a street mutt sharing a plate of spaghetti?"

He shook his head. "Not when I last looked. You do like to pop into people's dreams, don't you? I thought after our hike, you wouldn't want to venture out again."

"It's more like I don't have a choice. You sleep during the day?" She ignored the fact that she was catnapping herself.

"Night person, remember?"

"So you dream of an Italian restaurant straight out of the 1920s. I would think you'd choose a speakeasy." She allowed him to guide her to a nearby table.

"There's no better place for lasagna." He took the chair to her right. "Your appearance here is a nice surprise."

"It's a surprise for me, too." She looked up when a rotund man wearing an apron bustled out with a large tray in his hands. Smiling and greeting them in Italian, he placed the tray of antipasto on the table and snapped his fingers. A bottle of red wine and two glasses were added to the table.

"You really should try Marcello's lasagna," Declan told her with a smile that warmed his dark features.

"I love lasagna, so it sounds good to me." She smiled at Marcello, who gave a bob of the head and bustled off.

"I have to admit I'm glad you're here," Declan said. "I normally don't have company when I'm here, so this is nice. I hope you like garlic. He tends to go overboard with it."

"Obviously not a favorite place for vampires," she quipped, choosing a mushroom and then provolone before picking up a slice of warm bread and dipping it into olive oil alive with seasoning and then moving on to prosciutto-wrapped asparagus. She moaned with delight as the spices and flavor exploded inside her mouth.

"Best dream ever. Mine are never this fun." She picked up another slice of crusty Italian bread and knifed up some garlic spread. "It looks like Marcello does a great business even in your dreams."

"He always did." Declan looked pensive.

"So the restaurant is no longer around?" she gently probed.

He shook his head. "Not when one family enjoyed visiting the restaurant and another family moved in."

"Ah, you're talking family as in the Mob." She leaned back when a smiling Marcello placed platters of food in front of them and urged them to enjoy. She closed her eyes in bliss after the first bite.

"I should have asked you to come here before. Perhaps we're meant to talk here, since you can't use your magick." His teeth flashed white. "Interesting trick of yours, soaking me while my office and everything in it stayed perfectly dry."

Maggie blew on her nails as a gesture of triumph. "I thought it would be. I hate to turn someone into a toad or slug when I can come up with something more inventive. I thought you'd appreciate it more than being drowned in pink confetti."

"Then I give you my heartfelt thanks. Pink confetti would have definitely ruined my masculine image. Although it did provide Anna with hours of amusement as she continually asked me if she should contact you to give me another shower."

She grinned. "I've got to say this date in the dream realm is better than many I've had in the real world." She forked up another bite of lasagna.

"Dating not good, huh?"

"I'm not good with dating," Maggie admitted. "You know what I mean. There's all that small talk necessary to get to know one another, which doesn't work all that well when one of you has been around longer than most of your date's ancestors. Plus I can't talk about my work. It tends to put people off." She picked up her wineglass. "What about you? How do women handle your demon or human half?"

"I don't mention it." He leaned back in his chair, one arm draped over the back. He looked sexy, even dressed more casually in a black fine-cotton polo shirt and black *slacks.* "Female demons already can tell, and I don't see any reason to tell anyone who can't figure it out. Do you tell men you're a witch?"

"Touché. No wonder the two worst people in the dating world ended up here." She chuckled softly. "Maybe that's a sign." She nodded when Declan picked up the wine bottle and gestured toward her glass.

"Plus there are times when I need to leave immediately, and I can't say where I'm going or when I'll be back. I've probably cancelled more dates than I've kept. Elle's had a busier social life than I have, although her dates don't tend to survive to have a second one with her."

"Who's Elle?"

"Oh, that's short for Elegance, a black widow spider—when she's not tattooed to my arm, she does tend to have a life of her own."

Maggie noticed Elle was conspicuous in her absence. Hmm, maybe that meant she really was safe in this dream-world. She looked around, admiring the warm, family-style atmosphere.

"Of course, maybe if men had swept me off into the dream realm to a place like this, I might not have been so willing to abandon them." She turned back to him with a broad smile as she lifted her glass in a toast.

Declan inclined his head in a brief show of thanks. "Perhaps someone thinks we need to hook up."

"I can't imagine a dating service setting us up." She finished her food and pushed her plate away. A second later, Marcello appeared and whisked their plates from the table.

She looked around. "While the era is too early, I could see Bogie and Bacall or Gable and Lombard *coming in here. There's no sense of celebrity here, more a family atmosphere."*

"It was back then." He reached across the table and took her hand, lacing his fingers through hers.

"You must finish your meal properly." Marcello brought out rich, dark espresso and plates of tiramisu.

Declan stood up and picked up the plates and cups with the dexterity of a waiter. *"Let's have dessert on the patio."* He led the way.

Candles burned on the tables outside, the air smelling of spring and flowers.

Maggie felt a warm sense of intimacy as she relaxed into her seat and Declan took the chair next to her. He forked up a bite of tiramisu and lifted it toward her lips. She obliged by opening her mouth and allowing him to feed her. She wasted no time returning the favor.

"There's something about you, Maggie O'Malley," he murmured. *"You may be a member of the Guard, but there's no denying you're also a desirable woman."* His dark eyes gleamed like polished obsidian in the candlelight. *"You brought light into my dark world."* His gaze roamed over her like a warm caress.

Just as he liked looking at her, she enjoyed looking at him. Especially when most of the males she interacted with were either in serious need of manscaping or sported fur. She wasn't even going to think about how terrible most of them smelled.

"You do know how to make a girl feel good," she purred.

"Actually, this is the way I'd prefer making you feel good." Declan leaned over and covered her mouth with his.

Heat, the rich taste of coffee liqueur and chocolate, and Declan melded into a sensation that rocked Maggie's world. She gripped his wrists, her short nails digging into his skin. Her tongue danced with his, pulling him inside her mouth to keep him captive as she fully participated in the kiss that had her visualizing a big bed, lots of fluffy pillows, and a naked Declan.

Who needed dessert when a tasty man was right here?

She leaned into the kiss, feeling the warmth of his hand cupping her cheek.

"Maggie." *He breathed her name, making it sound as if it was something precious.*

She smiled against his mouth. "Declan." *It seemed enough just to say his name as his kiss deepened, intensifying the visions racing through her head.*

The idea of transporting them elsewhere tempted her, but Maggie had learned that her magick didn't work in Declan's part of the dream realm. It didn't stop her from thinking about it.

Slut, Mags. You're turning into a major hexy slut.

Maggie bitch slapped her common sense and gave in to the moment.

"I want—" *Something kept niggling at the back of her mind, starting to interfere with the serious make-out session going on.*

"What's wrong?" *He nuzzled her ear.*

Her nose wouldn't stop doing the Samantha Stevens twitch.

"I—"

The world suddenly started spinning like a carnival Tilt-A-Whirl, and she felt as if she was going to be catapulted into space.

—⁓—

Maggie opened her eyes to find a black ferret batting at her nose.

"Man, when you sleep, you sleep," Bickie told her. "You also snore." He hopped off the chaise.

"Why are you here?" Her voice was hoarse, and if she wasn't mistaken, she felt as if she'd just gone through a major hormone explosion. She swore her skin felt ready to split from the tightness. "And I do *not* snore."

"Came out for a break and found you sawing logs. You're also looking a little pink." He touched her bare shoulder, but even his gentle touch was enough to elicit a wince. "Even witches aren't immune from sunburn, ya know. Later, babe." He hopped off and scurried away.

Maggie sat up and flinched. The tautness in her skin was twofold. Sunburn and arousal.

Wow, if he's like that in a dream, what would he be like in real life?

Chapter 6

DECLAN DIDN'T NEED ANYONE TO TELL HIM THAT Maggie had stepped into his territory—for real. He sensed her presence immediately.

Moments later, the expected telepathic message from Anton rippled through the air. *The witch wants to see you, boss.*

He smiled at the grumble in the bouncer's voice. Maggie. *She's a member of the Guard, Anton. As much as you wish to, you can't keep her out.* He shook his head upon hearing a meaty grunt in reply that sounded a little pained. He counted to ten and started to wave his office door open, but there was no need. A blonde-haired whirlwind threw it open and stalked inside.

Maggie advanced on him with fire in her dark-emerald eyes and the expression of a witch ready and willing to create mayhem. He wasn't worried about her temper as much as surprised by the bright patch of pink skin marring her nose and the somewhat stiff way she moved.

"If I didn't know any better, I'd say you had too much sun," he said mildly. He arranged his features into a somewhat confused frown and leaned back in his chair. He continued to study her; pleased to see—more than just her temper—that hint of attraction she couldn't hide. He couldn't help but remember how kissing her had felt, even if it was in his dreams. Damn, he was getting hot just sitting here thinking about it, and that had nothing to do with his genetics.

"I didn't know witches could get sunburns. Don't you have ointments to treat that?"

She started to scowl but seemed to reconsider when her sunburned forehead wrinkled.

"To what do I owe the honor of your visit?" He leaned back, his fingers steepled in front of him.

"It has to do with Anna. What she needs, and what we can do for her."

He waved his hand in dismissal. "We will not have this discussion."

"No doing the talk-to-the-hand bit," she argued. "For once, think of her, not your macho demon ego. I need to talk to her. Better yet, Sybil needs to."

"She's an interrogator," Declan bit out. "Someone trained to inflict pain and nightmares if you lie. Your prisoners leave there bloody and damaged in the mind."

She rolled her eyes. "Don't tell me, page forty-five of the demon manual on what to do if you're captured by the enemy. You know what? That sounds more like what happens on your turf than on mine.

"We have a thing about turning our detainees bloody. Namely that it's a bitch to clean up blood and guts. The brownies who live in our compound may enjoy cleaning and keeping our quarters neat, but they're not too keen on the crime-scene cleanups."

She softened her tone. "So will you bring Anna? Will you let us help her? If not to Sybil, let her talk to Ravenna, one of our Seers."

"I'll think about it." He leaned forward. "Would you care for some lunch?"

"Lunch, and you'll bring her to the compound." She didn't budge.

"No one bargains better than my kind," he reminded her.

Maggie shifted in her chair, the hem to her top rising and revealing a hint of gold as her belly ring winked at him.

"You should see me when I visit the bazaars," she quipped.

Declan continued gazing at her with his hot dark eyes. "We could visit the Babylon Gardens or the Great Pyramid of Khufu. Visit Pompeii when the city was known for its culture and decadence. I could take you to places that existed long before your ancestors walked this earth."

Maggie prided herself on her ability to refuse any dip into temptation. Looking into Declan's dark eyes, with the hint of flames in the depths, was about as enticing as you could get. She didn't need to look south to know he was aroused. She could see it in his face. Judging by the way her breasts felt tight and full, she knew they were on the same hormonal wavelength.

"No thanks. My frequent-flier miles don't cover time travel." She smiled. "Shall we get back to Anna?" *Keep your mind on business, Mags. No thinking about that kiss in the dream realm.* "Listen to reason. Anna needs to come to the compound. She needs help with her gift. Ravenna can do that for her."

"She doesn't *need* to do anything she doesn't want to do. I'm in charge of Anna, and I will say what she does and doesn't do."

"Ooh, macho demon. Come on, Declan. You already

admitted you don't rule Anna, so you can't spin that tale now. For once, be willing to do what's right," she insisted.

"And I am."

"No, you're not when I'm talking about one of those 'Her words could save the world' situations." She nodded as he sat up at attention. "You got it, fireball. She knows something super-important, as in what I just said. Anna 'Saw' something important, and we need to make sense of it. I know someone who can help her do just that."

"You're only saying that to persuade me to send her with you." Except he had a sinking feeling that Maggie wasn't talking just for the sake of it. Anna's nightmares continued, and he had no way to stop them. What if someone at the compound *could* help her?

"You know what, Maggie? You could stand there and strip naked, and I still wouldn't go along with it. My people come first."

"Terrific, fine, whatever. They come first, but there are so many others we both need to consider. No matter what animosity goes on between the realms, there are times we all need to work together. It looks like this is one of those times."

Maggie shifted from one foot to the other, high-lighting her agitation. "Don't you really want to know what troubles are in the air? Just tea and a chat with Ravenna," she assured him. "Would you be willing to go along with that?"

Declan knew that if he didn't agree, Maggie would do her best to make life hell for him. No telling what she'd do to him, since he was positive she could use her determination to make life miserable for him both here and in the dream realm. "I want to be present the entire time."

"That's up to Ravenna, but knowing her, she'd agree as long as you didn't try to interfere." Maggie surveyed him. "I could be wrong, and that so very rarely happens, but now you sound as if you're willing to go along with this. Wouldn't it have been easier if you'd just agreed way back then?"

"I don't know. We wouldn't have had as much fun." He leaned forward and tapped a hidden button on his desk. "Have Anna come in here."

"Jeez, Declan, rude much? Where are your manners? You can't say please? Or is that against the demon code?" Maggie plopped into one of the visitor chairs and propped her feet up on the top of the desk's smooth black surface.

"Feet on the floor, if you don't mind. Where were you raised? In a barn?" He leaned forward and brushed her feet to the floor.

"I grew up in the Witches' Academy," she said, "and believe me, they believe in discipline. So I understand the importance of feet belonging on the floor and not on the furniture, but that doesn't mean I won't tweak you when I can. Every witch has to have a hobby." She looked over her shoulder when the door opened.

"You wish to see me, Declan?" The soft voice was hesitant as if afraid she would disturb something important.

"Come in, Anna." His voice softened at the female demon's entrance, meant to reassure her.

She started in and then almost bolted when she saw Maggie.

"It's all right, Anna." Declan stood up and walked over to her. He curved an arm around her shoulder in a protective manner and guided her inside while Maggie turned her chair around to face them.

"Hello, Anna." She greeted the visitor with a warm smile.

The young demon shot a look filled with panic at Declan. "Is she here to take me back there? Did I do something wrong?"

"You've done nothing wrong, Anna." Maggie kept her voice low and soothing. "Are you still seeing things? Perhaps having bad dreams?"

Anna sat on the very edge of the couch Declan guided her to but still looked as if she'd bolt if one wrong word were spoken.

"I still see things, but I also hear them." She flinched as Maggie and Declan focused all their attention on her.

Declan slowly lowered his body into the chair next to the couch. "What do you hear?"

Anna ducked her head, her hair flowing down to cover her face. "Chanting. Words in a language I don't understand. An old tongue. Not preternatural," she explained. "Human, yet not human. As if ancient magick is being used."

"Used for what?" Maggie asked.

Anna took a deep breath and shook her head. "Blood. Beating hearts eaten." She clasped her hands so tightly her knuckles turned white.

"Anna, would you be willing to talk to someone at the Guard compound?" Maggie said, then hurried on. "Not an interrogator. This is someone who can understand what you're feeling right now."

"No one can understand." Her hands tightened even more.

"Ravenna can because she's a Seer." Maggie abandoned her chair and moved over to Anna, kneeling down in front of her. She placed her hands over Anna's and squeezed lightly. "I spoke with her, and she knows you've seen horrible things. She can help you deal with it."

"Why would a Guard's Seer be willing to help a demon?" Anna's lips twisted in an ugly smile that warred with her delicate features. "I know what you think of us. You look at Declan and see a handsome male, but you also think of what's beneath the skin and you despise him."

Maggie refused to back down. "I'm a witch who's been judged for the last 700-odd years. Nothing fazes me now. I'm just asking you to meet with Ravenna."

Anna looked up at Declan. "What do you think? Do you wish me to do this?"

"It's up to you. You know I've always given you the freedom to make your own choices."

"But you think I should." Her dark eyes glimmered with moisture. She continued staring at Declan as if Maggie wasn't there.

Declan exhaled a deep breath. "Yes, I do. For all we know, the horrors you're dreaming could take over your mind and render you insane. And there may be bigger issues involved. Perhaps this Ravenna can help you."

"You will go with me." She looked at her demon lifeline.

"Of course."

She closed her eyes and took a deep breath. "Could we do it now?" Her request likened to wanting to get dental surgery over with as fast as possible.

"I'm sure we could, and knowing Ravenna, she's already readying the tea for your visit." Maggie smiled.

Anna looked down at the skimpy silver skirt and strapless top that comprised her barmaid's uniform. "Let me change first." She left the office, closing the door behind her.

"So the visions have moved into nightmare territory?" Declan nodded.

"I hope you let her catch up on her sleep," Maggie remarked a bit too casually.

His expression was grim when he faced her. "Maggie... Anna is my half sister, although as far as I'm concerned, she's full-blood to me. I brought her with me because our father wanted to mate her with someone who would pay a hefty price to own her. Someone Victorio considered appropriate. Namely anyone who could offer him enough power and money."

He felt satisfaction at her startled look. It wasn't easy to surprise the witch, and he could see his sudden revelation had thrown her off balance.

But Maggie merely stood up and said, "I'll alert the front gate to let you through."

Declan also rose to his feet. "You're not following us to make sure Anna doesn't change her mind?"

She shook her head. "I'd say from the look on her face she's hoping Ravenna can help take the horrors from her."

"Do you think a Seer can do that?" He had trouble believing someone could do what he feared might be impossible.

"If any Seer can, Ravenna can. She's incredible."

"And you're allowing two demons to get close to one of your Seers? Many Guards wouldn't allow that."

"If I were you, I'd worry more about Ravenna than me. She may seem like a pussycat, but she's a real tiger underneath." The moment her hand cupped the doorknob, Declan came up and covered her hand with his.

"I'm curious, Maggie," he whispered against her temple. "What's the name of the perfume you wear?"

She was quiet for so long that he didn't think she'd answer him. "Euphoria," she finally replied and then was out the door and down the hallway before he could blink.

"Euphoria. A very appropriate name for a woman who inspires strong feelings." Declan closed the door.

Maggie left a scowling Anton with a cheery "Bye now!" and a wave of the hand and then crossed the parking lot to where her Viper waited. She hadn't worried about her vehicle's safety when she was inside the club. The bouncer might hate her, but he knew better than to allow a Guard's car to be vandalized. Plus, the wards on the sports car meant some serious pain to anyone who approached it with threat and violence on their mind.

In the bright light of day, the part of town surrounding the club looked full of despair and anger. To call it seedy was an understatement. The alleys between buildings were narrow and filthy, more storefronts were abandoned and boarded up than were open for business, and the beings that walked the sidewalks hadn't known the meaning of the word "comfort" for years. Many who lingered near the street had the cold, dead eyes of humans with no soul.

Judging by the dark, empty eyes of the others, she'd

bet that they were on the Hellion Guard's Most Wanted List. An excellent reason to do a sweep late one night. It wouldn't hurt to come down here during the day as well. She ignored one gnome who turned around and pulled down his pants to show a filthy, bony ass with springy hairs popping out of the leathery skin.

"Guard whore!" he shouted.

"Yeah, yeah, like I haven't heard that one before," Maggie muttered, settling into the Viper's soft leather seats. "No one is original anymore." She made the calls to the front gate and to the Seers' Pavilion. Then she sat for a moment processing all she'd just learned.

She could hardly believe that Declan had diffused her anger so easily when she'd marched into his office. Or that he'd volunteered that Anna was his sister. And Anna was now willing to speak to their people, after previous exclamations that she never wanted to see them again. Although if Maggie were having the horrific nightmares and visions Anna was, she'd pretty much do whatever it took to make them go away.

While driving back to the compound, she thought of the dream and this visit with Declan. What was it about him that teased an inner part of her? That nurtured emotions she'd buried years ago?

Easy. All she had to do was think of Aleta, the sister she couldn't save. Declan was able to shield his sister when she hadn't been able to do the same for hers.

Then there was the fact he also appealed to her hormones in a big way.

He's a demon, Mags.

Uh, duh! Tell me something I don't know.

He can tear you apart with one thought.

And I can turn him inside out with a thought.

Then maybe the two of you are made for each other after all.

"I really hate it when that bitchy little voice has to chime in," she muttered, driving through the magickal shield that protected the compound from the outer world and making her way toward the large garage that housed the vehicles. "What's next?"

"You're talking to yourself, darling." Tita glided toward her. Oversize dark glasses protected her eyes from the sun while a long-sleeved catsuit protected the rest of her. "That's never good." She revealed her pearly fangs.

"Aren't you up early?" Maggie smiled at her team member as the vampire draped an arm around her shoulders.

"I have two days off, and I'm spending them in Paris. I was lucky to get a last-minute flight, and it will be dark by the time I reach the airport. I've always loved French food." Her eyes glowed red.

"Named Jean Paul or René?" Maggie teased.

"Why not both?" Tita smiled back. "I heard the demon is coming back to talk to Ravenna. How did you manage that?"

"My charm."

"Yes, I'm sure Declan was thoroughly bemused." Tita shot her a knowing smile. "See you in a few." She waved her hand over her head as she headed for her sleek, black Aston Martin with its dark-tinted windows.

"Bring me a souvenir!" Maggie called after her.

"Blond or brunet?" The vampire laughed and roared off.

Maggie took the time to duck into her quarters and

brush her hair, tucking it behind her ears, and add a swipe of lip gloss, blush, and mascara. Convinced she looked more presentable, she also changed into a cotton skirt in swirls of black, ivory, and hot pink, coupled with a pink tank top. She added a gold chain with chunks of pink coral and turquoise and matching earrings. Not once did she admit she was doing this because she'd be seeing Declan again soon.

Maggie was waiting at the entrance when Declan and Anna were escorted to the Seers' Pavilion. After making the appropriate request to enter, she gestured for them to follow. She smothered her chuckle when the duo looked down at the dark-green hooded robes that covered their clothing the moment they'd stepped over the threshold.

"See, wearing color isn't all that difficult, is it?"

She kept an eye on Anna, noticing her hesitation and the way she surveyed their environment. Maggie didn't blame her. Considering the seriousness of the Guard's work, it was always surprising to walk into the light and airy Pavilion. It looked more like the site of a lovefest than a building filled with Seers intent on discovering trouble in the realms before it happened.

"You're very lovely," an apprentice wearing a flower garland in her hair told Anna, giving her a hug and moving on.

"What is this?" Declan demanded in a low voice.

"They believe in their happy place," Maggie said.

"No kidding." He sneezed.

"Patchouli."

Declan and Anna gasped when they entered Ravenna's receiving room, and Declan started to step back as if he'd been seared.

"I apologize, but you must understand there are protocols," Ravenna said from her spot at the other end of the moonlit room. "We are considered very precious and must be protected at all costs. All you felt was a spell ensuring you and your sister could do me and mine no harm." Her smile warmed the room.

"Yes, I understand," he said in a low voice. "I am not like many of my kind. I prefer to save from harm rather than destroy."

"Can you really do it?" Anna blurted out. "Can you take the darkness away?"

Ravenna glided toward her and took hold of Anna's hands. "I can soften it for you, and together we will find the answers. Only then will the darkness be taken from you. But you must understand that you are a demon. Your race holds shadows within themselves the way we hold the light. But you can learn to push the shade away."

Maggie urged Declan to a corner that held two cushioned stools while Ravenna led Anna to the center of the room where two large pillows were arranged near a small brazier from which the scent of water lily and wild tuberose wafted in the air.

"What will she do?" Declan whispered.

"Only Ravenna knows."

"I require silence. Thank you."

Maggie mouthed an apology and made herself comfortable. She was just as curious as Declan about what would happen.

Ravenna and Anna sat on the pillows facing each other, their hands clasped.

The witch couldn't understand the words that left the Seer's lips, but the power that filled the room was potent. Declan shifted uneasily on the stool. On impulse, she reached over and grasped his hand.

"The time of darkness is near," Ravenna intoned. "A portal to evil is ready to open when blood falls on the sacred stone in the land of old beliefs where gods of the sun and moon are worshipped, but this time the sun will look down upon the sacrifice. Blood spilled to the gods.

"They require one with true blood to give up her heart to the god of destruction. She is near. The priests have not found her yet, but they will. Their only task is to find her and bring her to the temple for the sunrise that will reveal blood and fire. Once the Destroyer is returned to his rightful place, he will rule—and blood will flow like water."

"The true one," Anna whispered, her eyes closed.

"Who is the true one?" Maggie asked softly, forgetting she was to be silent, but no one chastised her.

Ravenna threw back her head and sang something that caused the power in the air to turn into a heavy mist. It lifted toward the ceiling and slowly evolved into a dark background for the colorful figure that dominated it. The faint sound of drums echoed throughout the room, the resonance seeming to bleed through the walls.

Maggie nearly had to pick her jaw up off the floor as she stared at the image of a teenage girl in ratty jeans and a Green Day T-shirt, her dark hair streaked with white blonde flowing past her waist.

"Wait a minute! Are you saying the one with the right blood is a teenage girl and the whole thing hinges on her?" She pointed toward the image. "Oh, we are so screwed!"

Chapter 7

"THIS IS NUTS!" MAGGIE BLURTED OUT, FORGETTING she was breaking the major rule in the Seers' Pavilion. *Thou shalt not interrupt a Seer during her vision.* She pointed to the image that still floated near the ceiling. "What is she, fifteen, sixteen at the most? She's barely out of her training bra. How could someone like her be that important to basically saving the world?"

Ravenna turned her head toward the witch. There was no anger in her voice at the witch's rude behavior, merely amusement.

"We See what is given to us. This young girl obviously carries the blood that is necessary for the ritual that is revealed to us."

"Blood. She has the right blood," Anna repeated in her musical voice. Her slender body shook violently, and she wrapped her arms around herself as if she was cold. She rocked back and forth.

"Death. Many will die once the ceremony is finished. Those who don't will be made slaves and die under the sacred knife when it is time."

"I don't like this." Declan started to get up, but Maggie grabbed his arm and shook her head.

"I've done enough damage here by opening my mouth," she whispered fiercely. "If you speak up, you'll be lucky not to be turned inside out and snared in a web of ice spiders. The Seers have protections that even the Guard doesn't understand."

Ravenna turned toward Declan. "Did you have something to say?"

He sat back. "Uh, no. I'm sorry for speaking when I shouldn't have."

Her head inclined in acceptance of his apology, and she returned her attention to Anna. A slender hand rested on the young demon's shoulder as Ravenna leaned forward and spoke for Anna's ears only. Several minutes later, Anna lifted her head, appearing calmer. Ravenna poured her a cup of tea and handed it to her, then stood and moved toward Maggie and Declan with her unique glide.

"I wish to keep Anna with me for a short while," she told Declan. "I assure you she will be perfectly safe here."

"I—"

The Seer placed her hands on his. Her skin glowed with the pearly essence of the moon, while her ethereal features betrayed no hint of her thoughts. "If you allow me, I can help Anna."

"She is precious to me," he told her.

"You may return when I call for you."

The door opened, and an apprentice stood there.

"Come on, I'll buy you coffee." Maggie rose to her feet and tugged Declan to his.

"I haven't given her my approval."

"You gave it. You just don't realize it yet." She pulled him out of the room. They had barely crossed the threshold before the door closed silently behind them.

"They'll do their talk. We'll do ours." Maggie gestured forward once they left the Pavilion. She hid her grin as members of the Guard shot Declan suspicious looks as they passed them. Only her presence kept anyone from challenging the demon, even though he wore a medallion signifying he was a protected visitor.

"I don't like leaving her there defenseless," he grumbled.

"What? You think Ravenna's going to eat her or something? Anna's safer there than she'd be even under your care."

The thought of something hot and soothing spurred her toward the dining hall with its variety of eateries catering to every species' tastes. She headed for a small bistro that offered coffee and pastries.

"This time you get your own muffin and leave mine alone."

Once inside, she inhaled the rich scents of coffee, tea, and spices. "What do you want? My treat."

She stepped up to a small screen. After she tapped in her order, she showed Declan how to make his choice and walked over to a table set in a corner where they wouldn't be disturbed.

"Someone will bring it to us," she told him. She waited until his drink, her peppermint tea, and a bowl of assorted muffins had been set before them. "What has Anna told you about what she's Seen?"

"Very little. She's always so traumatized after a nightmare or when she has a vision that I don't feel it's right to push her." He sipped his drink, grimaced, and set it down.

Maggie took a drink of what she thought was her peppermint tea, made a face, and switched cups. One cautious sip told her she now had the right one.

"What is that nasty stuff?" She mimed gagging.

"Something only demons like. And if you want to talk nasty, whatever you're drinking tasted just as bad to me as mine did for you." He cupped the mug with his hands.

"What's *he* doing here?" Meech stopped by the table, glaring at Declan while keeping a hand on the sword belted at his side.

"He's allowed," she told him. "What's that?"

"Look what I got off creaBay. Is this cool or what?" He held up a shrunken head and bared his jagged yellow teeth in a grin. "It's Rebus the Terrible, and I got him for only $800. I even have a certificate of authenticity."

"If you show that thing to Reesa, she'll probably pop the baby out right now."

"She's already seen it and told me I have to keep it in my office." He walked off with his prize.

"He collects shrunken heads of infamous tyrants?" Declan asked.

"No, he just loves cruising creaBay. One of my other teammates is addicted to watching *What Not To Wear*. To date, he's nominated himself eighty-three times, but so far Stacy and Clinton have ignored him, and I'm sure with good reason. There isn't all that much you can do with Frebus since he's a walking, talking fur ball. We're talking serious manscaping there."

"And you all live here in harmony?" Declan glanced toward a giant whose bald head was covered in elaborate tattoos that trailed down his cheeks and neck. The giant bared his teeth at Declan as he picked up a foaming mug and walked away.

"Not entirely, but if any of us has issues, we take them to the training ground and beat the crap out of each other." She delicately picked through the muffins and finally settled on one with cinnamon streusel topping. "That usually works."

Declan shook his head. "When we have issues, we don't stop until one of us is dead."

"That sure takes the fun out of it." Maggie nipped off a bit of muffin with her fingers and popped it in her mouth.

He leaned forward, resting his forearms on the table. "How much do you know about my race?"

"I know 99.9 percent of you are evil. You prefer killing to talking. You know some downright nasty spells that can skin a being in seconds. And I've met some demons who are just dog ugly, which really isn't very flattering to dogs."

"And you prefer killing us over talking to us."

She looked him square in the eye. "Damn straight. I've lost friends to demons. And if you had messed with any of my friends, you'd be dead already. I don't hesitate, Declan. I know my job, and I do it well."

"Yet you didn't shut down my club that night."

"No reason to. It was obvious you were as clueless as, sadly, I was about the Bloater. Plus I figured that the mess I left was punishment enough. And I really do compliment you on the swift cleaning job.

"But then, you'd want the business up and running right away, wouldn't you? All that nice coin coming in, because I'm sure you have to pay off the higher-ups who love coin even more than you do. Do you guys have, like, a demon mafia you have to pay tribute to?"

Declan smiled. "I enjoy the way your mind works. At times, it seems to scurry around like one of those hamsters on a wheel, and then you suddenly zero in on one thing with the precision of a well-placed bullet. How do you do it?"

"I'm a witch." She lifted a hand and snapped her fingers. A tiny hamster appeared in her palm, sniffing her skin and squeaking away. When she waved her hand, it was gone. "I learned to multitask a long time ago. What about you? Tell all, Declan. Who did you kill, bribe, or both, to get the club?"

"I didn't kill Ratchet, but I think you know that already." This time his smile wasn't warm and friendly but revealed the predator that lurked beneath the skin. The one who'd clawed his way to where he was now. "I bet you even know where the body's buried."

Maggie's smile showed she gave as good as she got. "All I heard was his death mentioned on the eleven o'clock news."

"You did me a favor, Maggie. He was in negotiations with my father to use Anna as one of his whores."

"And you protect your own." No way was she going to admit she knew where the pieces had been left.

"You came here without me? And with the hottie, no less." Elle skittered up the table leg and Maggie's arm and attached herself to the witch's upper bicep. The sparkly arachnid peered at Declan. She seemed to rub her front legs together.

"How I would love to have you in my web," she purred. "I can imagine you could last much longer than my other lovers. Perhaps that is what I require. Do you have demon arachnids?"

"Your tattoo is more than a little unique," he told Maggie.

"She'll be impossible after hearing that."

"I do not like people talking about me as if I am not here," Elle sulked.

"Declan meet Elegance, Elle for short."

"Charmed." He smiled at the spider.

"*Enchanté.*" She inclined her head in a regal manner. "You have lovely manners for a demon."

"Since I'm in the presence of a Hellion Guard, I thought it best to behave."

"I would like some of that banana nut muffin," Elle told Maggie.

Maggie crumbled a muffin and set it on a paper plate that she moved to the next table.

"I can still hear you." But Elle left with a graceful scurry.

"I've never seen a jeweled tattoo that was sentient," Declan commented.

"Elle watches my back. She also injects a lethal poison into any enemy who gets too close." She mulled over her choices and decided on a chocolate muffin that turned out to have a creamy coconut center. "Here, you look like an apple spice kinda guy." She handed him a muffin.

Declan looked around the room, shifting uneasily in his chair.

"Anna is fine," Maggie assured him. "Ravenna can help her a great deal, Declan. Isn't that what you want?"

"Yes, but I also want to know what all this means. Aren't you worried?"

She shrugged. "You forget. This is my job. I hear violence and death, and I see it as another assignment."

"What kind of existence is that? You're on duty 24-7." He shook his head, clearly not liking the idea.

"It's the one that suits me. In the past, I've protected nobility, worked as a spy more than once, and traveled the world many times. I've even visited various realms. Some I wouldn't care to repeat. I went undercover as a Pinkerton agent once they allowed women to join their hallowed male ranks, dealt faro in a Barbary Coast gambling hall, and once worked as a bartender in Whitechapel.

"I've made friends and enemies along the way. More enemies than friends, but I guess that's a given in my work. I've also lost friends along the way. Another given." She looked grim for a moment as she retreated to the past.

Declan opened his mouth to say something, then stopped when his gaze swiveled toward the entrance.

The Anna who walked in looked more assured and less frail as she moved toward them. There was even a smile on her face.

"Wow, Ravenna does good work," Maggie greeted her. "I guess she did something to help you. Would you like something to drink? There are muffins left."

She shook her head and took the chair Declan snagged from another table.

"What happened?" he asked.

Anna licked her lips, glancing at him nervously. "I've been invited to live at the Seers' Pavilion. Ravenna asked me to be her apprentice."

"No." No hesitation.

The female demon looked stricken at his immediate response. "Declan, this could be—"

His jaw tightened. "Absolutely not. That can't be the life you would want."

Maggie decided to chime in. "Her offer to bring Anna in is not a spur-of-the-moment invite. She must have Seen something in Anna."

"I want to do this, my brother." She showed an inner strength she hadn't shown before. "My visions have become stronger. They interfere with my sleep, and sometimes I've had them when I work. I'm frightened to sleep or even rest. I can learn to control the visions, and I can help with what's going to happen. We need to find the girl before the priests do. All our worlds will be affected if we don't."

Declan leaned forward, his eyes shining molten silver with flames in the center. "There is *no one* who can destroy us," he hissed.

"Uh, Declan, dial back on the anger," Maggie warned.

He turned on her. "Or what?"

She gestured toward his medal, which now glowed orange. "Or you're going to end up with a major headache. Besides, you said you brought Anna here to protect her. Fine, you've done your job. She's ready to take that next step. Let her go, Declan."

"Fuck you," he growled and then suddenly stiffened as Maggie flicked her fingers at the medal, which suddenly flared golden. Two seconds later, Declan was prone on the floor.

"Ooh, I love it when they do this," Elle crooned, peering down. "Men never listen, darling. They always think they're right."

Anna cried out and bent down. "You killed him!" She looked around in search of assistance, only to discover that no one was paying them any attention.

"He's fine. It's like a gallon of knockout drops. He'll

wake up with a killer headache, but that's it." Maggie was unconcerned. She grasped Anna's hand and pulled her to her feet. "Did Ravenna explain to you what's involved in your apprenticing to the Pavilion?"

Anna nodded.

"And you can't tell me all the details because they have so many secrets."

She nodded again.

"But it's what you want."

"She said I am the first demon she's met with such a strong gift of Sight. But I need training. I want to do it here."

"Demons must have Seers," Maggie commented. "Are you saying you'd rather have Ravenna train you instead of going wherever your Seers are trained?"

"We have Seers, but they're not like Ravenna. Ours tend to be... darker. They only search for trouble they can increase or enemies of our kind that need to be destroyed. Looking for any chance of good isn't allowed."

"I bet the depression level there is sky-high," Maggie muttered, looking down at Declan's unconscious body. A soft groan sounded. "Oh good, he's coming around."

He moved his body as if every bit of bone and muscle hurt. "What did you do to me?" He sat up and rubbed his hand over his face.

"You did it to yourself. That's why all visitors are given a medallion when they enter the compound. If they show any threatening manner toward one of the Guard, they're put down fast. You're lucky that I did some quick work to lighten it for you. Otherwise, you would have been out for a week." She wiped her fingers on a napkin and watched him slowly rise to his feet. "Next time I won't interfere, and you'll feel the full effect."

Declan stared at Anna. "If I deny you this chance, I'm acting like our father. I can't do that." He looked past her to Maggie. "You will look after her?"

"You can visit her any time you want, Declan. Just don't lose your temper." She smiled.

Anna's face lit up. She hugged him hard and then ran off.

"You're like the parent watching his kid go off for the first day of school," Maggie said, coming over and draping her arm around his shoulders. "She'll do fine. She'll make new friends, and it's actually a good thing. Anna's our first demon."

"Now! It's now!" Meech ran in and grabbed Maggie's hand, pulling hard on it and throwing her off balance

"No." She resisted.

"What's going on?" Declan asked.

"Meech and his mate named me the vow mother for their baby." Her heels slid along the floor.

"Come," Meech invited, keeping a tight grip on Maggie's hand.

"This won't be messy, will it?"

Maggie prided herself on having a cast-iron stomach. She'd been in battles where blood and gore was just a part of it.

But now she watched a panicky Meech try to comfort Reesa, who called him every name in the book along with some Maggie had never heard before. She tucked them into her memory for future reference.

She noticed Declan, who skulked off in a corner because she refused to allow him to leave the birthing room. His skin was the color of pea soup.

"Come on, I'm sure you've seen worse," Maggie hissed at him.

"I have, but this is different." He bared his teeth at her. "I could say the same to you. You're female. You should be used to this."

She shook her head. "Not childbirth." She straightened up. Battling a nest of smelly chupacabras was much easier than watching a woman giving birth. At least she had control then.

"You will never touch me again!" Reesa stated between clenched teeth.

"I love my passion flower," Meech crooned. "Don't worry, this will soon be over."

"How would you know, you insolent thing that belongs in a bog?" Reesa's scream was piercing enough to shatter the windows.

"The child is coming," the healer joyfully announced.

"Do not leave me here," Maggie ordered Declan as he started to edge his way out of the room. She threw out a hand. The door disappeared, and he ran into a blank wall.

She enjoyed watching the Guards' children play in the large playground, and she had wondered at times what it would be like to be a mother. But come on, she was a 700-year-old witch. Could she still have a biological clock ticking?

Maggie knew the mechanics of childbirth and had sometimes assisted over the long years, but she had never witnessed the birth of anyone from Meech and Reesa's race. She just hadn't expected the baby-size blue egg that Reesa eventually laid. She watched the midwife gently crack the surface and lift out a tiny mewling baby, quickly wrapping it in a blanket.

"I am beginning to think that my way is so much better," Elle announced. "Have sex, eat my mate, lay eggs, and leave them to hatch on their own."

"You're a regular softie, Elle," Maggie said.

"You have a girl," the midwife announced to the parents.

Maggie took one look at the miniscule wizened face and fell instantly in love with the tiny being.

"Hey, sweetheart, I'm your vow mother," she cooed, allowing the youngling to wrap her fingers around her forefinger. "I'm the one who's going to make sure you grow up to be whatever you wish to be. I'll keep you safe when your parents aren't here, and I'll teach you to stand up to bullies."

Declan realized he was seeing a whole new side of the witch. Instead of looking as if she'd happily break a few bones, she looked softer and more desirable than ever.

A few hours before, they'd heard word that the world could be destroyed, and now Maggie was smiling and cooing at a baby he thought looked like a tiny walnut with arms and legs.

What would she be like with my child? Would she still be out fighting enemies or turn into a witch of leisure?

"Don't worry, little one. I'll take you to the training room when you're big enough," he overheard Maggie say in a soft voice.

Definitely fighting.

Maggie waved the door back into existence, and they left the new parents.

"Now we'll be seeing baby photos all the time."

Declan stopped outside and looked in the direction of the Seers' Pavilion. "I need to say good-bye."

"Perhaps you should leave her alone for now. They'll let you know when you can see her again. They'll be helping her settle in." She pointed him in the opposite direction. "I guess when you came today you didn't expect all this to happen."

"Not even close." He took a deep breath. "I want to blame you for Anna's wish to be trained as a Seer, but deep down, I know that it's the best thing for her. As much as it galls me to say so, the Guard can protect her better than I can right now."

She cocked her head to one side. "Because of your father? So I guess he's not the Ward Cleaver type?"

"Not even close."

"And he's still alive?"

A smile touched his lips. "More than 1,000 years old and going very strong." He touched her arm. "I want to help with what you're going to do. I deserve to be involved if this god of destruction, whoever and whatever he is, could be targeting demons."

"I'd have to check with my superiors about that, but considering the crazy way this seems to be starting up, I doubt there will be any problems."

He was relieved she didn't give him an outright no. He wasn't the warrior his father was, but he did have fighting skills that could prove useful.

That it gave him a chance to spend more time with Maggie was just a bonus.

Declan drove back to the club, occasionally looking at the empty passenger seat. He missed his sister already.

"You left your blood with the Guard? What kind of brother are you, Declan?" The dark voice entered the car a millisecond before an equally dark presence drifted onto the seat. "Anna's a hot number. You could have made a fortune with her, and we both know your father wouldn't have minded if you accomplished what he couldn't. Of course, he would have insisted on a cut of the profits."

"Wreaker." There was no inflection in his voice to indicate he hated the uninvited visitor to the very marrow of his bones. "Who let you out?"

"The boss decided I needed a vacation. Lighten up, cuz. Aren't you happy to see me? It's been a long time."

The demon had a sinister beauty that appealed to women who enjoyed walking on the wild side. The trouble was that Wreaker always bled them dry of all emotion and vitality until they were nothing more than empty husks when he left their beds. Iron-gray hair hung loosely to his shoulders, obscuring the tattoos proclaiming his power that writhed around his neck.

Declan saw cruelty in the demon's black eyes and in the lines of his mouth, but he knew humans only saw the creature's unearthly beauty. While they were related by blood, even Declan didn't know Wreaker's true name. A demon's true name held power. Anyone with that information could summon them to do their bidding. Wreaker didn't trust anyone. Didn't matter to Declan, because he sure as Hades didn't trust his cousin either.

"And now it seems there's some serious shit going on around here. You sure you're up for it? I mean, if you're pussy enough to dump your sister on the Guard, who says you've got the cojones to go up against stone-cold killers? The Mayans think they invented sacrificial rituals while forgetting it was *moi* who taught them everything I know."

Wreaker was higher up the demon food chain than Declan and had let it be known he wasn't happy when Declan was given Damnation Alley. Declan knew his cousin had wanted to use the club as his own private hunting ground. He wished he could ban him from the club, but Wreaker had the credentials to freely come and go through the portal in the club's basement.

All Declan was allowed to do was make sure the undesirables were closely monitored in order to avoid any trouble—unless it was allowed by their rulers. He wasn't about to lose his club because a killer demon caught the eye of the Hellion Guard.

"And that's a new thing?" He flicked his fingers, extinguishing the cigar Wreaker had just lit up. "If you want to smoke, go elsewhere."

"What does the Guard know about the Destroyer returning to inflict havoc on the mortal world?"

Declan's fingers tightened on the steering wheel. "I see intel is still on top of things."

"The Guard isn't as impenetrable as they think they are. Plus, word about the Mayans has been floating around for the past few months. Good times back then." Wreaker smiled. "The women were incredible. I could have my way with them and then hand them over to the priests for the sacrifices. Bummer when they insisted on virgins. I was considered a god back then."

"I'm sure you were," Declan muttered. "And once again, why are you here?"

"You seem to be in the know where the Guard is concerned. You could tell us what they're up to."

"Because you intend to interfere with the Guard's intent?"

"Hades no!" Wreaker laughed, lighting his cigar again. "Because it looks like the Mayan fuckers think they can destroy us, too. They first tried back in the year 3500 BC and haven't given up since. I can't believe they've been in hiding all this time when blood is like food to them. We'll step in if the Guard fails, but why should we lose anyone when the all-high-and-mighty are ready to do their thing?"

He stroked the glove-leather seat the way he'd stroke a woman. "Nice car, dude. I need to look into getting me one of these. It's like sex on wheels. I don't suppose you'd let me test-drive it, would you? No, I guess not."

He shrugged at Declan's glare. "You need to be careful, Declan. And I'm speaking not just as your cousin but as a friend, too."

"We were never friends." And Declan had the knife scar to prove it.

One of Wreaker's tattoos flared a bright-red light and coiled its way down his neck.

"We could have been if you hadn't been such an asshole about your sister. Oh, I know Victorio had plans for Anna, but no reason why she and I couldn't have stepped out first."

Declan breathed deeply through his nose in an attempt to keep his anger under control. He idly noticed his car's temperature gauge starting to creep upward. It took a moment before it returned to normal.

"I only wanted to date her, Dec, not fuck her," Wreaker drawled. "You know. Dinner, maybe some dancing afterward. Or we could take in a movie."

"You'd never settle for dinner and dancing," Declan said tightly. "And you hate movie theaters unless you can find a quiet spot with your latest victim."

"We'll never know, will we?" Wreaker blew out a smoke circle. "Look, I'm just the messenger. Keep an eye on that Guard bitch you've been sniffing after. She's pretty hot looking, so I can't see it as a tough gig.

"Who knows? If you speak all pretty, she just might let you into her pants. I bet she's one hot lay." He grinned at Declan's ominous features. "I'll be around when you've got some info for me."

Wreaker was gone as quickly as he appeared, leaving only a haze of cigar smoke behind.

"And one day I'll turn you into a living torch," Declan muttered.

He made the forty-five-minute drive to the club in half the time. His employees took one look at his face and made sure to stay out of his way.

And no one dared ask him why Anna hadn't come back with him.

Chapter 8

"SO THIS IS THE TEENAGER WHO'S THE INTENDED sacrifice?" Maggie studied the photograph lying in front of her of a teenage girl and boy doing some serious PDA. "She looks more like a *Gossip Girl* wannabe. All she needs is the little dog. I gather that's the boyfriend with her, since they're sucking face."

She frowned as the soft sound of drums and chanting in a strange language floated through her head. She momentarily closed her eyes against the darkness that surrounded her. When she opened them again, it was gone.

"Courtney Parker," Mal announced from the end of the large conference table. "Fifteen years old, a high school freshman, and flunking most of her subjects. She's been suspended from school more than she's attended it. Although with what's going on now, it might be better she doesn't go, unless we slap some heavy-duty protections on her. Boyfriend's name is Mick Frasier. He dropped out of school last year, and they've been going together for the last six months."

All members of Maggie's team were assembled for the meeting, accompanied by Declan and Anna, garbed in her orange Seer apprentice robe and hood, seated alongside Ravenna.

"She is the one Ravenna and I Saw," Anna agreed.

"And she needs a home," Ravenna said. "Courtney is in Houston's foster system."

"She dresses pretty well for a foster kid." Maggie eyed the clothing. "Even the ratty jeans she wore in the vision had a designer label."

"Courtney has a job in an upscale clothing boutique. Since she's underage, she's paid under the table," Mal said. "No reason we can't set up a file showing Maggie's related to Courtney, so she can be named the girl's guardian." He shuffled through papers on the table, pausing to sign a few and hand them to the waiting messenger ferret.

"Uh, no," Maggie protested, sitting up straight. "I'm so not the mom type. I can't even be trusted to baby-sit a toddling ferret. I didn't know he wasn't supposed to have licorice."

"You're our baby's vow mother. You will be a wonderful guardian for the child," Meech said warmly. "You just need to tap into your inner female."

"Just because we have ovaries and you don't doesn't mean we automatically know what to do with a teenager," she argued.

"The only other female on this team is Tita, and no way can she be used."

"I resent that. I could be an excellent mother." The vampire examined her long red nails.

"I don't want to even think about what you'd teach the kid, Tita. At least Maggie'd teach her something useful, like how to properly handle a weapon." Mal raised an eyebrow. "We don't want to draw attention to this girl. She can't be brought to the compound, so we'll set up a safe house for you near her school. We'll make sure all the wards are up and running before you move in.

"I already worked up a cover story that you're a distant relative and seeking guardianship. Once we've got the paperwork looking authentic, you'll go in and take charge of her. Reports on her so far aren't too good. The kid's a regular hellion. Sounds like you'll get along just fine." He eyed Maggie thoughtfully.

Maggie thought of her fleeting moment of wanting to be a mother. She didn't expect it would mean a child who was already housebroken or one with behavioral problems.

"What about the rest of us?" Frebus asked. "It's not fair that Maggie has all the worries if the girl's in that much danger."

"We'll figure that out. Probably have to use some illusion spells, since you don't exactly fit in among the humans."

Frebus scratched his furry arm. "Just as long as you don't turn me into a dog. The last time I went undercover, I came back with fleas."

"What can I do?" Declan asked.

Mal paused. "I let you in here because your sister was instrumental in helping us find Courtney. That doesn't mean I'll put you to work."

"I'm not going to just sit by and do nothing," he said tersely.

"You could pretend to be Maggie's lover," Tita suggested, with a sultry smile that said she wouldn't mind having him for hers.

Maggie opened her mouth to argue that point when Mal spoke up.

"That might work." He puffed on his less than aromatic cigar. "What else do we know about this god of destruction?"

"He is to the south," Ravenna spoke up. "I see ancient temples, blood-stained stone altars, and people who were nothing more than slaves."

Maggie thought of the dreams that had begun haunting her sleep. They were nothing like the two she apparently had shared with Declan—not only had he been noticeably absent, but there had been a sense of fear, and she awoke very hazy on the details.

"South means Mexico or South America. How ancient? Incan or Mayan?" Maggie asked. "Aztec?"

"Mayan," Anna said without hesitation. She looked at Declan. "The Mayans were an offshoot of the demon race. According to our history, they were destroyed sometime in the tenth century because they wanted to annihilate all demons who didn't share their beliefs."

"And they've taken all this time to move up to everyone else? Talk about goals," Maggie said. "I only head south when there are chupacabras to kill or when I want a good margarita. I don't know all that much about the ancient cultures." She looked around expectantly at her team members.

"I once did the tourist thing and checked out some of the Incan and Mayan temples," Meech said. "About three hundred years ago, there were rumors that Mayan priests had reappeared in the temples and carried off women from the villages for blood sacrifices. When my team and I showed up, we found fresh bloodstains and a lot of human hearts that looked chewed on. No sign of anyone living in the temples, but the smell of dark magick hung over the place like a deadly disease."

"It's a terrible place," Frebus rumbled. "Too full of death and anguish. I didn't like it there."

Maggie looked at Mal. "Why weren't these places cleansed? It's not like we don't have enough sorcerers to sanitize the altars."

"They did go down there and performed cleansing spells. The death and violence were so intense there that they returned exhausted and could only sleep for days." Meech said. "Daily sacrifices had gone on until you wondered how there was anyone left in the villages. Let alone virgins."

"It couldn't have been any worse than some of the death houses we've raided over the years." Mal tapped a few keys on his netbook. "Ravenna, what else have you and Anna learned since that first connection? Any more visions?"

The Seer nodded her head, the silken fabric of her robe rustling in the sudden respectful silence.

"Anna and I have learned much since our first connection," she replied in her musical voice. "Seeing into the ether has not been easy. We suspect that those involved are blocking their activities, but with emotions running so high, some information filters out. One thing that has come through is the knowledge that a ritual will occur on the night of the blood moon."

"Makes sense." Maggie said, doodling impatiently on her notepad. Elle, residing discreetly between her shoulder blades, echoed her restlessness and began to fidget.

Declan glanced over and smiled at her artwork, a stick figure witch in a black pointy hat riding a jet-propelled broom. "That's your idea of taking notes?" he whispered.

"I don't need to. Mal sends out a transcription of everything said. He knows we all have a short attention span." She looked toward her boss. "Are we done here? What else do we need to know? Nasty god wants to take over the world, lots of blood—ah, now Tita perks up." She grinned at her vampire team member. "You little rascal, you."

"You said the magick word," Tita teased.

Mal glared at her. "Why? You gotta a manicure appointment or something that you consider more important, Maggie?"

"I need to find a ruffled apron and pearls for mommy patrol." She ignored Frebus's and Meech's snickers as the team rose to leave.

"Apron and pearls only. I've always been partial to naughty schoolgirl myself, but I could go for that," Declan murmured, the corners of his beautifully sculpted lips tipping upward.

Maggie "accidentally" ground her heel on Declan's toes as she stood up. She smiled. "Sorry."

"You two stay." Mal gestured Maggie and Declan toward him. He waited for them to take the chairs on either side of him before he zeroed in on Declan. "I'll be honest with you. I didn't want a demon in on this operation. I don't like your race. I don't trust your race. And I don't care who knows it. I've fought your kind for the last thousand years. It's only because of your sister that I'm allowing you in on these meetings."

"Gee, Mal, don't hold back. Just tell Declan how you really feel." Maggie grimaced.

Declan was unfazed by the gnome's diatribe. "I've never pretended to be anything other than I am," he replied. "I won't apologize if I make you uncomfortable. And I will also say that without trust, there's no reason for me to be here. I honestly don't know what I can bring to the party, if you want to put it that way."

Mal narrowed his eyes at him. "Terrific. We have a lover, not a fighter."

"Depends on the circumstances." Declan's smoldering expression was just as threatening. "If this is the kind of attitude Anna can expect here, I'll be taking her back with me."

"Okay, boys, enough with the pissing contest," Maggie interjected. "You're both da man. Mal, if you insist on giving Declan a bad time, we're gone. If you have something to say, just say it." She was unfazed by her superior's glacial stare.

The gnome pulled in a deep breath and exhaled. "I didn't want to tell the whole team, but this shit is really bad."

Maggie stilled. "Bad as in—?"

"As in what happened at Stonehenge in 1788. Word then was that a Destroyer like the one down south came through from another plane. Massacre so big it took us days to get rid of the bodies. Blood soaked the ground until it was nothing more than red mud.

"Just like in the ancient Mayan temples, there was so much dark magick smothering the place that our sorcerers almost died cleansing it. My best warriors were down for weeks. Some of them never recovered and were babbling idiots for the rest of their lives."

Maggie shifted uneasily in her chair. Even Elle paid attention, moving across Maggie's skin from her spine to her shoulder and up her neck.

"I do not like this," Elle whispered in Maggie's ear.

"The idea of becoming a babbling idiot doesn't sound all that great to me, either. Why didn't you say all this in front of the team?" she asked.

A computer flash drive materialized in front of Mal. He handed it over to Maggie. "Everything you need to know about the Mayans but were afraid to ask. The trouble is that there's next to no intel on the Destroyer."

"The same one we're going to prevent from being returned to this plane?" She palmed the drive and tucked it in her jeans pocket.

"Let's hope you succeed, because if this asshole is as bad as the last one, we're well and truly fucked." He waved them away as he shuffled off the chair and left the conference room.

Maggie and Declan were quiet as they left the administration building.

He looked around the compound, taking in the flurry of activity everywhere he gazed. "It's amazing how much power this place generates and that you can keep it so well protected. How do you make sure visitors don't go where they shouldn't?"

"How quickly you forget." She inclined her head toward his visitor medallion. "They're keyed to where you're allowed to go. If you try to enter the wrong building, you'll get a jolt that will make the last time feel like a love tap. We don't allow that many visitors in here or provide guided tours, so you should be honored you've been here more than once."

"Do I get a prize if I'm here a certain number of times?"

"Just the chance to live."

Declan grasped her arm and turned her to face him. "Why do you deny it, Maggie?"

"Deny what?" She wasn't about to state the obvious, even if he was.

"Our attraction to each other." His eyes glowed silver.

She felt her breath hitch in her chest. "Not so. We're the Hatfields and the McCoys. Capulets and Montagues."

"They were lovers." He moved closer, until she could sense the heat and scent of his skin.

She deliberately didn't look at his face. "Yeah, and look how that turned out. Witches tend to stay among themselves. We don't branch out because it never ends well."

"What about your friend Jazz who's with a vampire? Stasi with a wizard, and Blair with a Were?" he pointed out.

This time she looked up to meet his eyes. She felt the immediate pull but mentally dug in her heels to resist. He smelled so good and looked so good... although she wished he'd let go of the black wardrobe.

"I see you've done your homework. Fine, there are times opposites do attract, but there were special circumstances. Jazz and Nick have been together off and on for centuries. Stasi deserved someone special, and Trev was meant for her—even if Cupid started it as a joke. Except the joke backfired on him. As for Blair and Jake, well, he'd been visiting her in dog form for so long it was natural they'd take that next step. That's not us," she maintained.

Maggie, who could read the signs long before she was attacked, who knew how to avoid traps, didn't see it coming until she was in Declan's arms and his mouth was on hers.

Wow, even better than in my dreams. How can someone taste this good?

She wrapped her tongue around his, feeling his heat surround her while the world spun. Declan muttered strange words in the language of demons as he pressed light kisses around her eyes and back down to her mouth. She could feel her blood begin to boil.

For one insane moment, Maggie thought about dragging him back to her quarters. The idea of the two of them in bed was incredibly tempting. Declan naked on her sheets would truly seem like a dream come true.

"If you keep this up, I will have to spin a web to hide your activities," Elle hissed in her ear. "Just remember to make his death swift when you are finished with him. I like him."

Maggie blinked rapidly and stepped back. Mortification sent red up her throat while she looked around. She was stunned to see everyone walking around acting as if they hadn't seen her lose her mind for a few brief moments. She felt off balance and, for a second, thought about taking Declan down.

He waited quietly, watching the varied emotions cross her face. "You can't deny it now, can you? There's something there, Maggie. What's so wrong in pursuing it?"

"I have a job to do. You're a part of this as well. I don't know what exactly you are to me, but all that matters right now is the operation ahead of us." Despite her words, she gave in to her need to lean toward him. The heat of his skin called out to her, warming her better than any coat or blanket could. The idea of curling up with him on a cold winter's night was very appealing.

"And the way Mal made it sound, we could all be killed." His eyes flared with silver flame as he watched her.

"You're a civilian. You can bow out anytime." Her smile indicated she knew he'd do the exact opposite.

"Or seize the day, as they say." The sizzle in his gaze shot up her internal temperature. "Have dinner with me tonight. Not in the dream realm, but in the here and now," he said. He named a popular place in the city. "Eight o'clock?"

"Getting a last-minute reservation there is impossible." Dinner with Declan in the real world. Definitely too good to turn down.

Declan smiled. "Do you honestly think someone can resist me?"

Maggie smiled back.

"Eight o'clock and I will meet you there, because I'd hate for you to make the trip out here twice in one day." She tapped him on the chest.

"Very good. Oh, and Maggie," he leaned over to whisper in her ear, "the only weapon you'll need tonight is perfume."

For once, she was speechless as she watched him walk away.

"I am going along, am I not?" Elle asked from her spot on Maggie's shoulder.

"He said no weapons, and you're listed as one of my weapons."

"But I'm a fun weapon." The arachnid tipped her head to one side and then reared up, showing the red hourglass on her tummy. "I make sex an unforgettable pleasure for my partners."

"It's only unforgettable until they're dead when it's all over. This is why you have so much trouble finding dates on the Web." She dodged a ferret racing along and headed for her quarters.

"I know you won't go without me," Elle said, pointedly

ignoring Maggie's comment. "We must have Sybil help us choose what you'll wear tonight. Her taste is ultra-romantic. And which perfume is Declan talking about?" Elle chattered away while Maggie walked.

Except Maggie wasn't hearing a word. She was still wondering how dinner was going to go without either her or Declan ending up as dessert.

How would Declan feel about being covered in hot fudge with me holding a spoon?

"Your thoughts are giving you away."

Maggie felt warm all over.

"You have no idea."

Chapter 9

DECLAN'S EXPECTATION THAT MAGGIE WOULD BE LATE and make an entrance was mistaken. She arrived at the restaurant at eight on the dot and attracted more than her share of attention as she followed the maître d' across the dining area.

Her sapphire-blue dress was short and flirty with a saucy ruffle along the hem and narrow straps a man would ache to lower as he kissed her golden shoulders. She'd arranged her short hair in loose curls that curved around her cheeks.

He wasn't looking at a witch who could take down a hulking creature without breaking a sweat. He was looking at a witch who was pure female calling to his male.

She is mine.

"You look lovely," he told her, standing up as she approached the table.

"Thank you." She smiled, but he was convinced she didn't feel as confident as she looked.

Declan dismissed the maître d' and seated Maggie, inhaling the sexy scent of her perfume.

"Have you ever eaten here?" he asked as she was handed her menu.

"No, I seem to go more for burgers and chili dogs, but I always like trying something new." She looked up as the sommelier presented a bottle of champagne to Declan and the glasses were filled. "Are we celebrating something?"

"You having dinner with me." He held his champagne flute up for a toast. "To a successful mission—and to more dinners."

"To seeing you wear something other than black." She nodded toward his black shadow-striped silk shirt and slacks.

"Did Elle accompany you?" He glanced at her bare arms.

"Elle is always with me when I leave the compound." Maggie laid her small bag on the table. The jeweled spider was artfully placed on the sapphire silk fabric like a brooch. Elle waved one foreleg at him demurely.

"Don't worry… she'll behave." Maggie set the menu down. "Do you have any suggestions?"

"If you'd like, I'll order. Is there anything you absolutely don't like?"

"Don't order snails, and we'll be fine." She smiled, watching him as he spoke flawless French to the waiter and then turned to her to explain.

"To start, I thought of *gratinée de coquilles St. Jacques,* which is scallops with a crust of bread crumbs and grated cheese. For the entrée, *terrine de saumon aux épinards* and *riz spécial*—salmon and spinach terrine and rice pilaf—and for dessert, custard with fresh berries."

He fancied a soft spotlight shone down on her. "If we're meant to go into a battle soon, we may as well have a beautiful meal first. Perhaps get to know each other better."

"Tell me more about yourself as a child, Declan." She sipped her champagne. "Were you, pardon the pun, a hellion as a boy? Did you create mayhem and mischief everywhere you went?"

He suddenly wished he had something stronger to drink. If she had been any other woman, he would have brushed off her question and diverted her attention to another subject. But he knew Maggie wouldn't allow that. She wanted a truthful answer, or she'd get up and leave.

And for the first time, he wanted to speak the whole truth.

"As you know, my father raised me," he said quietly. "This was not the life you see on television. It was harsh. He wasn't happy if I didn't follow his rules and meted out punishment for the least infraction.

"While I was embarrassed anytime I burned something down, my father was proud. He said it showed the power I had, and he wouldn't have minded if someone died because of me. I'm grateful that never happened."

"Is Anna also half demon and half human?" she spoke softly enough that no one could overhear their conversation.

"No, she's my half sister but a full-blooded demon—and it appears she is a Seer." He leaned back as a bubbling dish of coquilles St. Jacques was placed before them.

"You never realized that was her gift, even with her nightmares?"

"That's the thing. Although I've always felt Anna was special, I only saw them as nightmares or night terrors. I never thought of visions because there aren't any Seers in our family tree."

"What would I see on your branch?" She smiled after her first bite of savory scallops and immediately took a second one.

"Warriors like yourself, some sorcerers, a few incubi,

and more than a few succubae. One cousin owns an S and M club in Manhattan." He preferred looking at Maggie to eating his food, but he wasn't about to insult the chef by ignoring the delectable fare in front of him.

"And what about you? What is your specialty?"

"Business and finance. When I showed a flair for numbers, my father," his lips twisted at the last word, "sent me to Cal Poly and then Wharton. He saw me as the next Donald Trump."

"And instead you're running a nightclub."

Declan shook his head. "I own it. I made sure every *i* was dotted and every *t* was crossed to ensure there were no loopholes they could use against me."

"No offense, but blood always tells."

"I leave the dirty work to my cousins." He paused while their plates were taken away and replaced with the main course.

Maggie fingered her water goblet. "I admit you're nothing like any demon I've met. Maybe it has to do with your mother's blood, since I haven't heard of many half-demons around."

"Most die before they're a year old, if not at birth. My father considered me a novelty and portrayed me as such in his household."

"I worked for a physician in 1803," Maggie said. "He had been under the eye of the Guard because supes in the area disappeared under suspicious circumstances and the not-so-nice doctor was the prime suspect. I didn't realize he knew what I was until I woke up one morning strapped to a table. He didn't know I was a Guard, so he didn't kill me.

"Somehow he figured out I was a witch, and he

wanted to find out what made me one," Maggie said softly. "I had no idea how he found out, since I never used my power around humans. By then, all that mattered was that I made sure he didn't try to dissect me."

"What happened to him?"

"His obituary read that he had a heart attack." She held out a hand, the fingertips sizzling with power.

"Seems we're getting too serious here. So tell me, Maggie, what's your sign?"

Her laughter was just what he wanted. He saw it as the next step, because there was no way he was going to back down from this woman.

⁓

Maggie had to admit that Declan knew his food. Every bite melted in her mouth, and a few times, she was positive her taste buds experienced an orgasm.

At the end of the meal, she sipped coffee and nibbled on rich champagne truffles while Declan enjoyed a glass of cognac.

"I enjoyed this. Thank you very much." She noted the disappointment in the back of his eyes at the idea the evening was coming to an end. "I wonder if you'd like to do some surveillance work tonight."

"Not my idea of after-dinner fun. I thought we might visit a club—no, not mine—and listen to music or dance."

She reached inside her bag and pulled out a slip of paper. "Even if I have the address of the home Courtney's staying in? I'd really like to get a look before I start playing my role."

He took the paper from her and studied the address.

"I know where this is... not all that far from a favorite club of mine that plays excellent blues."

"Spy, then music. I can do that." She lifted an eyebrow.

"I'll drive." He gestured for the bill and guided her out of the restaurant.

Maggie eyed Declan's BMW 335 convertible with open avarice. "Very nice," she said as he helped her into the passenger seat. She pulled the paper out of her bag and gave him the address.

As he roared away from the restaurant and glided through traffic, Maggie noticed her hair wasn't ruffled from the wind.

"Protections for passengers," Declan said, easily reading her mind.

"Female passengers who don't like getting their hair mussed." She watched the buildings fly by, changing from city high-rises and apartment buildings to homey neighborhoods.

"It's a group home," she said. "About ten kids live there. I also told Mal it's better if I'm like a third cousin instead of an aunt."

"Here's Oaktree Lane," Declan announced, making a sharp left turn.

"That must be it." She felt the car slow down as they neared the two-story house. "Hide us from curious eyes, keep us silent, and do it now." Maggie invoked a protection spell. Soft gray light floated over the car, starting at the hood. "If anyone senses anything, they'll think it's a dog," she told him. "Just don't try any fancy moves or rev the engine."

"A couple of lights are on upstairs," Declan commented, pulling over to the curb. "Did you think you could see her by parking out here, or do you have a spell for that?"

"I have a crystal that works great for that, but this time around I just wanted to see where she was living." Maggie studied the house. With the moonlight, she could see it was painted cream with burnt-orange trim and that the yard was well cared for with several bicycles lying on the wraparound porch.

"Why her?" she mused.

"Ravenna said she has true blood in her veins." He switched off the engine.

"If so, you'd think they'd want to make her some kind of priestess or something."

"I don't have to tell you that blood sacrifices offer a lot of power. Since somebody's planning to raise the Destroyer, they'll need all the magick they can get. How do you know they won't look for anyone else who carries what they call 'the true blood' if we manage to stop them?"

"This is why I hate those who use blood magick. All they do is create chaos," she murmured. She cocked her head and threw out her senses. "Do you hear that?"

Declan stilled. "A window opening. Whoever is doing it is experienced, because very few humans could hear it."

"It sounds like it's coming from the back." Then she noticed a motorcycle rolling toward them with its headlight and engine off. She touched Declan's arm, but he'd already seen their visitor.

A sprightly figure ran from the rear of the house and down the lawn. The motorcycle rider hopped off his bike and grabbed her in his arms. After a long kiss, she climbed on the bike behind him. They rolled silently up the street at first, and then he switched on the ignition.

"Do you hear it?" Maggie lifted her face.

"Hear what?"

Darkness momentarily surrounded her. "Drums," she whispered. Seconds passed when she shook her head indicating there was only silence now.

"Shall we follow her?" Declan asked, already turning on the engine.

"Definitely. I'll keep the invisibility spell going so they won't know they're being tailed."

"No problem there."

Maggie wasn't surprised to find that they were returning to the center of the city. She thought the young couple might be heading to a local fast-food restaurant or somewhere for coffee. Instead, they parked near a warehouse.

"The Hallows?" she said, reading a signboard propped up outside the door. "What is this idiot kid thinking? No way she'll be coming down here when I've got hold of her, because she won't be able to sneak out as easily."

"Come on." Declan parked the car and went around to the passenger door. He glanced at the patrons entering the club, none of whom appeared to be over the age of twenty-five. "Any illusion spells up your alley so we can blend in and not arouse the bouncer's suspicions?"

"You don't have any magick of your own?" She got out and looked around.

"I told you. If you don't count controlling fire, my magick mainly has to do with figuring out profit and loss." He took her arm. "Are you going to hurt the bouncer if he gives us trouble?"

"Why would I do that?"

"You seem to thrive on it."

"Only at your place." She patted his arm and then kept her hand there. "We are not fiends. We are teens. We wish to hide in plain sight and do it now." She looked up and saw Declan the way he must have looked in high school. "You were a cutie back then. How about me?"

"The black eyeliner is a bit over the top, along with the barely there pink dress, but you'll blend in."

Maggie's ears started hurting the moment they entered the club. "And here I thought your club was bad, sound-wise."

She took his hand, looking from right to left until she saw a flash of dark hair with blonde streaks. "She's over there."

She started forward, but Declan pulled her back.

"Let's just observe. There's something about the boyfriend that bothers me."

Maggie knew his hearing was good enough that she didn't have to shout over the loud music. "Is he a demon?"

She studied the kids dancing with a frenetic energy that tired her just by watching. She also felt a wave of something that she could only describe as feeling wrong. Even with all her years as a Guard, she couldn't remember sensing something like this.

"I do not like this place," Elle moved up to embrace Maggie's neck. Considering the tattoos covering some of the kids in the club, a shiny black widow spider wouldn't look too odd.

"No kidding," Maggie murmured.

Declan continued staring at the young couple.

"I don't know. He doesn't feel demon, but there's still something off about him. I can tell you that I'm positive he's hiding something."

"I felt that, too."

With the club so dark, Maggie couldn't easily see what the boy looked like, but she sensed that Declan could give her any details she missed.

"Wanna dance?" A black-haired boy with multiple piercings on his face approached her.

"Back off," Declan growled, draping his arm around Maggie's shoulders and pulling her close.

The kid took one look at him and backed off. "It's cool, man."

"He only asked me to dance, Declan. No reason to get the testosterone going. She sneaks out at night, goes to a rave, and has a boyfriend who might not be what he appears," Maggie mused, still checking the participants and not liking what she was seeing. She sensed magick but couldn't identify a source.

Declan was looking around uneasily. He took her by the hand. "We need to leave."

"Not yet."

"Someone's noticed us." He pulled on her hand and practically dragged her toward the exit, although he kept a slow pace as if they weren't retreating.

"My illusion spells are perfect," she argued.

"And you, of all witches, should know that even perfect can be broken by the right being." He didn't stop until they reached the car.

"What did you sense that I didn't?" Maggie curled her legs under herself and turned in the seat to look out the back as they left the parking lot. Two men exited the building after them and watched as they drove off. "And please tell me that they can't get any info off your license plate."

"Not a thing." He kept driving until they left the area and then headed for a coffee place. "They won't even be able to connect the car to the club."

—⁓—

Maggie snagged a corner table while Declan ordered for them.

"Peppermint tea." He placed the cup in front of her.

"Yum!" She took a sip, savoring the rich taste. "There was magick all throughout that rave."

He nodded. "If I'm not mistaken, someone, if not more than one someone, is feeding off the energy of the teens."

His words chilled her to the bone. She kept her voice low, even though they were the only customers in the shop. "That's demon."

"Other creatures siphon off energy, but yes, some demons are notorious for it. It's the only way they can exist. It's their food and drink."

Maggie looked at Declan, seeing the sorrow etched in his features. "It hurts that you have to think of your own kind as monsters." She held up her hand, halting him from speaking.

"No, hear me out. Yes, I used to consider all demons as evil, but you've shown me that's not the case. And no way Anna's dark. Let me tell you, every race has its good and its bad. I've killed witches because they practiced baneful magick. I destroyed them because they were harming the innocent.

"Did I feel bad? Only that those with so much power

would use it for evil." She took another sip. "If demons are running the raves, we need to take them out. Just what happens when they siphon off the power?"

"It's like tapping into one's life force," he said wearily. "Many only take a sip, enough to keep them going until they find another human to do the same with. All it will do is shorten a human's life a day or so. Some might even lose a month. But what I felt in there was much stronger. Those kids were losing years."

"Okay, not good at all. First the god of destruction needs to go down, and now we have this." She nodded. "It's not as if the Guard doesn't have enough teams to cover pretty much everything, but how did this fly under our radar?"

"How many incidents involving children have you dealt with?" He finished his triple-shot espresso and went back for a second.

"And I thought the ferrets lived on super-caffeine." Maggie waited until he was seated again. "As for children? We have special teams that deal only with children. I can't even fathom how they can handle it."

"The demon behind this is old. I felt ancient power in there."

"I wondered what I sensed. I only knew it was wrong."

"They're very good at hiding."

"I'll let Mal know, and he can send in a team."

"You know they won't find anything. Raves move from building to building with little advance word."

"All those kids are in there, not knowing what might happen to them. And even if they're gone, there might be traces," she insisted, pulling out her cell. She made a quick call, giving Mal all the info. "Okay, we have to go back and make sure Courtney and her boyfriend are out of there." She picked up her cup.

The drive past the building showed the motorcycle was gone, but more teens streamed inside.

"Do you think they figured out exactly who we were?"

"They might have sensed a demon was in there, but I didn't make any threatening moves. That's why it's still open." He glanced at her. "Are we waiting for your team to move in?"

She shook her head. "They wouldn't like me being here."

Declan drove back to the restaurant parking lot and waited while the valet brought Maggie's car.

"I had a lovely evening," she told him.

"I've got to say, you do make dinner out more interesting." He smiled, and she felt her insides heating up. "And informative."

"Scary to be on the good guys' side, isn't it?" She reached up and kissed him lightly on the lips. "Good night, Declan."

"We could go to my place for a drink," he offered.

"Next time."

It wasn't until she drove away that Maggie realized she'd admitted to Declan that she wanted to see him again.

Now it's getting complicated.

"What the fuck have you done?"

Declan hadn't been in his apartment for more than fifteen minutes before Wreaker materialized in a dark swirl of power. His gray hair was pulled back in a tight ponytail.

Declan turned around and faced his cousin. "If I remember correctly, you're not welcome here. This is my haven." He stalked over to Wreaker, his face harsh with fury. "I was promised none of you would enter my private quarters without my permission. And you *do not* have my permission."

"You're turning traitor, cuz." Wreaker plopped on the couch and conjured up a bottle of beer. His boot heels scarred the coffee table as he propped his feet on the polished wood surface. "The old man's not happy with you at all."

"Do you really think I care how he feels about me?"

"You should when you're acting like some frat boy looking to date the prom queen. Although the witch is a great-looking piece of ass." Wreaker chugged his beer and then belched.

"If the women you seduce saw you like this, they'd run the other way." Declan walked over to his bar and poured himself a stiff Scotch. He feared this wouldn't be the only one he'd be downing.

"The women I fuck love me this way. Nothing like a bad boy to get them ripping off their clothes." He gestured toward the black leather vest that revealed his living tattoos and chaps. His dark eyes glinted with sinister humor. "But we're talking about you, stud. You were spotted in a club tonight that you had no business being in—and to make it worse, you were there with the sexy Guard."

"Nothing wrong with clubbing."

"There is when the average age at that rave was seventeen." Wreaker finished his beer, stared at the empty bottle, and watched it refill itself. "And I know you're not into tender flesh." He eyed Declan.

Declan knocked back the Scotch in one gulp and re-filled the glass.

"Why do Maggie and the Guard worry our kind so much? They rarely interfere with our politics unless one of us catches their attention by making a splash in the world of humans." Declan turned around and leaned back with his elbows resting on the bar. "Such as you might do, if you're not more careful. The Guard protects humans."

"If they rarely interfere with us, why were they at Damnation Alley?"

"I told you. She was tracking down a rogue Bloater. Nothing to do with me—or even the club." He watched his cousin closely. His lack of expression had Declan wondering if Wreaker knew more about the Bloater incident than he let on.

"You've tightened up the portal. Not letting so many through." Wreaker looked at him over the brown bottle. "What's that about?"

"Keeping the numbers even. Ratchet let so many through that there was chaos everywhere," Declan said, curious about his relative's inquisitiveness.

"She killed him, you know. Your sexy Maggie turned Ratchet into pâté."

Declan got a sick feeling in his stomach. Wreaker wasn't saying anything he hadn't thought of before, but he didn't want any demons focusing on her. "No one knows what really happened to Ratchet."

"Maybe we don't have rock-solid proof, but many feel she had something to do with it. It's been said that his pieces were scattered to the winds." Wreaker made his bottle disappear and stood up. "Make sure she doesn't do the same to you, cuz. We'd like to keep you around." With a smile and salute, he was gone in a puff of smoke.

I should have killed him when I had the chance. Declan picked up the Scotch bottle and carried it to bed. He knew it was going to be a long night.

Chapter 10

CHANTING. WORDS IN A LONG-FORGOTTEN LANGUAGE FILLED the air. The smell of smoke, the scent of death in the air, coming from the victims as each was stabbed through the heart with the sacred knife.

Blood flowed down the stone steps while the sky turned dark and ominous as the ritual progressed. Clouds turned orange; fire rained down; and the portal swirled open in a mass of black smoke.

A tall, bronze-skinned man wearing a coat of brilliant feathers and a feathered headdress made of gold smiled at her. Not until then did she realize she was lying naked on stone, her hands bound with leather cords and words of power painted on her skin.

"You and the girl will finish the ritual." Even though he spoke in the ancient language, she found herself able to understand him. He raised the stone knife, the tip red with blood. "Once I have eaten your heart, I will be invincible."

Even though she was securely bound, she refused to give up. "Then expect some heartburn. Heart. Burn. Get it?" she grinned.

But then she really looked at the priest and felt horror fill her body.

This wasn't someone from an ancient race. This was someone she knew.

The face she looked into was Declan's as he brought the knife down to her chest.

—nn—

"Whoa!" Maggie shot up in bed and struggled to catch her breath.

"Sleeping here," Elle said in a groggy voice from her silken web.

"Good for you." Maggie pressed her hand against her chest, feeling the rapid rise and fall as air failed to fill her lungs. A blind grope showed there were no wounds, no blood streaming down her body, even as she was convinced she still felt the pain from the blade piercing her flesh.

A wave of her hand gave life to the candles scattered around the bedroom. The soft yellow light was meant to be calming, but her heart rate didn't show any signs of slowing down. She grimaced as she realized her hair was damp with sweat and her skin was slick.

"Did you have a nightmare?" Elle asked, finally rousing herself.

"A whopper—and one I'd like to forget." Maggie pushed back the covers that suddenly felt too heavy.

The spider skittered her way to the bed and across the comforter to Maggie's pillow and attached herself to Maggie's shoulder. "What happened?"

"I dreamed I was the sacrifice along with Courtney." She made her way into the bathroom and used a damp washcloth to sponge the sweat from her body. "And Declan was the priest performing the ritual. But why should I have this vision?"

"Perhaps it is nothing more than a nightmare. You could have had this because this is the day you will meet the girl face-to-face. Could you have fear that you will fail in protecting her?"

"Thank you, Sigmund Freud." Maggie splashed cold water against her face and leaned against the sink.

"If I was Freud, I'd compare the knife to Declan's penis."

"Not going there!" Maggie turned the shower up as hot as possible so it would warm her blood, which now ran cold. The shower and a change of pajamas made her feel marginally better.

"Have sex with the demon. You will feel much better. I always feel better after sex."

"Elle, *please*. If it happens, it will happen on my time, not yours."

A wave of Maggie's hand had the bedsheets stripped and fresh ones on in a flash, and she crawled back under the covers. She left the candles flickering in an attempt to keep the darkness at bay, since she knew sleep would be a long time coming.

And fearless Maggie jumped a foot when her cell chimed "All Star." A glance at the Caller ID told her it was Declan.

"Do you know what time it is?" she said by way of greeting.

"Did you just have a nightmare about Mayan priests?" he countered with his own.

"How did you know?" *Because he was there, Mags!*

"Because I had one, and you were there," he spoke in a clipped voice.

"Don't tell me. You were the priest, and I was the sacrifice. You carved out my heart. You were pretty sloppy about it, too. Or were you the sacrifice, and I was the scary priestess?"

He swore under his breath. Some of the curses were new to her, and Maggie mentally cataloged them for future reference.

"Someone knows we're coming," she said.

"I could have done without that nightmare," he muttered.

"Couldn't we all? But there are two ways of looking at it. We're being targeted specifically, or the bad guys sense something and only sent out a blanket spell to warn off whoever is on their trail. It's like a two-way mirror. They know someone's watching, but they can't see who."

"I tried contacting Anna, but they wouldn't let me through. I need to talk to her. To know she's all right. For all we know, she's a target, too."

"The Seers' Pavilion is warded more heavily than the entire compound. No psychic dreams would get through their protections." She picked up on his panic. "She's safer there than she'd be anywhere else."

"But if she has the same nightmare." He took a deep breath. "What if she dreams she's the sacrifice and I'm the—"

"I will check on her and call you back." She knew she wasn't going to be returning to sleep any time soon. She disconnected and then punched in the extension number for the Pavilion. Ten minutes later she was assured Anna was asleep and that whatever horror had visited Maggie and Declan hadn't invaded his half sister's slumber.

"She's all right?" were Declan's first words.

"Haven't you ever heard of 'hello'?"

Before she'd called him, she'd gotten herself a glass of wine and returned to bed with the covers wrapped around her. A grumbling Elle had returned to her web. She'd declared that since she wouldn't be sleeping any time soon, she might as well check her email in hopes someone had found that illusive immortality spell.

"It's one of those polite things most of us do. And yes, Anna's fine. She's asleep with no sign a beastie is ruining her snooze."

"I'm sorry."

"You're stressed and worried about her. I get it." She lifted the glass to her lips.

"No, I'm sorry I killed you in the dream."

That stopped Maggie cold. The last thing she wanted was a reminder of her horrifying illusion. "Apology accepted, and we really don't need to revisit that." She could hear him breathing on the other end of the line. "Umm, haven't you ever had a nightmare, Declan? I mean, with your family background…"

"We create nightmares. We don't have them."

"Well then, welcome to my world. If we're lucky, we're still flying under the radar and they're just sending out feelers. Better a bad dream than something tangible."

"What about Courtney? Do you think she's going through this, too?"

"I don't know. This is new to me. I'm usually the one sent to take care of the baddies. I'm told where the rogues are, and my team and I go in and clean them out. I don't deal with kids. I don't deal with ancient cultures, and I don't go up against bloodthirsty cults.

"Well, there was one in Bolivia." She thought back. "They were actually idiots playing with something they couldn't handle, so we had to handle it for them. Very messy."

"Are you always so glib about your work?"

"It makes it easier. That's why I'm not addicted

to creaBay or watching *What Not To Wear*. Although Frebus does give me good fashion tips."

She paused and thought of Declan on the other end of the phone line; she sensed he was more vulnerable than she'd yet known him to be.

"And I'm doing it again. Okay, here goes. There are times when I'm so scared, I can't breathe. More than once, I've gone on a mission with the knowledge I might not survive. And then I wonder who will mourn me.

"I know my team will, but they'll go on because they have to. The way I've moved forward every time we've lost a team member." She plumped her pillows behind her so she could sit up. "I value the friends I've known for more than 700 years. I know they'll always be there for me, but sometimes I want…"

"More." He finished it for her. "Something that's just for you."

"Exactly." She lit up, pleased he understood.

"Love."

"I told you, it's not in my future, and I'm surprised you'd think of that word." Maggie shifted uneasily, since Declan's voice had lowered to a caressing tone that stroked her nerve endings. She wasn't ready for this.

"Call it my human half. And you can't deny there's something between us. *Hey*! Dammit!" He paused. "You did that, didn't you? I've got Scotch all over me."

"You get personal, you get a bath. I'm going to get some sleep. I have to look bright eyed when I meet my new 'cousin,' and concealer can only do so much." Her voice softened. "Good night, Declan."

"Good night, Maggie. Sweet dreams."

His words hit her as soon as she extinguished the candles and pulled the covers over her chest.

"No dreams for me. No dreams at all. No dreams to see. No dreams that will gall. A good night's sleep for me." She smiled as she felt the magickal sparkles drift over her. A moment later, she was sound asleep with the image of Declan's face in her mind.

"Why didn't you call me last night?" Sybil sat cross-legged in the middle of Maggie's bed and watched her friend dig through her closet. The elf's wings rustled softly, sending calming fragrance through the air.

"We could have sat up and talked, experimented with makeup, or told ghost jokes. I heard a good one from Janus a few days ago," she said, referring to the compound's resident spirit.

"Declan called. He had the same nightmare and was afraid that Anna might also be experiencing it. I was able to find out she was okay and let him know."

"And…?" She lifted an arched eyebrow.

"And we talked for awhile." Maggie pulled out a dress, held it up against herself, and looked at Sybil. The elf shook her head, and Maggie threw the dress back into the closet. The second and third dress met the same fate.

"This isn't working. I don't even know how to *dress* for the role Mal thought up for me."

"That's because you're trying to look either too professional or too boring. There's no reason for you to do either." Sybil climbed off the bed and gently pushed her friend to one side. Within thirty seconds, Sybil had pulled out a bright-pink-and-turquoise-print V-neck blouse paired with a black skirt and turquoise jacket.

"And when did you get these cute shoes?" She held up black peep-toe pumps that sported a small pink bow. "I would have borrowed them in a second. I like how you kept your makeup simple. You won't need an illusion spell to charm the authorities."

"Tita could pull this off." Maggie quickly dressed and took the jewelry Sybil held in her hand.

"She'd show up in black leather and scare everyone. You're protecting someone important, Maggie," she said softly.

"Then why don't I feel that way? Yes, I know the young are easy targets, but there's so much going on here. And now there's that rave Declan and I followed Courtney to. Who knows how much damage is done to the teenagers who attend them? How do we know that demons aren't somehow involved with the Mayans and managing to keep themselves under wraps?"

"No one we've brought in has even hinted that," Sybil told her. "The team that went to the warehouse only found traces of the demon power, but no hint where they'd moved to. Mal sent witches to cleanse the area, so the demons can't return there."

"They're off somewhere else, and more teenagers are being affected," Maggie mused, fluffing her hair and spraying on perfume. She adjusted her blouse, gratified that her push-up bra did its job. "Okay, I'm gone."

"You'll do great." Sybil followed her out of the room.

"You better come visit me in that house Mal set up for me." She hugged her friend and hurried out of her quarters with the elf walking behind her.

"Wait up!" Mal ambled up to her as she exited the building. He handed her a sheaf of papers. "Don't forget your ID, backstory, and credit cards. Just don't go overboard charging up a storm." His wizened face looked her over. "You look downright harmless, O'Malley."

"And what will you be doing while I'm playing mommy?" She stuffed it all in her bag.

"Looking into how you and the demon were visited by nightmares. And make sure the kid wears this." He handed her a necklace made of hammered brass links. "Tracking and protection. This is for you to use if you have to track her." He added a bracelet to it. "You wear this. Touch the links, and you'll see where she is. If she feels fear, the bracelet will alert you. If she's hurt, you'll find that out, too. Keys to the house."

Maggie nodded. "Are you sure someone else can't do this?" She hated the whine in her voice.

"Witch up, O'Malley. You're the one." He waddled off in a haze of cigar smoke.

"Easy for you to say." She glanced at her watch and realized she'd have to race to make it in time for her meeting.

"You think you can dump me with a perfect stranger?" A teenage whirlwind rounded on the judge, the attorney, and Maggie. Her glossy black hair with its white blonde streaks flared around her shoulders. "How do you know she's not some perv just looking to sell me into white slavery?" She glared at Maggie.

"Or a drug dealer who plans to use me as a mule? Or put me in porn movies? I won't go with her." She crossed her arms in front of her chest. A chest that Maggie sadly noticed was a bit more abundant than her own.

Maggie's first thought was *All righty then, she's all yours*. Her second was *This kid has a pretty good imagination*.

"I realize this is upsetting to you, Courtney," she said, doing her best to put across total normalcy. "I'm just sorry I couldn't have been here sooner. I didn't hear about your parents' deaths until a couple of months ago. I've been living in Europe for the past ten years, and we didn't keep in touch like we used to." She used the cover story Mal and company had cooked up for her. "When I heard what happened to you, I knew I needed to come here and offer you a good home."

Courtney glared at her from wide eyes lined with kohl. Her dark-red skirt looked more like a Band-Aid, while her matching top was postage-stamp size. Maggie thought of her own outfits when she went clubbing, and none of them were that miniscule.

The administrator of the group home sat in a corner looking relieved that her charge was being handed off to someone else.

"I won't go."

Courtney continued to repeat those three words as the judge signed off on the paperwork and added his good wishes to Maggie.

"We'll pick up your things and go over to the house I've purchased," Maggie said, just as happy to get out of there as Courtney was.

"Didn't you hear one thing I said? I'm not going anywhere."

Maggie matched her glare for glare. "Yes, you will."

Courtney drew out her cell phone, but Maggie took it from her and tucked it in her bag. "How about we grab some lunch and get to know each other?"

"That's mine. I paid for it."

"And you'll get it returned. I just want to talk, Courtney."

"I have to get back to school."

"You're excused today." She led the teen down to the parking lot.

"This is your car?" Courtney's eyes bugged out at the sight of the Viper. "Can I drive it?"

"No."

"I have a learner's permit."

"Still no. Any choice of where to go for lunch, or do you trust me to come up with something fun?"

"Gee, how noble of you." Courtney sulked in the passenger seat.

Maggie glanced at her charge as she started up the car.

Anyone whose biological clock is ticking overtime only has to meet Courtney. Adopting a cobra would be a much better bet.

Maggie didn't expect lunch with the girl to be easy. She was right. Courtney ordered enough food for a third-world country and then only nibbled at it. Her replies to Maggie's questions were monosyllables.

"For someone who was convinced I was here to kidnap her, you're not all that curious about me," Maggie said, finishing her food.

"You're my dad's third cousin. You haven't kept in touch with him for several years, and my parents never mentioned you. You don't even look like anyone in my family. Your hairdresser makes it look natural." She eyed Maggie's blonde hair.

"I'm from the Scandinavian side of the family."

"You are so full of shit," the girl hooted. "My ancestors came from South America. Not the North Pole."

"Sounds like you need to learn your geography. And being a third cousin doesn't mean my bloodline is the same as yours."

"Whatev." Courtney slumped in the chair and looked around the restaurant.

"If you're finished, we'll stop by and pick up your things." As Maggie said the words, she saw the first flash of real emotion in Courtney's brown eyes. She caught a hint of sorrow and insecurity and wondered if it came from the girl's troubles. Losing her parents, no hint of family members, and she would have been stuck in the system for three more years if the Hellion Guard hadn't found her. That left Maggie wondering what would happen to the girl if they all survived what was ahead.

She took a deep breath. "Let's go."

"Can I have my cell back?" Courtney followed her.

"Once we settle in at the house." She hoped she'd find a large bottle of aspirin there. "I may not be used to having a teenager around, but that doesn't mean I don't remember what it was like."

"Huh. You haven't been my age in years."

"Something like that," she said dryly.

Maggie knew her clothing and personal items would have been moved over to the house while she was at the courthouse. Her magickal supplies would remain in her quarters at the compound.

Courtney didn't take long to gather up her things at the group home. Maggie observed, noting none of the girls wished her well and the boys only gave her sly looks. Mrs. Whitney, the administrator, displayed the same relief she had shown at the courthouse.

"Do you know what happened to your family's things?"

"The court appointed a guardian who sold the house and furniture and put the money in trust until I'm twenty-five." The teen acted as if that were a hundred years away. She looked down, her dark hair falling forward to obscure her features. "The other stuff is in a storage unit."

"I'm sure I can arrange it if you want to go through what's in there and take anything you'd like," Maggie offered.

"No thanks. It's all junk." Courtney shrugged.

Oh, yeah, a *really* big bottle of aspirin.

Maggie easily found the two-story, creamy-yellow Victorian house with blue gingerbread trim. It was part of a quiet neighborhood. The building with its wrap-around porch was set at the end of the block and somewhat secluded by a row of trees along the driveway that offered a windbreak.

With colorful flower baskets hanging from the porch ceiling and wind chimes near the glass-fronted double door, it looked like something out of a storybook. The name of the street was Spinning Wheel Lane, for Fates' sake. Maggie wouldn't have been surprised to see a shaggy-faced dog peeking out over the back fence. She felt the strength of the wards as she drove up the driveway.

"Nice house. And you've got a hot car. You must be rich." Courtney eyed her speculatively. "What do you do?"

"I'm a consultant, so I work out of the house."

"Consultant's a fancy way of saying you run an escort service."

Maggie stopped the car and half turned in her seat. "Where do you get these ideas?"

Courtney shrugged as she looked away. "It's the way the world is. Good things go away. Bad things happen." She pushed open the door and climbed out.

"Your room is the third door on the right." Maggie walked into the kitchen and wasted no time setting up the coffee.

"If it's pink, I'm going to projectile vomit all over it." Courtney headed for the stairs.

"If the room is pink, it will stink. Change to a color she will love, and look kick-ass," Maggie muttered. "And please don't be black."

"You did one thing right!" floated down. "The green isn't so bad."

"Glad to hear that." Maggie palmed her cell and connected with Mal. "We're here."

"She fell for the story?"

"Not really. She's debating whether I'm a madam or a white slaver. She's one troubled and confused kid."

"She's a teenager. They're all like that," he said with the authority of one who'd never been a father. "You'll be good for her." She could hear him puffing away on his cigar. "I've got Zouk Rattail tracking the dream you and the demon shared. We're hoping he'll have some info for us soon."

Maggie shuddered at the thought of the troll's job, which was finding ways to backtrack someone's dream to the originator. If she thought her nightmare was bad, she didn't want to think what his must be like.

She winced as loud thumps from overhead made it sound as if the ceiling would fall at any second.

"Hey! You've got the bigger room with its own bathroom!" Courtney shouted down.

Mal chuckled. "Yeah, the two of you are the perfect pair." He turned serious. "I'm going to email you some updated intel on this god of destruction. That somebody's able to invade your sleep isn't good."

"Gee, ya think?" She searched for coffee mugs and poured herself a cup, inhaling the rich cinnamon scent of fresh-brewed caffeine. Tea wasn't going to help her one bit in dealing with a teenager. "They've got another thing coming if they assume this will make me back off."

"There are some special sachets you're to use in your pillow. They should keep the bad dreams away. Gotta go." He hung up.

"Nice to talk to you, too." She sipped the hot liquid.

"Oh good, coffee." Courtney grabbed a mug, poured some, and took a sip. "Not bad."

"Thanks. I gather you're okay with your room?"

"It's all right and not a sucky color."

Maggie leaned back against the counter and watched Courtney prowl through the kitchen. Although they'd eaten barely an hour ago, the girl was already investigating the refrigerator contents and looking through the cabinets.

She was glad that the kitchen was bright and cheerful, painted white with bright-red accents and appliances. The knowledge the morning sun would come in the window over the sink was another plus in her mind. She realized it was something she could get used to.

But even with the cheerful atmosphere of the house, she felt darkness creeping up around them like an encroaching fog. She knew the wards were strong enough to hold it back, but she'd still never let down her guard.

"At least you don't believe in stocking nothing but healthy food." Courtney chose a bag of chocolate marshmallow cookies. "Mrs. Whitney was positive we were better off eating so healthy I thought I'd turn into a vegetable. She'd even make veggie lasagna because she felt too much meat wasn't good for us. How wrong is that?" She hitched herself up onto the counter even though there was a chair nearby.

"Some people prefer it that way. As for me, I like mine with lots of meat."

Courtney tore open the bag of cookies, took out several, and belatedly offered the bag to Maggie, who took one.

"Why didn't you keep in touch with my dad? They've been gone for three years. Didn't you think something was wrong when you didn't get a Christmas card?" She demolished her snack in two bites and then dipped her second cookie in her coffee. "Didn't anyone tell you about them?" *About me?* was left unspoken.

"I didn't keep in contact with anyone while I was in Europe." Maggie continued with her cover story. "It was one of those self-discovery journeys."

"Wish I could do that." Courtney looked out the window for a moment before zeroing back on her. "Why are you doing this? I mean, Dad was only some million-times-removed cousin. It's not like you were brother and sister. You didn't have to do this."

Maggie saw that the girl was a lot smarter than they'd anticipated. She'd have to step carefully with her, or Courtney would easily see through her lies. If that happened, Maggie didn't want to think of the consequences. How could she explain to the girl?

Why couldn't she be four years old and just accept whatever I say?

"We were close as kids, and while we didn't keep in touch as we got older, I did think about him a lot," she lied. "When I heard what happened, I didn't want to think of you sharing a house with basically strangers."

"But you're a stranger. I told you, Dad never mentioned you. The only cousins I knew were on Mom's side."

"After time I won't be a stranger to you." Maggie couldn't help but wonder what would happen to Courtney if they all survived this. She hated to think the girl would be returned to the system.

Courtney shot her a look filled with calculation. "Are you going to let my boyfriend come over without giving me a lot of grief?"

Not in this lifetime. "What's he like?"

For the first time, Maggie saw joy in the girl's face. "Mick is… he's just fantastic. He listens to me. I mean *really* listens to me and doesn't just say what I want to hear. He even found me my job. I work at Peach Moon at the mall. They give me an awesome discount on clothes there. FYI, I'm *not* giving up my job." Belligerence.

Maggie understood her insistence. She thought guiltily about how Courtney was going to be laid off when she next went in to work.

She considered what she knew about Courtney. So far it was only what she'd read in reports, what she and

Declan had noted at the rave the night they followed her and her boyfriend, and what little Courtney had let drop so far. Not a lot, but it was enough to tell her that what she'd expected to be a smart-mouthed teenager was really a scared little girl.

The way Maggie had been a frightened child the first day she entered the Witches' Academy. The fears she first felt when she and her class were banished from the academy, and she had no idea what she would do to survive in an unknown world.

But she'd carried on, and she intended to see that Courtney did the same.

"I don't eat eggs. Why can't we have pancakes?" Courtney poured herself a cup of coffee.

Maggie touched her forehead where the pounding had intensified. "Pancakes have eggs in them."

"That's different." Courtney looked through the refrigerator and freezer. "We don't have any kind of toaster pastries? Or microwavable waffles?"

"Eggs and bacon. You better hurry up so we can get you to school on time."

"Mick takes me."

"Mick doesn't know where you live."

"I called him last night after you gave me my cell back." Courtney's phone chirped, and she dove into her pocket for it. "He'll be here in about fifteen minutes. I guess I'll just have toast. Do we have jam?"

"Text him back and tell him I'm taking you."

After dropping the sulky teen off at the high school and making sure she was wearing the new necklace with the tracking spell embedded, Maggie drove back to the suburb that was part of her new life.

With more coffee in hand, she checked her email to find the additional research Mal had for her.

Every word she read sent more boulders to the pit of her stomach.

Elle skittered up Maggie's shoulder and peered at the laptop's screen. "Does that say what I think it says? We are doomed, *ma chere*. Or should I say, more doomed than usual."

"No kidding," Maggie said softly, reaching for her phone.

Chapter 11

"YOU'RE RIGHT. THIS IS DEMON MAGICK," DECLAN pronounced after reading the report. "The worst kind." He'd wasted no time driving to the house after Maggie called him.

"Tell me something I don't know." Maggie's brain buzzed from all the coffee she'd sucked down that morning. She fidgeted at the kitchen table. More proof she should have stuck with her tea. "This is absolute proof that the Mayans were—and are—demons."

"That's in our history books. But there's more than I've ever heard before. According to what's here, they're a branch that's about as evil as you can get. Some of us can be reasoned with. Most can't. What you're looking at here are ones who believe that blood is the only path to power. They will do whatever is necessary to obtain that."

"The more blood, the more power."

"Exactly." He took the mug out of her hand and drank.

Maggie sighed and got up to get herself another mug. "I still don't understand why they chose Courtney. She's a kid barely out of training pants. How much power could be in her blood that they'd be so desperate to use her for a sacrifice?"

"Did you sense anything unusual during the time you've spent with her?" Declan asked.

"No, but to be honest, I didn't push it. I thought I'd

give her a few days to get used to me and keep this time as normal as possible. For the first time, I hate the lies, because I think lying will only make things worse in the long run."

She picked at a loose thread on her multi-striped, linen calf-length skirt. Her lace-trimmed lime tank top matched one of the colorful stripes in the skirt, and her hair was tucked behind her ears.

"She needs stability, not the prospect of ending up as a piece of meat on an altar if we screw up."

His eyes softened with understanding. "Have you talked to Mal about this?"

"He'd tell me to suck it up and do my job. Mal doesn't have a speck of compassion in his roly-poly body."

"So you called me first. I'm flattered." He smiled and reached forward, picking up her fingers, bringing them to his lips, and nibbling gently on the tips.

She felt the heat of his mouth against her skin. It brought to mind other parts of her body where his lips could travel.

"Maybe you've proven to me that you're not a nasty like most of your brethren." She was relieved her voice didn't betray the depth of her arousal.

"That's good to hear." He kept her hand in his as he moved her laptop to one side. He idly played with her fingers, rubbing his thumb over the moonstone ring on her ring finger. "Interesting choice of stone."

"All of the banished witches have a piece of moonstone jewelry. The meaning of the stone is sanctuary, so it seemed appropriate. There's a small mountain town in California called Moonstone Lake. Rumor has it there's a monster in the lake." She smiled.

"When any of us can get away, we visit there during the full moon and hold a centering ceremony at the lake. Two of my friends settled in the town years ago." She looked down, noticing the stone glowed a soft blue under his touch. She wondered at the gem's reaction, since she hadn't seen that happen before.

"Stasi and Blair. I did my homework, remember?" He brought her fingers to his lips again, nibbling. "You always taste so good." His charcoal eyes turned silver. "And now that business is over, we can move on to other things. Such as pleasure."

"Are you sure you're not an incubus?" She looked down at their entwined fingers.

"My cousin has that duty. I usually advise that anyone who meets Wreaker should run the other way. Something tells me you'd be more likely to create a little damage to his body."

"It sounds like he's devoted to his craft."

"He does enjoy his work a great deal, but he leaves a dry husk behind. He knows I don't approve, which is why he likes to show up now and then just to irritate me." Keeping hold of her hand, he stood up and drew her to her feet. "When I look at you, I understand why he enjoys women so much. You're very delectable."

"I think you've picked up a few of your cousin's moves." She didn't protest as he brought her flush against him. "Honestly, Declan, it's not even lunchtime yet."

"I don't know. I find myself very hungry." He nuzzled her neck.

She closed her eyes, savoring the touch of his mouth against her skin. "Be grateful you're not a vampire. Our blood is poisonous to Nightwalkers."

"Sounds dangerous. I like danger." He nipped her earlobe, his tongue curling around the twist of gold that dangled down. "It adds a sexy seasoning. Just as you do." His mouth now moved closer to hers. "We haven't had much alone time."

She angled her lips toward his, inhaling the slightly spicy scent of his skin with the barest hint of sulfur. "No, we haven't," she agreed, nipping the corner of his mouth.

When Declan kissed her, Maggie felt that zing of connection she'd felt from the moment she'd laid eyes on him. Something she couldn't recall ever sensing, even when she'd been with men for whom she cared deeply. But that emotion was faint compared to what she was experiencing now.

Her mind loudly warned it didn't make sense. After all, Declan had demon blood. Demons were the enemy. Mal didn't trust him and only had allowed him access to this mission because of Anna, who insisted that Declan be part of the team.

The warning left Maggie's mind as quickly as it had entered it. She was too caught up in the feel of the man holding her so possessively, as if nothing mattered to him more than this moment.

He trailed his hand down her thigh, inching her skirt upward until he could feel bare skin before reaching a wisp of silk. He stroked her once and felt the moisture against the fabric. He needed nothing more to know that she wanted him as much as he wanted her.

"Where's your room?" he asked in a raw voice.

"Upstairs, end of the hall." Deep down, Maggie had known this moment would come. She had alternately feared and anticipated it, since she felt once they made love, things would never be the same again.

Declan kept his arms wrapped around her and sent them upstairs in a cloud of dark smoke.

Maggie stumbled against him, coughing and waving the smoke away. "I thought you said you didn't have any magic. That's an interesting trick."

He picked her up and tossed her on the bed. "It's only the first."

Maggie's laughter as she bounced on the covers was pure music to Declan's ears, and he knew he'd never tire of hearing it.

He stood at the end of the bed watching her sit up, ignoring the fact that her skirt was still hiked up over her thighs. The gleam in her emerald eyes was also a potent warning.

"Come on, big boy. Show me what you've got," she said throatily.

He toed off his boots and then started to work on his shirt buttons. "I'm only too happy to comply as long as you know you'll have to return the favor."

Maggie's smile was pure mischief—and sunshine to the demon who had lived so long in the dark. "Don't worry. I'll make it worth your while."

Declan unbuttoned his shirt with sensuality a male stripper could only envy, slowly drawing it open to reveal a bronze-skinned, sculpted chest. Once the garment was tossed to one side, he worked on his black jeans, leisurely lowering the zipper and then pushing the denim down. He hid his smile as her eyes widened.

"It seems our studies of demons forgot to mention a few things." She licked her lips. "And I don't mean about you going commando."

He watched her with the same hunger. "Your turn."

Maggie didn't climb off the bed but stood up on the covers, easily keeping her balance on the mattress. She hummed a haunting tune as she shimmied out of her skirt with a slow wiggle of hips and then stepped out of it before tossing it toward him.

"Too bad I don't have seven veils," she told him, grasping the bottom of her tank top. She hesitated.

"You can't stop now." His voice was raw with need.

"Uh, I'm not…" she chewed on her lower lip. "Well, I'm not exactly…"

Declan moved forward and gently peeled the fabric from her tight grip. He slowly raised her top over her head.

His mouth went desert dry as he looked at her wearing only a tiny blue thong. Maggie's lightly tanned skin glowed in the morning sunlight streaming through the window over her bed. "You are beautiful," he said softly.

"I'm sure you've seen women with a lot more," she said uncertainly.

"Quality." He palmed her breast, rubbing his thumb over her nipple until it tightened to a dark pink nub.

She had the body of an athlete, a warrior. He recognized white scars made from knife wounds and swords. Even the puckered scar of a healed bullet hole marred her taut belly. The idea she'd been injured hurt him, but that she bore the scars and hadn't allowed magick to erase them told him what kind of woman she was.

Her shyness about her breasts was surprising, considering that she was otherwise comfortable with her body. A sense of possession welled up inside him. He experienced the need to make Maggie completely his.

This woman is mine.

He held her gaze with his as he walked around the bed and pulled her toward him. She hooked her legs around his waist as her arms circled his neck.

"Why are you smiling?" he asked even as he couldn't help but smile back at her. To have this kind of light in his life was a new experience.

"Of course I'm smiling. You make me smile. Honestly, you need to lighten up." She arched back so far, Declan had to quickly turn around so he would take the brunt of the fall as they tumbled backward onto the bed.

"You have such beautiful eyes," he whispered, taking a hand to brush a lock of hair from her face. "They go from the green of a baby leaf to a deep emerald."

"Be careful, Declan. Someone might think you have the soul of a poet." She took a deep breath, pressing her breasts more tightly against his chest while his cock nestled against her moist center.

"I feel as if I do every time I look at you." He brought his fingertips to her face, memorizing the delicate planes. His thumbs traced her lips, one pressing down on her lower lip, until they parted. The tip of her tongue appeared, moistening his thumb, and then wrapped around the digit, laving the skin as he ripped off her thong.

He felt his balls tighten at the sight and moved his hips under her slight frame, arching up to rub his cock against her. She moaned softly and countered his move with one of her own.

Declan rolled onto his side, keeping Maggie tight against him. She draped one long leg over his hip, angling her body in just the right position. He cupped her face with his hands, kissing her deeply as he thrust into her and stilled, experiencing emotions he'd never known existed.

He was home.

The demon race didn't have typical families. A male and female fucked, and if the female gave birth to a boy, she gave up the child to the male to raise. A girl was usually left to the mother to take care of unless the sire wanted her.

There were no warm fuzzy memories of Mom holding you when you had a stomachache or bad dreams.

Now Declan knew that the sex he'd had before was just an empty promise. It had been nothing more than pure and total fucking. What he had with Maggie transcended space and time. She pulsed around him and drew him in tighter.

He now understood what it meant to find your other half.

I am so screwed. Oh well, but in a good way.

Maggie watched the colors shift in Declan's eyes. He whispered words in his strange language and moved in and around her with a fervency that matched her own as she arched up under him. She met him with the same power while magick sparked all around them like tiny fireworks.

She'd resisted his insistence that they had a strong connection, even though she knew deep down his words were true. She'd been independent for so long she couldn't imagine having someone in her life.

And no way would she have imagined that someone would be Declan.

It wasn't just the heat of his body wrapped around hers or the fire in his gaze as he looked at her. It was the inferno he stoked inside her as the blaze of their joined bodies flared up to engulf her.

Her body tightened just when she felt his do the same. Their bodies were so in tune with each other it was natural they'd come at the same time.

"Now," he whispered to her, reaching down first to stroke her clit and then pinch the ultrasensitive hooded flesh.

That was enough to send her soaring, and Declan went right along with her.

It took time for Maggie to find her brain, and the man sprawled beside her seemed to have the same problem. She studied his features, seeing them relaxed. It was easy to envisage what he'd been like as a little boy. She had a brief inclination to tousle his spiky hair, but she already knew there was nothing truly childlike about him.

"Better than any dream I've had about you," Declan said sleepily.

"Oh, no, you do *not* do the guy thing and fall asleep." She playfully pushed at him.

He rolled onto his back, showing himself in all his glory. Maggie suddenly felt very greedy. And happy she had this house, since it gave them a lot of privacy.

He smiled and grabbed her hand, threading his fingers through hers. He rested their hands on his chest. She stretched her fingers out, lightly rubbing the taut skin, feeling the warmth sear the tips.

"I suppose you're waiting for me to say, 'You were right, Declan,'" she teased. "I gave in to your manly attributes because it was meant to be."

"No reason to."

"Good. I hate men who gloat. I tend to turn them into potted plants." She felt his chest rise and fall with his laughter.

"And what would you have turned me into?"

"Hmm, maybe water hemlock, since they're found in swamps, or I could give you that color you need and zap you into a daffodil."

"I'm surprised you didn't say nightshade."

"Nah, too boring."

"Who's the little girl in the picture on your dresser?" His voice rumbled softly against her ear.

Maggie stiffened even as Declan's hand moved gently down her back in soothing strokes.

"She was someone precious to you, wasn't she?"

She nodded. "Aleta, my baby sister."

"I gather she didn't die of natural causes." He wrapped his arms around her, allowing his body heat to seep into her skin.

Maggie nodded. "Aleta loved being outside where she could gather flowers and play with the lambs. Sometimes we complained she was underfoot, but then she'd look at you with her big, blue eyes and smile at you, and you'd forget why you were angry." She swallowed the tears that threatened to fall.

"There was a boy in town, Axel. He…" She pulled in a deep breath to center herself. "He had a very mean streak. He liked to spook the sheep, frighten the girls, and he'd pick fights with the smaller boys. And as he got older, he would do more than frighten the girls, but since his father was a local landowner, no one dared do anything."

Declan pressed his lips against her hair.

"One of the local girls had spurned his unwanted attention, and he decided to frighten her father's herd of sheep. Except Aleta was nearby picking flowers. She wasn't able to get away in time, and by the time I got to her…"

A harsh sound erupted from her throat. "By that time, she was crying that she hurt, and blood was seeping from her mouth. She didn't have a chance. After that, I vowed I would protect as many innocents as possible."

He turned her to face him, kissing her tears away. "And you have," he assured her. "No wonder you are so fearless. Aleta would be very proud of her big sister."

"The man knows just what to say." She smiled through her tears and dipped her head to kiss him, feeling the old pain drain away and the heat of their loving begin to burn again.

She rubbed her free hand over his chest and downward. She'd just cupped his cock and raised up to bend her head over him when the phone rang.

"Let your voice mail pick up," he advised, breathing heavily, prepared for a second go-round.

The second ring brought her head back up. "Damn." She glanced at the Caller ID. "Double damn! It's Courtney's school." Maggie barely said hello before she was off the bed and running to her closet. She kept the phone tucked against her ear as she fought her way into her clothing.

"What happened?" Declan asked.

"It seems my 'cousin' has been fighting and I need to meet with the principal," she said grimly, pulling on a short, pink cotton cardigan over a pink-and-black print top and black jeans. She took a quick look in the mirror, finger combed her hair, and added a swipe of lip gloss.

"I'm coming with you." Declan was off the bed and gathering up his clothing.

"Not a good idea. I have a feeling I'll be doing a lot of yelling." She was gone before Declan could argue any further.

He'd barely gotten into his clothes when his cell rang.

"Call this an oops. You won't be able to leave the house until I get back because the wards automatically set when I leave," she told him and then disconnected.

Then I guess I may as well take my time.

Maggie made it to the high school in record time.

"Don't lose your temper," she told herself, walking down the tile hallway to the offices. Once there, she gave her name and waited.

"Ms. O'Malley? I'm Mr. Turner." The tall man walking out of the principal's office paused and looked at her quizzically. "You are Ms. O'Malley, Courtney Parker's cousin?"

"Yes, I am. You have a copy of the paperwork on file." She stood up and offered her hand. "I understand Courtney is in trouble?" She looked past him and saw the girl seated in a chair by the desk. Since she wasn't hunched over, Maggie guessed she hadn't gotten the worst of the fight.

His lips firmed. "Let's go into my office."

"You didn't need to drag her in," Courtney drawled once the door was closed.

"She's your legal guardian." He took his chair.

Maggie realized they weren't the only ones in the office. A burly man was also there, along with a boy sporting a cut lip, a black eye, and assorted bruises.

"What happened?" Maggie asked, noting bruises on Courtney's arms and legs and another bruise on her cheek.

"I thought we would wait for you before we discussed the situation." The principal wasn't happy to have the proceedings taken out of his hands. "This is Mr. Reynolds and his son Troy."

"Fine. I'm here. What happened?" She sat down and looked at Courtney.

"The bitch tried to kill me," the boy shouted.

Maggie half rose in her chair.

"Enough. Troy," Mr. Turner said. "We don't use that word. Women are to be respected."

"I'm pressing charges," Troy's father rumbled. "And I'm suing you for my son's medical bills."

"I don't see any need for stitches or X-rays," Maggie said. "But I also see that Courtney has her share of injuries." She stared down the boy. "Who taught you it was all right to hit girls?" She glanced briefly at the father, who looked ready to inflict some damage of his own.

"I was defending myself."

Maggie ignored his belligerence and looked at Mr. Turner. "Were there any witnesses?"

"Who the fuck are you to question us like we're in the wrong? It was that girl who almost killed my boy," Reynolds demanded.

"We have zero tolerance for fighting in this school," the principal interjected, sensing he was rapidly losing control.

"So both of them are suspended?"

"Courtney is expelled, and Troy will have a two-week suspension."

"He's the victim here," the father insisted. "Troy doesn't deserve to be suspended for even one day."

"If you have zero tolerance, then I should think that both would be expelled. Courtney is revealing enough wounds to show that Troy did his part," Maggie said. She stood up and walked over to the girl, leaning down to examine the teen's face and picking up her arms. "What was the fight about?" she asked her charge.

Courtney refused to look at her.

Maggie turned to Troy. One fulminating look shut the father up. By then, the principal was letting her take the lead.

"Why don't you tell me what happened?" She was secretly pleased to see the boy's temper was starting to rise. She hoped that meant he'd actually tell the truth.

"She got all over me, punching and kicking and biting me. I could have rabies."

Maggie waved Courtney back into her chair when she started to stand up. "I think you're safe on that score." She glanced at the principal. "No witnesses?"

"None that would speak up," he said wearily.

I could be rolling around in bed with Declan instead of playing Law & Order *here*.

"Tell me what happened, Courtney, and tell me

everything." She stared into the girl's dark-brown eyes. It would have been easy to use magick to get the truth out of her, but Maggie wanted her to volunteer it.

Courtney looked ready to explode again. "I'm tired of him groping me," she snarled, looking Maggie in the eye. Not once did her gaze veer from the witch's stare. "He and his asshole friends think it's funny to brush up against the girls and cop a feel.

"He palmed my ass, and I told him to knock it off. I also told him if he didn't back off, I'd make sure my boyfriend turned him into hamburger. He laughed and grabbed my breast, and it hurt." Her face flamed a bright red. "So I hit him, and he hit me back."

"You're lying. My kid wouldn't touch a skank like you," Reynolds growled, flexing his meaty fists.

Maggie spun around and stared the man down while Mr. Turner sputtered.

"Now I see what's going on. Your son started it, and Courtney finished it. Yes, she was wrong to fight. She should have come in here and made a complaint. But if Troy's been sexually harassing her for some time, she obviously was fed up and finally did something about it."

"You're right. Courtney should have reported this to me," Mr. Turner stated officiously. "She also should take her share of responsibility for her actions. I realize you are new to parenting, but allowing a child to get away with such grave actions can only lead to more dangerous situations. Courtney has shown emotional problems in the past, and what happened today is proof she needs more intensive counseling."

"And what about Troy? Let's talk sensitivity training,

anger management, and a personality transplant." She was one second away from throwing down some serious magick.

Maggie looked around the office and then focused on Courtney.

"Are you happy in this school?"

The teenager shrugged. "The teachers don't suck. Just some of the students." She glared at Troy, who smirked.

"Then we're outta here." Maggie pulled her to her feet and tugged on her hand, pausing long enough for Courtney to pick up her backpack.

"We really need to discuss this further," Mr. Turner pointed out, holding up a hand to stop them.

"We've discussed this enough. All you've done is make Courtney the villain in this without any hint there's shared responsibility."

"I'm calling the cops," Troy's dad threatened.

"Don't. Even. Think. About. It." Power swirled around her like a whirlwind, leaving the room airless.

The large man backed down immediately.

"What are you?" he whispered.

As she and Courtney walked out, Maggie leaned over to murmur in his ear, "Your worst nightmare."

"What happened in there?" Courtney demanded, as Maggie practically dragged her down the hallway. "Why did the room turn all weird?"

"Because I can make it that way," the witch said grimly. "It might be something you'd be wise to remember."

Maggie didn't speak again until she drove off the school's campus.

"You're blaming me, aren't you?" Courtney asked, slumping in her seat. "You didn't want to do it in front of them, but you feel that way. No wonder. Troy's a total scuzzball, but no one's going to say that. Everyone's afraid of him."

Maggie pulled the car over to the curb and shut off the engine.

"Never *ever* feel like a victim," she told the girl. "As for what I believe and don't believe, what really matters is the truth. You told me what happened, and I believe you. But what I saw in there was proof you fought like a girl."

"I am a girl!"

"If someone touches you when you didn't ask for it, then you fight dirty. We'll work on that." She started the car up again. "Right after we find another school for you."

"Boy, you pull me out of there, and you're already thinking of dumping me in another school? FYI, do *not* even think about one of those schools that require everyone to wear those lame-ass uniforms. I don't care what they say, those schools are scary. I mean, for all you know they pour chemicals in the school drinking water to turn the kids into Stepford students," Courtney declared.

Maggie closed her eyes. "Note to self. Restrict Courtney's cable TV."

The girl scowled at her. "You're really getting into this guardian shit, aren't you?"

Maggie thought back to that fleeting moment when she thought what it would be like to be a mother. Except instead of starting out with a tiny baby, she was saddled with a cranky teenager whose moods jumped around faster than the speed of light. Then there was the sexy demon waiting for her back at the house, and she really wished she were going back there alone.

"Not really. I'm just making it up as I go along."

Chapter 12

"I SHOULD HAVE KICKED HIM IN THE NADS," COURTNEY said, following her into the kitchen. "I mean, who would seriously want to have kids with that moron? The only thing he knows how to do is play football."

Before Maggie could tell her she'd had more than enough of Courtney's "I should've's," the girl had skidded to a stop.

"Whoa!" All of a sudden, the teenager slouched in what she obviously thought was a sexy stance but what actually looked as if she had back trouble.

Maggie silently echoed her emotions. "Oh, yeah, this is Declan. And this is Courtney. As you can tell, she's feeling a bit bloodthirsty toward the male sex, but I think one look at you has changed her mind."

"Hi," Courtney practically purred. "And there's only one guy I want to tear apart. You're perfectly safe."

Declan, who'd been sitting at the table with a cup of coffee, smiled up at her. Courtney immediately straightened up and ran for the coffeemaker to pour herself a cup.

"Thank you." Maggie plucked it out of her hand.

"So what happened at the school?" Declan asked.

"Troy is pure pus," Courtney announced with a touch of theatrics. "I'm going to text Mick that I want him to beat him up." She pulled her cell from her bag.

"I don't think so." Maggie confiscated the phone and stuck it in her pocket.

"*Hey*! Isn't that illegal or something?" She turned her attention to Declan. "So who are you exactly? Maggie's lover? Old friend?" Courtney plopped down in the chair across from him.

"Business associate."

"She said she wasn't a prostie, so what do you guys do?"

"Consulting," Maggie said.

"Consulting what?" She looked from one to the other. "I watched a show on TLC once where a drug dealer called himself a consultant. But you don't look as scuzzy as he did."

"I own a club, and Maggie oversees security for me."

Maggie stood behind Courtney shooting Declan a *'Nice touch!'* smile.

"Really? What's the club's name?"

"Damnation Alley," he replied. "And no, you can't go there." He neatly anticipated her next comment. "You have to be over twenty-one to get in, and we enforce that rule."

"I can look twenty-one."

"You can look twenty-one in six years." Maggie took the chair to Declan's left. "And any ID claiming you're of age is now promptly impounded."

"Ha! You'll have to find it first. It's probably a sucky club anyway." She resorted to slouching again, but no sexy teen stance this time. "So why are you here?"

"We were going over some reports when the school called me. Why don't you go upstairs and do your homework while we finish up here," Maggie suggested, aware that once Courtney checked her hiding place, she'd find her three false IDs gone.

"Uh, helloooo! Expelled, remember? I am so off homework duty." She hopped off the chair and executed a little happy dance.

"Then go upstairs and clean up your room. You've barely had the room for twelve hours, and it already looks like a war zone. I want to see that place looking immaculate."

"Fine, but I'll be down for lunch." Courtney rolled her eyes before sweeping a knowing look over them. "It's okay if he stays." She nabbed some cookies and left.

"Thank you," Declan called after her. He turned back to Maggie. "That wasn't some airhead of a teenager."

"No kidding." She rubbed her forehead. "She also doesn't understand the meaning of the word 'silence.' I bet she even talks in her sleep."

"What will you do with her now that she's been expelled from school?" Declan asked. "Although I guess you know something about that kind of punishment."

She flicked her fingers at him, releasing a bit of magic that attacked him like a swarm of gnats.

Declan growled and batted at the intruders until Maggie took pity on him and banished them.

"I need to get her into another school, but at the same time, I wonder if that's a good idea. I didn't sense any magick in that idiot Troy or his equally inane father, but that doesn't mean someone didn't set her up for this. All anyone had to do was cast a short spell on Troy to act like a chauvinistic jerk, knowing he could set her off."

She sipped her coffee and looked at the cabinet holding the chocolate marshmallow cookies. A moment later, the bag was on the table. There was nothing like the best part of the cocoa bean to make life seem brighter.

"But what will I do with her if she's not in school? And it's not like I can take her out to the compound, although it would be tempting. And wouldn't Mal just love that?" she mused with a soft laugh, taking a bite of cookie and savoring the rich taste.

"Why not? Where else could she be better protected?"

Maggie's laughter burbled out. "Uh, maybe because he'd take off my head if I did. Very few humans know about the Hellion Guard. Yes, they know about magick in the world and the creatures that use it. The Vampire Protectorate, the Witches' Council, and the Ruling Council are recognized as peacekeepers among our kind, but the Guard is special ops.

"We're the SEALs, Recon, Green Berets, Rangers, and Black Ops all rolled into one violent package. We do the dirty work and make things go away. The compound here isn't the only one. There are three in Europe, one in Australia, and even one in a hidden realm. I do this because it's important to me. I want to keep others safe, and this is the best way to do it."

"I've been to your compound. I saw children there. A school and a playground any child would kill for," he persisted. "You feel Courtney needs to know the truth about what could happen to her. Fine. Take her there. Give her the chance to help you fight back. You could still keep the house as a cover, since you're being watched."

"So you felt it, too? I sensed it last night, but no one tried to breach the wards. They'll probably settle for surveillance until then." She stopped and lifted her head. "Something's wrong." She was out of her chair and running for the stairs before Declan could blink. But he was quick on her heels.

Maggie's heart thumped in her chest as she raced up the stairs, almost skidding to a stop when she reached Courtney's closed bedroom door. She didn't bother knocking but barged in.

"Privacy here!" Courtney's head snapped up. She sat in a cleared section of the floor, hastily pushing some things under a pile of clothing.

But Maggie had already seen enough. She threw out a hand, extinguishing the candles that circled the girl, and broke the circle with her foot.

"*You stupid child! What do you think you're doing?*" Another wave of her hand sent the clothes tumbling away from what Courtney had tried to hide.

The girl scrambled backward, alarmed by Maggie's fury. "Me? What about *you*?" She made her way onto her bed. "And those are mine!" She looked at the doorway where Declan stood looking at the scene before him. "She's gone nuts!"

Maggie snatched up the cloth doll and tore off the small photograph glued to the face. She crumpled up the picture of Troy and stared at a tiny dot of red on the cloth. Her rage was so great, she was shaking.

"Who taught you this?" Her voice was hoarse with her anger.

"No one." The teen retreated into her sullen self as defense.

"Courtney, you have to tell her." Declan stepped inside the room and almost shuddered from the energy still roiling in the space. "This is very bad."

"What? It's a joke. I was just going to send it to Troy with a bunch of pins stuck in it. Who knows? Maybe it would even work."

Maggie swooped down and picked up a black silk bag, tucking the doll inside. She'd have to deal with it later. "This is a poppet," she said in a low voice. "And it isn't something you play with lightly. This isn't a toy. In the right hands, it's very powerful, and in the wrong hands, such as yours, it's a disaster in the making. Now tell me who told you how to do this."

Courtney recoiled from her. Maggie's magick sent a thick cloud through the room, making it hard for them to breathe. Maggie was past caring.

"Maggie, you need to calm down," Declan said softly, still keeping a bit of a distance from her. "If you don't, we all could implode. It's obvious she has no clue how serious this is. Please, Maggie."

"What the hell is going on?" By now Courtney was plastered against the head of her bed as magick translated itself into electricity, sending sparks into the air and their hair flying around their faces.

Declan spun around. "The wards. You could destroy them," he warned Maggie.

"The wards will hold," she said grimly as she stared down the girl. "Are you going to tell me?"

"*Mick*! Mick gave it to me. He told me if anyone ever really pissed me off, I could use it to make their life miserable!" she shouted. "He said it was a joke. One of those things where you can mess with their minds. I could send it to the person I meant it for, and they'd think I was really going after them. They'd think something really bad would happen to them. No big."

"No big?" Maggie loomed over her. "Courtney, a poppet is not a toy! It's dangerous magick. Not only could you have killed that boy, but it would also direct itself back to you because the magick would know you were doing a wrong thing. And you added blood to it! Bad enough with the poppet, but blood takes it to a whole other level."

Courtney started to straighten up. "I don't even know what you're talking about. Is this what you did in Europe? You practiced all that supernatural stuff?"

Maggie breathed in deeply through her nose, doing her best to bring her temper under control. She knew if she didn't do it soon, she'd be fighting a losing battle.

"I told Mal I wasn't mom material," she muttered. "I *told* him someone else should do this."

"Do what? Who's Mal?" Courtney looked from Maggie to Declan. "You're not really my cousin, are you? You lied to that judge. And who are you really? Someone tell me what's going on!"

"I am the person who's taking care of you." Maggie bent down and picked up the candles. "If I ever catch you trying any form of magick again, I will lock you away in a tower that will make Rapunzel's prison look like a resort."

She flexed her fingers, finally slowing down the magick that was seeping out of her pores. She shook her head and turned away. "I can't do any more of this right now. We will talk later." She left the room with Declan following.

"You just scared the shit out of that kid," he told her.

"Good." She muttered a layering spell for the wards to ensure Courtney wouldn't sneak out of the house.

"You need to sit down and talk to her."

"I need to give her a good spanking," she snarled, throwing open the back door and walking outside into the large fenced-in yard.

"She's a teenager who didn't understand what she was dabbling in."

"You're defending her?"

He held up his hands in defense. "Not when you're pissed off like this. I remember that waterhemlock threat."

Maggie circled the yard. "You don't understand, either. All you are is a nightclub owner," she spat out. "What do you know about danger and wars and the magick that feeds it?"

Declan crossed the yard in a few steps and grabbed her wrist so hard, bruises would be left behind.

"You think I don't know what it means?" he hissed. His temper had risen to the point where a shadowy mist swirled around him. They both felt the sensation of flames flickering around them. "That every day in my father's house wasn't a battle just to stay *alive*? That there weren't beatings and other punishments you couldn't even comprehend?

"My father didn't reach his position by being an easy mark. If you looked at him wrong, you could lose a limb. If a slave dared say a word, he'd cut out their tongue. The only reason I don't bear the scars from my childhood is because he knew I would rise further in this world if I didn't have them. If you saw the real me, you'd turn your head away in disgust."

Her brow furrowed. "He beat you?"

"On a good day. He had a special dungeon built for playing his sadistic games. Three of my brothers didn't survive his actions."

He could see her fury subsiding. He only wished it hadn't happened at a cost to himself. He'd told her more in those few lines than he'd ever told another woman.

"What about Anna? Was she beaten, too?"

"She was largely ignored until she grew of age to be useful," he replied. "Then she was groomed for a position that would further our father's aspirations. When she refused to go along with his plans, she was beaten to within an inch of her life, healed, and beaten again."

"How did you get her away from there?" she asked curiously.

"I called in a lot of favors and told a lot of lies. There's no way he will ever know where she is, because he'd see that as his chance to infiltrate the Guard."

Maggie shook her head. "Not possible. Not even demons can do it. There are too many protections on us. Plus the Ruling Council would step in then. The treaties might be few, but they are there." She took a deep breath. "So in essence you're saying I need to go easy on Courtney even if she almost did something incredibly stupid?"

"No, I think you need to sit down with her and explain just what was stupid about it."

"What do you think I just did?"

"You just yelled at her, scared the shit out of her, and almost strangled her with magick. Not a good thing for a girl's guardian to do when you need to keep her on your side."

She looked off to the side. "I really hate it when people are logical."

"I thought all Nordic types were calm and collected."

"Yeah, well, I missed that chromosome. I lost my temper. I almost lost all control, and now there's a teenage girl in there who probably hates and fears me."

Declan wrapped his arms around her and brought her

against him, enfolding her in the warm embrace. She buried her nose against his shoulder and sniffed loudly.

"I'm no expert on teenage girls, except as a former boy who chased them on a regular basis, but what I do remember is their moods changed like the wind." He rested his chin on top of her head, inhaling the soft fragrance of her shampoo.

"She'll destroy her room to punish me," she mumbled against his shirt. "Or shave her head. Or find a way to sneak out and get a tattoo."

"Says the witch with her own tattoo." He tapped her right hip where he'd found a colorful sketch of a witch's hat riding a broom. "And here I thought the spider was your only one."

"Elle likes to think of herself as part of my jewelry. I'm of age for a tat. Courtney's not." She sighed. "And no age jokes either."

"You need to go in there and talk to her."

The way she relaxed in his arms told him she knew he was right.

"I don't suppose you want to come in and help."

"I have to get to the club."

"You wouldn't use that excuse if she was still at school. You'd be trying to seduce me in the kitchen or on the stairs or in the family room."

Declan smiled at the sound of her grumbling. His Maggie was back.

"Why don't you let me out of here, and if all goes well, give me a call, and I'll come back tonight with a pizza," he suggested.

"All right, but no anchovies."

"No problem there." He kissed her briefly and waited

while she made an opening in the wards. He wasted no time going past it and waited while she returned the wards to normal. "I'll talk to you later."

As she watched Declan drive away, the glass-shattering sounds of Evanescence's "Haunted" roared from upstairs.

"Sound so loud. Sound in air be taken away," she said, waving her hand at Courtney's bedroom window. Silence coated the patio except for the twittering of birds using the birdbath. "Better than earmuffs."

She went inside, not prepared to face the wrath of a teenager but knowing if she didn't do it now, she would never do it—and she would have to leave Courtney locked in her room until after the date of the ritual.

—·w·—

"She's crazy," Courtney babbled into her cell. After five minutes of loud music, she turned it down so she could call Mick and relate the events of the day starting with the fight with Troy. He laughed when she told him what she did to the jerk.

"Yeah, she took me out of that lousy school and that's a good thing, but now she's acting really weird. I think she lied to the judge, too."

"Why?" Mick's voice rumbled in her ear.

Courtney settled back in the disaster known as her bed. "First she tried to be my friend and now she's got this guy here and she just does this stuff."

"Courtney, you're not making much sense," her boyfriend insisted. "Calm down, okay? Do you want me to come over?"

"The way she is now? She probably wouldn't let you past the front door. I just needed to talk to you. I don't know why Maggie got so pissed about that little joke doll you gave me."

"Adults can get bent out of shape over stuff they don't understand."

"But she acted like she did understand. She said it was really bad stuff."

"She probably saw some movie that said that or read a book. If you want to give Troy a good scare, I'll get you another one, and this time you'll be more careful that she doesn't find it. In fact, if you want, I'll go have a talk with the asshole myself."

She was so tempted to let him. She knew Mick would go after Troy and beat the shit out of him in her honor. The idea was appealing.

She had been flattered the first time he showed interest in her. It had only been in the last year or so that she started to look more like a girl than some little kid other kids made fun of.

With his sun-warmed skin and dark shaggy hair, Mick was the kind of guy moms warned their daughters about. Except Courtney didn't have a mother to look out for her. Not that it would have mattered where he was concerned. She was in love with a guy who treated her like she was the most precious thing in his life.

She already had the idea that Maggie didn't like him, even though she hadn't met him. But Courtney wasn't giving Mick up for anyone. Once she was of age, she was outta there and with Mick full time. And if Maggie really was totally crazy, then Courtney would be gone even sooner. She could look older and get a better job. It wasn't until then she heard Mick shouting her name.

"I'm here. Just thinking."

"I'm coming over. You're worrying me, babe. What if she does something bad to you?"

"I don't think that will happen." She conveniently forgot her first accusations that Maggie could be a white slaver. "I don't think she's so keen on me having a boyfriend, although hello, you and I've been going together like forever. So let me talk to her about you more. Maybe you could come over tomorrow night for dinner. Or we could meet at the mall tomorrow." Again, conveniently forgetting she'd have to ask permission.

"Since I'm expelled, I've got a lot of free time." She examined her nails. "At least I do until Maggie dumps me in a new school, which will probably be as bad, if not worse, than the one I just left. Hell, for all I know, she'll send me away to a boarding school that's more like a high-security prison."

"Don't think that way, baby. I'll talk to you later."

Courtney disconnected the call just as Maggie walked in.

She warily watched the woman formerly called her guardian, whom she now called her jailer, circle the room.

"I'll get it cleaned up," Courtney told her.

"I'm sure you will," Maggie said softly, picking a top and jeans off a chair and tossing them to Courtney before she sat down. "I apologize for coming down on you so hard earlier, but what you were doing was so risky that I feared what would happen if you completed the ritual. Some things shouldn't be trifled with."

"I understand that," Courtney said, wanting to reassure Maggie that she knew the risks and wouldn't have done anything to harm anyone but the intended victim. "Mick told me exactly what to do, Maggie. He's done stuff like this for a long time, and he said as long as I'm careful and don't use Latin or anything, I'm okay."

As she spoke, she noticed the older woman's moonstone ring start to give off an eerie glow. She put it down to the sun coming in the window and returned her attention to Maggie's face, but it didn't stay there long. She found herself distracted by the spark of gold on Maggie's ankle. Some kind of charm hung from the chain, but she couldn't figure out what it was.

"Courtney!"

She almost shot off the bed. "I'm sorry. I'm sorry. And I'm not one of those kids with ADD either. It's just that I don't know how many times I can say Mick taught me how to be cautious so that I wouldn't really hurt anyone or myself."

She paused, searching her brain for how to say what had been bothering her since Maggie's meltdown. Plus she was *really* curious about Declan. The guy might be old, but he was really hot.

"Did… uh… Declan think I was doing black magick or something? I could tell you guys are close and all, but is this really something he'd know about? I mean Mick's parents taught him, and they were really good. They live in New Orleans," she added, as if their location added to their credibility.

"And that means they know what they're talking about." Maggie knew she sounded sarcastic, but she couldn't help it. She knew of warlocks and voodoo queens who lived in small towns in other states. "And that Mick knows what he's talking about."

"Yeah." Courtney brightened, pleased Maggie understood.

Maggie nodded, as if listening to a voice deep inside. "So when you finished your spell and sent the poppet to Troy, he'd think something bad was going to happen to him. You'd find out his reaction from friends at school, and you'd be one happy kid, right?"

"Yeah." *Except for her using the kid word.* "No harm, no foul. I don't want you thinking bad of me." She was honest about that. While she hadn't known Maggie for long, she realized she did like her. Her new guardian hadn't treated her like a little girl or talked down to her.

She had even stood up for her at the school and didn't automatically think it was all her fault, the way Mrs. Whitney would have. If Mrs. W had been around, Courtney would have been grounded for two months and had kitchen duty for three. Maybe that was why she didn't want Maggie to think she was some crazy teenager who went around wearing black all the time and thought it would be cool to hold a black mass or something.

She also wanted her to like Mick. Mrs. Whitney hadn't and didn't allow Mick inside the house. She claimed that he was too old for Courtney, and she was positive he was nothing but trouble. All because he owned a motorcycle instead of a car and he looked dangerous. That's why Courtney loved him. Because he wasn't like the boys at school.

"Courtney, you're in another world again." Maggie sounded amused.

"It hasn't even been one day, and it's like you've only seen me as some kind of troublemaker. I know Mrs. Whitney told you I have 'problems.'" She made

air quotes. "Mr. Turner told you I have behavioral problems, and then there's what happened a little while ago.
I bet you want to take the next plane back to Europe."

"Amazing. You're making yourself sound like Public
Enemy Number One," Maggie quipped. "Let me explain
something. There's nothing you can do to scare me off.
Trust me on that."

Courtney's brown eyes lit up. There was nothing the
girl loved more than a dare.

"Really?"

Maggie nodded. "Definitely. There's nothing you can
do to put me off. Nothing you can come up with that I
won't figure out. And if you'd managed to finish that
ritual, I would have vanquished it. I wouldn't have been
happy, but I would have done it."

"Uh, Mick's stuff is really good, and there's no way
to do that," Courtney said knowingly.

"Oh, but there is."

"And you know because…?"

"I know because I'm a witch."

Chapter 13

MAGGIE HADN'T DROPPED THE W BOMB ON ANYONE IN some time. She waited for one of the usual reactions: eyes bugging out, jaw dropping in shock, and so on.

This time, she was able to add a new response to the list as she watched Courtney roll around laughing so hard, the bed shook under her. It took her a few minutes to gain control.

"Wow, you have a sense of humor." She sat up, wiping the smeared mascara away from around her eyes. "That's really good, Maggie. First you go all drama queen on me about the doll, now this. So what's Declan? A vampire or something?"

"What he is doesn't matter. What *I* am does." Maggie lifted her hand. "Time is nigh. Lift her high. Show her my words are true with what I wish."

"Wha—?" This time Courtney's jaw did drop as she found herself hovering a good three feet above her bed. She started to wave her arms and then stopped as her body tipped from side to side. "It's a trick!"

"Clean her room and make it soon." Maggie waved her hand around, sending magickal energy everywhere.

From her vantage point in the air, a wide-eyed Courtney saw her clothes hang themselves up or fold themselves before flying into her dresser, and even her bed was made. The minute the covers were in place, she was gently lowered onto the bedspread.

"Okay, what was *that*?"

"I told you. I'm a witch. Don't say you don't know what they are. We've been in this world a long time, along with vampires and shape-shifters." She relaxed in her chair; discovering this was almost as much fun as she'd had in her bed with Declan. Well, not *that* much fun, but it was amusing.

Maggie regretted her flippancy when she detected a hint of fear in the girl's eyes. Before she could blink, Courtney grabbed her Coke can and threw the contents at Maggie.

She sputtered and swiped at the sticky fluid. "What was that for?" she demanded.

Courtney sat back. "You don't melt."

"Sorry to disappoint you, but I'm not the Wicked Witch of the West. First clue, my face isn't green." She picked up the hem of her tank top and wiped her face clean.

"Second clue? No flying monkeys. Trust me, you don't want anything like them around. Messy and disgusting doesn't even begin to describe them." She was pleased to see the wariness leave the girl's face. "And don't even think you can find a way to make a house fall on me, either."

"Mrs. Whitney said witches are evil. That you do these horrible spells and…" The light bulb snapped on over her head. "That's why you said what you did when you came in here earlier. You really do know what I was doing. Not that I planned on hurting that bastard," Courtney added hastily.

"And more," Maggie agreed. "When I told you it was unsafe, I wasn't kidding. Your boyfriend might know the basics, but if he doesn't know all the ramifications of fooling with a poppet, he won't know what can happen to you. Magick like that exudes an energy that feels, well, wrong."

"So you didn't just barge in here. You came in because you felt the spell?"

Maggie nodded.

"And if I wasn't careful, that thing would have done to me what I wanted it to do to Troy?" She gagged.

"That and much more. Repercussions are always hefty, because the Fates want you to remember not to ever do it again. Trust me, their idea of payback is a bitch." She waited for her ward to take it all in. She knew Declan was right. Courtney was smart, but this was still a lot of information to be given in a short amount of time.

Courtney frowned, starting to pick at the bedspread. "So you're not really my cousin?"

"No, I'm sorry. You really don't have any other family members that we know of. The organization I work for set up false paperwork so I could take custody of you. And I would appreciate it if you didn't say that outside of this room. There was a reason why it was done, Courtney, and it was for your own good."

"My own good." Her lips twisted. "Do you know why I wasn't killed when my parents were? They wanted to go away for a weekend. They told me I wouldn't have any fun, and it was really for my own good.

"Then a judge told me there weren't any family members to take me in and how sorry he was about that. So I'd live in a group home until I reached eighteen, and that was for my own good. I left my friends at my old school because there was no group home in that school district. Again for my own good. Now you're telling me you faked papers and lied to a judge *for my own good*?"

Maggie didn't look away from Courtney's bitter disappointment. "I can't explain it all right now, but I promise you I will. I've already given you a lot to think about. Why don't we take it a step at a time?"

"Can I tell people you're a witch?"

"I'd rather you didn't. At least for now," she amended, hoping to keep the girl on her side. She already knew that Mal would have apoplexy when he heard what Maggie had done, but she was confident she could handle the grumpy old gnome until he thought it was all his idea. "Declan offered to bring a pizza over for dinner. Does that sound good to you?"

"No anchovies."

Maggie laughed. "I already told him that. Anything else?"

"Mushrooms make me gag. So, is he a warlock? You know, a guy witch?"

"Warlocks practice dark magick. Men and women are called witches. And no, he's not either. We'll let him stay a mystery for the time being." Maggie pushed herself out of the chair and looked around. "That's right, I told you to clean your room, didn't I?"

"And you did it for me. Thanks!"

"As much as I like what I see, reverse what I did, fiddle-dee-dee." She waved a hand, leaving behind a tornado of clothing and bedcovers whirling around. "*Now* you can clean it up," she told Courtney as she walked out of the room.

"So what are you exactly?" Courtney asked, nibbling on her slice of the sausage pizza that Declan had brought over along with a beef-and-veggie pizza and cold drinks. "Maggie said you're not a vampire or a witch. I can already tell you're not a vampire, since you're eating all that pizza. You don't look like an elf, and you're way too cute to be a troll. Are you a Werewolf?"

He glanced toward Maggie. "You're right. She doesn't stop talking."

"Hey!" Courtney waved her cheese-laden slice in his direction. "C'mon. Give me a break. Because Maggie made me clean up my room, I couldn't do enough research on the Net before you showed up. There's no information on Damnation Alley online, either. You really should have a website."

"We do, but it's not where you'd find it."

She tossed her long hair over her shoulder. "Maggie hasn't given me the whole story. So why did she tell me stuff now? Am I magick?" She looked at them with hopeful eyes.

"Is that it? I mean, why would anyone with magick want me unless I had it and they needed it for something?" She caught the sharp silent exchange between Maggie and Declan. "That's it, isn't it? So why can't you tell me? Am I going to save the world or something?"

"It's not time for you to know everything yet." Maggie chose to keep a little mystery. She'd said enough but wasn't about to admit it. "Just remember what I told you. You can't tell anyone. Not even Mick," she added when Courtney started to open her mouth.

"He won't tell anybody if I ask him not to. He can keep a secret as well as I can."

Maggie grabbed her hand and held it tight. "Silence is golden. Secrets must be kept. Tell no one what you have heard, or what escapes your lips will sound absurd. Do it now."

Courtney started coughing so hard that Declan jumped up and clapped her on the back.

"What was that?" she wheezed.

"A spell to make sure you can keep a secret as well as you claim to."

"What do you mean?"

"Tell Declan what I told you this afternoon," Maggie suggested.

"You mean about you being an armadillo?" Courtney stopped. "That you practice piano ten times a day?" Frustration started to cross her face. "You ride a tricycle. Augh!" She threatened Maggie with her pizza and then looked at Declan. "I don't know what you are, but it's probably a rowboat."

Declan snorted and then sobered at her glare. "Sorry. I've just never been called watercraft before."

"You did a trampoline on me so I can't tell anyone?" Courtney looked at Maggie.

"I did. I wanted you to know I did it because it was the right thing to do, but I realized I also need safeguards in place. No one can change it either." She happily munched on her pizza.

"This sucks."

"So do vampires."

Declan snorted again at Maggie's quip. He started coughing as his beer went down the wrong way.

"Since tomorrow's Friday, I won't worry about getting you into another school until Monday," Maggie said.

"As if any school will take me with fighting on my record."

"I'll have a talk with Mr. Turner about that."

Courtney finished her slice and pushed away from the table. "I'm stuffed. I haven't had pizza in like forever."

"Forever as in a week or two?" Declan teased.

"At least." She turned to Maggie. "Can I go upstairs now? Because if I stay down here I'll try to ask more questions, and you'll just laugh at what I come up with."

"You're excused after you pick up your plate and napkin and throw them away."

After the girl did as Maggie asked, she left the room. Declan looked at Maggie and smiled.

"What?"

"You said you weren't mom material, but you sure acted like one."

"At first I thought she was a disaster in the making, but I'm already seeing a different side to her. Maybe she's scamming me. I understand teens will do that. But I'd like to give her the benefit of the doubt, because she's going to have enough to deal with when she finds out just why she's with me.

"I really hate it when the universe is in peril." She pulled a stringy bit of cheese off her slice of pizza and nibbled on it. "I'm not Batgirl."

"I bet you'd look great in black leather—and that mask." Declan sprawled back in his chair, rolling his beer bottle between his fingers. "Very S and M."

She rolled her eyes. "You would think that's hot." She winced as music thumped overhead. "It's a good thing we don't have neighbors living all that nearby."

He cocked his head to one side. "What's the problem? She's got good taste in music."

"You would think so." She picked up the now empty pizza boxes and put them in the trash along with their paper plates. When she opened the refrigerator and indicated the beer bottles, Declan nodded. She got one for him and refilled her wineglass.

"This feels... homey. The kid's upstairs doing her thing, and the parents are downstairs worrying about what mischief she'll get into next."

"I'm still on bodyguard duty." Maggie sighed. "In hindsight I shouldn't have let her go to school, but I hoped to allow her to keep her life as normal as possible."

"Right, 'normal' living in a house covered in protective wards with a witch for a guardian. And if things go wrong, she'll end up as a blood sacrifice for a Mayan priest. You can't get more ordinary than that." He tipped his beer bottle upward and drank deeply.

Maggie thought about turning the bottle into a dribble bottle and then discarded the idea. She'd have to be the one to clean it up.

"Well, enough talking about it. I want to go out there and seriously kick some Mayan ass. I'm not meant to sit around and wait for them to come to me. I go to them." She settled back in her chair and sipped her wine. "I want to throw down magick. Send shock waves through the baddies' systems. Maybe explode a few brains in the process."

"Bloodthirsty much?" Declan muttered with a grimace.

'What can I say? When the nasty guys show up, I take them down." She blew on her nails and polished them against her top.

"Along with your band of merry creatures, which sound like something out of a kid's movie: Frebus, Meech, Tita. All you need are Grumpy and Sleepy."

"You mean since I already have Dopey." She bared her teeth at him.

"Ha, ha." He finished off his beer and pushed away from the table. Catching Maggie's pointed glance at the abandoned bottle, he picked it up and took it over to the sink to rinse it out.

"Good boy." She beamed as she stood up and walked with him to the front door. She whispered a few words to release the wards so Declan could pass through safely.

Before he opened the door, he turned around and drew her into his arms.

"I could always come back later after you've tucked the kid into bed," he said softly.

"Good night, Declan." She softened her refusal with a smile. "Go play club owner, and don't call me if any Bloaters show up."

Not to be outdone, he kissed her deeply, not letting up until she melted against him.

"A hint of what you're giving up." With that parting shot he left.

Maggie blew out a deep breath as she collapsed against the closed door.

"Is Declan gone?" Courtney shouted from upstairs.

"Yes."

"I figured out what he is." She hung over the railing. "He's a pothole, isn't he?" Her face twisted in a grimace as she threw her hands up. "This really sucks!" She stomped back to her room.

Maggie thought of Declan leaving when she would have preferred tempting him back to her bedroom.

"Yes, it does."

~~~

"You have been away too much." Snips appeared by Declan's side the moment he came through the club's private entrance. As usual, the imp held his PDA in one clawed hand. Colors scrolled downward as he alternated his attention between the screen and Declan.

"What's going on?" Declan walked into his office with his assistant close on his heels and sat down at his polished ebony desk.

"There's something going on with the portal. We've had…" Snips hesitated, "situations."

"Such as?" Declan allowed his power to darken. He had learned right off the bat that he had to show domination over the creature or he would be doomed. There was no doubt Snips would have preferred to be in charge of the club, although he'd never be allowed any position of power. Demons ruled imps, not the other way around. But there was no doubt Snips could wreak havoc of his own if not handled properly.

"Some of the workers used to restore the club did not return through the portal. And someone used it without permission earlier today."

"And I'm just being told this *now*?" Declan ran his hands through his hair, feeling aggravation heat up inside. "Why didn't you call me on my cell when you found out?"

"I wanted to investigate the matter more thoroughly first, so I would have all the information you might require." Snips took the chair by the desk. He tapped a few keys on the PDA. Two minutes later, a soft knock on the door preceded one of the waitresses bringing in a mug of ale. She smiled at Declan as she set it down before him.

"Thanks, Eva." He noted the slight shift in her bone structure. For a brief moment, her true nature revealed itself to him. He saw scales the color of wet cement and slitted yellow eyes. A black forked tongue briefly appeared to wet her lips.

He was positive if he gave the right sign she'd be all over him and wouldn't care if Snips stayed as an audience. He wouldn't have been interested even if he hadn't made love to Maggie earlier that day.

He was also aware of Snips's avid attention.

"We must talk sometime," he told the waitress.

She preened as she left the office with the slithering gait of her kind.

Declan pushed the flagon to one side and speared his assistant with a dark look. "Now tell me what's going on with a worker not going back through the portal."

"When I recruited laborers, I stressed that it was only a temporary job and they would be returning to their world as soon as the work was finished," Snips stated in his precise voice. "Apparently, one of them was able to slip away after the final count was made."

"Anyone we need to worry about?" He felt pain settle in behind his eye.

"A very minor demon. A drone."

"But?" Declan knew there was a *but* in there. He could feel it all the way through his bones.

The imp licked his dry lips. "It also appears the portal has been used for some unauthorized travel between the worlds."

"By who?"

"I don't know yet."

This really worried Declan. Either Snips was lying, or someone was very good at hiding his tracks. Declan always felt there was more involved in this portal deal than he knew. Something that Snips hadn't told him. Now the imp stared at him slightly bug-eyed but not giving away whatever thoughts traveled through his devious mind.

"What else?" Declan tapped his fingers on the desk's polished surface. "There has to be more than what you just told me."

He was surprised to see Snips look uneasy. Declan hadn't worked with the imp for long, but it had been long enough that he knew the creature was about as unflappable as they came.

"There are rumors."

"Rumors about what?"

The imp's mismatched eyes of peridot and sapphire remained focused on his boss's face. "About you and the witch."

His blood iced. "Why would anyone care?"

"You allowed your sister to live in the Hellion compound and be apprenticed to one of their Seers, even though we have competent Seers of our own."

"Do you honestly think Victorio would have allowed her to apprentice to one of our Seers when he preferred to see her mated to a monster?" Declan's voice simmered with fury. "He's whipped her bloody more than once. It won't be allowed again."

He mentally cursed himself the moment the words left his mouth. He'd never said a word of what happened the night Anna got up the courage to tell their father she refused to mate with Gaston. That she wouldn't turn into a victim the way his previous mates had.

Declan would never forget the night he found his half sister cowering in her rooms, her body torn and bloodied. No healer would touch her, so Declan had taken her to a sorceress who healed Anna while Declan called in enough favors to safely take her with him when he moved to Damnation Alley.

He hadn't wanted to leave Anna at the Guard compound, but when he saw how happy she looked, he knew he had made the right choice. He knew she would be protected from their father there. That was what mattered.

"Victorio has requested that Anna be returned to him. The contract with Gaston was binding and must be fulfilled." Snips didn't react when a sconce on the wall shattered and the candle flowed down in a waxy river. The acrid scent of sulfur filled the room.

"Then he may as well bind himself to Gaston, because there's no way he'll get her now." He felt the fire burning deep in his throat. "She's now under the Hellion Guard's protection." *And they can provide her with much more than I ever could.*

Snips hopped off his chair. "As the humans say, you can't buck the system."

"I want that worker drone found and immediately sent back to where he belongs. Make sure he's made to understand that he will not be welcome back here," Declan said, determined to hold on to his authority.

He'd worked damned hard to get to where he was, and he knew going up against his father would create problems. He just hadn't expected so much insanity to happen so quickly. Or that the portal below that had been routine for so long would suddenly be so problematic.

He pushed himself away from his desk and left the office.

It looked like he needed to remind his staff just who was in charge here.

He walked down a side hallway until he reached the end. A pressing of fingertips against the wall activated a hidden panel that silently slid to one side.

Declan descended the ancient stone steps until he reached the subbasement. Power swirled in the area like a suffocating cloud. A giant that looked like Anton's twin stood nearby.

"Declan." He inclined his head politely.

"Alexi." Declan gazed at the large portal, blacks and grays churning in front of him. "Has anyone come through today?"

"No, sir. Not for two days."

Declan picked up a small leather-bound notebook and perused the contents. Names, dates, and times of those who crossed the portal were meticulously listed. He didn't doubt Alexi's attention to detail. But he was starting to doubt that Snips was entirely to be trusted.

He wasn't happy to see his cousin's name on the log showing he'd gone back and forth through the portal a great deal. He leafed backward through the log.

"Is there anything wrong, sir?" Alexi stood back from the shimmer of fire circling Declan.

"No, nothing." He offered up a reassuring smile. "You do an excellent job, Alexi. Thank you." He left quickly.

All he had wanted was the club. Something he could

call his own—and he'd done anything and everything to achieve that.

Now it looked like if he wasn't careful, he could lose it all.

The surprising part was that the idea of losing the club wasn't as frightening as the idea that if events catapulted out of control, he could lose Maggie.

Chapter 14

MAGGIE HATED READING INTEL REPORTS.

They were always filled with dire predictions at worst and were boring at best. When you merged the two, you had a report that could scare the crap out of you and put you to sleep at the same time.

Yeah, yeah, yeah, the world could end if the Destroyer came back to this realm.

Yeah, yeah, yeah, it would take the Hellion teams to bring a balance to humankind.

"There are days when being me sucks," she groaned, closing her laptop and leaving the table in search of more coffee.

"I need to go to the mall." Courtney skidded into the kitchen, a riot of color in bright-pink leopard-print pajama pants and a pink tank top. "Now."

"Did some catastrophe happen that no one told me about?" Maggie asked.

"Yes." She held up a narrow tube.

"And that is?"

"I need to replace my mascara." The teen waved the tube in front of Maggie. "So you need to take me to the mall."

"We… uh… don't have a mall. Just that lovely little shopping center in the center of town."

"Houston does, unless…" the teen eyed her speculatively, "you want to do some tricycles and make some for me." She made a face at her word choice. She had thought the spell would wear off by morning, but this was proof Maggie wasn't about to undo the hex. Especially when it was hysterical to see what word would tumble out of Courtney's mouth. "You really think this is funny, don't you?" She glared at Maggie.

"Oh, definitely." Her lips twitched. "So why don't you tell me why you running out of mascara is a life-or-death situation."

"I can't live without blush and mascara. And it's not like I can go to a drugstore for it, either," she interrupted Maggie before she suggested just that. "If you want quality, you have to pay for it. Chloe at Peach Dreams taught me that."

"Then I guess you'll have to suffer through a mascara-less existence, because we're not driving to Houston just for that." She waited for the last of the coffee to spit into her cup and pulled it out from the coffeemaker. Ah, caffeine nirvana! Since Courtney had burst into her life, she'd discovered that tea just didn't give her the energy she needed.

"Then I'll drive myself if you give me the keys."

"No driver's license. No keys."

Courtney's expression turned sly and sent Maggie's suspicion meter soaring. "Mick could take me."

"Another no."

The teen opened her mouth, fully prepared to offer up the argument of all arguments, when Maggie waved a hand in front of her. Magick shimmered around her.

"Now, I could have you forgetting why you feel the need to wear mascara or perhaps silence you for the rest of the day—or month," she said conversationally.

"But I'd rather give you a warning. No road trips today. I have work to do, and since you're not going anywhere either, you don't need to worry about your makeup."

"You…" Courtney snapped her mouth closed before she made another verbal faux pas. She spun on her heel and left the kitchen.

Maggie collapsed against the counter. "Anyone who thinks they want to be a mom needs to have Courtney for a few hours." The first chords of "All Star" barely sounded before she picked up her cell. "This had better be good."

"More like bad," Meech said without bothering with a greeting. "That rave you and the demon invaded?"

Maggie instantly waved a silence bubble around her. She didn't think this was something Courtney should overhear.

"What about it?"

"Another rave went on last night, except this time a couple of kids ended up dead."

She froze. "How were they killed?"

"All their life essence was sucked out of them. There was nothing left but the husks of their bodies," he exhaled a deep breath. "They look a good fifty years older."

Maggie's mind raced with the news. "Declan sensed something like that the night we were at that club, but it was minor. A sip here and a sip there. Nothing of the magnitude you're talking about."

"It's not easy to get a handle on these parties, because they're always moving locations," Meech said. "Mal's having his usual temper tantrum. He wants this to go away before the humans realize what's going on."

"I thought Zouk was handling this."

"He's missing."

Okay, not what she expected to hear.

"What about his team?"

"MIA, too."

She groped for a chair and dropped down into it. "No. An entire team never goes missing."

"This one did," her second-in-command told her in a voice that revealed how badly this piece of news affected him. "Communication was lost not long after they went into the building."

"How long ago?" She licked her lips, finding them as dry as her throat.

"Last night. Fuck, Maggie. Zouk's one of the best."

"Yeah." She glanced upward. "I'm coming in."

"You're on bodyguard duty."

"I'm still coming in."

"Mal will take a strip off your hide. I wasn't even supposed to call you."

"He doesn't need to know you called, and I've got a tough hide."

"What will you do with the kid?"

"Find a baby-sitter." She disconnected and dissolved the silence bubble at the same time.

Maggie already knew that sneaking on to the compound wasn't possible. That she was transported to Mal's office the second she set foot on the property was more than proof of that.

The calming atmosphere of the temple background dissipated under the gnome's infamous temper.

"Tell me why you're here." He paced the never-ending space.

"We're missing a team. No man, or creature, left behind and all that." She sprawled in the chair by his desk that, as usual, overflowed with papers. She flicked her fingers to straighten the listing pile.

"What about the kid?" He lit up a cigar.

"She's fine." She hoped.

"She has no idea what's going on?" He puffed away, sending noxious smoke curling through the columns and out into the darkness beyond. Elle glared at Mal as she sneezed loudly and made her way to a protected corner of Maggie's neck.

Maggie wrinkled her nose, forcing herself not to sneeze. Next Yule she was going to buy the gnome a box of good cigars.

"All she wanted to do today was have me drive her to the mall so she could buy mascara. She's your typical teenager."

"Typical with a boyfriend who has a hinky past."

"Hinky? You been watching those cop shows again, Mal? I sent in what I knew about him. What can you tell me about Mick Frasier?"

"Jack shit. A punk kid who should have a police record a mile long but doesn't. Works as a mechanic and hooked up with the kid about six months ago." He swore at the tower of papers and slapped his palm on them. They instantly shrunk to the height of one sheet. "Shoulda done this months ago. You didn't need to come in because of Zouk."

"Yes, I did. I've known Zouk for three hundred years, Mal. He's had my back in the past. I can't just let him disappear." She thought of the rave she and Declan had attended. "What happened? Please tell me you didn't send the team in there with the intention of clearing the place out. Human teenagers go there. Talk about major risk factors."

His walnut visage wrinkled even more. "He said he had it all under control. Dispatch heard them go in. Zouk later was heard muttering he knew what was going on and they were coming back. Except they didn't come back. By the time another team got out there, they couldn't find anything except two bodies lying in the middle of what had been the dance floor."

"Did you send any trackers out there to find out what happened to the team?"

He nodded. "Nothing. No indication any of our people had ever been in that building. No signs of where they went. Not even a hint there had been a portal in there to transport anyone out. So that means…" he lifted a brow.

She felt that sick sensation that meant the same thing Mal left unspoken. "Demon technology. They have a way of masking their portals that we haven't been able to break yet.

"Do you think MacGyver was a demon?" Maggie asked, tongue tucked firmly in cheek. "He probably used a paperclip to mask a portal."

"Cute. Real cute." Declan walked in and grinned at Maggie.

"Yes, I am." She preened as she tipped her head back to study the cloud-dappled ceiling filled with chubby-cheeked cherubs that she now swore bore Mal's grumpy features. How scary was that? "We need to find out when and where the next rave will be."

"*We* are on it. *You* are not."

Maggie smiled at the disgruntled voice. "You have no idea about the next one, do you? Neither do the Seers."

"We have the experts." He looked at her. "So go back to your duties of looking after the potential sacrifice so she doesn't end up under a ritual knife."

"You have such a way with words, Mal." She stood up. "What I'd really like to do is gather up my team so we can figure out where the next rave will be. Then we'd go in and take them out." Her voice softened. "For Zouk."

She pulled in a deep breath. "But instead, I'm going to go and make sure that Courtney doesn't end up on that sacrificial altar." She walked out of the office.

"You sounded very *Norma Rae* in there," Elle told Maggie as she headed for her quarters. "Or whoever said, 'Attica.' For a moment, I thought you would whip out a wand and etch sigils in the air. I do love the magickal images you create." The gem-encrusted spider crawled further up Maggie's shoulder and settled down into position.

"Mal was never a team player." Maggie reached her door and whispered the words to open the door.

"Maggie!" Sybil fluttered down the hall, trailing lavender along the way. The lovely elf hugged her friend tightly. "How is motherhood?"

Maggie dragged her into her suite. "Scary. I had no idea human teenagers were like that. Courtney can go through a whole mass of emotions in two minutes."

Sybil settled in one of the chairs while Maggie chose a few more changes of clothing and personal items. She stuffed them haphazardly in a duffel bag she'd set on the bed.

"What a wonderful spell!" Sybil chuckled, after

hearing about Courtney's verbal mishaps. "Something like that could come in handy in so many ways."

"It's driving her crazy, too. Although not as much as what she's going through with Rickie as her baby-sitter," she confided with a giggle.

"Rickie? He's the most hyper of all the messengers. How did Courtney take it?"

"Not well." Maggie was positive she'd get an earful when she returned to the house. From both parties. "Right now, I'd rather wade into a nest of angry ice spiders than face them."

"Why did you bring a rodent into the house?" Courtney almost shrieked, keeping a chair between herself and the ferret.

"She's crazy." Rickie downed half the liquid in his coffee mug. "The next time you want me to baby-sit, don't ask." The ferret settled his paws on his hips and glared at Maggie.

"One pound of Kopi Luwak," she reminded him, naming the world's most expensive coffee.

"You didn't tell me she was so much trouble. I want five."

"*Five*? Do you know how much a pound of that stuff costs?"

"Five or else," he threatened just before he winked out of sight.

"I don't need a baby-sitter. Especially that thing that just disappeared," Courtney huffed.

"There was a reason." Maggie rubbed her fingertips across her forehead. She feared the day would come when even the most powerful spell for headaches wouldn't work.

"All he did was talk like a chipmunk on speed and drink coffee." She was now on a roll. "And he ate all the cookies!" She searched through the cabinets and pulled out flour and sugar. "Where's that cookbook? Oh, good, here it is. Do we have any chocolate chips?"

"Top shelf." Maggie shot magickal energy to the mentioned shelf to provide the necessary chips. "So you can cook?"

"Baking's a no-brainer, and Mrs. Whitney insisted the girls learn to cook. You'd think she was still back in the 1950s. Plus, all you do is read the instructions, put everything together, and throw it in the oven." Pretty soon the teenager had the fixings in a bowl and was happily mixing away.

"Wow! Why didn't you tell me you were making cookies!" Rickie popped back in. He scampered over to the coffeepot and refilled his mug. "I love cookies."

This time, Courtney's scream was only a bit below the implosion level.

"He's box, isn't he?"

"I'm no box." He reared back.

"She can't use any words pertaining to magick," Maggie explained. "You get used to it. You already cleaned us out of cookies, and you're getting a small fortune in coffee. Off with you, and I won't tell Mal that you moonlight."

The ferret disappeared with a muttered curse left behind.

"You live in a totally crazy world," Courtney said, now spooning dollops of cookie dough onto a baking sheet.

"Yeah, well, it's only going to get crazier," she muttered, thinking of her conversation with Mal. She needed to talk to Declan. She had thought about calling him, but she wanted to wait until she sorted more of it out in her head. She sipped her coffee and watched the girl pile dirty utensils in the sink and rinse them off.

"Courtney, how do you find out about the raves in town?" she asked casually. She didn't miss the way the girl stiffened at her question.

"People just know," she said evasively.

"How? It's not like flyers would be distributed among the teens. Texting?" she probed.

"Sometimes. Passing the information on at Starbucks or wherever we tend to be." She spoke slowly, clearly not wanting to say too much. "It just happens."

"How many raves have you been to, Courtney? How many times did you sneak out of the home and go to one?"

"Not as many times as you think I did." She moved to the oven when the timer dinged and brought out a sweet-smelling batch of chocolate chip cookies.

"Did you always go to them with Mick? Is he the one who heard about them?" Maggie had a feeling she sucked at interrogation. Sybil could do it so subtly that her victims never realized just how much they revealed.

"Why are you so down on Mick? You haven't even met him yet. You won't let him come here so you can get to know him."

Her accusation dug deep because Maggie knew she was right. Plus, it was a failure she shouldn't have allowed to happen. She should already have checked further into the boy to see just who, and what, he was.

"Fine, invite him over tomorrow for dinner. We'll barbecue."

"Really?" Courtney squealed. "Okay, I'll call him after he gets off work. Are you going to ask Declan to come so the two of you can gang up on Mick?"

"For Fates' sake, is there anything more suspicious than a teenager?" Maggie threw up her hands. "Tell him to come around six."

"It's not like I can tell him what you are, and I still don't know what Declan is," she muttered, sliding a new tray of cookie dough into the oven. "Because while he's totally cute, he sure isn't normal."

"Normal's just a word. In my world, I'm normal and you're not. In Declan's world, you and I aren't normal."

"So what's his world?"

"Not a place you'd want to visit." She singed her fingers stealing a cookie off Courtney's makeshift cooling rack. It almost burned her mouth, but the chocolaty goodness melting on her taste buds was worth it. She snatched up two more cookies.

"So when are you going to tell me why you had to pretend to be a relative?" Courtney pursued, waving a spoon. "I know, I know, I won't be able to tell anyone because of that stupid thing you did to me. So there's really no reason why you can't tell me. I mean, you already sent that talking, coffee-swilling ferret here."

"When I know more." Maggie figured that was promise enough.

Courtney didn't see it that way. "Not fair when you're asking questions that you feel I should answer. Such as about raves."

She looked too sly for Maggie's comfort. "Meaning?"

"Meaning I bet you want to know when and where the next one is being held."

"You won't be going."

The teenager was clever enough to ignore that statement. "But for some reason you want to know, don't you? Maybe even know who puts them on." She dangled the carrot in front of Maggie.

"Forget the fibs, Courtney. Your nose is growing."

She squealed and ran to the refrigerator's polished stainless surface to study her face. "Is not!"

Maggie smirked. "It could have, though. These cookies are good. Better than what we got from the store. What would you think about making a cake or something for tomorrow night?"

"Great. Now I'm nothing more than the kitchen help." But she looked pleased by the suggestion.

"No, call it a shared responsibility. You baked the cookies. I'll clean up." Maggie did just that by loading the dishwasher. Once finished, she snagged a few more cookies and went upstairs to her bedroom while Courtney headed for the family room and switched on the TV.

She took a quick look at Courtney's room, relieved to see that it only resembled a mess and not a war zone, and then moved on to her room. She'd set her duffel bag on the bed when she returned. Now it was time to tune out Courtney's choice of television programs and unpack.

She also thought of calling Declan and inviting him to dinner the next night. A tingling sensation started at the back of her neck and continued around front.

"My spidey senses are on alert, *ma chère*," Elle said, moving down Maggie's arm and landing on the dresser. In no time, she'd spun a silken bed. "What of yours?"

"I leave that to you." She dropped onto the bed and fell backwards, her head neatly resting on the pillows.

"We heard all that Mal said, and we listened to Sybil. It is one of those situations that will get worse before it gets better, and it all has to do with the girl's blood. But there is more to it. You know that." Elle preened in front of the mirror, polishing her jeweled surface. "I have not had a male in so long," she sighed. "You did pack my computer, didn't you?"

"Yes, I did. You can hook it up to your new web in no time. That's right, Elle, talk about your lack of a love life. All you do is seduce a guy, screw him silly, and kill him. If only the rest of us had such an uncomplicated life."

Maggie didn't think it was crazy talking it over with her spider. She missed Sybil, but Elle was more than just a pretty accessory. She had more smarts than most and was fun to talk to.

"The Mayans were very cruel and very intelligent. So are demons." Elle left the statement hanging in the air. "Declan will help you because the two of you are lovers."

Maggie closed her eyes, feeling mortification wash over her. "Please tell me you didn't tune in during that time."

"Do not worry. You had all the privacy you needed." Elle yawned. "Call your handsome demon and whisper sweet nothings. I must hook up my computer." She practically flew up to her web while Maggie magicked it up to the ceiling. In no time, Elle was happily checking email.

"Terrific, romantic advice from a black widow spider," Maggie muttered, nibbling on another cookie. She winced when the TV's volume increased. "How do adults survive a kid's teenage years?"

She closed her eyes and mentally ran through her day.
Mayans, demons, Courtney, Mick Frasier.
Declan.
So where was the connection?

———

"Declan." Anton's deep voice rumbled around the office as he stood soldier straight in the open doorway.

Declan looked up from the array of paperwork he needed to get caught up on. Thoughts of Maggie had jumbled his brain, along with his hunger to spend time with her. Hopefully they could have time alone when he could inhale her scent mixed with the fragrance of black orchid, violets, and lotus blossom that made up her perfume. Where her legs would wrap around him in a loving embrace and she'd whisper in his ear.

Get your mind off your cock, Declan.

"What is it?" He kept his voice harsh. The reminder he had to always be in charge was constant.

Anton paused a moment. "Alexi is gone."

That Declan hadn't expected. "I assume you don't mean he's gone out for coffee."

Anton shifted from one foot to the other, a sure sign he was uneasy. "The log was on the floor, and the portal was left open. I don't think he went through it willingly."

Declan was out of his chair and down the hallway before the bouncer finished the last word.

He found the entrance to the lower level open and Snips waiting by the portal, which was now closed. The imp looked at him with a flash of fear that vanished as quickly as it appeared.

"There is nothing here," Snips informed his master.

Declan stared at the log his assistant held in his purple claws and at a black smear of blood near the portal—and noted that no one was guarding the area.

"On the contrary, there's a great deal here." He glanced at Anton, who hovered anxiously in the background. "I want you standing sentry down here. Put Elias on the door." He turned back to Snips. "And I want a tracker here immediately. Alexi must be found."

He returned upstairs with the sensation that darkness was not just lingering, it was right there waiting to pounce.

Chapter 15

DECLAN PARKED HIS CAR IN THE DRIVEWAY AND TOOK the walkway that led around the side of the house to the backyard. He heard Maggie's exasperation along with Courtney's whines as he reached the rear gate.

"You have to do it again," Maggie said in a tone that brooked no refusal.

"*Again?* It hurt the last million times you made me do it. I'm nothing more than a bunch of cuts and bruises."

"Then the best thing we can do is keep doing it until you develop enough calluses on your ass that it won't hurt anymore."

"You are so mean!"

Declan paused at the gate before opening it. He felt the wards throbbing all the way into the wood. He sensed touching it would give him an unwelcome shock, at the very least. He looked over the top and saw Maggie and Courtney facing each other in the middle of the lawn. Courtney's dark hair hung in sweaty coils, and her yoga pants and tank top were grass stained, while Maggie looked as if she'd just stepped out of the shower. The slight tilt of her head told him she was aware he was there.

"Come at me again, and this time put some effort in it," Maggie ordered.

Declan watched as Courtney, looking about as frustrated as a kid could look, ran at Maggie with her arms outstretched. He cataloged her first mistake and swallowed his laughter when Maggie easily avoided Courtney's attack and neatly flipped her over.

"I really hate you," the girl snarled from her prone position.

"Then you must not hate me enough, because if you did, you'd try harder." Maggie put out a hand and pulled Courtney to her feet. "What were my first words to you when we came out here?"

"To forget about fighting like a girl and fight dirty using my nails, feet, and teeth." The teen dug dirt out from under her fingernails. "Guess what? I did fight dirty, and I've got the crud to prove it." She held up her filthy hands.

"She means you do whatever it takes to cause your opponent serious pain." Declan felt the magick wards give enough for him to open the gate and step through before they closed up behind him.

"Declan!" Maggie turned on him in a way that had him feeling wary. He took a step back and then jumped forward as the gate sparked against him.

"I'm *so* glad you're here because you can help me with Courtney's self-defense lessons." Maggie practically floated toward Declan.

"I thought she was kicked out of school for fighting."

"She was, but she fought like a girl," Maggie explained. "She needs to learn to fight dirty enough to handle anyone—and anything—that might come her way." She stared straight into Declan's eyes, her gaze a deep-green glow that looked like pure seduction. "So I need you." A faint pink lit up her cheeks as his grin deepened.

"Oh jeez, if you two are going to get that way, I'm

going inside." Courtney started to do just that, but without even looking her way, Maggie grabbed the back of the girl's tank top and pulled her back. "Some R-rated things shouldn't be seen by this kid."

"Not so fast, grasshopper. You have some work to do here. So watch and learn." She backed up, still grinning at Declan. She wiggled her fingers at him. "Come and get me, big guy," she purred.

Declan grinned. "You do know I wasn't taught to go easy on females."

"I was hoping you'd say that." She bounced on her toes. "Let's see what you've got."

"Oh my God, he's going to pulverize you." Courtney dropped to the grass, prepared to watch the show. "And after what you've put me through, I'll be happy to see you get your butt whipped."

The two moved in a circle that slowly grew smaller as they each gauged the other, looking for the perfect opening.

"Oh, no, the big, bad man is after me," Maggie sang out, gazing at him with a wide-eyed innocence he wasn't buying for anything. "What will I do?"

"Who let you out all alone, little girl?" Declan spoke in a voice that rumbled with the darkness he'd been raised in. "Didn't anyone tell you it's not safe?"

She clasped her hands together in mock fear. "Please don't hurt me."

He advanced on her with the intent of leaving a few bruises just to teach her a lesson, nothing too harsh. Then lightning quick, he was on her.

Just as fast, Declan found himself flat on his back with Maggie's boot resting lightly against his chest.

"Normally, I would have aimed a bit more south just to make a point," she murmured. "But I thought this would be enough to get your attention."

She moved back and danced away some more steps when he tried to grab her ankle to throw her off balance. She immediately twisted in a spin kick, and only Declan's quick reflexes kept him from getting his jaw broken. "Uh, uh, uh, none of that."

Courtney's mouth dropped open. "So cool! How did you do that?"

"Magick." Declan grumped, slowly rising to his feet. Served him right for holding back. It appeared the one who ended up with bruises was him.

"No, just my impressive skills." Maggie grinned.

"That's not fair because I can't even say the words, much less do anything with it. No way I'm embarrassing myself tonight by even trying to say them." The teen jumped up. "I wanna learn what you just did," she told Maggie. "Maybe I can't do it the way you can, but you can teach me other ways, right?" She danced in place.

"If I'd known this was all it took to inspire you, I would have had Declan come over sooner," Maggie teased.

"Tell me you have beer inside." At her nod, Declan limped into the kitchen and headed for the refrigerator. Once he plucked a beer out, he returned outside and settled into a patio chair.

"You do know that we guys consider girl-on-girl fighting pretty hot," he commented as he watched Maggie instruct Courtney in moves and then had the teen perform them on her. There was no doubt Maggie held back to give Courtney some beginning confidence, and each time the girl tried, she got faster. She even connected once.

"Remember that, kiddo. Men only have one thing on their minds. Now it's time to step up your game. Come at me fast and hard. I'm not going to give you any quarter."

"But kicking you down there won't give the same effect as it would if I kicked him." Her gaze slid sideways toward Declan.

"Oh, no." He held his hands up. "I'm not going there. You can figure that out without using me as a punching bag."

"You should have brought Anton," Maggie said.

He sobered at the thought of Anton losing his brother. She caught the change in his expression and sent him a silent question. He shook his head, mouthing *later.*

Declan watched Maggie turn into an instructor and put Courtney through her paces, showing her what moves were effective and even how to use her femininity to her advantage.

By the time they were finished, Courtney was dragging.

"I'm taking a shower," she announced. "I'd crawl into bed and die, but with Mick coming in an hour, I need to look gorgeous." She turned to Maggie. "I guess you don't want me telling him about this either."

"Only if you want to tell him you're learning to kick his ass."

"Guys don't like that."

"Well, since you're convinced you need to look gorgeous, here's a reward for working so hard," Maggie said, producing a slender tube of mascara from behind her back and handing it to the delighted girl. "It's the good stuff."

"Thanks." She favored them both with a dazzling smile and headed into the house.

Maggie dropped into the chair next to Declan's and stole his beer bottle. "You couldn't save any for me?" She waved the empty bottle back and forth.

"You have more in the house." He was content not to move. Now she looked as if she'd had a good workout, with her face and body gleaming with sweat. She pulled the clips from her golden hair, letting it swing forward.

"I guess I need a shower more than I need this." She pushed herself out of the chair.

"No chance of my joining you?"

Maggie smiled and patted him on the head. "Sorry, no. But you can start up the barbecue. I bought steaks and thought we'd roast corn and potatoes to go with them."

"Sounds good."

She started walking backward into the house. "So, do you fire demons just stare at a barbecue to fire it up?"

He grinned. "What can I say? We like it easy. The sad thing is we can't add mesquite or hickory to it. Go take your shower... alone." He cocked an eyebrow, reminding her that he had high hopes for the future.

Maggie blew him a kiss and scampered inside.

Declan continued grinning as he headed for the state-of-the-art barbecue set up on a corner of the patio.

That witch will drive me crazy yet.

———

It was official.

Not only did Maggie dislike Mick Frasier, but she wouldn't trust him as far as she could throw him. And she especially didn't want him around Courtney, who sat there hanging on his every word and looking the picture of a teenager in love. Since the evening was warm, Courtney had chosen a pair of bright turquoise shorts with a yellow-and-turquoise halter top and pulled her hair up in a long ponytail.

Maggie looked at her and saw a sweet girl. She was positive Mick looked at her and saw someone he wanted to nail. She tamped down her violent thoughts. Such as watching his head explode like a cantaloupe.

If he touches Courtney anyplace he shouldn't, he will be leaving here in a body bag.

At first glance, the nineteen-year-old was the picture-perfect image of the bad boy all girls lusted after. Ed Hardy T-shirt, artfully ripped jeans, a wicked-looking tat of a skull on his bicep, coffee-brown hair pulled back in a short ponytail, and a hint of dark beard on his jaw. He was catnip to Courtney's kitten.

Maggie also knew she couldn't fault his manners, which were pretty damn perfect, and he treated Courtney with the right amount of deference.

He and Declan had done the male bonding bit talking about motorcycles. Declan also did the guy thing by offering a beer to Mick, who was smart enough to turn it down when Maggie turned a dark eye on them both. Mick flashed her the patented bad-boy grin and accepted a Coke from Courtney.

He wandered into the kitchen while Maggie wrapped corn on the cob and seasoned potato wedges in foil.

"It's nice that Courtney now has a relative who is willing to take her in," he told Maggie as he leaned against the counter. "It's always a shame when a sweet kid like her loses her family the way she lost hers. Now she looks happy."

"I'm glad I was able to finally be here for her." She sent out her senses, hoping to pick up something odd from him, but all she got was a blank slate. Humans tended to show up that way to her, but this was different. Deliberate. Something deep inside her said he wasn't completely human. Question: *What* was *he?*

"She's a good girl, and I intend to see she stays that way." She gave him the adult eye.

She knew that just not being human didn't mean he was a danger to Courtney. Many creatures wandered out of their playgrounds to seek different chums. But she was determined to keep a close eye on him until she could find out what his agenda was.

He showed a flash of teeth and held his hands up in surrender. "No worries. Court says no, and I'm fine with it."

Maggie bared her teeth. "Good."

"Especially since I've seen your boyfriend." He glanced outside where Declan and Courtney stood by the barbecue, with Courtney chattering away. "Something tells me he'd hurt me good if I got out of line."

"Maybe he would, but I'd be the one to turn you inside out and stake you in the boiling sun." Her smile wasn't meant to take the sting out of her words but to enforce them.

"Wow, bloodthirsty." He eyed her closely as she handed him the serving platter filled with foil-wrapped corn and potatoes. "You women are dangerous."

"Why do you think many warriors handed their captives over to the women?" She gave him a gentle push toward the door. "Take those out to Declan while I bring everything else."

She waited until he was outside before she pulled a small bag out of her jeans pocket and tucked a hair inside.

"Messenger needed. Safe to come now."

"Hey, baby." A dark-gray ferret appeared on the counter in a spark of light. "You got something for me?"

Maggie handed him the bag, which he tucked into his tiny leather bag. "Hand this over to Forensics, Zickie. Tell them it's a rush job. I need to know what he is."

The furry critter peered out the window. "Looks like a fire demon to me."

"The other one," she told him. "Have them leave the info in my private message box. I'll pick it up the next time I'm at the compound. Thanks."

"No prob." He paused at her coffeemaker and poured the last of the brew into his cup. "You want this copied to Mal?"

She shook her head. "I'd rather give him an oral report after I read what comes up."

"The big guy won't like it, but who am I to say? Later." He was gone as quickly as he appeared.

Pasting a perky hostess smile on her lips, Maggie picked up the rest of the dishes and carried them outside.

"Everything's coming along well," Declan announced, giving her a searching look.

"Good." After she set everything on the round glass table, she walked over to the barbecue. Out of the corner of her eye, she could see Courtney and Mick sharing the wooden swing at the edge of the yard.

"What do you think?" she said for his ears only.

"Even with the James Dean attitude, he seems too good to be true. Polite but not too polite. Looks badass, but not so much you'd want to call the cops on him," Declan replied, putting the food on the grill. "He even has decent manners."

"The key words are 'too good to be true.' Courtney's

smart. She isn't taken in that easily, but she's totally blind where he's concerned."

"Testosterone does that to a girl." He bumped his hip against hers. "We guys blind you with our charms so you don't see the real us."

"All I want to know is what the real him is." She did her best to keep a subtle eye on the duo. "I should have done it from the beginning. Especially since he doesn't show any back history. I can't believe he was hatched like this, but then, who knows."

"A lot of kids fall off the grid. Get fake IDs so they can do their own thing. He could be one of those."

"I told Mal I wasn't up for this gig," Maggie muttered. "I don't deal with humans if I absolutely don't have to, so it's not easy for me to get into their minds. To understand them well enough. Jazz interacts with humans all the time. So do Stasi and Blair. Lili is a doctor and treats them. Some of us have lived among them all the time. Others stay away from them."

"And you stayed away as much as you could," he guessed.

She nodded. "When I could, but it wasn't easy when a lot of my bodyguard jobs dealt with humans. You can't show emotion in my work. Emotion can get you killed. When I protected someone, I thought of that person as my charge. Not even as a name. Now my charge not only has a name but a personality that gets under my skin, and the knowledge that if I fail…"

"You won't. It's not in your genetic makeup not to succeed."

"Are we eating soon?" Courtney called out. "Starving kids here!"

"It won't be long," Declan told her. He looked down at Maggie. "Think you can be subtle with him so you can find out about the raves?"

"He'd be too suspicious. Courtney's been a little open about it, and if I step carefully, she'll tell me enough. Or I'll just activate the tracker necklace when she does the expected and sneaks out of the house." She fingered the bracelet on her right wrist.

"Witches and their jewelry." He eyed her ankle brace-let with its emerald winking brightly. Like Courtney, Maggie wore shorts, hers the color of ripe watermelon, with a white tank top edged in dark pink.

"Girls gotta have their bling." She felt unease wash over her like poisoned water. "You know what? Let's get this over with." A wave of her hand, and the food was done cooking. "I should have known I couldn't do the family barbecue thing."

"Come on, Samantha, no using magick," he teased.

"I really hated *Bewitched*. What witch refuses to use her magick? No wonder she couldn't do what Darren wanted." She looked at the young twosome. She was beginning to think dinner couldn't be over soon enough.

Maggie forced herself to laugh and smile, talk as if nothing was wrong, and eat food that held no taste at all for her. She was fairly sure that Courtney and Mick had no clue, but she couldn't hide her feelings from Declan. He didn't betray her worries, but a dark look in his eye told her he saw through her mask as the perfect hostess.

This is why I go to parties, not host them. I have no idea how to do this.

But for just a moment, a tiny spot deep inside her whispered that she could have a different life if she wanted it. A normal one like they show in TV sitcoms, complete with a white picket fence, a dog, and a minivan in the driveway.

The question was: Did she want a life like that, or were her hormones just telling her that was what she wanted?

Maybe hitting that 700-year mark meant it was the time for a midlife crisis.

———

Courtney was positive something was up. She was really glad that Maggie had invited Mick to dinner. She wanted to know about him. And Courtney wanted her to see what a nice guy he was.

Sure, Mick had his dark side. She'd seen it a few times, and while it scared the hell out of her, it also excited her. He was hot, and he loved her. He'd even said so. How many guys are willing to use the L word? Plus, he hadn't pressured her into anything she didn't want to do.

She enjoyed sitting next to him, feeling his thigh brush against hers under the cover of the table.

While they'd sat in the swing, he'd whispered to her that he knew of a party the next night—and could she sneak out to go with him?

She wanted to tell him the truth about Maggie and Declan, even if she still didn't know what the dude was. But after that whopper of whatever junk (she couldn't even think the words because they never came out right) Maggie threw at her, she couldn't say a word without sounding like an idiot.

She had thought about texting Mick, but she quickly learned that didn't work, either. Luckily she deleted the message before sending it out. She didn't know what Maggie had done, but she sure wanted to learn. Knowing that would be better than anything she'd learn in a school; that was for sure.

"Mick asked if I could go to the movies with him tomorrow," she announced, smothering a giggle when he nudged her foot. "Can I go?"

"While I'm new at this guardian job, I know I should ask what movie." Maggie looked at Mick.

He named the new Hugh Jackman action-adventure film.

"I can't fault your taste in movies. And while it's a school night, yes, I know you're not in school right now." She glanced at Courtney, who made sure to keep a small smile on her lips and no expression of triumph. "I won't say no if you go to an early show and come back right afterward."

Courtney nodded and almost stomped on Mick's foot with her excitement.

Declan started.

Crap, wrong foot!

He looked at her but said nothing.

"I think we could be out by nine," Mick said.

"Maggie!" she whined, because she knew it was expected of her. "Do we have to go to an early show? It's not like we're driving into Houston for the movie. We're just going here in town. We could stop for pizza or something afterward, couldn't we? I'd be back before curfew. And my cell phone would be on all the time," she promised. "You've met Mick, and you can see how nice he is. And he makes me wear a helmet when I ride with him on his motorcycle." Surely that was the clincher.

She waited with bated breath while Maggie and

Declan exchanged that silent conversation that adults seem to share. The two might not be married, but they might as well be, with the way they were always in sync. She also thought if Maggie concentrated more on Declan, she'd focus less on her.

"The show lets out at nine?" Maggie asked Mick, who nodded. "Fine, you can grab something to eat afterward, but I want Courtney home by 10:30."

"We can do that." Mick smiled at Maggie and then grasped Courtney's hand and squeezed it.

Courtney felt a smidgen of guilt that she'd lied to Maggie. Sure, she and Mick would go to the movies, but later tomorrow night she'd be sneaking out to go to a rave.

Maggie had talked to her about the raves, hoping Courtney would tell her where they were. No way she'd do that. The last thing she wanted was Maggie showing up at one. Besides, Maggie and Declan were too old for the kind of parties Courtney and Mick went to. If Declan wouldn't let her go inside his club, she wasn't going to talk about where she went.

She'd already scoped out the house and knew the easiest ways to sneak out. It was a good thing Maggie didn't have an alarm system. And so far Declan hadn't stayed over, although Courtney was positive they'd done *it*. There was something about them that said so.

But she's a kitten. She knows plumbing. What if she's put something on me so she knows where I am all the time?

Great, now Maggie's got me feeling paranoid. She seems to like Mick, so she must see he's okay. She said yes to the show and our going out for pizza afterward.

Courtney decided to just relax and enjoy the moment. And tomorrow night, Mick had promised, they'd attend the rave of the year.

———————

Maggie exhaled a breath of relief after Mick left with a polite thank-you for dinner. Courtney immediately disappeared upstairs. Maggie was positive the girl was up there calling or texting him.

"It wasn't as difficult as you thought it would be, was it?" Declan settled on the couch next to her. "Now it's just us old folks," he told her, turning her around and draping her legs across his lap. "I could get to like this."

"No, you wouldn't. You like the edgy life in your club." She noted the fleeting change in his expression. She straightened up. "What's wrong? It has to do with Damnation Alley, doesn't it?"

"It's something I've had to keep quiet," he said in a low voice.

"Such as something the Guard should know?" Her voice took on an edge. "You need to tell me, Declan."

"You can't let anyone else know," he told her, his eyes turning a dark silver.

"No promises, and you *will* tell me."

Witch and demon personalities warred, thickening the air in the room.

"There's a portal in the club's subbasement."

Maggie sighed. "Sorry, Declan, but that's old news."

He nodded. "It's always been under strict control. A guard is on duty 24-7 and keeps a log on who comes through."

"What kind of control?" she asked tautly.

"Heavy restrictions, but not the kind you'd appreciate. Don't forget we're talking about demons. Remember, Anna's talent makes her exceptional. There are no warm and fuzzy demons around. Just mean and meaner. Then you move up to psychotic. Coming through the portal is a privilege, but bribes are nothing new if you want to go through badly enough. There are no visas given, but time limits can be enforced."

"You said it's guarded," she reminded him.

"Alexi, Anton's brother, was the guard."

"Was?"

He nodded. "He's gone. No trace of him at all."

Maggie's mind whirled. "Do you know when he disappeared?"

Declan shook his head.

"Or who could have come through after he was gone."

"Amazing how your mind works."

Maggie resisted the urge to scream. "Can't I have just one piece of good news?"

"How about that I think you're as sexy as Hades, and I'd enjoy hauling you upstairs to your bed?" he quipped. "I told you about the portal, something you're not supposed to know, and I have someone checking into this."

"And it's common knowledge that demons don't like the Guard messing in their business." She blew out a deep breath and drummed her heels against the couch cushion. "Fine. It's your headache, not mine. I'll have mine tomorrow night when Courtney sneaks out of the house to go to a rave."

"Do you want some company?"

"I think I'll take this on myself." She slid over until her butt settled snugly in his lap.

"Looks like you're doing that already." He rested his hands against her waist, edging his fingers under her white cotton top until they met bare skin. "Think you can make sure the kid doesn't sneak downstairs? We wouldn't want her receiving a live version of adult education."

"Easy peasy." Maggie looked upward. "Lullaby and good night. No ears, no sight. Just slumber and sweet dreams for young girls. Do it now." She threw her power upstairs. She waited a moment. "She's probably sound asleep in that pile of clothing she never cleared off her bed."

"Good." He pulled her closer to him and angled his mouth over hers.

Maggie realized she was quickly getting addicted to Declan's kisses, the hot taste of his mouth, and the way he made her insides tumble around like an Olympic gymnast.

She pulled his shirt out of his waistband so she could spread her hands over his heated skin, feel his taut abs, and listen to the rough sounds of his breathing, aware his reaction was all for her.

"We." She nipped the corner of his mouth. "Have." She moved to his ear. "All." She sucked on his earlobe. "The." She returned to his tempting mouth. "Time." Then down the rough underside of his jaw. "In the world."

She returned to his mouth and licked the seam of his lips. "I can't make time stop," she whispered against his skin. "But I can slow it down a bit. Make it all ours."

Declan moved his hands up her bare back before bringing them around to cup her breasts, his thumbs circling her nipples, which peaked under his touch. The tune he hummed under his breath was familiar and a bit haunting.

Maggie smiled, recognizing the Rolling Stones' hit "Time Is on My Side." "Do you think that's possible?"

"Sure, if we want it to be." He nuzzled her throat. "We're a powerful team. I knew you were trouble the minute you first walked into the club."

"The Bloater was trouble. I was just the catalyst." She combed her fingers through his hair. As spiky as it looked, it felt soft as silk.

It would have been so easy to suggest they go upstairs and finish what they were starting here. But the idea wasn't perfect with Courtney in the house, even if she was now sound asleep.

Maggie felt greedy. She wanted a large space of time where nothing mattered but the two of them. Where they could indulge in each other and feel the intimate connection tighten between them. No teenagers. No Mayan priests looking to take over the world. No Mal ruining her day.

Maggie pulled back just enough to look at Declan's face. *Fates help me: I'm falling in love with a demon.*

Chapter 16

IT SHOULD HAVE BEEN EASY.

Maggie acted the part of the clueless guardian when Mick arrived the next evening to pick up Courtney for the movie. She even thanked him for adhering to her rules when he returned the girl at ten-thirty on the dot. The witch pretended she didn't notice Courtney whispering something to Mick as she hugged him good-bye. She nodded when Courtney yawned and said she was going upstairs to listen to music before going to sleep.

Maggie settled in the family room with the TV on. She knew to the second an hour later when Courtney crept out her bedroom window. A moment later, the medallion on her bracelet lit up.

"Thank you for wearing the necklace," she whispered, fearing the girl would take it off. But Courtney had loved it the moment Maggie gave it to her and hadn't taken it off since.

Maggie went out to her car ten minutes later and used the tracking medallion to keep tabs. She cursed when the tracker flickered in and out a few times—and cursed even more when the light dimmed and then died. She felt as if she was driving in circles and was ready to throw out a locator spell.

"Not now," she snapped when her cell rang and she activated her Bluetooth.

"Yes, now." Declan's voice came out of the speaker. "We've got trouble."

"I'm following Courtney and Mick to the rave."

"There's no rave." A tone in his voice alerted her that what he had to say was very bad. "Or if there is, they aren't at it."

She pulled a one-eighty in the road and sped off with a squeal of tires. "Do not tell me she's at Damnation Alley."

"Fine, I won't tell you, but she is." Anger coated his voice.

"How the Hades did she get past Anton?" She pounded her dashboard as she increased her speed.

"Anton's not on the door. He's on portal guard duty. Believe me, someone's head will roll for this."

"Not if I get to him first. I'm on my way. And if anyone claims I'm not fitting the club dress code, I will turn them into a boggart." She ignored that she had just blown through a red light.

Declan sighed. "I'll alert the door. Or maybe I won't, after what happened." He disconnected without saying good-bye.

Not that Maggie's feelings were hurt. She had other things to think about. Such as dragging Courtney out of there before something happened. The only thing that kept her temper in check was the knowledge that Declan was there to make sure the girl was kept safe.

Mick was another matter.

In record time, Maggie was at the club's parking lot, leaving the car in a No Parking zone as she moved toward the entrance.

"You are not allowed inside, Guard," the troll sneered

when she reached the door. "No one in there has need of your aid, nor would we call you if trouble happened."

Her smile grew wide with anticipation of a good, old-fashioned knockdown drag-out fight, if need be. Yep, she was in that bad a mood.

"Oh, good, Declan didn't tell you I was coming. I could just kiss him for that because I'd like nothing better than to cause a few bruises. Someone in there absolutely needs my aid because you were a bad boy and committed the ultimate no-no.

"You allowed a human girl and boy in there. That's about as illegal as you can get. Automatic death sentence, in fact. So," she drew out the word, "you don't give me any crap, and I won't tear your gullet out."

The troll growled and started to reach for her but froze in place. His eyes rolled frantically as he struggled to move.

"Be grateful I let you breathe." She brushed past him and entered the dark interior.

Nothing had changed since her last visit. Even Seether screaming "Fake It" out of the speakers in the walls was enough to turn her deaf.

She ignored the vampire that snarled at her as he passed by and the trio of imps who looked at her as if they'd like to kill her but still kept a careful distance.

"They're in one of the back rooms." Declan appeared at her side.

"Did they see you?"

He shook his head. "Everyone's been told that if they ask about me, they're to be told I'm not here tonight. So far, I've managed to keep an eye on them without them seeing me."

"Why did they come here?" she ground out, feeling her blood boil. "Courtney knows she's underage and this isn't the place for her."

"Because it's forbidden and Mick obviously talked her into breaking the rules big time." He steered her around the edge of the crowded dance floor. "I understand you threatened Paxil."

"Paxil? He named himself after an antidepressant?" She laughed. "I know many races refuse to allow their real names to be known because of the power the names hold, but you have to admit that's more than a bit much. There are plenty of baby-name books out there, so why go through a pharmacology textbook?"

She looked up and saw humor flickering in his eyes. "You know what, Sparky? Talk to the wand. Right now, I'm so pissed at Courtney that I'm surprised the club hasn't gone up in flames."

He held out his cupped palm, a tiny flame flickering. "That's my job. Come on. Let's surprise the kids, shall we?"

She shook out her hands, ignoring the magick that filtered out. "Surprise will be the least of it. Right now, I want to take the punk down." She looked down to find Declan's fingers threaded through hers.

"Just don't destroy anyone. I do have a business to run."

"Be happy I don't feel like blowing something up. Yet."

Declan felt Maggie's anger flow through her body. She fairly smoldered, with her power threatening to erupt like Mount Vesuvius. He looked at her, seeing the sharp gaze of a Guard, her form tight, ready to fight if need be.

It was easy to remember the first time he saw her. Sexy as hell in a skimpy clubbing outfit, with high heels that showed off the golden tanned legs that he fondly recalled having wrapped tightly around his hips. But her smile was what had caught him that night. The way she smiled at the Bloater, drawing the rogue creature in until there was no escape.

Just as there had been no escape for him. That was fine. He had no desire to leave her. She was already imprinted in his blood.

He cocked his head to the side, listening to a telepathic message from Snips, whom he'd ordered to stay a safe distance away while still keeping an eye on Courtney and Mick. The imp's words weren't what he wanted to hear.

Declan guided Maggie toward one of the back rooms that offered private tables and booths.

"Just how many private rooms do you have in this place?" she asked, noting the hallways and couples making their way down them. She doubted they were looking for the restrooms.

"More than you'd like to know about. Her human blood won't allow her to enter any of the more clandestine areas. I can't keep an eye everywhere," he said by way of an excuse that he knew wasn't going to fly with her. Judging by her expression, he was right. "What goes on there is nothing illegal, since humans shouldn't make it past the front door."

"And since Courtney did, you have no idea how many others have in the past," she argued, pushing past him.

Declan swore under his breath when he saw Snips standing by a filmy curtain that opened to a room he would prefer to shut down, but keeping the room available at all times was an ironclad clause in the contract he'd signed to get the club.

The imp looked at Maggie as if she was a piece of filth he'd find on the bottom of his shoe. A warning rumble moved up Declan's chest and left his lips before he could think twice.

Snips looked from Declan to Maggie and back to Declan. His knowing look was also a warning.

Demons and witches didn't mix, and now Snips had figured out that Declan had mixed very well with Maggie.

"The human girl is in there and looking very uneasy," Snips reported, ignoring Maggie's presence. "The boy with her appears to be content to stay there. So far, there has been no trouble, and Elena has been instructed to serve them no drinks."

"Who else is in there? Or should I say, what else?" Maggie demanded.

Snips hesitated.

"Tell her," Declan ordered harshly. "Who is in there?"

The imp's response was reluctant. "Wreaker is there with several ladies. Otherwise, the room is empty."

Declan looked away in hopes Maggie wouldn't see his reaction, but he wasn't fast enough. Her eyesight was more than good enough, even in the dark surroundings.

"Who is Wreaker?"

"My cousin." He gestured for Snips to get out of there fast. He didn't know what the witch might decide to do to the imp if she believed in the axiom *Kill the messenger*. Snips wasted no time disappearing.

"Your cousin the incubus?" Her moonstone pendant started gleaming with an eerie light that lit up their little corner.

"Let me go in first."

But she already had her hand on the curtain and was pushing it aside. "Ladies first, remember?"

"Please remember my request not to wreck my club again, okay?" He followed her in.

Declan was familiar with this room, although he preferred to stay out of it unless there was trouble. Unfortunately, trouble erupted in here more frequently than in any other room in the club.

Large privacy booths along the walls gave couples, or more, seclusion to indulge in their wildest fantasies. Healers were kept on call for when the games got out of hand.

He kept close to Maggie's back while scanning the room for his cousin.

Red filmy curtains sectioned off the booths and tables, while almost naked waitresses circulated with trays of drinks, most of them mixed with potent aphrodisiacs.

As he expected, Wreaker held court in one corner, his large body sprawled on a red velvet couch while several females watched him with rapt attention. Mick sat nearby, looking as if he were mentally taking notes of what the incubus was saying. A very unhappy Courtney sat next to Mick. He shrugged her off every time she plucked his sleeve and said something to him. Clearly, she wanted to leave and he didn't.

"That son of a whore."

Declan didn't miss the dangerous magick thrumming

through Maggie's body. "Umm, Maggie, could you dial it back just a little?" he murmured. He tried to loosen his hand from her tight grip but was unable to do so. "Even demons need to breathe."

She took a deep breath. "I'll kill him."

"Things will get out of hand fast if you make a scene, so don't kill him until after you leave the club." He didn't like that Wreaker noticed their entrance. Judging by the avid interest on his face, trouble could easily follow.

There was nothing his cousin liked more—other than willing female flesh—than creating trouble. A pissed-off witch would be the perfect target for him.

"Cuz! Good to see you. Our lovely Elena over there said you weren't in tonight, but I found that hard to believe, since the club is so important to you." His obsidian eyes glowed with dark light. "Come join us."

Courtney's head snapped around, her face a mixture of pleasure and relief followed by a hint of guilt. "Maggie! Declan!" She started to get up, but Mick grabbed hold of her hand.

"Hey, you're with me, remember?" he reminded her with a snap in his words. He stared at Maggie with open threat. "You don't need that bitch anymore."

Declan shook his head. "Boy, you've done it now, because if I don't take you apart, she will."

Mick threw back his head and laughed, an edge of howling in the sound. "Her? All she's good for is spreading her legs. I bet you've had her more than once, haven't you?"

Courtney gasped and struggled to free herself, but she could only cry out in pain when he tightened his grip.

Declan looked at Maggie. "It's my club, my rules, so feel free to hurt him first."

The witch lit up like a Christmas tree. "Do you know that is the nicest thing anyone's ever said to me?" She rolled her shoulders and shook out her hands again.

Wreaker straightened up more, watching the two. "Is there something I don't know?" He flashed Maggie a dazzling smile.

She rolled her eyes. "Honestly, Declan, I can't believe that Neanderthal is related to you. I'd sure hate to see the rest of your family tree." She dismissed the other demon and advanced on Mick, who stood up and stared at her with menace in his manner.

"I knew you'd try to mess up her mind," he told Maggie.

"I didn't want to come here," Courtney cried out. "Last night, Mick said we were going to a rave. But when we left tonight, he said no, we'd come here. Declan had said we couldn't get in, but Mick said he could get us in." She stared at what was her former boyfriend with fear in her eyes, "I—he took my cell phone so I couldn't call you."

Maggie stared at Courtney's bare neck. Now she knew why the tracker had failed. Mick had taken it from Courtney and somehow managed to dampen its use. Did he know what it was for?

This close up, she could see the beginning of a bruise on Courtney's cheek. Oh, yeah, she really hated this guy. She was looking forward to making sure he'd never hurt a girl again.

"You might want to stay out of the way," she advised Wreaker, who straightened up and watched her with an odd look in his eyes. While he knew she was a Hellion Guard, he obviously hadn't taken her very seriously. Until now. He moved off to one side, taking his harem with him. The women wasted no time exiting the room.

Declan spoke quietly into the air. A moment later, a familiar giant guarded the doorway. "No one gets in or leaves," Declan told him.

Maggie smiled. "I could really get to like Anton." But for now, her target was the asshole in front of her. She stared at his hand, which still held Courtney's wrist in a bruising grip. "Release with pain to him and none to her. *Now*."

Mick yelped as fire encircled his hand. The moment he let go of Courtney, she ran to Maggie, who gently pushed the girl behind her.

"What the fuck are you?" Mick started to advance on her.

Maggie's smile just got wider. "Oh, honey, I'm the witch your mother, if you even had one, would have warned you about."

She walked forward until she could wrap her hand around his throat. She kept her hold just tight enough and kept walking until she had him up against the wall. Mick's words gurgled deep inside his throat as he struggled against her.

"Don't bother talking," she said in a low voice, squeezing her fingers just enough to get him to shut up. "I just love it when they get all stupid." She glanced over her shoulder at Declan and then returned her attention to Mick.

"I... can't... breathe," Mick rasped.

"Ask me if I care." Maggie felt her face tighten with

the fury that rippled through her body. "You called me a bitch. You lured an innocent girl into thinking you loved her," she spoke in a deadly soft voice. "You played the part of the bad boy because you knew, with her past, she was ripe for the picking. You brought her to a club that is strictly forbidden."

With each word, her hand tightened around his throat. "But you know what really pisses me off? You put your hands on her." She ignored his gasps for air.

"You're killing him!" Courtney cried. "Please, I don't want you to get into trouble."

"By the time I finish, he'll wish I had—and don't worry, nothing's going to happen to me."

"Do me a favor and leave something for me," Declan spoke up. "I'd like to ask him a question before you tear him to pieces. Just how the fuck did you get into my club?"

Maggie loosened her grip just a fraction and arched an eyebrow at Mick. "Answer fast. My patience is very limited."

Mick shrugged, showing a bit of bravado. "A guy told me what to do. He said it would be easy to get in. And it was."

Declan and Maggie looked toward a corner of the room.

"Not me." Wreaker held up his hands in surrender. "This is the only club where I have any fun. No way I'd want to be banned from here."

Maggie tipped her head to one side when a soft gleam flickered off Mick's chest. She reached out and snatched a medallion from around his neck without caring if she left a welt behind. She held it up, studying the sigil shifting across the metal.

Declan looked over her shoulder. "Demon made," he said softly. "By wearing that, he wouldn't appear to be human to the bouncers here, so he could get in without any problems." He took the medallion from her. "I'll find out where this came from."

Maggie knew whoever gave Mick the charm would find himself in a heap of trouble. She'd let Declan have that fun. She was already in the midst of her own.

"I paid good money for that!" Mick argued, trying to grab it back, but he faltered when Declan's demon side appeared. Flame seemed to flicker over Declan's skin and leap from his eyes. The room's temperature rose by a good twenty degrees. "What the fuck are you?"

"Something that makes sure assholes like you don't last long."

"Enough chitchat." Maggie focused back on Mick after taking a moment to admire her fiery demon lover. "Turnabout's fair play. I'd also like to know what you are, because I'm positive you're not totally human."

"What do you mean, I'm not human?" He tried to fight her hold but found it was all in vain. "Just because you're a witch and he's something else doesn't mean I'm a freak like any of you."

Maggie released him and stepped back as he fell to the floor. He slowly stood up, rubbing his throat, which was reddening by the second.

She got in Mick's face. "Then I guess there's only one place for scum like you." She pulled her cell phone out of her pocket and punched in her speed dial. "Hi, I've got a package pickup at Damnation Alley. We'll be in the parking lot."

The moment she disconnected, she punched in

another number. "Hey, Syb. I'm sending someone to you for a chat. And I'll be there later. Thanks!"

"I'm not going anywhere with you," Mick said, regaining his courage. "You're not a cop, so you can't make me. That's kidnapping, and I'll press charges so you're in jail until you're an old lady."

"No, I'm not a cop. I'm worse than any cop you've ever dealt with in your short lamentable life because I don't have to play by their rules. Trust me, they won't care about you, nor will they believe I kidnapped you, so don't try that story with me, bub. I'm also older than you could ever guess."

She shook her head. "It's amazing that everyone says they're not going with me, but they still do, willing or not. You have a choice, Mick. You can walk out of here on your own two feet, or I will toss you out of here, which would involve bruises at best and broken bones at worst. Declan doesn't like having his club messed up, so I suggest we do the adult thing and walk out of here."

By now, Mick was doing his best to keep out of her reach.

"I'm serious, Mick. If you screw with me, I will screw with you—and my way is very painful."

"Don't bother asking for help from me or anyone else in the club," Declan advised the boy as Mick looked in his direction with a silent plea. "Especially when we leave this room. Some of my clientele might offer to assist you, but they would do it only for their own benefit. Trust me, their plans wouldn't be anything you'd like." His eyes turned to molten silver.

Mick turned to Wreaker, whose eyes now sizzled like charcoal. "Sorry, kid, you're not my type, but I can set you up with a revenant who enjoys fresh meat every now and then. You look like you'd provide him with a tasty meal."

Courtney grabbed hold of Maggie's arm. "Can you get my cell from him?" she whispered fiercely.

"Don't expect to get it back any time soon." She plucked it out of Mick's jacket pocket and secured it. She shoved Mick hard enough that he almost lost his balance. "Just move."

The sound of applause came from the side of the room.

"Brava, witch!" Wreaker's handsome face was wreathed in a broad smile as he leaned back in an artful slouch while clapping his hands. "You are truly a lovely sight to behold. Beauty and violence, hand in hand. I had no idea members of the Hellion Guard were so comely." He sketched a low bow. "If only I'd met you before my cousin did. I think we would make an excellent pair, what with your fighting skills and my good looks."

Maggie shot him a *You have got to be kidding* expression. "We'd make a great pair only if I turned you into a mud slug, because it's obvious you're extremely annoying." She planted her hand against Mick's back and gave him a push. He walked without any further argument. Courtney remained close on Maggie's heels.

"Cuz." Wreaker reached out to halt Declan before he followed them. "As sexy as she is, she's also poison for you," Wreaker told him. "She's a Guard, Declan. If push came to shove, she'd destroy you as quick as you can blink an eye. The Guard would be happy if we were all gone. So don't shit a brick if she decides she wants nothing more to do with you."

"Thanks for the family chat, Wreaker," Declan said, brushing past. "And *cuz,* if you ever bring a human back here again, even more so an underage human, I will make sure you never leave the deepest and darkest realm I can find, where exquisite pain will be the least of your worries."

Maggie ignored the suggestive remarks as she escorted Mick through the club to the exit. And did her best not to laugh, since most of them were directed at Mick. She heard Courtney whimper and keep a tight hold on her waistband, trailing her like a chick following a mama hen. After tonight, she doubted the girl would do anything to get into trouble for a very long time.

Mick paled when a vampire swept in front of him, dropping fang and revealing eyes red with hunger.

"He's too anemic for you," Maggie said, grabbing Mick's arm and pulling him around the vampire.

"Tell me you wish my assistance, human, and I will kill the Guard for you," the vampire said.

Maggie conjured up a needle-sharp stake and spun around. "Do you really want to get into it with me? Because I wouldn't mind dusting you." When she didn't receive a reply, she continued on until they were outside.

A black SUV sat with its engine running near the entrance. The creatures lined alongside the building waiting to get into the club were properly subdued, as if they knew just what waited inside the vehicle. The Hellion Guard didn't need shiny decals on their transportation nor did they wear fancy patches on their clothing to identify themselves. And yet it was apparent who they were and what kind of justice they dealt.

It was an unspoken secret that the Guard was

everywhere—and woe be to any creature that messed with them.

Courtney squeaked when Frebus climbed out of the driver's seat. He shook himself lightly, his thick blond fur settling into place while his pink eyes surveyed the parking lot. He grinned, showing his razor-sharp teeth.

"Is there a reason why you can't go out and have a bitchin' time like anyone else, Mags?" he asked, walking around to the rear and opening the back. "How much of the place did you mess up this time?"

"Just the kid here." She pushed Mick forward. "Here's your package. When you get back to the compound, hand him over to Sybil. She knows he's coming."

Mick spun around, his arm cocked back and ready to punch her in the face. Before he could move his arm any further, Maggie flipped him around and had him on the ground with her foot resting against his throat. He coughed and choked.

"You just don't listen, do you?" Her magick sparked around her. "I could make fireworks go off inside you. So I suggest you get up and behave yourself because Frebus doesn't have my patience." She stepped back and watched him struggle to his feet.

Mick started to limp over to the SUV.

"Wait a minute." Courtney edged around Maggie and walked over to Mick, who turned around to face her.

He smirked at her. "Can't get enough of me, can you? Too bad you're nothing more than a little kid."

She placed her hand on his shoulder as if she was going to hug him, and then she quickly raised her knee to connect with his groin. Mick's mouth opened in an O of pure pain.

"You asshole," she snarled. "Eat shit and die."

Mick's mouth opened and closed like a fish out of water before he crumpled to his knees.

"Now that's nasty." Maggie commented serenely.

Frebus walked over and grabbed Mick by his collar, lifting him easily to his feet. He threw the boy into the back of the SUV and slammed the door with the boom of heavy metal.

"Good for you, kid." He sketched Courtney a salute and got in the SUV and drove off.

"What is he?" Courtney tugged on Maggie's arm.

"One of my team members. Frebus is really an old softie, but no reason to let Mick think so." Maggie lightly grasped the girl's chin and lifted her face so she could see it better under the sodium-vapor lights.

"I'd say the son of a whore should pay for that bruise, but I think you already took care of that." She smiled briefly. "I hope you enjoyed your much-deserved revenge. But you're still grounded for the next hundred years."

"Why did you tell him you're a hedgehog when I couldn't say it?" Courtney asked, smart enough not to say anything about the grounding.

"Because I wanted to make sure to put the fear into him, plus he'd find out in there anyway."

"Are you taking her out to the compound?" Declan asked.

"It's too late to get a baby-sitter, and no way can I ask you to baby-sit her, so yes, she's going with me." She cut a quick glance at the girl to make sure she wasn't watching and then blew him a kiss. *Later*, she mouthed.

As Maggie drove off, she noticed Snips had come out and stood by Declan's side with a proprietary air.

"I'm really in trouble, aren't I?" Courtney asked, bringing her back to the moment at hand. The teen slumped in the passenger seat, not even looking out the window.

"What part of *grounded for the next hundred years* don't you understand?" Maggie punched the Viper's accelerator, ready to catch up with Frebus.

"Knowing you, you'll find a way to keep me alive that long just to make me suffer."

Maggie started laughing, feeling freer than she had since she first realized what had happened to Courtney.

"I'm sure I can find a way. For now, consider that every privilege you think you have has been revoked." As she spoke the words, she realized just what it meant.

Maggie sounded just like a mom.

Chapter 17

MAGGIE WATCHED COURTNEY'S FACE AS MAGGIE'S CAR crossed the invisible shield that protected the compound.

"This is magick?" Her mouth dropped open. "I said the word! You're a witch." She squealed with delight as she danced around. "How come I can say it now?"

"Because you're in a place where all is magick, so it doesn't matter. Once we leave here, you'll have your old alternate vocabulary again."

She parked the car and waited for Courtney to bounce out. "But there are rules you have to follow. No staring, no screaming, no calling anyone a monster—and you obey everything I say. Trust me, this isn't a good place to break any rules."

When they reached the entrance kiosk, Maggie stopped long enough to sign in and pick up a visitor medallion for Courtney. "Do you know what Mick did with the necklace I gave you?"

"He said he could get good money for it. He gave it to someone at the club," she mourned. "This creepy guy told him it was valuable."

"Don't worry about it. Whoever has it will discover it's not what they thought it was." She knew anyone not associated with the Guard would find that the necklace was nothing more than cheap metal. How she loved the safeguards that were always in place.

Maggie had to keep grabbing Courtney's arm as the

girl tended to wander away, staring at the creatures that bustled about. "Remember my rule about not staring? It's also known as rude."

"But I've never seen anything like this," Courtney explained, her head almost spinning around as she tried to take it all in. "How many ferrets are there here?" She pointed at a silver one that flashed by.

"More than you can count. They're our messengers. And don't get in their way. They will run you over. Are you hungry? We offer pretty much anything you can think of here." She gestured toward the building holding the dining halls.

"No, I'm good." Courtney had to be pulled along as she scanned the grounds. She finally dug in her heels, forcing Maggie to stop. "I think I've figured it out. It's because of what almost happened at Declan's club. That's why you taught me to fight, wasn't it?"

Maggie looked at Courtney's face, seeing fear in the young features. She thought of all the girl had lost: her family and home, the boy she thought loved her, and if Maggie didn't do her job, she could lose her very life.

"We will talk," she said softly. "I promise you will know everything. But right now I have to see what's going on with Mick. I'll take you to my quarters. You can take a shower and borrow some clean clothing, because... well, you smell like demon."

"Demon?"

Maggie steered her around a cluster of trolls who looked at the duo with curiosity.

"What is this place?"

"Where I live and work. A lot of it you don't need to know about, and you're best off not knowing."

Maggie settled Courtney in her rooms and left Elle to keep an eye on things.

"Does it have to stay here?" Courtney asked, gaping as the spider popped off Maggie's skin and skittered up to her web. The girl looked as if she wanted a shoe to smash Elle with.

"Tell the girl I do not harm humans," Elle said demurely, her ruby eyes flashing.

"I'll be back as soon as I can." Maggie pointed out the TV remote and controls for her CD player. "All I ask is that you don't leave my suite. That medallion you're wearing lets them know you're a visitor here, and it also ensures you can't enter all the buildings. But don't think of it as absolute protection."

"You don't have to worry about that." Courtney plopped down on the couch. "I'm totally finished walking on the wild side." She looked up. "I don't have to see Mick again, do I?"

Maggie looked at the forlorn expression on Courtney's face. She knew no girl should go through so much in such a short time. She hated to think what Courtney's reaction would be when she found out a Mayan priest had her on the menu to be sliced and diced.

"No, never again. Think of him as a bad dream that won't be revisiting you."

Maggie held up her hand in a *wait a second* gesture and ducked into her bedroom. She returned with a large cream-colored teddy bear in her arms and set him in Courtney's lap.

The teen almost crawled up the back of the couch. "What does he do?"

"Nothing. He's just there for you to hug. He's only a toy, Courtney." She leaned down and dropped a kiss on top of her head. "Sometimes the best magick isn't magick at all." With that she left.

"Mal's busting a gut you brought a human here." Meech met Maggie as she reached what she called Sybil's lair, even if the lovely elf wasn't the only interrogator in there.

"I call it not having a choice. Good childcare's not easy to come by." She pulled open the door and stepped inside. She paused and leaned against the wall. "What else is there?"

He grimaced. "He's also wondering what's going on between you and the demon."

"Demon as in Declan." The pit of her stomach warmed at just saying the name. Was she turning into one of those moonstruck heroines in a romance novel or what?

"That's the one. The girl shouldn't be here."

She felt her face tighten with remembered anger. "The girl was taken to an underground preternatural club, and I'm convinced the one who took her would have gladly sold her to the first skin trader he encountered. That bastard had an agenda, and I mean to find out what it was."

"Hey, keep all that temper for him, then," Meech teased. "I did hear the kid took out the guy's gonads."

Nothing like laughter to relax the body. "She did me proud, Meech. I honestly thought she was going to hug him and cry all over him. Instead, she let him have it where it did the most good. She may only be fifteen, but she's got grit I didn't see in her at first. And it's a good thing, because she's going to need it. How's the baby doing?"

His ugly face wreathed in a broad smile. "Great. She eats more than I do. She'll be a fine Guard one day."

"She might take after her mother and become a weaver or a spell caster," Maggie said. "She's got the world in front of her, Meech." She pushed away from the wall and started down the hallway with her team member walking beside her.

"I saw the thug Frebus brought in," he told her. "Frebus said you felt something was off about him, and it seemed that way to me, too. Forensics should have something for you soon. Sybil's in Room Two with him now. First thing the asshole did was try to hit on her." He chuckled. "She set him straight real fast."

Maggie shook her head. "You'd think he would have learned his lesson after Courtney."

"You don't call. You don't write. Why the Hades do I keep you around?" A door slammed against the wall, and Mal waddled into the hallway. His glare was directed at Maggie.

"I didn't want to bother you until I knew something for sure."

"And that's why the girl's in your quarters when she shouldn't even be here?" He pushed past them.

"We both know this is the safest place for her, and no way I'd leave her home alone while I was here." She ignored the moaning sounds coming from the cells below, although one drawn-out sound almost made her jump.

"Banshee," Meech said. "Tried to take out a village, and the compound in Ireland didn't think they should keep it there." He smirked and coughed out a laugh. "I sent them a water dragon in return. Let them deal with that fucker."

Mal puffed away on his ever-present cigar. He made an abrupt turn and pushed open the door with Maggie and Meech following.

Instead of a two-way mirror, they had an entire wall to peek into the interrogation room, making them feel as if they were in there, although Mick couldn't see them. Maggie could tell by the slight tilt of Sybil's head that she was aware of their presence.

Mick sat slouched in his chair, one arm draped over the back, while he faced Sybil with a smirk on his face.

Maggie was pleased to see the bruises on his throat and that when he spoke his voice was a little raspy.

"Why Courtney, Mick?" Sybil asked in a soft voice that invited confidences. "You're nineteen, good-looking, and you like to party hard. So why a fifteen-year-old virgin?"

"I felt sorry for her. I mean, look at her. She needed someone to show her a good time, and I could do it." He preened. "You didn't see that foster home she was in. It was more like a prison, and she hated it there."

"That doesn't tell me why." Sybil's wings fluttered with the calming scent of lavender.

"It didn't affect him," Maggie murmured, leaning forward and almost touching the invisible barrier. "Usually it relaxes the suspect, but he hasn't changed his position."

"You know all I gotta do is call the cops and all your skanky asses will be in jail for kidnapping," he told Sybil. "So I took an underage kid to a club. It's not like it hasn't been done before. Courtney's not all sweet and innocent the way she makes Maggie think she is. And what the hell are you, anyway, with the freaky wings and purple face?"

"Nothing you need to worry about. We're just curious why you chose her. She isn't your usual type, is she?"

"What does it matter? Some guy paid me to pick her up six months ago. Said all I had to do was keep an eye on her. Only way to do that was to date her. At least she's cute, but yeah, not someone I want to spend a lot of time with. I'd get texts with suggestions where to take her."

"Bingo," Maggie whispered. "The raves."

"Do you mean like the raves?" Sybil picked up on what Maggie wanted to know. "Why would they want you taking her to raves?"

"To keep an eye on her." He shifted around in the chair, lifting his hand to pluck at his T-shirt neckline. "Can't you turn on some air in here or something?"

"What do you know about the raves?" she pushed.

"Just that weird stuff goes on there. Kids disappear." He shrugged, clearly not considering it important.

"That tells me you know more about the supernatural than you let on." Sybil jotted down a few notes on the paper in front of her.

"Yeah, so?" He fidgeted again. "I'm serious. Turn on the AC or something." His face looked flushed.

"Oh, no." Maggie started for the door with Meech on her heels. She whipped open the door to the interrogation room and grabbed Sybil, almost dislocating the elf's shoulder as she threw her out of the room.

"What the fuck is going on?" By now, Mick's face was the color of a ripe tomato and looked swollen. He started to get up and then fell back. "What are you doing?"

Maggie exited the room and slammed the door behind her, leaning against it. A moment later, a loud pop was heard followed by a squishy sound.

"He was booby trapped," she said, disgusted with herself for not thinking of it sooner. "That way, if he started to say too much, he'd be pureed." She turned around and glanced in the small window. "Not as bad as that Bloater, but bad enough."

"So what do the raves have to do with Courtney?" Sybil asked.

"Maybe nothing more than what he said. Just a way to check on her." She turned to Mal. "Nothing else about Zouk and his team?"

He shook his head. "The trackers couldn't find any kind of scent. Two teenagers turned up dead in the next town over. Same thing as before. They were nothing but empty husks. The local sheriff managed to keep the parents from seeing the kids by saying they should remember them the way they were."

"Then we track down the raves. There's got to be a connection. Maybe the kids are early sacrifices for the final ritual." She threw up her hands. "As if I know what I'm talking about. Knowledge of the Mayan culture has never been high on my reading list." She paced back and forth and then stopped. "Wreaker."

"The incubus?" Mal asked. "How do you know him?"

"Along with being a total party animal, he's Declan's cousin. If anyone would know about these raves, he would. Plus Mick was with him at Damnation Alley. Who's to say he wasn't Mick's contact?" She didn't want to think that was it, because it would bring Declan under closer scrutiny of the Guard. "I don't think we'll be able to bring him in unless we can prove he's had something to do with one of our cases."

"Don't quote the law to me, witch!" Mal snapped. "Just find a way to learn what he might know." He left the building trailing a cloud of noxious smoke.

"You should have known the demon would get you into trouble," were Meech's parting words.

"What about you?" Maggie turned to her friend. "Do you have anything to say?"

Sybil's lips tipped upward. "Is he good?"

Maggie couldn't hold back her chuckle. "On a score of one to ten, he's probably in the millions."

Sybil faked a swoon. "You have all the luck!"

"What about Elweard?"

Together they walked out of the building.

"Let's just say that Elweard cares more for his grooming than he cares for a gorgeous elf. Are you staying here tonight?"

"Since it's so late, I might as well. For all I know, Courtney's already taken over my bed. Something tells me getting her up would be like waking a boggart. And it's a well-known fact that Humphrey refuses to get up before noon if he doesn't have to."

She looked longingly at the dining hall with the idea of a sugar-laden bedtime snack. But the late hour, coupled with the sudden loss of the adrenaline that had fueled her body for too long, had her aching for ten or twenty hours of sleep instead.

She thought of Declan and wondered what he was doing. The club would remain open until dawn, so he'd be busy taking care of his business.

Maggie and Sybil parted company at Maggie's door.

"Let's meet for breakfast," Sybil suggested.

"Okay, I'll meet you at eight."

When Maggie entered the parlor room, she found the lights dimmed and Courtney curled up on the couch with her arms around the teddy bear.

"A warrior one moment. A child the next." Maggie retrieved a light blanket from her room and draped it over Courtney, along with carefully nestling a pillow under her head.

Maggie was never so happy as when she crawled into her bed and wrapped her arms around her own pillow.

It wasn't Courtney who cluttered her mind as she burrowed under the covers. It was the fiery image of Declan that had her smiling as she drifted off.

"This is different." Maggie turned around to study her surroundings with great interest. *"You make sleep so interesting."*

"I thought you'd like to be at the top of the world." Declan spoke, walking out of a kitchenette. A pair of black silk pajama bottoms hung low on his hips.

"And we are." She walked over to the wall of windows that overlooked a forest. *"Whatever made you think of a tree house? Is it somewhere you've come before?"*

"Off and on." He brought in two glasses of wine and set them on a rough-hewn table.

"I've got to say you have these dreams down to a science." She took a seat on the couch next to him. *"Even the wardrobe."* She glanced down at the soft blue, silk-and-lace ankle-length gown that flowed over her body.

"Personally, I would have preferred you naked, but I had an idea you would object if I brought you here in that fashion." He picked up the glasses and handed one to her.

"Why are we here?"

"Privacy." He looked around the warm and cozy room. *The perfect hideaway, even in a dream realm. "No teenagers. No imps demanding my attention. It's just my beautiful Margit and me."* Amusement chased across his features.

"No sex-maniac cousins," she added, half turning on the couch to face him. *"I like that. As long as we keep to one rule."* She wasn't about to ignore the opportunity that Declan set up for them. *"No discussing the Mayans, previously mentioned teenagers, succubae, the club, you name it. Just us."*

She picked up one of the wineglasses and dipped her forefinger into the liquid. She bathed his lips with the wine and then dipped her finger in again and did the same with her own before she leaned forward and kissed him as she blindly returned the glass to the table.

The wine was dry and tart, the perfect counterpoint for a kiss that rapidly turned sizzling.

"Beautiful." The word was a breath of air against her mouth. *"I missed you."*

She smiled. *"You just saw me, what, a few hours ago?"*

"Not the same when we have company." He pulled her on top of him and then rolled them over so he was on top.

Maggie laughed as the couch suddenly morphed into a large bed piled high with pillows.

"And I thought I was gifted with magick. I could get

used to this." She angled up so she sat on his hips, her gown flowing around his legs.

"Not all in my bloodline can create dream realms or manipulate what's within them. I like to keep my hand in."

"Yes, I noticed," she purred, shimmying her hips just enough to keep his attention. Not that she had to work at it too hard. Declan's interest was right there. "A world all our own." She rolled off him and lay alongside him, draping one leg over his. She rested one hand against his chest, feeling the heat radiating off his skin.

"I was thinking about you when I fell asleep," she confessed.

He took her hand and threaded his fingers through hers. "I like the sound of that. I wanted more time with you. I couldn't stop thinking about that day in your bed. At least the part before we were so rudely interrupted."

"So you decided if we couldn't be together for real, we'd have something just as good."

"For now." His eyes turned dark, the flames glimmering within.

Maggie idly ran her hand over his chest, enjoying the skin-to-skin contact. She lost herself in his gaze.

"I don't want to talk," he said huskily. "I want to…" He bent down and nibbled on her earlobe. "…ravish you. To make love to you until you scream my name." He bit down a bit harder.

"Let's try screaming together."

Declan pushed down his pants and pushed up her gown. He brushed his fingers across her center, finding it damp and inviting. He inserted two fingers, rubbing them against her clit until she mewed and arched her body, pushing down on him.

Maggie returned the favor by wrapping her hand around his cock. "Mine." She let her body and facial expression echo the word as she rose up, then down on his erection. She pulled off her gown and tossed it to one side.

Declan's hands spanned her narrow waist and then moved up to cup her breasts. "Mine." But his eyes told her he was talking about the whole package. He pulled her down to him, licking each nipple and then softly blowing on them.

She gasped at the exquisite heat that raced through her body and moved her hips, rising and lowering them in a rhythm that sang a sensuous song inside her head. She hungered for more, the need to wrap herself around Declan and never let go. Greed roared in her veins as she felt Declan's body tighten beneath her. Wanting to prolong the moment, she slowed her motion and cupped his sac, gently squeezing the velvety skin.

"Damn!" he rasped, his hands digging into her waist so hard he left finger marks.

She allowed it when he started to direct her move-ments, and this time, she felt the world momentarily turn black as they came together, each shouting the other's name.

—⁓—

The only word that came to mind was "satisfied." Declan was happy to lie there with Maggie in his arms and inhale the sensual scent of her skin. He wanted his time with her to be extended as long as possible before their individual worlds intruded again.

A shift in the air above alerted him. He snapped open his eyes, looking into eyes that reflected the deeper realms of Hades.

"Hello, cuz." Wreaker revealed his pearly whites. "Wakey, wakey."

Chapter 18

DECLAN FELT THE SHIFT IN THE REALMS THAT transported him back to his apartment and his bed.

"What the fuck are you doing here?" He was fully prepared to beat the shit out of the incubus, relative or not. He climbed out of bed to do just that.

"Whoa, too much." Wreaker picked up a pair of jeans and threw them at him. "Get dressed. You've been summoned."

Declan pulled them on and accepted a T-shirt the color of blood. He smiled in the back of his mind. And here Maggie thought he wore only black.

"Hurry up." Wreaker wandered around the room, picking up Declan's key ring and setting it back down.

"Who sent you to get me?" Declan feared he already knew the answer.

"Victorio." For the first time, Wreaker's usual flashy grin was missing. "And he wants to see you now. He couldn't get hold of you on the phone."

Declan dropped his shirt. "I don't accept his calls."

"That's not stopping him. He's moving up the career ladder, cuz. We can't afford to ignore him anymore. Not if we want to stay in one piece."

A tingling of unease shot through Declan's body. "What's this about?"

"What do you think? That witch you're fucking." Wreaker held up a dark crystal and tapped it.

Declan was instantly transported to the place he'd fought long and hard to escape.

At least he was fully clothed when he arrived. Ineffective armor, yes, but when facing the one who sired him, he took what he could get.

"How nice to see you, my son." The gravelly voice was as grating as it always had been.

For Declan, looking at Victorio was like looking into a mirror. His father might be over 1,000 years old, but he still looked more like an older brother than an ancient one. The main difference was in the elder's eyes. Victorio's eyes were a deep, dark charcoal that betrayed no emotion. The fire demon wasn't happy unless he was making someone's life miserable.

It appeared to be Declan's turn now.

"I understand your club is turning a nice profit," Victorio commented, pouring wine into two glasses and handing one to Declan.

He sipped the bitter liquid, ignoring the faint hint of sulfur that wafted upward. What he wouldn't give for a shot of Johnny Walker Black Label right then.

Wreaker moved to a nearby doorway and slumped against the wall. Declan wasn't fooled. His cousin might look like the laziest son of a whore in the universe, but he had an excellent sense of self-preservation.

Victorio seated himself in a black lacquered chair. A young female wearing only a filmy skirt was tethered to the leg. She gave Declan a smoldering look while caressing her master's calf. Victorio gestured for Declan to take the seat facing him.

"You have been very busy, my son," he said, drinking his wine. "Making a profit in the club despite the

Hellion Guard witch invading your new domain. And you even protected a human child. Yes, yes," he waved a languid hand, "she shouldn't have been allowed to enter, but I understand she was a tasty morsel." His smile didn't reach his eyes.

"I would have thought you'd be tired of human females," Declan replied. "You always complained they were too frail."

"They are, but they can be amusing. What about witches? Do they have more stamina? How was she, my son?"

Declan needed every ounce of his will power to keep from looking at Wreaker. He was positive the incubus had said just enough to ensure Declan showed up on his father's radar. He also knew that meant Wreaker had done some trading to further his own ambitions.

He was always good at protecting himself.

"I was told to keep her occupied, to find out what I could." *Show no fear. He'd snap your neck and then kiss your cheek, telling you what a good son you could have been.*

"The Guard shouldn't concern themselves with the Mayans." Victorio thrust his empty glass toward his slave, who filled it and carefully placed the glass back in his hand. "The Mayans' activities have nothing to do with them."

"And they have to do with us?" Declan asked facetiously. His smirk disappeared when he saw the look on the elder demon's face. "What do the Mayans offer that you want so badly?"

"Nothing that concerns you, my son." Victorio peered at him over the rim of his glass.

The wine turned to acid in Declan's stomach. "What exactly are you saying?" One thing he always hated was a roundabout conversation where no one could be nailed for making a rock-solid statement.

"That the wording in treaties between demonkind and the Mayans can be changed for many reasons."

"I realize secrets are impossible around our kind, but why would we bother with the Mayans and a sacrifice that would ensure the return of destruction to all but them?" Declan said. "When we could be in danger also?"

Victorio smiled. "That would never happen. As to bothering with them, would that be so bad? Those days were filled with feasting, song, and blood. While ritual anthropophagus was rare, cannibalism did happen back then." He appeared lost in memories. "It was a fascinating time."

By now, even Declan's blood held a bitter taint.

"Why didn't I ever hear these stories?" he asked curiously.

"There was no reason. Also with you being a half-breed, there were many parts of our history you didn't need to learn."

As a child, Declan had been hurt by his father's dismissal of a heritage Declan couldn't help. Now he was grateful he had the human half to temper his demon heritage. He knew enough of his relatives that he had no desire to emulate their behavior.

"Yet you're telling me now."

"Only because you have an 'in' with the Guard." Victorio's eyes sliced toward Wreaker. "We thought of sending your cousin, but it didn't take us long to see she would prefer you over him."

Declan had always wished his father would talk to him. Treat him as an equal. Now he realized some wishes shouldn't be granted.

"The club." His mouth suddenly felt dry, as if dust had been poured down his throat. He'd worked damn hard to earn that club, and now he was hearing that all his work was for naught!

Victorio beamed. "A reward in advance. Oh, yes, you've worked hard and gained enough favors to be granted such a boon, but it still would have been years before you could rise that high. You're lucky that you have relatives with the right connections.

"The witch killing Ratchet sped up the process, which only helped us. While she never admitted to destroying him, we know she was behind his death. No loss there— all in all, it was a boon. And it was a simple matter to have the Bloater visit Damnation Alley, bringing her there so the two of you could meet."

If there's ever a time to be sick, this is it. Declan didn't know who he hated more: his father for arranging his life or himself for being so blind he didn't see the truth.

"It should have been me," Wreaker muttered. "I could have gotten things done a lot faster."

"If you can't shut up, leave," Victorio snapped. "All you've done is create more problems than solutions. Declan may not be a full-blood, but he seems to have the ability to do what I need."

"You mean there's more?" Declan inquired, although he had a fairly good idea what the elder demon wanted. And Declan wasn't about to do it.

"Throw them off the trail. I'll give you documents to show that the ritual is false and someone gave them the wrong information. Once you convince them, they'll release the girl, since they can't be bothered with keeping a human around. They don't appreciate pets the way we do."

He ran his hand over his slave's hair, which flowed in deep-purple waves down to her hips. "Isn't she lovely? Very attentive, too." She looked up at him with adoring eyes.

Please don't give him a blow job while I'm here.

"You *want* the god of destruction returned to this plane? He'll try to take us out, too." Declan always knew when it was a good time to deny his human heritage. This was definitely that time.

"Not all of us."

"Not all the families," Wreaker chimed in.

"*Out.*"

The incubus slid out of the room.

"Did you ever think he might have been adopted?" Declan watched his father and saw the glimmer of anger and tight lines around his finely sculpted face.

"Or snatched from another family." Victorio blew out an exasperated breath. "There are plans in play, Declan. If you do your job, you will have much more than that club. You will be revered. A god in your own right."

Victorio's eyes showed orange flames while the scent of sulfur filled the room. The pet tried to back away from the chair, but her leash didn't give her much room. "If you wish, you can even keep the witch as a pet."

"How in Hades did you make a deal with them?" Declan demanded, setting his glass to one side. No way he'd ever eat or drink again while down here. After all, look what happened to Persephone.

"Treaties were drawn up centuries ago. Just do as I say. Ensure that girl is released so she can fulfill the agreement. Once the sacrifice is completed, we will be the ones in charge and the Guard will be no more."

"Give me the papers. I'll handle it all." One lesson Declan had learned well from his father was the art of falsehoods. He could lie with the best of them.

Victorio's smile of satisfaction would have been a joy to many. For Declan, it only evoked the strong desire that the demon would become someone's pet instead of the other way around.

For now, he'd let his father think he was willing to do what the ancient demon wanted.

Once Victorio realized that his son had double-crossed him, Declan knew he'd have only one choice—a choice that would land him a starring role on *Jerry Springer*.

He'd have to kill his father.

—∾∾—

"Hey! Are you waking up anytime soon? Maggie. Wake up."

Maggie managed to prop open an eyelid. "Go 'way. Dammit, Courtney! I haven't had enough sleep."

"There's a purple person outside who said you have to wake up," the teen whispered. "Do you think I'd look good with her color hair?" She hopped on the side of the bed, sending Maggie bouncing upwards.

"Maggie, get your lovely butt out of bed so we can go to breakfast!" Sybil shouted.

"No, you wouldn't look pretty with that hair color, and honestly, Sybil, I just got to sleep!" That dream realm was too good to leave.

Actually, Declan was much too good to abandon. Why did Courtney have to wake her up? With him around, she'd never need a vibrator again. Except the teenager wasn't about to let her laze in bed and relive every hot and heavy moment.

Sybil appeared in the doorway. She arched an eyebrow and mouthed *Declan?*

"I'm getting up." Maggie pushed Courtney off the bed and got up.

"You said I could borrow something of yours. This is really cute. Can I keep it?" Courtney preened in a French-blue flutter-sleeved top and white Bermuda shorts. "Too bad we don't wear the same size shoe. You have an adorable pair of sandals that would go great with this." She'd clipped her hair up in a loose ponytail.

"I said you could *borrow* some of my stuff. Nothing in that statement meant you could keep it." Maggie blindly pulled clothing from the dresser and her closet, and stumbled into the bathroom. "Give me five minutes."

"I'll give you ten so you can put on makeup," Sybil told her.

"So what are you?" Courtney asked Sybil curiously.

"*Courtney!* Rules."

"It's all right, Maggie. I'm an elf." She proceeded to explain her lineage to a fascinated teenager who looked as if she wanted to take notes.

"At least I can say all the words here," she told Sybil. "Maggie put some spell on me that had me speak all sorts of stupid stuff, because she said I couldn't tell anyone she was a witch." She whooshed. "Before I'd call her something like a frying pan.

"And now I'm here, where everyone is magickal and

I can call them what they are. That's if Maggie tells me what they are. She said I'm not supposed to stare or ask them questions. But jeez, this is like a weird Disneyland. Some have fur, others have scales, or…"

She stared at Sybil's gossamer wings that wafted soothing scents. "And all those ferrets running around. They sound like hyped-up chipmunks. Did you know there was someone outside throwing these balls of fire like baseballs?"

"You left the quarters after I told you not to?" Maggie peeked around the bathroom door.

"Just for a minute. She's got more rules than school ever did," Courtney confided to the elf.

"They're for your protection," Sybil told her. "This is a new world for you."

"No kidding." Courtney moved over to Maggie's dresser and started to rummage through the jewelry box. A movement from Elle had her backing away. "Are we eating soon? I'm starved. They'll have, like, my kind of food here, right? Nothing that's squirmy or crawls?"

"Bacon, eggs, waffles, pancakes, and probably some fancy Danish." Maggie walked out of the bathroom, pulling her lapis tank top down over the waistband of her cargo pants.

Courtney watched wide-eyed as Maggie strapped on a couple of knives and added her handgun. Elle skittered up her arm and took her place decorating Maggie's bicep.

"I thought it was safe here."

"It is, but sometimes you still have to be prepared for anything." Maggie gestured to the door.

"So what do elves do around here?" Courtney asked, latching on to Sybil while Maggie followed. "Can you fly? You always smell so good. Do you wear perfume to do that or sprinkle it on your wings? Are you like pixies? Grant wishes? Are there any guy elves that look like Orlando Bloom?"

Sybil shot Maggie a panicked look. The witch smirked and slowed her steps a bit more. She was enjoying this way too much.

Luckily, Courtney was so focused on Sybil that she didn't stare at the various Guard members they met along the way.

"Food." The girl almost ran to one of the tables. Maggie snagged her by the collar and steered her to a corner.

"No need for a menu. Just let me know what you want," she said.

Courtney thought for a moment. "Coconut pancakes, bacon, and two scrambled eggs?"

"I thought you didn't eat eggs."

"I changed my mind. I'm a growing girl, and I need protein."

"My usual," Sybil told her.

Maggie set up the orders. She almost inhaled her coffee, grateful for the caffeine, while Courtney, for once, sipped delicately.

"Where's Mick? Sharing a cell with something nasty, I hope. The asshole," Courtney muttered. She looked up in time to see Maggie and Sybil exchange looks. She set her coffee cup down. "He's dead, isn't he? Did..." she gulped, "did one of you kill him? Did he do something that made you do it?"

"He is dead, Courtney." Maggie knew she couldn't soften the truth, and it was better the girl know now.

"But not by my hand or Sybil's. I think something had been placed within him so that if he tried to tell us the truth, he'd be destroyed."

Courtney looked down at the table, her fingers loosely wrapped around her coffee mug. "He lied to me. And he planned something horrible for me, didn't he?"

"Yes, he did," Maggie admitted.

"That's why you showed up, pretending to be my cousin. And why you met Mick. You didn't trust him, did you?"

"He was only using you, Courtney," Maggie said gently. "I'm sorry."

Courtney stared at the food that was set in front of her. "It's not over, is it?"

"Let's eat first." Maggie poured warm syrup over her sourdough pancakes. She thought that the girl would pick at her food. Instead, she didn't stop until her plate was empty.

"Men are scum," she pronounced, on her third cup of coffee.

"Always," Maggie and Sybil agreed.

Courtney glared at both of them as if they were teasing her. She relaxed when she realized they were serious.

"So did he like have a heart attack and keel over? Choke and turn blue?" She gurgled with laughter. "Blow up?" She stopped when she saw their faces. "*He blew up?*"

"Like an overfilled balloon. But he choked and turned red and purple first."

Courtney paled and then turned a soft pea-green color. "You're not kidding, are you?"

"I decided I'd tell you the truth from now on," Maggie said, still working on her pancakes.

Sybil waved her hand over the table, and a small glass filled with pale-pink fizzing liquid appeared. "Drink this."

"What is it?"

"It's perfectly safe and will settle your stomach."

Courtney picked up the glass and sniffed the contents. Judging it had to be safe, she downed it quickly. Her color soon returned. "That was really good. So what else aren't you telling me?"

"Mal will have a stroke," Sybil murmured, concentrating on her breakfast of fresh berries and yogurt.

"He's too mean to die," Maggie mumbled, her mouth full of pancake.

"Now what?" Courtney persisted.

Maggie winced at the higher pitch. "Just let me finish my breakfast. We'll get out of here and walk around. I have a baby to see."

By now, Courtney was fidgeting in her seat like a five-year-old child. It wasn't easy for the witch to ignore her, but she did her best. Not even a restless teenager was going to interfere with her meal.

Sybil finished her food first. "I have appointments this morning," she told them and then smiled at Courtney. "You're in excellent hands, sweetie. Maggie may be grumpy at times, but I wouldn't trust anyone else with my life." The scent of lavender and vanilla lingered in the air after she left.

"What does she do?" Courtney inquired. "I can ask that, can't I?"

"She's a counselor." Maggie decided it wouldn't be a good idea to say interrogator.

"Like a psychologist?"

"Sort of."

"But you had her talk to Mick. Not that he probably didn't need a shrink's help," she grumped. "No offense to Sybil, but she looks like Mick could run over her."

"There was a book about a woman named Sybil who had multiple personalities," Maggie said, now finished with her food. She stood up. "Our Sybil doesn't have as many faces as that one, but she can handle the nasties without blinking an eye. Now for some walking. I haven't trained in a while. If I keep that up, I'll turn into a slug." She laughed at Courtney's look of horror. "Not for real."

"How many live here?" Courtney looked around as they left the dining halls.

"About two hundred in all. Five teams of four Guards who cover this part of the country and points south, along with family members and support staff."

"And Guards protect everyone," Courtney guessed. "Even humans like me."

"You're a special case. We generally keep the peace among other races."

"So what's Declan?" She skipped ahead and walked backward in front of Maggie. "I've already ruled out vampire and shape-shifter, and he's too gorgeous to be a troll or gargoyle. No pointed ears, so not an elf like Sybil. What else is there?"

"He's a demon." She enjoyed the girl's reaction.

"You mean like—?"

Maggie nodded. "Actually, he's half fire demon, and the other half is human. If you want to know anything more, you'll have to ask him."

"I think that's enough for now. And you're a witch, complete with wand and cauldron."

"We've updated our look since those days. No pointy hats, ugly black dresses, or striped stockings now. Even my warts are gone." She waved her hands over her face.

Courtney rolled her eyes. "Ha, ha."

"You're taking this all very well," Maggie commented, waving at Meech, who had appeared across the main courtyard. "You've had a lot to process in a short amount of time."

Courtney turned around to walk beside her. "When I was little, my mom used to read me this book of fairy tales that came from around the world," she said softly. "She said that there were many things out there that I might not understand, but if I allowed myself to believe in the impossible, I could have the universe in my hand. There weren't that many supernaturals around, but I knew that didn't mean they didn't exist."

"Yet, you didn't believe me when I first told you what I was," Maggie teased.

"You didn't look like my idea of a witch. And I wasn't thinking pointy hats or warts, either." She skipped to one side when a ferret raced up to Maggie and handed her a small scroll.

"The report you wanted," he told her.

"Thanks, Bickie."

He glanced at Courtney and raised his eyebrows. "Hey, babe." Then he was off.

"Terrific. My former boyfriend was a psychopath, and now a ferret is hitting on me." She mimed gagging. She stopped when Maggie turned the scroll to ash. "What did it say? It was about me, wasn't it?"

She shook her head. "No, it was about Mick."

"You said you'd always tell me the truth."

"And I'm already regretting that notion."

"So what did it say about Mick?" Courtney pressed. "He wasn't human, was he? Not human like me."

"No, he wasn't," she said slowly. She drew a deep breath. "I don't know how anyone missed it, but he had a few drops of demon blood in him. So he lied to us. That's how he got into the club without anyone stopping him."

"I was dating a demon? What did he plan to do with me?" Her voice continued to rise in pitch.

Maggie gripped her arm. "But nothing happened. You need to remember that. And nothing will."

"I don't know what can be any worse than Mick blowing up, unless someone's trying to kill me." Courtney stopped short as the realization of what Maggie *wasn't* saying sunk in. "*Ohmigod!* Someone wants to kill me?"

Chapter 19

COURTNEY BENT OVER WITH HER HANDS ON HER KNEES. "Why would anyone want to kill me?" she gasped. "I can't breathe!" She started to wave her hands around, eyes bugging out, her mouth open to take in air her body seemed to be rejecting.

Maggie conjured up a paper bag and forced it over Courtney's nose and mouth. "Just breathe in and out," Maggie instructed.

The girl pushed it away. "Who wants to kill me? Why?"

Maggie returned the bag to its position and kept her grip tight. "Just breathe."

"Is she all right?" One of the healers paused in her morning yoga workout and came over. "I can take her to the infirmary."

"She's hyperventilating."

"Poor thing." The healer gently rubbed Courtney's back in long, soothing strokes while murmuring therapeutic words under her breath. A few minutes later, Courtney's color returned to normal and she was breathing more naturally.

"Are you feeling all right now?" the healer asked, touching the teen's forehead and cheeks with delicate fingertips. The diminutive shaman turned to frown at Maggie. "What did you say to her to cause this, Maggie? Humans are very fragile."

Maggie held her hands up in surrender. "I'm sorry, Shayla. It's not my fault."

"Do you want to come to the infirmary with me and be checked out?" the healer asked Courtney.

"No, I'm fine. Thank you." She managed a wobbly smile. "This is all new to me."

Shayla didn't look convinced. "Well, if you start feeling faint or anything, you make sure to have Maggie bring you to see me." She shot the witch a warning look. She walked over to pick up her yoga mat and towel, and walked away.

"I haven't had so much attention since the school expelled me." By now, Courtney's face was pink with embarrassment.

"Shayla is very caring and an excellent healer. I'm sorry. I shouldn't have piled so much on you at one time."

"I asked for it. Where are we going now? The dungeon? Do you have torture chambers here?"

"Something a lot more positive. I think even you'll like it." Maggie headed for the bungalows housing mated couples. She stopped at one where a large female with bluish-white skin sat on the front step, rocking a tiny cradle.

"Maggie!" the female called out, her broad smile revealing jagged yellow teeth. "How wonderful you came to visit."

"Hi, Reesa, I came to see our shared baby," she said. "I'm sure you already know about Courtney. Court, this is Reesa, Meech's mate. And this is Atisha." She touched the side of the cradle.

Courtney leaned over. "Wow, she's cute."

Reesa laughed. "Thank you. Her hair's coming in

nicely. I imagine you thought she'd look more like me." Shimmering, sleek white fur covered the baby's face and body.

"Uh, yeah." Courtney perched on the step, fascinated with the cradle's contents. She reached out a tentative finger, laughing when the baby latched onto the digit.

"Don't let her put—"

"Ow!" Courtney stuck her injured finger in her mouth.

"A baby's teeth are very sharp," Reesa explained. "Let me get us some coffee. I assume you also drink it?"

Courtney nodded around her finger. "You could have warned me," she hissed once Reesa was out of earshot.

"I tried. It happened to me once, except my finger was almost taken off."

"It's a good thing I'm off guys, because no way I'd want a baby now. Even if this one is cute."

Maggie and Courtney visited with Reesa and Atisha for an hour, Maggie enjoying the short time of normalcy. They hadn't experienced much of that lately, and she hoped it would cheer Courtney up to spend time with a family. Judging by the teenager's smiles and laughter, it was working.

It was even working for Maggie.

~~~

"You really are going to throw the witch under the bus, cuz?" Wreaker waylaid Declan the moment he stepped inside the club.

After he'd left his father, Declan had escaped his apartment and driven as fast and as far as he could in hopes of blowing the meeting out of his mind. It wasn't until he'd discovered he was halfway to New Orleans that he stopped to grab something to eat.

He had always known his sire was greedy for power. He would never have been surprised if Victorio traded him at a moment's notice, as long as it pushed his father further up the career ladder.

Except this time, a human girl's life was forfeit. Declan had always watched his back before. Now he'd be even more cautious.

"Don't you have a woman to ravage?" he growled, heading for his office.

"Been there, done that. What else did Victorio say?" Wreaker's question was couched in a casual manner, but Declan didn't miss the sharpness in his cousin's eyes.

"Just that the girl is more important than I thought." He noted that Snips was rapidly coming their way. *Did he know all this already? Was he one of Victorio's drones?*

"That kid was too cocky. When things got tough, he had no clue how to handle it. No wonder his inner grenade went off." Wreaker slid into the office ahead of Declan. He immediately went to the bar and fixed himself a drink, and then sunk into a chair. "Once the blood thins, anything can happen."

"He didn't give off any kind of hint he was demon." Declan glanced at the report Snips handed him, relieved to see there were no problems, even with the portal that the loyal Anton was still guarding. "Still no word about Alexi?" he asked in a low voice.

"None. We fear he is truly gone." Snips cast a disapproving eye at Wreaker, who grinned back at him. "It is thought the missing drone is behind Alexi's disappearance. That he took him back through the portal. But we can find no reason why."

'There's always a reason. You just need to find it." Declan signed several forms. "My cousin is not to associate with any females while in the club, nor to have the use of any of the private rooms," he said only for the imp's ears.

Something passed for a smile on Snips's face. "It shall be done." The imp left as quietly as he'd arrived.

"How can you work with that thing?" Wreaker shuddered as he took a healthy swallow of alcohol. "He gives me the creeps."

"He's efficient." Declan searched in the office-size refrigerator and pulled out a bottle of Coke. "I'm very busy, Wreaker. What do you really want?"

The incubus's usual laid-back demeanor changed to the greedy creature he really was. "I don't want to be left behind. I want to share what you'll receive."

"You're blood. You will." Declan welcomed the cold carbonation down his throat.

"You forget how much Victorio hated his sister—all the way up to the day he killed her. He tolerates me barely. But if you put in a good word for me, I'd have a chance." Wreaker waited.

"You'd have a better chance than I do. At least you're pure-blooded." Declan didn't want to think about what was ahead. Time was growing short. Victorio had hinted at that. He also had strongly suggested that his son make sure Maggie abandoned Courtney. Declan doubted that would happen. It was apparent that the comely witch was mother hen to her teenage chick. For someone who didn't consider herself maternal material, she was doing a damn good job of it.

Wreaker pushed his hair away from his face. Declan realized he didn't look as smooth and sexy as usual. Signs of dissipation showed on his features, and his eyes were heavy with fatigue.

"You look like shit. Aren't you getting your quota of women?"

"Fuck off." Even that was said with a weary sigh. "I might not know the whole deal, but I know enough that if the Mayans finish that ritual, there will be hell on earth for sure. Did you read up on the god of destruction, cuz? He doesn't even have a name. There's little information in the records. Not even any drawings on temple walls. All that's known is when he's revived, the world will never know any kind of peace."

"You afraid you'll lose your sex partners?" Declan was tired and well on his way to cranky. Only memories of his time spent with Maggie kept him from snapping Wreaker's neck.

Of course, that could change at any moment.

"I'm afraid of losing the only family member I like," Wreaker admitted. "You, of all people, know that Victorio can't be trusted. It's obvious that you have more than just the usual hard-on for the witch. Thinking with your dick can get you in all sorts of shit. I'm talking about the kind that can get you killed."

He drained the glass and set it down on the table with a thump. He stood up. "Just remember, it's family who stands behind you. She won't." With that, he walked out.

Declan leaned back in his chair. *They only stand behind you if it protects them from being in the line of fire.*

—✦—

"You never think of them having kids," Courtney chattered. "And that Frebus is so adorable. He's like a real, live teddy bear, except with sharp teeth." She looked around with open delight. "This place is so cool."

"O'Malley, when did you turn into a tourist guide?"

Maggie turned to face her boss. Mal managed to share his glower between her and Courtney.

"Courtney, this is Mal, the head man around here. He keeps us all in line."

"I wish," he muttered around his cigar. He frowned at Courtney. "You're not what I expected."

"Cuter?" She'd developed enough immunity during the day that the grumbling gnome didn't frighten her off. "So I understand you're a gnome, but where are your little red cap and blue jacket?"

Maggie closed her eyes, not wanting to watch Mal fly into one of his usual snits.

"Girl, you need a good education in our worlds," he rumbled. "I'm not one of *those* gnomes. You'll never find me in someone's garden—and no way I'd wear one of those damned red caps." His gaze fell on the medallion hanging around her neck, and he leaned forward to finger the metal. "It's not active."

Maggie ignored his accusation. "Of course it is." But she examined it and saw that he was right. "It was active when I picked it up for her."

"I already heard about lover boy turning into confetti. Take her to the infirmary and have her tested. Then both of you come to my office." He ambled off, the smoke coiling behind him.

"What a nasty little man. And what did he mean by having me tested? Tested for what?" Courtney dug in her heels. "Mick turned into confetti? So when he blew up, he blew up in pieces? Ick!"

"I don't know. Yes, he did, and 'ick' is a good description for what happened. Let's see Shayla."

"You keep putting off telling me why someone wants to kill me. Are you ever going to tell me?" Courtney followed her like a good little puppy.

"Yes, but I thought you'd like a nice day first. Plus, I have an idea Mal will lay it all out."

"Terrific. A nasty cigar-smoking gnome looks happy that he'll be giving out bad news to an innocent teenager. How great will that be?" She continued dragging her feet even as Maggie gave her a gentle nudge to quicken her steps.

In no time, Shayla performed a few tests and then took Maggie aside.

"Mal wanted proof that Courtney has Mayan blood," she said in a low voice. "She does, but there's also something else in her blood."

"Please don't tell me she's sick or something!" Maggie rarely experienced fear, but she did right now.

Shayla smiled. "Oh, no, but I saw a very faint trace of demon in her blood. It's probably why her medallion isn't reacting the way it should."

"How could that happen?" Maggie kept her voice low.

"Why not? I have Aztec and Irish blood in my veins. You're Scotch-Irish and Nordic. Courtney's merely a blend the way so many of us are. And think about it. That might be another reason why the demons want her so badly for that ritual."

"Do you realize how Mal will react to this?"

"He's already received the report. I suggest you waste no time going over there."

"Where are you dragging me now?" Courtney appeared in the doorway.

"To the cigar-smoking gnome."

"Gross." But she followed Maggie. "Do you actually do any work here?"

"I'm doing it now. You're my job." What she wouldn't give to roust a nest of revenants or even a man-eating crocodile. They descended into the Dungeon.

"At least I'll finally get the whole story." Courtney stepped inside the Grecian temple and looked around with her mouth open. "How cool."

Maggie didn't bother looking at her boss. She was too busy looking at Declan seated in front of Mal's desk. She didn't need to be psychic to know he was worried about something, but the small smile he gifted her with held the memory of their time in the dream realm.

"Kid, you've got an interesting bloodline," Mal said without greeting, gesturing to two chairs by Declan. "You have any idea of your ancestors?"

"Dad once started a family tree. The papers are in the storage unit. Why?"

Mal looked at each one of them and then focused on Courtney. "What has O'Malley told you?"

"That she's a witch, Declan's a demon, and from everything that's happened, I figured somebody wants to kill me. Although I don't know why." She moved around in her chair.

"You better let me tell her, Mal," Maggie spoke up. "You're not exactly the most tactful."

"Shit, I'm more tactful than any of you," he groused, lighting up another cigar. He offered one to Declan, who politely refused.

Maggie looked at the girl's face. The sullen, smart-mouthed teenager was gone. In the space of twenty-four hours, Courtney had grown up. The last thing Maggie wanted to do now was relate things that no child should learn, but she knew it had to be done. And better from her than from Mal.

"Just tell her!" he barked, causing Courtney to jump.

"Yeah, tell me, Maggie." Her dark eyes pleaded for the whole story. "And don't leave anything out."

"Do you know who the Mayans are?" Maggie began.

"Sure. We went to Mexico when I was little and took one of those corny tours where you see these big stone temples and stuff." Courtney laughed. "So, what, you think I'm some long-lost Mayan priestess or something? Is that why you wanted blood tests?"

"Not exactly, although you do have some Mayan blood in you. But we already knew that, and that was why Mick chose you. There's a small cult of Mayan priests who've been around for centuries. They plan to bring back one of their gods."

"And marry me off?"

"More like use you for a ritual sacrifice in order to bring that god back. He's the god of destruction, and his return would mean pretty much the end of the world as we know it. We need to keep you safe past the night they plan this ritual."

She watched the girl closely. "Are you going to hyper-ventilate again?" Courtney shook her head. "Throw up?"

"Seriously thinking about that," she said shrilly.

"Well, don't. Mal hates messes," Maggie told her. "Courtney, I know it's been a lot to take in."

"There's more," Declan spoke up.

"*More*? Some crazy priest is going to kill me, and there's more?"

Maggie leaned over and took her hand, squeezing it gently.

"Is this why you're here?" she asked Declan.

He nodded. "My father summoned me today. After Mal heard what was said in the meeting, he felt I should come out." He looked at Maggie. "Victorio knows all about Courtney. He was the one who sent Mick to her. I heard what happened to Mick here, and my father set that up, too."

He took a deep breath, clearly not wanting to continue.

"He... has a deal with the Mayan priests in the works. They gain the god of destruction, and he gains power." He glanced at Courtney with sorrow giving his eyes a charcoal sheen. "I'm sorry, Courtney. He arranged your parents' deaths. He figured if you had no one, you would be an easier target for them when the time came."

If Maggie hadn't been holding Courtney's hand so tightly, she feared the girl would have slid off the chair.

"Your dad killed my parents?"

Even Mal looked uncomfortable with the pain that emanated from the girl.

"He made the arrangements. He prefers not to get his hands dirty."

"But why? He didn't know them, did he? He doesn't know me. *Why*?"

Declan looked at Maggie, now clearly at a loss.

She shook her head at the stupidity of the male sex. She stood up and pulled Courtney to her feet, hugging her tightly.

"Everything that happens to us has a reason behind it," she whispered, keeping her firm hold even as Courtney struggled against her. "You lost your family, but you went on. You developed that tough outer shell and, think about it, you even had a psychopathic boyfriend and survived that. You are a great kid."

"You're only saying that because you have to. Because it's your job."

Maggie paid no attention to her mumbles. "No, I'm saying it because it's true. I really like you, Courtney. Yes, at the beginning I wanted to throttle you, but you've managed all these twists and turns without freaking out. Most adults couldn't even do that."

"Everyone's gone."

Maggie shook her head and framed Courtney's face with her hands. "No, you have us." She cut a quick warning glance in Mal's direction. "And you have more than Mayan blood. You have demon blood."

Declan shot to his feet. "What? She couldn't. I would have sensed it."

"Shayla ran the tests, and it's very minor. Less than the Mayan connection," she replied.

"Okay, overload now." Courtney released herself from Maggie's hold and dropped into her chair. "I'm a demon like Mick? Euww!"

"There are all kinds of demons," Declan explained. "Trust me, you're nothing like him."

"Does this mean I can't be sacrificed? I mean, I'm part demon, and your dad wouldn't want to sacrifice a demon, would he?" Her words slowed as she read the truth in his eyes. "Okay, he would."

"Did he say how they planned to snatch Courtney?" Maggie asked.

"The kid doesn't need to be here for this," Mal said.

"The kid does," Courtney insisted.

"I promised her the truth from now on," Maggie said. "If Courtney wants to stay, she does."

"She does," the girl said.

Mal puffed away on his cigar. "What are Victorio's plans, Declan?"

"He didn't implant some kind of booby trap on you, did he?" Courtney questioned.

Declan shook his head. "I'm to convince you that the ritual is a sham and Courtney is in no danger. The ritual is scheduled for a week from now during the night of the blood moon." He looked tired.

"Victorio has been doing a lot of planning over the years. Not just Courtney, but he arranged my gaining the club, and he even sent the Bloater into the club so the Guard would show up. I can't imagine he made sure Maggie would be the one who would come in, but the way things are going, anything is possible. He loves to play puppet master, and he will do what it takes to make sure the ritual is carried out."

"And what about you? What will you do?" Maggie asked, feeling her hackles rise. One hand rested against her favorite blade.

He captured her eyes with his. "I'll kill him along with anyone else who tries to hurt Courtney."

"Good answer."

"So where did Mal get an office that looks like one of those old Greek temples?" Courtney asked after Mal threw the three out of his office. "It sure doesn't fit his personality. The guy seriously needs a new decorator."

"It *is* a Grecian temple. Aphrodite learned the hard way not to play poker with him," Maggie replied. "I admit the cherubs fluttering around are pretty much overkill."

"Maybe you could add some gremlins," Declan suggested. "I can hook you up with a few."

"Guys, there aren't any more surprises, are there?" Courtney smiled when Maggie conjured up a Tootsie Pop and handed it to her. The teen immediately unwrapped it and stuck it in her mouth.

"Of course, what more could there be after finding out I'm Mayan and demon—and a Mayan priest wants to kill me?" She paused. "That *is* it, right?"

"Well, there is the part where you're naked and covered with snakes," Declan said with a straight face. He laughed and danced out of her way as she threatened him with her sucker.

Maggie smiled, watching Courtney chasing him.

"There's nothing like those Kodak moments."

"Are we eating soon? Lunch was forever ago." Courtney bounced up with Declan behind her. She looked back. "Do demons have fast metabolisms? I never seem to gain weight, although my friend Brooke said it would eventually catch up to me. She could just look at a salad and gain weight."

"If I was a truly cruel person, I'd send her to The Library to gain an education," Maggie told Declan with a wry smile. "Although The Librarian would probably bar my entrance for the next thousand years." She looked at the girl who walked briskly ahead of them. "Look at her. She's so resilient, even with all that's happened to her."

"It's probably the demon blood. We tend to bounce back quickly. Even with her having that small amount, a family would take her in. I could find a good one for her."

She skidded to a stop and pulled on his arm so hard, she almost dislocated his shoulder. "You'll *what?*"

"Find a family for her. Not all demons are like my father or Wreaker," he said, confused by her anger.

"Oh, no, she's staying here."

"Hey, are you coming?" Courtney stopped and started back toward them.

"Go on and get us a table in the dining hall I took you to," Maggie ordered, not taking her eyes off Declan. "We'll be there in a minute."

"She's not an abandoned puppy, Maggie," he said fiercely. "Even with a tiny amount of demon blood, she could have latent power. If so, she'll need to learn to control it. You're a witch. You have no idea what to do. She'll need to be with her own kind."

Her fingers twitched, power sparking off the tips. "Guess what. She's with her own kind. If Courtney shows some power, I'll work with her on it. And just maybe I'll let you work with her. But no way am I handing her over to any other demons. Get it?" She poked her finger in his chest, setting off tiny fireworks.

Declan yelped and jumped back, extinguishing the heat that seared his shirt.

"You're not being rational." The moment the words left his mouth, he knew he'd made one of the biggest mistakes of his life.

"Rational? So because I'm female and a witch I'm not *rational*?" Her entire being started to glow with a yellow-orange light. She snatched his visitor medallion from his neck and crushed it in her hand. Two large males appeared on either side of Declan. "Escort him out," she ordered.

Declan didn't say a word, just stared at her with a mixture of confusion, frustration, and anger. Maggie's expression was pretty much the same.

"And to think I fell in love with you," she confessed.

He opened his mouth, ready to say something, but the Guards winked him out of sight.

Maggie stood there, unsure if she was going to scream or cry. She thought about settling for both, but she knew she couldn't appear upset when she joined Courtney.

Instead, she walked slowly toward the dining hall, feeling about as sick as a witch in love with a stubborn half-demon could feel.

Chapter 20

DECLAN DIDN'T KNOW WHO HE WAS ANGRIEST WITH: Maggie for telling him she was in love with him right before she had him tossed out of the compound; Victorio for ruining his life when he thought he was finally free; Wreaker for helping Victorio: Or even Courtney for showing him what a normal life could be like.

"Master, we have discovered what happened to Alexi," Snips announced, coming into the office.

"What?" He prowled the room, unable to stay still for too long. Even with the dampening spells, he was convinced he could hear the music and laughter coming from the club.

"His body was found in the lower depths." The imp placed something wrapped in black silk on Declan's desk. He unwrapped the fabric to reveal a wickedly sharp blade. "This was found beside him, and his heart was missing."

Declan placed his hand just above the curved blade that shimmered with color in its depths. Something dark and menacing seemed to cover the weapon. He was loath to pick it up, since some metals were dangerous to demons. "Not gold or brass."

"It is *Quetzalitzlipyollitli*, the stone of the bird of paradise, otherwise known as fire opal," Snips said. "The Mayans use it for rituals and mosaics."

"Mayans again." Declan flipped the scarf back over it. "Does Anton know?"

"He was the one who found Alexi. Anton slipped through the portal every chance he got. He should be punished for breaking the law. I can arrange for him to be lashed."

Declan shook his head. "No. He's had enough sorrow. Close the portal." He took no notice of his assistant's astonishment.

"But Master—"

"*Close it*!" he barked. "One of our own has been taken and viciously killed. I have a perfect right to close it. I should have done so in the beginning." He poured himself a whiskey and downed the contents in one gulp, savoring the burn traveling down his throat. "I'm not Ratchet. I won't take bribes to allow just anyone through it. It's been a headache from the beginning."

Snips's dark eyes widened with shock. "There will be repercussions."

"Right now, I don't care. Just do it. Tell the trackers they aren't to stop looking for that drone until they find him. After that, they can do whatever they wish with him as long as there's nothing left. His death is to be slow and agonizing. And leave the knife here," Declan ordered when the imp started to pick up the silk bundle.

Snips turned away and then spun back around again. "I have served many masters during my thousand years," he said. "You are the only one who has been… kind to me. Who hasn't punished me for being what I am." His purple claws flexed. "I realize I have been distant with you, almost hostile. But I have come to see you are an honorable male.

"There have been rumors. Words of blood and sacrifice. That your sire plans a coup that could destroy many of us. I will keep my ears open and inform you of anything else I might hear. If there is any way I may assist you, Master, please let me know." He bowed his head and slipped out of the office.

Declan looked at the closed door, still processing the imp's speech. "And here I thought I couldn't be any more surprised."

He closed his eyes, sensing dark and dangerous words flowing through his mind. He heard promises of violence, rich with flowing blood and power, while his inner eye viewed images of a huge moon, tall stone temples, and rhythmic chants. For a moment, the rich taste of copper filled his mouth.

He was positive the sensations were coming from the knife lying not all that innocently on his desk. It wasn't something he wanted to keep here any longer than he had to.

Maggie might not want to see him, but he was damn well going to see her.

"I thought school was over for a while," Courtney whined as Maggie guided her into a classroom furnished with desks and chairs. "And why do I have to come here at night? *Smallville* is coming on."

"That's what DVRs are for," Maggie said with a lack of sympathy. "You're here at night because it's the only time he would agree to come—and it wasn't easy to get him here as it was. And he is coming because there's a lot you need to learn about your heritage."

"Is this the one?" The imperious voice from the front of the room brought Maggie to attention. She wasn't afraid of much, but The Librarian always seemed to stoke the fear in her heart.

As always, he wore old-fashioned, bottle-green knee britches, a faded brocade waistcoat over a linen shirt the color of old parchment, and a bottle-green long-tailed coat. The front desk he presided over was covered with ancient scrolls and leather-bound books and even a few stone tablets. Narrowed black eyes peered at her over the rim of ancient half-spectacles perched on his beak-like nose. His scant brown hair held a neat comb-over.

"The Librarian." Maggie inclined her head in respect, even if the grumpy old wizard refused to acknowledge it. "This is Courtney Parker." When the girl didn't move, Maggie gave her a strong enough shove to move her forward. "We are grateful you are willing to help us educate her in the ways of her ancestors."

The Librarian frowned. "Speak up, girl," he snapped. "You must have a voice."

"Uh, hello?"

"It is a good thing I appreciate a challenge, since I can see this girl will need a great deal of work." He gestured toward the empty desk. "Sit. We have much to do and little time in which to do it. I only hope you have the intelligence to follow what I have to say."

Courtney had a frantic look on her face as Maggie pushed her into the chair.

"Don't leave me with him!" she pleaded.

"Just show respect, and you'll get along with him fine." Okay, she was lying, since The Librarian didn't like anyone. "I'll be back later." She stiffened her spine and walked out, feeling as if she'd left her chick with the fox.

"Do not bother returning until I send for you," The Librarian called out after her. The door closed with a final click.

"O'Malley, *now*." Mal's voice echoed from the walls.

Shoot me. Shoot me and put me out of my misery. Maggie wasted no time making her way down to her superior's office.

"Hey, Maggie!"

She spun around at the sound of a familiar voice. "Zouk!" She almost ran over to the team leader then stopped short at the sight. "No offense, dude, but you look disgusting." She grimaced at his yellow, leathery skin covered with red spots that oozed a nasty-looking pus. His three team members didn't look any better. "And smell worse." She pinched her nostrils with her fingers. "What happened? Mal said you and your team disappeared."

"We did. Fuckin' building was a portal to a plane world populated with a goblin nest," he explained. "They were the ones sucking the life out of the teens then popping them back to this plane." He shook his head in disgust. "We managed to capture the leader and brought him back. The rest didn't need to come along. Mal took one look at us and told us to get out of his office." He grinned.

Maggie nodded, understanding his unspoken words. The rest were killed and, as far as she was concerned, good riddance. She would have done the same.

"You think there's more out there doing this?" she asked, figuring that's why Zouk brought back the leader.

"Oh yeah. We want to know where so they can be taken care of." He winced at another spot popping with the putrid-smelling pus. "We gotta get to the healers. This shit itches like a son of a whore."

"I'm glad to see you back," she told him before moving on to Mal's office. Knowing there was a good outcome to her fellow team leader's situation put a spring in her step.

"I just saw Zouk and—" her words to her boss halted when she saw who else was there.

Seeing Declan was a welcome surprise, although she schooled her features not to betray her. After thinking about it, she knew she might have overreacted the last time they were together, but being the stubborn witch she was, she wasn't anxious to apologize.

His offer to find Courtney a family of her own wasn't unusual among demonkind. Many times, demon families had fostered children who lost their parents. Except Maggie already saw Courtney as one of her own. The teenager might chatter like a magpie and might as well have her iPod surgically grafted to her ears, but she also showed an inner strength that Maggie admired.

She was positive she saw warmth flash across Declan's face when she walked in.

"Declan," she said quietly.

"Maggie."

Mal looked at them and shook his head. "This is why I remain single," he muttered, finishing one cigar and lighting up another. "Declan brought us a present." He pointed his cigar at a lump of black silk on his desk. The object was encased in an iridescent bubble.

Maggie walked over, feeling the strength of the protection spell as she looked down. The fire-opal blade winked multiple colors at her while darkness tried to sneak into her mind.

Drums, chanting, the wet smell of vegetation. The musky scent of skin anointed with herb-infused oils. All of it overlaid with the metallic smell of blood.

She shook off the vision before it overtook her and stepped back from the knife. How could it do that even with the protection spell on it?

"What is it?"

"It's called *Quetzalitzlipyollitli*, the stone of the bird of paradise," Declan replied. "Fire opals are used in Mayan rituals. This one was found near the body of my missing portal keeper. His heart had been cut out." His eyes turned silver. "You felt it, too, didn't you?"

She didn't need to ask him what he meant. "It's almost as if it's looking for more death, and by winding its way into someone's mind, it can tempt that person into killing someone."

"That's how I felt, too. That's why I brought it here. I knew I couldn't keep it secured at Damnation Alley."

"And you don't trust your father not to find out you have it and come for it," she guessed.

He inclined his head. "Victorio would love to have this knife. It's obviously been baptized in blood and seeks more."

She watched the bubble as if the knife would find its way out. "Such as Courtney's."

"I've had scouts down in Central and South America," Mal said. "A few of the temples are suddenly not available for visitor tours. Signs are up stating they're closed while restorations were going on, but there's no hint of anyone working there. There's also a dark cloud covering a temple well-known for sacrifices. The time is fast approaching, you two. That means the kid can't even step one toe off this compound. And we need to go down there and take out the trash."

"Take out the trash?" Maggie parroted. "Sheesh, what movies are you watching, Mal? Fine, my team will head down there the day before the sacrifice is scheduled," Maggie said. "We can take care of it."

"I'm going with you," Declan said.

"No civilians allowed. I can't afford to be worrying about you," she retorted.

"You won't be." He leaned forward. "I didn't have to bring this to you. I've been a part of this situation from the beginning. You're not leaving me out of it now."

"He's going with you," Mal said. "And he'll look after himself. Something tells me you'll need someone with demon blood down there. Where's the kid now?"

"She's with The Librarian. He's giving her a crash course in Demonology 101."

"Someone she won't be able to talk the ears off," he muttered. "Fine, go set up the mission. And Declan sits in on the planning session."

"What about that?" She nodded toward the knife.

"Someone will be here to pick it up."

"I hope you like the tropics," Maggie told Declan as they walked out into the courtyard.

"I'm half fire demon, remember? The heat doesn't bother me a bit." He was quiet for a moment. "Did you mean what you said?"

"Yes." She didn't bother to pretend to misunderstand him. Without warning, she was spun around and into his arms.

Declan's kiss said it all. The way he felt about her—whether it was aggravation, lust, or the other L word that turned a male upside down and caused a female to see stars and hearts—was all mixed up in the heat of his mouth.

Maggie embraced it and returned the emotion.

"Get a room, Mags!' someone hooted.

Applause soon followed.

She pulled back, shook her head at the grinning audience, and pulled on Declan's hand.

"Tell me we're getting some privacy very soon." His words tickled her ear.

"Oh, yes."

"No Courtney?"

"I doubt The Librarian will release her until close to dawn." She almost dragged him along. "Plus, she has her own quarters now." She laughed when Declan looped his arm around her waist and hugged her against him. Then realized something was different. She stopped and took a close look from head to toe.

"You're not wearing a visitor medallion." She touched his chest, savoring the heat of his skin through the silky cotton of his shirt.

"Mal seems to think I need open access." He flexed his arm. "He didn't tell me it required an implant. Hurts like a son of a bitch. But I was even able to spend a few minutes checking on Anna. She's completely absorbed in being a Seer-in-training."

"Then let's get going, so I can kiss your boo-boo, along with a few other places," she added with a significant look further south.

"I'm yours."

Maggie liked hearing that and made sure they wasted no time going to her quarters.

Elle looked down from her computer surfing, realized she wasn't needed, and returned to her task.

"Very nice," Declan commented, admiring the rose-pink wall behind the bed that echoed the rose in her bedspread. The room was deep rose and cream, sparked here and there with jewel tones, and adorned with paintings and a few figurines that reflected a life of travel to exotic locales.

His attention was caught by the blonde Barbie doll dressed in fatigues and armed to the teeth, and he had to smile.

"Blair gave her to me last Yule," Maggie said. "She gave us each one that reflects us. I guess she sees me as a Lara Croft type."

"Our worlds are so different. Even with what you do, you have color in your life," he commented, picking up a pillow and setting it back down before fingering the silken spread.

"Don't tell me. Your place is all black and chrome."

"Pretty much." He sat on the bed and grasped her hand, pulling her to stand between his spread thighs. Her hands landed on his shoulders. "I think the only color that's ever come into my life came from you. You make me think of the sunlight. How am I supposed to return to my murky life after meeting you?"

"Watch out, Declan," she whispered in his ear. "People might think you're a real softie. Besides, you don't have to go anywhere without me. Who knows, I might get you wearing bright colors yet." She punctuated her words with a kiss that trailed down the side of his neck. "Now if your implant is where mine is…"

She pushed up his T-shirt and tossed it to one side.

Only a faint spot of red showed on his skin where the implant had been inserted. She bent down and kissed it gently and smiled when the redness disappeared. She trailed her lips up his arm, back to his throat, and then up to his mouth while she slipped off his shirt and then worked on his pants.

"I do love you," he whispered. "More than life itself. You've found a way into my heart."

Maggie pushed him backward and straddled his hips. "How perfect a match is that?" Her smile dimmed. "I was really ticked off at you for wanting to take Courtney away from me."

"I figured that out." He kept his hands resting on her hips. "I was only thinking of her. I thought it would be good for her to have a chance to learn about her heritage."

"The Librarian can help with that. That wizard may be cranky, but he knows his stuff." She caressed his face, enjoying the rough texture. "Plus, it gives us all this alone time."

Declan inched his way up the bed, carrying Maggie with him. Along the way, he tossed her T-shirt to one side and her pants to the other.

"You don't need this." He unfastened her bra and threw it across the room. "So beautiful." He cupped her breasts as he arched up, covering the dark rose-colored nipple with his mouth. He sucked gently, pulling it into his mouth and sending shock waves through her body. "Perfect." He transferred his attention to her other breast.

Maggie blindly ran her hands down his chest, feeling the heat of his skin against her palms, taut skin over bones. It was easy for her to intertwine her legs with his, lying fully on top of him. His cock was hard against her belly, silky to the touch. She rubbed against him, feeling it jump against her.

"I can't wait," she told him, inching down and rising up, taking him inside her. She hissed with relief as he stretched her inner tissues. She rocked, adding to the friction, but Declan wanted more. He flipped her over with ease and loomed over her, thrusting as she arched up to meet him.

"Mine," he reminded her.

"Mine," she agreed.

As she echoed what sounded like a vow, flickers of flames encircled them, giving off heat that echoed the love between them but was harmless to their surroundings.

Maggie threw her head back, laughing with joy and the sensation they shared of such strong emotions that she wanted to fly.

That was all it took for them both to fall into the abyss that sent them spiraling out of control.

"The last time we made love, I woke up to Wreaker's ugly face," Declan told her as he fought to catch his breath. "That's enough to make sure I never close my eyes again."

"That sounds more like a nightmare." Maggie snuggled in against him. "Don't worry. He can't show up here."

"He's an incubus. That gives him pretty much *carte blanche* wherever there are females." He trailed his fingers along her spine.

"Not here. Not even a bug could cross the boundaries without ending up as a spot of ash." She nibbled on his shoulder while she snuck her hand down his abs. "Short recovery, mister."

Declan rolled over to face her. "Some might call it witchcraft."

This time was soft and tender. The warrior and the demon whispering words of affection and exchanging light touches and featherlight kisses. This time, Maggie brought golden snowflakes falling down around them, and Declan reveled in the clean, cool magic.

"Everything's changed," he said as they lay in each other's arms.

"For the better."

"I can fight, but not the way you can." He rose up on his elbow, resting his head on his cupped hand. "I'm a businessman. Mal's offered me free entrance here, but I've got the feeling he has something more in mind for me."

"He's like that, and I'm sure he does. Hellion isn't just about the Guard. As you know, we have the Seers, healers, teachers, and families who live here."

"But no demons."

She nodded. "You always kept to yourselves and didn't want us around."

"I want *you* around." He whispered a kiss across her forehead.

"It will work out. I'll set up a meeting with the team in the morning so we can take out those priests, and afterward, life will be as boring as it was before."

"I don't think the word 'boring' is in your vocabulary," he teased.

"You just wait. There will be one day when the most exciting thing we'll be doing is lying outside, soaking up the sun and drinking Long Island iced teas."

"I'll look forward to that day."

—⁓—

"According to the blood tests, you come from a revered line," The Librarian droned, passing over a large book. "Albeit a somewhat violent one."

Courtney took a look at grayish-colored creatures that sported spikes along their spines. Razor-sharp teeth finished the picture of faces that leered with malevolent glee.

"Oh, no. There is no way I'm like them." She pushed the book back at him. "There was a mistake with that blood test. Just like there's no Mayan in me. I got sick the only time I went to Mexico. I didn't care to go again. See, no thought of 'home.' I think that's all proof I don't have any Mayan in me."

"Someone who talks as much as you do does not have the chance to learn because that requires the mouth to be closed and the ears open. As with every race, the beings change over the years." He glowered at her over his half-spectacles. "I am sure with time I could trace back your family tree."

Courtney looked down at her watch only to see it was missing. A look at the wall, where she knew a clock had been hanging, showed it was also bare. All she saw was a large brass hourglass sitting on The Librarian's desk. She was convinced that if the sand flowed any slower, it would be going up instead of down.

"What time is it?"

"No matter to you." The Librarian turned to a scroll and frowned. "This is not right." He started to roll it up.

Convinced it had to be something he didn't want her to see, therefore something she had to see, she jumped out of her chair and ran over to his desk.

"What isn't right?" She snatched the scroll from him.

"Here, here! This is inappropriate behavior," he scolded, reaching for the parchment. "This is very fragile."

Courtney unrolled the scroll and studied the drawing. She knew she couldn't translate the writing beneath it, but it didn't matter.

"I know this," she said under her breath. "It's—"

The air around her started to thicken and darken, while the sounds of drums and men's voices echoed inside her head. For a moment, she imagined the smell of rotting leaves, and the feel of humid air enfolded her.

"What's happening?" Courtney cried.

The Librarian hopped to his feet and started shouting, but she couldn't understand anything he said or why he waved his hands the way he did. Whatever magick the wizard was doing didn't seem to have any effect on the unseen hands that had grabbed hold of Courtney.

"*Help me!*" she screamed just before her invisible captors snatched her from the room in a swirl of black air.

—⁓—

"What the hell?" Declan yelped when the shower water suddenly ran ice cold and the lights blazed in the rooms.

"It's the compound alarm. Something's happened." Forgetting that they were having a cozy shower time,

Maggie ran out, toweling off quickly and tossing a second towel to Declan.

"Maggie!" Sybil's panicked voice, along with her pounding on the door, backed up the alarm.

Wrapping her towel around her body, Maggie ran for the door. Sybil, disheveled in her sleep pants and tank top, hugged her tightly.

"It's Courtney," she announced. "She was taken from the classroom."

"How? It can't happen with all our wards surrounding the compound. The Librarian has power. Couldn't he stop them?" Fear flooded her body like acid. *It was too soon! She should have still been safe.*

Sybil shook her head. "He said whatever took her was unseen. No matter what spells he threw at them, the spells just seemed to slide off."

If Declan hadn't grabbed hold of Maggie, she would have fallen to the floor.

"I brought her here to be safe. I told her nothing would happen to her," she said woodenly. "I *promised* her!"

"We'll get her back." He kept his arms around her to keep her upright.

"I have to call the team together." She fought to keep her mind on the business at hand. "There must be a trail we can follow, and I know Tita can find them. We already know which temple they most likely will have gone to." She was still shaky as she moved to her dresser and pulled out clothing.

"Where can I get some other clothes?" Declan asked Sybil.

"I'll find some," she told him, looking past him at Maggie. "I'm going with you—and no arguments. I'll be back with appropriate clothing for you," she told Declan before she left.

Maggie picked up a communicator and ordered her team to meet her in ten minutes.

"You can catch up with us there," she told Declan as she finished dressing and went through her weapons chest, looking for what she felt she would need in the upcoming fight. "I'm not going to leave you behind." She anticipated his protest. "Just come with Sybil when she returns with the clothes. Feel free to take anything you want from the chest." With a kiss she was gone.

Maggie noted controlled chaos as she left the living quarters and ran across the grounds toward the armory where the team would meet. Standard procedures went into play any time the boundaries were breached. She knew the children would be herded underground; the medical building would go into lockdown; and every Guard on the property would be armed and ready for battle.

As she passed the Seers' Pavilion, she saw Anna standing in the doorway. The female demon looked serene, even contented.

"Keep my brother safe," she called out with a tremulous smile.

Maggie smiled back. "I intend to." She stopped for a moment and touched Anna's arm. "You've helped us with your visions, you know."

"I think it is you who have helped me." She hugged Maggie and kissed her on the forehead, leaving a warm imprint of her lips there.

Maggie hugged her back and took off. She looked around, aware the Guard was ready to fight those who dared invade the compound's borders. Except the enemy had already left, and they had taken with them something precious to her.

Her mouth firmed with determination as she thought of Courtney in the hands of sadistic murderers.

She wouldn't need magick to kill them. She would be only too happy to do it with her bare hands.

Chapter 21

"How did they break the wards?" Maggie asked, once her team was assembled.

"It was a dark spell that had been set centuries ago." The Librarian mopped his face with a linen handkerchief. He looked paler than usual and uncharacteristically agitated.

"I don't understand." She collapsed in a chair, only sparing Declan a brief glance when he and Sybil entered the room and took chairs nearby.

"I was only able to do a brief amount of research on this, but it appears the Mayans knew they would be calling forth their god in the future and would require the right sacrifice for their ceremony. I had in my possession a scroll." He held up the parchment. "I assure you it's perfectly harmless now." He handed it to Maggie.

Declan got up and walked over to stand behind her as she unrolled it.

"It's the knife. One of Declan's employees was killed with a knife like this drawing. It gave off images." She went on to explain what she and Declan saw.

"To do with the sacrifice." The little wizard nodded. "I wasn't even aware of this piece until I found it to bring with me tonight." He wasn't happy at being fooled. "I should have known."

"Something this intricate could be planned that long ago?" Declan frowned at the scroll.

"If the sorcerer is gifted enough and had sufficient blood to fuel the spell." He wiped his hands on his handkerchief. "That scroll will be burned in a cleansing fire. Just because the spell has been used doesn't mean it couldn't happen again. The scroll is harmless in itself but can be used for evil in the wrong hands."

"Always the blood," Maggie murmured. "You'd think they'd get bored drawing blood and casting dark magick."

Tita reached across the table and plucked the scroll out of her hand. She closed her eyes and ran her palm over the surface. After a moment, she opened her eyes and looked around the room.

"It isn't a secret where Courtney is being held," she announced. "She's at the temple we were going to anyway."

"Except the ceremony is set for a couple days hence. Why would they take her now?"

"There will be rites to follow before she is led to the altar," The Librarian explained. "Cleansing of the body, ceremonial clothing, and even food. She will be treated like a goddess during this time."

"The condemned always has a hearty meal," Meech said. He glanced at his team leader. "When do we leave, boss?" He was already armed and ready, as was the rest of the team.

"As soon as we outfit Declan and Sybil with weapons."

"I am also going," The Librarian declared.

"Excuse me?"

"I am a bit of an historian in my spare time," he told her. "This type of ceremony hasn't been seen in ages. I wish to record it."

"Except we mean to stop it, and someone who spends

their time in a Library won't have any ounce of self-preservation," she said flatly.

"Perhaps I should mention my own lineage."

Maggie growled. She didn't need a reminder that while The Librarian was low wizard on the totem pole, he did have relatives in high places. It was just that he preferred the dank and dusty archives.

"You will stay out of the way."

"Of course."

Maggie looked around at her team of well-trained warriors who would fight to their very last breaths. And now she had a demon, with as far as she knew no formal training in hand-to-hand combat; an elf whose biggest asset was a pair of wings that wafted calming fragrance and a steely look that brought confessions flowing from prisoners; and a wizard Librarian who was stuck back a few centuries.

A witch walks into a bar one night. Kills a Bloater, meets a demon, semi-adopts a teenage girl, and finds herself traveling south with the craziest group ever. Fates help us.

"Get your nasty hands off me!" Courtney didn't bother batting at the fingers removing her clothing. She kicked, punched, and even used her teeth. Maggie would be so proud of her.

The three women, dressed in simple gowns, had appeared the moment Courtney was dropped into a stone room decorated with ancient colorful paintings on gem-encrusted walls. No matter how much the girl fought them, they silently continued with their tasks of removing her clothing and guiding her to a large tub of scented water set into the earth.

"You wait until Maggie finds you," she threatened, wondering why there was no reaction when she pinched one woman's arm hard enough to leave a bruise even as she was dumped into the water.

"No one will find you, revered one." A skeletal man wearing a brilliant-colored loincloth and a feathered cloak entered the room. His shaven head gleamed with oil, and colored images were tattooed on his skin. "And no matter what you do to the serving girls, they will not speak to you."

Courtney squealed and ducked down in the water.

"Why did you take me? And where am I? Tell me that and get out!"

"You are the last of our kind. With you, we can be whole again."

"Well, if you're looking for a virgin sacrifice, forget about it," she sneered, and then was unsettled by his laughter. "That's way long gone."

"We do not require a virgin for this," he told her. "If you are quiet and do as we ask, it will go better for you." He turned away.

"Wait! Why did you say they wouldn't speak to me?" She'd hoped to get information from them, such as where she was and if there was a way to escape this place.

His smile was as evil as his laugh. "They do not speak because their tongues were removed, as were their thought processes. They only obey the simplest of commands. Think about that, revered one. We do not need you to have a tongue when we cut out your heart to present it to our god." With that, he left.

Courtney refused to show any sign of weakness. Looking at the serving girls' blank eyes told her apologies wouldn't matter because they wouldn't understand.

Until Maggie arrived, she was on her own. One thing she had no doubt about was that the witch would rescue her.

After all, Maggie had promised nothing would happen to her.

Maggie saw minutes as hours. Every minute she was in the compound was a minute Courtney was in the enemy's hands.

Everyone was dressed and armed for jungle fighting. Well, except for The Librarian, who scoffed at the idea of changing from his sixteenth-century coat and knee breeches. The only concession he allowed was wearing a pith helmet he'd settled on his balding head—and his spectacles now had a brown tint.

"This will keep you in contact with the team if any of us get separated," she said, handing Declan a tiny mic.

"No magick communicators?"

She shook her head. "Magick going up against magick can go bad. Especially when you're dealing with the old ones. Although these mics do have their own protections, so no one else's magick can interfere with them. No one can even mimic someone else's voice with these." She stopped and took a breath.

"She'll be fine," he assured her. "The kid's got grit and a mouth to match."

"Which may have them wanting to kill her sooner."

She wanted to walk into his arms and just stay there. To act like a total girl.

"Not if they want the ritual to succeed." He cupped her shoulder. "Let's go get our girl."

She nodded and then turned to Tita, who wasn't happy at all. "I wish you could go, but it will be broad daylight. Even with your age and strength, I don't want to take the chance of losing you."

"Then bring me back one of the priests," the vampire said. "I'm in the mood for some Mexican food." She flashed her fangs.

"The jet's ready." Frebus came in, loaded down with enough weapons to make him look like a walking armory.

"The Librarian refuses to use a portal, so we're taking the Lear jet," she muttered to Declan. "All right, everyone. Let's head south to rescue our new mascot."

Maggie couldn't sit still during the flight. She paced the length of the cabin, muttered to herself, mapped out plans in her head, and occasionally stopped to look out the window. She thought of using a spell to increase the aircraft's speed, but she didn't want to tire herself out.

"You need to rest," Declan told her, pushing her into one of the seats and then taking the one next to her.

"I need to think."

"He's right. Rest." Sybil pressed a cup of warm liquid into her hands. "It's only tea," she told her. "Nothing else in it, I swear."

She wanted to argue; instead she obediently drank the beverage.

"The pilot plotted a landing spot several miles from the temples," Meech told her. "We should be far enough out to avoid any of their wards. He'll silence the engines so they won't know we're coming in."

Maggie nodded and settled back in the seat. She had to admit the soft leather felt good, even if she still couldn't relax.

"I've got something to tell you." She didn't look at Declan. "I was the one who killed Ratchet."

"I already figured that out. It was no loss, and I got the club." He grasped her hand. "Although I'm curious about what you did with the body."

"Chippers chop more than wood, you know. Even more so if they're cursed."

Declan winced. "Remind me never to piss you off."

The humid air was thick enough it could have been eaten with a spoon. Maggie felt the sweat start to pour off her body as soon as she walked down the stairs.

"I have never liked the tropics," Elle said from her spot on Maggie's bicep.

"What are you worried about?" the witch muttered. "You don't have any sweat glands."

Once everyone had exited the jet, Maggie invoked an invisibility spell to hide the plane and ordered the pilot to get out of there if he didn't hear from them in two days.

The sounds, sights, and smells were all that she experienced in her vision. The rich, moist scent of vegetation wafted around them while the plants appeared to have a life of its own. Once they entered the dense jungle, they were fighting dark-green vines that snaked around their ankles, threatening to jerk them off their feet. Meech hissed when he brushed against a leaf that sliced a deep cut into his arm. He wasted no time slapping a healing poultice on it and moving on.

Exotic fragrance from the brilliantly colored flowers was an intoxicating assault on their senses and made it more difficult to breathe the thick, moist air. Each step was a struggle as their boots sank into damp earth that squished around their footwear.

"Don't get too near the flowers," Maggie advised, frowning at a bright-red bloom that seemed to seek her out. She stepped out of its reach even as the blossoms tracked her movements. "For all we know, they're poisonous."

"They are," The Librarian intoned, studying the colorful blooms from a respectful distance. "Just watch."

A large flying insect got too close to the flower that had stalked Maggie. The blossom expelled a foul-smelling mist. The bug instantly turned to dust and fell to the damp ground.

It wasn't long before the faint sound of drums and a metallic sound from a horn filled the air.

"They can't do the ritual now. It's not nighttime."

"With adjustments, they can," The Librarian said.

"Remind me again why I wanted to come," Sybil moaned, slapping yet another mosquito that wanted to make a meal out of her. Her lavender wings wilted in the tropical heat.

Meech and Frebus picked up the pace, using their blades to cut the attacking vines and vegetation that got in the way. Declan grabbed hold of Maggie's arm one time when she slipped and kept his other hand on Sybil's arm to help her over fallen logs.

"She has to be all right," Maggie muttered, repeating

the words inside her head like a mantra as they grew closer to their destination.

They stopped several yards from the clearing, staring at a multitiered temple that seemed to kiss the sky. Vibrant drawings of long-gone deities decorated the bottom stone blocks.

But it was the sight at the top of the temple that had Maggie's heart flying into her throat.

A tall man, his face and body adorned with colorful paints, stood before the stone altar with a gleaming knife held high. There was no doubt about the identity of the figure lying there.

The priest spoke in a loud carrying voice.

"He's calling on the god of destruction to honor his gift of the last one with noble blood," The Librarian whispered.

"That's what he thinks," Maggie said grimly, pulling her Hisshou knife from its sheath. She hefted the blade in her hand.

"Trouble," Frebus warned, pointing to the land surrounding the bottom of the temple.

Men carrying spears poured out of the temple, heading straight for them.

"I just love to dance!" Meech howled. "We'll keep these fuckers busy. You get Courtney!" He unsheathed a heavy sword and ran forward with the others after him.

"I must come with you," The Librarian insisted.

"Then you'll have to do it on your own." Maggie looked at Declan. "Ready to rock and roll?"

He had his own knife out. "Ready and willing."

They flew up the tall steps, Maggie pushing her magick to keep them going as fast as possible. As she neared the top, the sky turned pitch-black, with clouds rolling in and thunder booming overhead.

"You are too late!" The priest bared his teeth, all filed to jagged points. He held the knife aloft. "We call upon the one to bring us prosperity and riches! The one who will rule our world the way it should be!"

"Courtney!" Maggie shouted.

"Maggie!" The girl struggled against the leather bonds that kept her tethered to the stone altar. She wore a finely woven linen gown with intricate colorful embroidery decorating the neckline and a hem that fell to her bare feet. "I knew you'd come."

"Once she is dead, I will kill you as well," the priest declared.

"Kill the witch now!"

Declan spun around at the sound of the familiar voice. "Victorio." Hate colored the word.

"You are more resourceful than I thought, my son." The elder demon smiled. "You brought us a wonderful prize. I didn't think you'd do it. The witch's death will add so much more to the ceremony."

Maggie glanced at Declan once and then returned to stalking the priest.

"Honestly, Declan, Wreaker was bad enough, but your dad barging in on the party is just a total downer." She divided her attention between the demon and the priest.

A demon and a priest walked into a bar one night. She started to giggle.

"It has already begun. You cannot stop it now," the priest intoned, keeping the fire-opal blade just above Courtney's heart.

"That's what you think." Maggie knew enough not

to make any quick moves. She just wanted to distract him long enough... As she sidestepped, she whispered words that floated through the air and reached Courtney, loosening the bonds securing her to the altar.

Lightning split the sky as Courtney rolled off the flat stone.

"No!" The priest reached for her. As he fell forward, the knife nicked the girl's arm.

"Shit!" Before Maggie could utter words to stop the blood flow, a drop dripped off the knife blade onto the sacrificial stone. She didn't hesitate and threw her knife at the priest, the blade finding its way to the man's heart. He fell dead onto the altar.

"It's too late!" Victorio shouted, triumph spilling from his voice. He threw up his hands to the sky. "Welcome to the one we have summoned!"

Maggie ran to Courtney, sealing her small wound with a spell and pushing the teen behind her as she retrieved her knife. "Elle, protect her," she ordered. The spider immediately left Maggie and landed on Courtney's shoulder, sinking her fangs into a guard who tried to grab hold of Courtney.

"You won't win," Declan declared, advancing on his father, his knife resting easily in his hand.

"I've already won," Victorio taunted. "And if you choose the witch, you will become fodder for the god while I will rule."

Black clouds covered the temple top, making it difficult to speak.

"Who summons me?"

All four turned at the musical voice.

The woman who faced them was barely over five

feet tall, slender as a reed, with the golden skin of her Mayan heritage and lush black hair that hung to her hips. Her blood-red gown was accented with a girdle of gold circles, along with an elaborate collar of hammered gold and matching earrings. Her lips matched her gown, and her teeth, when she smiled, were white and very sharp.

"Only one of you wishes me here," she spoke. "While I wish it were one of the females, I sense that is not so. Nor you." She glanced at Declan. "So it must be you." She turned to Victorio, who couldn't hide his shock. "You are surprised, demon."

"The history we have studied so many centuries and the reports all say *god* of destruction, my lady," he said formally, quickly recovering from his surprise. "Naturally, I am happy to see a beautiful woman instead, and I welcome you to our world."

Maggie kept Courtney behind her and at a safe distance from the goddess, whose power felt like a million nuclear plants ready to melt down. It was a struggle just to breathe. She glanced at Declan, who had managed to move a few steps away from his father, although he hadn't sheathed his knife.

The Goddess of Destruction stared at her priest, touched his back, and impassively watched while his body turned to ash.

"You thought to tempt me with a child's blood? Such weak fare is not a suitable offering for one such as I," she said, with a toss of her head. "And I sense that the world is not what I wish at this time."

"But I was promised much." Victorio made the mistake of protesting. "I brought you the heart of a warrior my son valued." He waved his hand. A mass of black muscle appeared in his palm, dripping dark blood.

"Alexi! You bastard!" Declan roared, moving toward his sire. "You had him killed." He looked ready to tear Victorio's heart from his body.

The Goddess of Destruction ignored Declan's fury as she turned toward Victorio. "You are merely a demon, not even one of my lineage. You are also one that cannot be trusted. You have the heart of a deceiver and bring me the heart of one I did not ask for. A sacrifice such as this would only be accepted if the younger one had brought it to me. There is no power in your gift. I do not like deceivers, nor would I allow one to become a part of my court." She looked at Declan. "You have the eyes of one to be trusted, but I also know you would not join me. What a pity." She showed her pearly whites that looked razor-sharp.

"Is she hitting on him?" Courtney hissed in Maggie's ear. The girl was immediately shushed.

"I will not be denied!" Victorio advanced on Maggie, an obsidian blade in one hand. "The witch's blood will finish the ritual, and you will take me as your consort. I have worked too hard to see my plan fail now!"

Declan didn't hesitate. He pushed his knife into his father's back and then pushed his bloody body toward the goddess.

"He's yours!" he shouted. "Take him back where you came from, and do not return!"

Victorio's eyes widened with shock as his son's words sunk in. "*No!*"

The goddess smiled. "I welcome your gift and will be happy to return to my home with this sacrifice. I have been in need of a new pet since my last one expired." As petite as she was, she had no trouble wrapping her arms around Victorio's torso. With a swirl of acrid smoke, she disappeared with Victorio's cries a mere echo.

The threesome felt the rumble beneath their feet a second later.

"Time to go!" Maggie grabbed Courtney's hand, while Declan guided them through the lingering smoke.

As they ran and slid their way down the steps, the topmost blocks of the temple tumbled down around them. By the time they reached the bottom, the rest of the team had dispatched the guards and were ready to help them back into the jungle.

It wasn't long before the temple was reduced to a pile of rubble, the intricate drawings having disappeared and the fire opals in the stones melted.

"I knew you'd come!" Courtney hugged Maggie.

"Court, I have to breathe!" Maggie gasped with laughter, hugging her back.

Declan was treated to the same, along with every team member.

"You came, too?" Courtney stood in front of The Librarian.

"Someone had to record the rite," he informed her.

Courtney danced around, the hem of her gown flaring around her bare feet. "Can you use magick for shoes?" she asked Maggie and sighed with relief when she found hiking boots on her feet. "Not cute, but they'll work. Can we go home now? All they fed me was some kind of nasty-tasting liquid and berries!"

"I barely fought. Only one was my victim." Elle pouted as she returned to Maggie's arm.

"You were almost sacrificed. No hysteria?" Maggie was stunned by Courtney's attitude.

"Oh, I'm sure that will come later, but I supposedly come from a line of nasty demons. We don't have to walk far, do we? And does anyone have any food? I'm starving! Who can survive on nuts and berries? I *told* them I wasn't a vegetarian, like that did any good," she chattered away to Sybil as they walked back to the waiting jet.

Maggie felt Declan's arms around her.

"You know what?" he said softly. "I think we'll keep her."

She tipped her head back to receive his kiss. "Yes, I think we will."

Epilogue

"WHAT GOOD IS COMING FROM A LINE OF KICK-ASS demons if I can't throw a knife in a straight line?" Courtney groused. "And look at this. Blisters!" She held out her hands. "Frebus made me practice on the punching bag all afternoon." She blew her bangs out of her eyes.

Maggie laughed, much to the teenager's disgruntlement. "It will take time."

Courtney collapsed on the couch. To maintain a cover for the human courts, they remained in the house on Spinning Wheel Lane, although they spent most of their time at the compound and Courtney slept there when Maggie was on a mission. The only difference was that the attic at the house had been turned into a studio set up for Maggie to teach Courtney basic magick. Elle had her own corner as she continued her search for a way to have a longer-lived lover. So far, the teen had blown holes in the roof twice and turned the attic stairs into rubber.

They had yet to learn what Courtney had a flair for, but Maggie knew it would come when the girl was ready to embrace it.

She looked at her ward, feeling a warmth that was new to her. While Maggie had plenty of friends, she hadn't known anyone who relied on her in so many ways. She also discovered that going to the mall had a whole new meaning when shopping with a clothes-hungry teenager. And that junk food didn't last long in the house.

But her life had taken an even more interesting turn. The object of that turn could be heard coming through the kitchen.

"Hi, honey, I'm home!" Declan walked in and kissed Maggie.

"You guys are so corny." But there was affection in Courtney's teasing. "Okay, I'm off to die on my bed. You can tell Frebus I can't make my next class because he *killed* me!" She bounced upstairs.

"Gotta love the dramatics." Declan dropped down on the couch beside Maggie.

"Anything more said about Victorio's death?" She knew he'd been dealing with the administration of Victorio's extensive holdings.

"I heard from one of the Demon Committee members an hour ago that it's all settled. Wreaker put in a claim for his pets and some of the money." He grimaced. "I told Wreaker he could only have the females as long as he doesn't drain them. It's in writing with his signature in blood, so they'll be safe. With luck, he'll get tired of them and release them.

"The Committee decided that Victorio's greed for power got the better of him and they're better off without him trying to usurp their positions. He will not be missed. They're not happy I closed down the portal, but I won't be punished for it. It's not as if the club needs it."

"Does that mean I can get in?" Courtney called downstairs. "I've got demon blood anyway."

"No!" they shouted in unison.

"Changes all around." Maggie admired the navy tone-on-tone shirt Declan wore. She saw it as too close to black, but she figured by year's end, she'd have him in forest green or even a nice burgundy.

"How about some more? Think we can make a go of it as a family?" He brought her fingertips to his lips. "I move in here, and we tackle Courtney together. With Courtney, it would probably be best to have backup."

She stilled. "I'll still be a Guard."

"I wouldn't have it any other way. I just want to know you'll come home to me." He smiled. "I'll even throw in a tree house."

The sounds of Linkin Park screamed overhead, along with sounds of Courtney chattering away on her phone.

Maggie climbed onto Declan's lap. "I already cleared out half the closet for you."

"Good to know." He leaned in to kiss her and then reared back as his nose twitched. His face grew a bright red, and he turned away to sneeze.

Maggie yelped and started to jump away as a corner of the coffee table went up in flames. Declan waved his hand, smothering the flames with a word.

"New perfume?" he asked, rubbing his nose.

She nodded. "I'll give it away. By the way, the next time you feel the need to sneeze, aim at the fireplace."

─ ∿ ─

"I've found it! I've found the perfect hex!" Elle's voice could be heard from upstairs. "I must choose my next lover wisely because I will be able to make him immortal!"

The next minute, Maggie fell off Declan's lap as the

house rocked on its foundation and the explosion had them staring up at the ceiling, which now sported a multitude of cracks and scorch marks. There was silence, and then came the tiny voice.

"Never mind."

Acknowledgments

A thank-you to the lovely and imaginative Meredith Clark, winner of my name-that-character contest.

And a bless-you to Michael Charton, who researched the Mayan culture for me and saved me so much time.

Mega thanks to my family, who puts up with my muttering spells and creature names and sometimes grabbing pen and paper at the oddest times.

My totally awesome agent, Laurie McLean, who's always there for me. Sourcebooks's Deb Werksman, who's also there for the witches; Susie Benton; Danielle Jackson who gets the word out; and fantastic illustrator Lisa Mierzwa, who illustrated my first four gorgeous covers and Tony Mauro who illustrated *Demons Are a Girl's Best Friend*.

My Witchy Chicks family, who've been there from the beginning. I love you all.

The Casababes and my beloved Lair mates, who are always there.

And much chocolate and champagne to my friends who listen to me whine, giggle, and everything in between. You keep me just sane enough.

About the Author

Linda Wisdom was born and raised in Huntington Beach, California. She majored in journalism in college and then switched to fashion merchandising when she was told there was no future for her in fiction writing. She held a variety of positions, ranging from retail sales to executive secretary in advertising and office manager for a personnel agency.

Her career began when she sold her first two novels to Silhouette Romance on her wedding anniversary in 1979. Since then, she has sold more than seventy novels and two novellas to five different publishers. Her books have appeared on various romance and mass-market bestseller lists and have been nominated for a number of *Romantic Times* awards. She has been a two-time finalist for the Romance Writers of America RITA Award.

She lives with her husband, one dog, one parrot, and a tortoise in Murrieta, California.

When Linda first moved to Murrieta, three romance writers lived in the town. At this time, there is just Linda. So far, the police have not suspected her of any wrongdoing.

50 Ways to Hex Your Lover

BY LINDA WISDOM

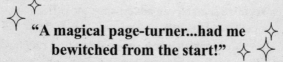

"A magical page-turner...had me bewitched from the start!"

—Yasmine Galenorn,
USA Today bestselling author of *Witchling*

JAZZ CAN'T DECIDE WHETHER TO SCORCH HIM WITH A FIREBALL OR JUMP INTO BED WITH HIM

Jasmine Tremaine is a witch who can't stay out of trouble. Nikolai Gregorivich is a vampire cop on the trail of a serial killer. Their sizzling love affair has been on-again, off-again for about 300 years—mostly off, lately.

But now Nick needs Jazz's help to steer clear of a maniacal killer with supernatural powers, while they try to finally figure out their own hearts.

978-1-4022-1085-3 • $6.99 U.S. / $8.99 CAN

Hex Appeal

BY LINDA WISDOM

"Kudos to Linda Wisdom for a series that's pure magic!"

—Vicki Lewis Thompson,
New York Times bestselling author of *Wild & Hexy*

JAZZ AND NICK'S DREAM ROMANCE HAS TURNED INTO A NIGHTMARE...

FEISTY WITCH JASMINE TREMAINE AND DROP-DEAD GORGEOUS vampire cop Nikolai Gregorivich have a hot thing going, but it's tough to keep it together when nightmare visions turn their passion into bickering.

With a little help from their friends, Nick and Jazz are in a race against time to uncover whoever it is that's poisoning their dreams, and their relationship...

978-1-4022-1400-4 • $6.99 U.S. / $7.99 CAN

Wicked by Any Other Name

BY LINDA WISDOM

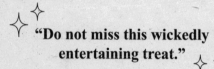

"Do not miss this wickedly entertaining treat."

—Annette Blair,
Sex and the Psychic Witch

STASI ROMANOV USES A LITTLE WITCH MAGIC IN HER LINGERIE shop, running a brisk side business in love charms. A disgruntled customer threatening to sue over a failed spell brings wizard attorney Trevor Barnes to town—and witches and wizards make a volatile combination. The sparks fly, almost everyone's getting singed, and the whole town seems on the verge of a witch hunt.

Can the feisty witch and the gorgeous wizard overcome their objections and settle out of court—and in the bedroom?

978-1-4022-1773-9 • $6.99 U.S. / $7.99 CAN

Hex in High Heels

BY LINDA WISDOM

Can a Witch and a Were find happiness?

Feisty witch Blair Fitzpatrick has had a crush on hunky carpenter Jake Harrison forever—he's one hot shape-shifter. But Jake's nasty mother and brother are after him to return to his pack, and Blair is trying hard not to unleash the ultimate revenge spell. When Jake's enemies try to force him away from her, Blair is pushed over the edge. No one messes with her boyfriend-to-be, even if he does shed on the furniture!

Praise for Linda Wisdom's Hex series:

"Fan-fave Wisdom… continues to delight."
  —*Romantic Times*

"Highly entertaining, sexy, and imaginative."
  —*Star Crossed Romance*

"It's a five star, feel-good ride!" —*Crave More Romance*

"Something fresh and new."
  —*Paranormal Romance Review*

978-1-4022-1819-4 • $6.99 U.S. / $8.99 CAN

Strange Neighbors

BY ASHLYN CHASE

HE'S LOOKING FOR PEACE, QUIET, AND A MAYBE LITTLE ROMANCE…

Hunky all-star pitcher and shapeshifter Jason Falco invests in an old Boston brownstone apartment building full of supernatural creatures, and there's never a dull moment. But when Merry McKenzie moves into the ground floor apartment, the playboy pitcher decides he might just be done playing the field…

———

What readers say about Ashlyn Chase

"Entertaining and humorous—a winner!"

"The humor and romance kept me entertained— a definite page turner!"

"Sexy, funny stories!"

978-1-4022-3661-7 • $6.99 U.S./$8.99 CAN/£3.99 UK

The Werewolf Upstairs

BY ASHLYN CHASE

SHE SHOULD KNOW BETTER...

Attorney Roz Wells is bored. She used to have such a knack for attracting the weird and unexpected, but ever since she took a job as a Boston Public defender the quirky quotient in her life has taken a serious hit. Until her sexy werewolf neighbor starts coming around...

Roz knows she should stay away from this sexy bad boy, but she can't help it that she's putty in his hands...

What readers say about Ashlyn Chase

"Entertaining and humorous—a winner!"

"The humor and romance kept me entertained— a definite page turner!"

"Sexy, funny stories!"

978-1-4022-3662-4 • $6.99 U.S./$8.99 CAN/£4.99 UK

IN OVER HER HEAD

by Judi Fennell

"Holy mackerel! *In Over Her Head* is a
fantastically fun romantic catch!"

—Michelle Rowen, author of *Bitten & Smitten*

○ ○ ○ ○ ○ HE LIVES UNDER THE SEA ○ ○ ○ ○ ○

Reel Tritone is the rebellious royal second son of the ruler
of a vast undersea kingdom. A Merman, born with legs
instead of a tail, he's always been fascinated by humans,
especially one young woman he once saw swimming near
his family's reef...

○ ○ ○ ○ ○ SHE'S TERRIFIED OF THE OCEAN ○ ○ ○ ○ ○

Ever since the day she swam out too far and heard voices
in the water, marina owner Erica Peck won't go swimming
for anything—until she's forced into the water by a shady
ex-boyfriend searching for stolen diamonds, and is nearly
eaten by a shark. Luckily Reel is nearby to save her, and
discovers she's the woman he's been searching for...

978-1-4022-2001-2 • $6.99 U.S. / $7.99 CAN

WILD
BLUE
UNDER

by Judi Fennell

"Bubbly fun in a sparkling 'under the sea' tale." —
Virginia Kantra, *USA Today* bestselling author

THE UNDERWATER KINGDOM IS HIS...

○ ○ ○ ○   **AS SOON AS HE CLAIMS HIS QUEEN**   ○ ○ ○ ○

Rod Tritone is gorgeous and irresistible—he could snag any queen he wants for his Mer kingdom, but unfortunately, it's not up to him. As fate would have it, the one woman destined to rule with him lives in land-locked Kansas and has no idea she's a princess. Somehow Rod has to prove to Valerie Dumere who she really is. But when she learns the truth, will she ever forgive him?

○ ○ ○ ○ ○ **PRAISE FOR *IN OVER HER HEAD*:** ○ ○ ○ ○ ○

"A delightful, quirky blend of humor, adventure, and passion."
—*Star-Crossed Romance*

"A wondrous undersea adventure—molten moments, waves of sensuality, ripples of emotion, and depths of fun. Not to be missed!"—L.A. Banks, *The Vampire Huntress Legends Series*

"A witty, funny, fabulous story." —*Passion for the Page*

978-1-4022-2427-0 • $6.99 U.S. / $8.99 CAN

CATCH
OF A
LIFETIME

by Judi Fennell

"Judi Fennell has one heck of an imagination!"
—Michelle Rowen, author of *Bitten & Smitten*

WHEN HE DISCOVERS WHAT SHE REALLY IS,

○ ○ ○ ○ **THEY'RE BOTH IN MORTAL DANGER...** ○ ○ ○ ○

Mermaid Angel Tritone has been researching humans from afar, and when she jumps into a boat to escape a shark attack, it's her chance to pursue her mission to save the planet from disaster—but she must keep her identity a secret. For Logan Hardington, finding a beautiful woman on his boat is surely not a problem—until he realizes his life is on the line…

○ ○ ○ ○ ○ **PRAISE FOR *IN OVER HER HEAD*:** ○ ○ ○ ○ ○

"A charming modern day fairy tale with a twist. Fennel is a bright star on the horizon of romance." —Judi McCoy, author of *Hounding the Pavement*

"Fennell's under-the-sea suspense will enchant you with its wit, humor, and sexiness." —Caridad Pineiro, *NYT* and *USA Today* Bestseller, *South Beach Chicas Catch Their Man*

978-1-4022-2428-7 · $6.99 U.S. / $8.99 CAN

SLAVE

BY CHERYL BROOKS

"I found him in the slave market on Orpheseus Prime, and even on such a god-forsaken planet as that one, their treatment of him seemed extreme."

Cat may be the last of a species whose sexual talents were the envy of the galaxy. Even filthy, chained, and beaten, his feline gene gives him a special aura.

Jacinth is on a rescue mission… and she needs a man she can trust with her life.

PRAISE FOR CHERYL BROOKS'S *SLAVE*:

"A sexy adventure with a hero you can't resist!"

—Candace Havens, author of *Charmed & Deadly*

"Fascinating world customs, a bit of mystery, and the relationship between the hero and heroine make this a very sensual romance."

—*Romantic Times*

978-1-4022-1192-8 • $7.99 U.S. / $9.99 CAN / 4.99 UK

OUTCAST

BY CHERYL BROOKS

◇◇◇

Sold into slavery in a harem, Lynx is a favorite because his feline gene gives him remarkable sexual powers. But after ten years, Lynx is exhausted and is thrown out of the harem without a penny. Then he meets Bonnie, who's determined not to let such a beautiful and sensual young man go to waste...

◇◇◇

"Leaves the reader eager for the next story featuring these captivating aliens." —*Romantic Times*

"One of the sweetest love stories...one of the hottest heroes ever conceived and...one of the most exciting and adventurous quests that I have ever had the pleasure of reading." —*Single Titles*

"One of the most sensually imaginative books that I've ever read... A magical story of hope, love and devotion" —*Yankee Romance Reviews*

978-1-4022-1896-5 • $6.99 U.S. / $7.99 CAN

FUGITIVE

BY CHERYL BROOKS

"Really sexy. Sizzling kind of sexy...makes you want to melt in the process." —*Bitten by Books*

A mysterious stranger in danger...

Zetithian warrior Manx, a member of a race hunted to near extinction because of their sexual powers, has done all he can to avoid extermination. But when an uncommon woman enters his jungle lair, the animal inside of him demands he risk it all to have her.

The last thing Drusilla expected to find on vacation was a gorgeous man hiding in the jungle. But what is he running from? And why does she feel so mesmerized that she'll stop at nothing to be near him? Hypnotically attracted, their intense pleasure in each other could destroy them both.

PRAISE FOR THE CAT STAR CHRONICLES:

"Wow. The romantic chemistry is as close to perfect as you'll find." —*BookFetish.org*

"Fabulous off world adventures... Hold on ladies, hot Zetithians are on their way." —*Night Owl Romance*

"Insanely creative... I enjoy this author's voice immensely." —*The Ginger Kids Den of Iniquity*

"I think purring will be on my request list from now on." — *Romance Reader at Heart*

978-1-4022-2940-4 •$6.99 U.S. / $8.99 CAN / £3.99 UK

THE
FIRE LORD'S
LOVER

BY KATHRYNE KENNEDY

IF HIS POWERS ARE DISCOVERED, HIS FATHER WILL DESTROY HIM...

In a magical land ruled by ruthless Elven lords, the Fire Lord's son Dominic Raikes plays a deadly game to conceal his growing might from his malevolent father—until his arranged bride awakens in him passions he thought he had buried forever...

UNLESS HIS FIANCÉE KILLS HIM FIRST...

Lady Cassandra has been raised in outward purity and innocence, while secretly being trained as an assassin. Her mission is to bring down the Elven Lord and his champion son. But when she gets to court she discovers that nothing is what it seems, least of all the man she married...

"As darkly imaginative as Tolkien, as richly romantic as Heyer, Kennedy carves a new genre in romantic fiction."
—Erin Quinn, author of *Haunting Warrior*

"Deliciously dark and enticing." —Angie Fox, *New York Times* bestselling author of *A Tale of Two Demon Slayers*

978-1-4022-3652-5 • $7.99 U.S./$9.99 CAN/£4.99 UK

WHAT WOULD
JANE AUSTEN
DO?

BY LAURIE BROWN

Eleanor goes back in time to save a man's life, but could it be she's got the wrong villain?

Lord Shermont, renowned rake, feels an inexplicable bond to the mysterious woman with radical ideas who seems to know so much…but could she be a Napoleonic spy?

Thankfully, Jane Austen's sage advice prevents a fatal mistake…

At a country house party, Eleanor makes the acquaintance of Jane Austen, whose sharp wit can untangle the most complicated problem. With an international intrigue going on before her eyes, Eleanor must figure out which of two dueling gentlemen is the spy, and which is the man of her dreams.

978-1-4022-1831-6 • $6.99 U.S. / $7.99 CAN

The TREASURES of Venice

BY LOUCINDA McGARY

"Bursting with passion."
—Darque Reviews

An Irish rogue who never met a lock he couldn't pick…

With danger at every corner and time running out, Keirnan Fitzgerald must use whatever means possible to uncover the missing Jewels of the Madonna. Samantha Lewis is shocked when Keirnan approaches her, but she throws caution to the wind and accompanies the Irish charmer into his dangerous world of intrigue, theft, and betrayal. As the centuries-old story behind the Jewels' disappearance is revealed, Samantha must decide whether Keirnan is her soul mate from a previous life, or if they are merely pawns in a relentless quest for a priceless treasure…

"Lost jewels, a sexy Irish hero, and an exotic locale make for a wonderful escape. Don't miss this charming story."
—Brenda Novak, *New York Times* bestselling author of *Watch Me*

"A brilliant novel that looks to the past, entwines it in the present, and makes you wonder at every twist and turn if the hero and heroine will get out alive. Snap this one up, it's a keeper!" —Jeanne Adams, author of *Dark and Deadly*

978-1-4022-2670-0 • $6.99 U.S. / $8.99 CAN